The Crime

and

Cards of Death

TWO CLASSIC ADVENTURES OF

by Walter B. Gibson
writing as Maxwell Grant

plus **"The Red Macaw"**
a lost radio classic by
Edward Hale Bierstadt

with new historical essays by
Anthony Tollin and Will Murray

SANCTUM BOOKS

International Standard Book Number:
978-1-60877-031-1

First printing: July 2010

Series editor: Anthony Tollin
anthonytollin@shadowsanctum.com

Consulting editor: Will Murray

Copy editor: Joseph Wrzos

Cover and photo restoration: Michael Piper

The editors gratefully acknowledge the assistance of Scott Cranford, Sergio Aragonés, Karl Schadow and Michael Ogden in the preparation of this volume.

Published by Sanctum Books
P.O. Box 761474, San Antonio, TX 78245-1474

Visit The Shadow at www.shadowsanctum.com.

THE Shadow™
Volume 40

CONTENTS

Two Complete Novels From The Shadow's Private Annals As told to Maxwell Grant

Thrilling Tales and Features

Cover art by George Rozen
Interior illustrations by Tom Lovell and Edd Cartier

THE LAUGH HEARD AROUND THE WORLD

It started with a laugh—mocking mirth that first emerged from radio receivers 80 years ago on the premier broadcast of Street & Smith's *Detective Story Magazine Hour.*

For a half-hour each week beginning July 31st, 1930, the sibilant host of CBS' *Detective Story Magazine* program narrated dramatized stories from the upcoming issue of the world's premier mystery magazine, beginning with Herman Landon's "The Serpent Stings" and concluding a year later with H. M. S. Titus' "Fugitives' Retreat."

Radio's famous mystery man was first conceived by Ruthrauff and Ryan advertising executive Dave Chrisman and radio director Bill Sweets, but it was young scriptwriter Harry Charlot who suggested the perfect name for the phantom narrator—The Shadow!

The mysterious host of Street & Smith's *Detective Story Program* was network radio's first sinister story-teller, and took broadcasting by storm. Sinister-toned imitators soon filled the airwaves, including *The Witch's Tale*'s Old Nancy, *Suspense*'s Man in Black, *Inner Sanctum*'s Raymond, The Mysterious Traveler and The Whistler.

James LaCurto portrayed the mysterious narrator during the earliest broadcasts, but soon left to perform on Broadway. His successor, Frank Readick, was one of the finest character actors on the airwaves, whose venomous tones soon made The Shadow a national sensation. The following year, Readick reprised his famous radio role in *Burglar to the Rescue,* the first of six two-reel "filmettes" released by Universal Pictures, and continued to voice the ethereal tones on Street & Smith's *Love Story Dramas,* the *Blue Coal Radio Revue* and two seasons of The Shadow's own mystery anthology series on NBC and CBS.

When Street & Smith circulation manager Bill Ralston heard that listeners were asking for "that Shadow detective magazine" instead of *Detective Story,* he quickly decided to reenter the long-dormant "character magazine" field with a new periodical built around the popular radio host. A Philadelphia magician-turned-journalist was assigned the task of bringing literary life to radio's mystery man. From the shadowy reaches of his own imagination, Walter Gibson recast radio's mysterioso host as literature's first Dark Hero, a crimebusting supersleuth who embodied the iconic charisma of Dracula and other classic melodrama villains. Only now, the sound of mocking laughter signaled rescue instead of doom.

The first issue of *The Shadow Magazine* arrived on newsstands on March 6, 1931. In just 18 months,

Sh-h-h- —listen!

TONIGHT AT 9:30 [Daylight] [Sav. Time] ON WJAS

Double murder mystery puzzles famous detective

MASTERSON was stumped. A daring jewelry robbery — two ruthless murders! Was all this the ingenious work of some "master-mind"? Was it the Wolf? Shorty? Margy? Mrs. Wakeling? Masterson had nothing but suspicions until . . . .

Get the inside story. Tonight, and every Thursday night, a smashing detective drama will be presented by Street & Smith, publishers of the famous Detective Story Magazine.

Detective Story Magazine
A Street & Smith Publication

it jumped from quarterly to monthly to twice-monthly frequency, revitalizing a pulp industry devastated by the Great Depression and inspiring a small army of imitators including the Phantom Detective, the Green Lama, the Spider, the Black Bat and The Avenger.

Gibson's Shadow novels were soon reprinted in Canada, France, England, Spain and Argentina, while The Shadow's mocking tones spread beyond national borders into Latin America and Australia via a radio transcription serial starring Carl Kroenke.

In 1937, *The Shadow* returned to the airwaves as a revamped series based on Gibson's pulp novels, which helped propel its 22-year-old star Orson Welles to national fame. During the next 17 years, the role would be voiced by Bill Johnstone, John Archer, Steven Courtleigh and finally Bret Morrison, who owned The Shadow's famous laugh for a decade.

"By 1940 The Shadow was more than a household word; it had become a household commodity," Walter Gibson recalled. "People could buy the magazine on a Friday and bring it home to read over the weekend while the kids were going to the Saturday movies to see Victor Jory in a Shadow serial and other members of the family were listening to *The Shadow* radio program on Sunday afternoon." *Shadow Comics* debuted that same year, along with a syndicated newspaper strip by Gibson and cartoonist Vernon Greene. By 1941, *Shadow Comics* was selling 450,000 copies each month, and the Dark Avenger was featured in Macy's Thanksgiving Day Parade and the department store's Christmas Toyland.

In March of 1942, *The Shadow* owned the airwaves, commanding a Hooper rating of 17.2 and 55.6% of the listening audience for its time period, "the highest daytime rating of the entire week."

American GIs and overseas listeners soon heard The Shadow's adventures over the Armed Forces Radio Network, while Lloyd Lamble supplied The Shadow's filtered tones when American scripts were rebroadcast in Australia. *The Shadow* also aired in South Africa and was transmitted to England by Radio Normandy, while nearly 300 scripts were translated into Portuguese for Brazilian listeners and Alejandro Ciangherotti starred in a Mexican series.

The Shadow ended its MBS network run on December 26, 1954, but the legendary series triumphantly returned to the airwaves in 1963 via syndicated rebroadcasts, launching a radio drama revival that continues into the 21st century.

And it all started 80 years ago with a laugh—the laugh heard around the world!   —Anthony Tollin

*Jewels—crooks and clinics—
death and danger. All pack
a terrific punch in this amazing
story of*

THE CRIME CLINIC

CHAPTER I
COMING EVENTS

A SHORT, stocky man was strolling beneath the superstructure of an East Side elevated. The collar of his brown overcoat was upturned. His gray hat was tilted down over his forehead. His hands were thrust deep in his side pockets. The man had all the appearance of an idler. He looked like a typical denizen of this dingy district in Manhattan.

Jostling shoulders with bums, the saunterer continued his slow pace. He growled at those whom he encountered, and there was a challenge in his air that commanded immediate respect. He seemed to be as tough a rowdy as any in the neighborhood, which abounded in tough characters.

The street was gloomy; nevertheless, the stroller showed a marked aptitude for turning his head away from any lights that he approached. Shop windows were lighted, for there was some evening business even on this tawdry thoroughfare. The muffled man avoided the glare from the little stores, sought only the shadows.

Only once did the stocky individual relax his effort to remain unrecognized. That was when he reached the entrance to a side street, where he idled in meditative fashion. He wanted to be sure that he was unobserved, and in convincing himself that this was the case, he unwittingly eased his vigilance. The glow of a streetlamp temporarily revealed the man's upturned features. That light showed a swarthy, square-jawed countenance.

The muffled man was Detective Joe Cardona, ace of the Manhattan force. A prowler in the borderlands where crime was fostered, he had every reason to keep his identity unknown. After short, quick glances along the street, Cardona turned and entered the alleyway.

Perhaps there were those who knew Cardona's gait; perhaps there were spying eyes that had caught that momentary revealment of the detective's face. Whichever the case might be, there was a distinct activity along the street immediately after Detective Cardona's departure.

Another idler across the street turned suddenly and walked away. A sneaky, stealthy man slipped from the protection of an obscure doorway. He passed a lounger who was standing beside the steps of an elevated station. This fellow sidled away as though a relayed message had been given.

NEWS was going through the underworld that Joe Cardona had arrived within the realm of crime. The grapevine telegraph was hard at work, reporting this event. Such was the way in the badlands of Manhattan.

Yet amid the subdued excitement, no one had noted the activities of the first individual who had taken action after viewing Joe Cardona's face. This fellow had passed as one of the underworld. He looked like a husky gangster, who had every right to be in this forlorn district. Hence he had passed unchallenged.

In the light of a dingy cigar store, this man who had seen Cardona appeared as a different type. His face, though firm and determined, showed a keenness lacking in the usual gangster. Ensconced in a telephone booth, he called a number, and announced his identity in a low voice.

"Marsland reporting" were his words.

"Report," came the order, in a quiet voice.

"Cardona in vicinity," announced Marsland. "Entered alley alongside Climax Brass Shop. Went into third house on the left."

"Report received."

This secret conversation had a meaning. Cliff Marsland, pretended gangster, had reported Cardona's arrival. The man to whom he had spoken over the wire was a chap named Burbank—one whom Cliff had never seen, yet with whom he had much in common.

For Cliff Marsland was an agent of The Shadow; and Burbank was The Shadow's contact man. As a prowler in the underworld, Cliff picked up data of importance, and sent it to Burbank; the contact man, in turn, relayed it to The Shadow.

To the underworld, a secret visit by Joe Cardona was a matter of importance. Whatever concerned the underworld, concerned The Shadow also. For The Shadow, mysterious personage whose very identity was unknown, battled crime and swung the balance of power into the hands of justice.

Cliff Marsland, sensing suppressed excitement in the neighborhood, had picked up the information that Joe Cardona had been seen. He had passed the word along to The Shadow. From now on, it would be The Shadow's province to learn why Joe Cardona had set forth on a secret mission.

JOE CARDONA was a detective of capability. He had a tendency, however, to rely upon grit rather than craftiness. He had come to this district, confident that he could conceal his identity. So sure of that had Cardona been that he did not suspect that he had been recognized and trailed.

The detective was laughing gruffly as he ascended a pair of dilapidated stairs within the building that he had entered. He stopped in front of a door on the third floor and gave two short, quick raps; after a pause, he repeated the double knock.

The door opened, and a peaked, wild-eyed face stared through the crack. A sickly grin appeared upon the hunted countenance as the door opened farther.

Joe Cardona stepped in. The little, stoop-shouldered man who had admitted him quickly closed and locked the door.

"Nobody seen you?" he questioned, in a hoarse, frightened voice. "Sure nobody seen you, Joe?"

"Not a chance, Scoffy," returned Cardona, with a grin. "Look—I had my collar up—my hat tilted. I looked like any other mug on the avenue. Sit down—sit down—"

"Don't stay long, Joe," pleaded the little man as he sank to a tumbledown chair. "I ain't got much to tell you tonight. I took a big chance, Joe, when I told you to come to this hideout. Say—if anyone wised that I was playin' stool—"

"Forget it, Scoffy. You're safe. Let's hear what you've got to tell me."

"It ain't much, Joe"—"Scoffy's" voice was a hoarse whisper—"but it may mean a lot—later on. I just got the word that The Jackdaw is workin' again."

Scoffy's lips twitched as his beady eyes stared toward Cardona. The little stool pigeon was anxious to see what effect his words had on the detective. He expected that Cardona would be startled. The expectation was fulfilled.

Cardona's eyes narrowed. His jaw hardened. His fists tightened. The star detective sat down upon the only other chair in the dilapidated bedroom and looked firmly at his informant.

"What do you know about The Jackdaw?" he demanded.

"Nothin' at all, Joe," pleaded Scoffy. "Nothin'—honest. I'd blab if I knew who he was—"

"Tell me what you think about him."

"Nothin' you don't know, Joe."

"Tell me, anyway."

"Well," asserted Scoffy, in a confidential tone, "he's a real guy, all right. Everybody knows how he used to work. He went after swell stuff—jewels—bonds—the kind of swag you'd find in a big banker's home."

"Alone?"

"Sometimes—an' sometimes with a mob. All dependin' on the lay. Then he scrammed—an' came back. But he scrammed again. Now I think he's comin' back."

"Why?"

"Because I seen Bennie Lizzit back in town—and Bennie was workin' in The Jackdaw's mob."

"Do you know any others in the outfit?"

"Not a one, Joe—honest. Say—Bennie an' me used to be pals. If he knowed that I was squealin' to you, Joe, I'd get the works, sure."

Cardona eyed the furtive-faced stool pigeon. There was no question about Scoffy's sincerity. The palefaced gangster was telling all that he knew. Joe was determined to take advantage of Scoffy's potential usefulness.

"All right," said the detective, rising. "I'm counting on you, Scoffy. Keep your eyes open. Pal around with Bennie Lizzit again. Find out the fellow he's working for. If The Jackdaw is back again, I'm going to crack his mob and get him, too."

"It ain't goin' to be easy," volunteered Scoffy, with a shake of his head. "I knowed Bennie was workin' for The Jackdaw. I was the only guy that knowed it. But I never got no hookup on the rest of the mob.

"The Jackdaw is a silk hat, Joe. He may use some gorillas when he needs 'em, but he ain't in their class. He's a guy that moves high. He knows the swells, an' he works alone whenever he can."

"I know his game," nodded Cardona. "If he had stayed around long enough, I would have grabbed him. Now that I know he's back, I can get to him. But I may have to do it through the mob. That's where you come in. Understand? Watch Bennie Lizzit."

"All right, Joe," nodded Scoffy reluctantly.

"Give me a call," ordered Cardona. "Tell me as soon as you have any new dope. Nobody knows that you're tipping me off. Don't worry."

With this assurance to the stool pigeon, Cardona closed his coat collar about his chin. He slouched his hat down over his eyes, opened the door, and thrust his hands into his pockets as he stalked down the stairs.

Scoffy listened at the door. He heard the thud of Cardona's footsteps. He was glad that the detective

had gone. The interview had taken only a few minutes. Scoffy tried to convince himself that no one had recognized the detective. The stool pigeon realized that he had taken a long chance in bringing Cardona here.

Satisfied as to Cardona's departure, Scoffy closed the door. He stood trembling as he fished in his pocket for a pack of cigarettes. Matches rattled as a wooden box came out in the shaky hand.

Scoffy's gaze was toward the window. Suddenly, it turned to the door. With a wild gasp, the stool pigeon sprang to lock the barrier.

He was too late.

SIMULTANEOUSLY with the sound of footsteps, the door swung open, and a big-shouldered, ugly-faced ruffian thrust himself into the room. In his right hand, this fellow held a big revolver. He covered Scoffy with a weapon, and a fierce grin appeared upon the pockmarked countenance.

"Bennie Lizzit!"

The name was gasped from Scoffy's lips. The intruder laughed as he closed the door behind him.

"Didn't expect to see me, eh?" he snarled. "Who'd you think I was—that smart dick comin' back?"

"What dick?" questioned Scoffy, trying to bluff.

"Joe Cardona," jeered Bennie Lizzit. "Say—that clodhopper was lamped when he hit the avenue. Everybody knew he was down here. I heard where he headed. I figured maybe he was comin' to see you."

"What'd he want to see me for?" asked Scoffy. "I ain't said nothin' to him, Bennie. You an' me—we're pals and—"

"We was pals," retorted Bennie. "But not no more—you squealin' rat!"

Scoffy saw what was coming. Bennie Lizzit was between him and the door. With a frenzied cry, the trapped stool pigeon made a dash for the window. Bennie overtook him; with a sweep of his arm, the big gangster sent the little man spinning into the corner.

"Honest, Bennie!" Scoffy was pleading. "Honest—I didn't squeal!"

"You mean you ain't goin' to squeal no longer!"

With these words, Bennie shot his left hand forward, and pinned the stool pigeon's neck to the wall. Before the cornered squealer could manage to squirm away, Bennie made a vicious swing with his right arm. His revolver landed squarely upon the side of Scoffy's head.

The little fellow sagged. Bennie Lizzit delivered another skull-crushing blow. He released his left hand. Scoffy's body tumbled to the floor. The stool pigeon was dead.

Bennie gloated as he surveyed the work which he had done. Still holding his revolver, he turned toward the door.

The murderer's eyes began to bulge. His fist tightened on his revolver. His hand, however, did not rise. Bennie Lizzit, killer though he was, felt pangs of fear at the uncanny event which was taking place before his gaze here in this gangster hideout.

The door was swinging open, of its own accord. As Bennie stared into the darkened hallway beyond, all that he could see was a pair of blazing eyes. As he stared, the murderer saw a form materialize. He gasped as he observed a being in black that appeared just within the doorway.

"The Shadow!"

Bennie's blurted recognition was a fitting tribute to the mysterious presence of The Shadow. A tall form garbed in black, The Shadow had arrived as an avenger from the night. His shape seemed spectral beneath the folds of a black cloak. His features—all save those terrible, blazing eyes—were invisible beneath the shade of a broad-brimmed slouch hat.

THE one symbol of realism was the huge automatic that projected from a black-gloved hand. The sight of that weapon brought terror to Bennie Lizzit. The mobster had killed. His victim lay at his feet. The Shadow had trapped the murderer.

An ominous laugh came from unseen lips. The Shadow had arrived too late to prevent the death of Scoffy, the stool pigeon. He was here, however, to learn the reason why Scoffy had been slain. His sinister laugh was the token of his power.

Had The Shadow trapped Bennie Lizzit at any other moment, the gangster would unquestionably have quailed. From his lips, The Shadow would have learned the reason for the murderer's crime.

But with Scoffy's body at his feet, Bennie Lizzit still was dominated with a savage thirst for murder. At the sound of The Shadow's laugh, the killer spat a fierce oath and swung his gun arm upward to fire point-blank at the avenger who had caught him on the scene of crime.

The room re-echoed to the roar of an ear-splitting report. The flash of flame came from The Shadow's automatic. A split second before his enemy, The Shadow had delivered his message to prevent the gangster's shot.

Bennie staggered backward, clutching his left shoulder. Crippled, he still snarled his rage. With clawing finger, he managed to pull the trigger of his revolver. Shots went wide from his wavering gun.

Once more the automatic thundered. The bullet clipped the gangster's arm. With a shriek of pain, Bennie Lizzit sprawled sidewise. He was against the window as he fell; his useless hand, as it lost the revolver, struck against the drawn window shade. The sash beyond was open. Lurching, where he had sought solidity, Bennie Lizzit floundered head-foremost over the low sill. He made a wild clutch with his left hand; his fingers slipped as they clicked against the window frame.

The window shade snapped loose. Wrapped like a shroud about the hurtling gangster, it accompanied Bennie Lizzit on his three-story plunge to the paving beneath the window. A hideous scream ended in a crash below.

Silent, The Shadow stood within the door of this room where death had been delivered and avenged. Shouts came to him from the street below. The black cloak swished. The tall form disappeared into the darkness of the hallway.

Coming events had brought The Shadow to this spot. Joe Cardona had talked with Scoffy. The stool pigeon had died at the hands of Bennie Lizzit. The murderer, in turn, was dead. These startling occurrences were but the prelude to a trail of crime.

The Shadow, though he had not heard the words from Scoffy's lips, foresaw the coming conflict. Though Joe Cardona, alone, had received word that the smooth crook called "The Jackdaw" had returned, The Shadow soon would know what the detective had learned.

The stage was set for the events that were to come.

CHAPTER II
THE SHADOW BEGINS

LATE the next afternoon, Detective Joe Cardona was seated at his desk in headquarters. The place was deserted. Cardona, alone, was giving vent to his feelings by means of a sullen scowl. The chief object of Cardona's annoyance seemed to be the evening newspaper that was lying on the desk before him.

Leaning back in his chair, Cardona spent a few minutes in reflective thought. Then, in a decisive manner, he arose, picked up the newspaper, and strode into another office.

He sat down in a chair on the opposite side from a gray-haired man who was busily engaged in completing a report sheet. This was Inspector Timothy Klein, Cardona's superior.

Klein did not appear to notice Cardona's arrival. When he had finished his report sheet, however, the grizzled inspector looked up and greeted the detective with a friendly smile.

"What's the matter, Joe?" he inquired.

"Plenty," admitted Cardona. "This, for one thing."

He pointed to the newspaper as he spoke. Klein looked at the item indicated and shook his head.

"Why does this bother you?" he questioned. "A couple of small-fry mobsters killed—that's all. There have been other shootings in that neighborhood."

"Listen, inspector." Cardona's voice was serious. "I've got a hunch that there's trouble coming. There's something big behind this. I'll tell you why.

I was using this fellow Scoffy. Just breaking him in as a high-grade stool pigeon."

Inspector Klein arched his eyebrows. The statement aroused his immediate interest.

"Last night," went on Cardona, "I went down there to see him. He told me about this fellow, Bennie Lizzit. Scoffy was afraid of Lizzit. More than that, he told me Lizzit was hooked up with a big game. I told Scoffy to keep an eye on Lizzit. Then what happens? This. Lizzit kills Scoffy; and someone gets Lizzit."

Inspector Klein began to nod thoughtfully.

"Which leaves me out," declared Cardona. "My stool's dead; so is the man he was watching. That's why I think the game is going to break."

"What do you think it's all about, Joe?"

"I know what it's about," asserted Cardona. "You know the trouble we had with those swell society robberies. You know how little we learned. Some rumors about a smart crook they called 'The Jackdaw.' Whether he was a gentleman burglar or a gang leader, we didn't find out. The only way we figured that he'd ducked out was when he quit operating.

"Well, last night Scoffy tipped me that Bennie Lizzit had worked for The Jackdaw. With Bennie back in town, Scoffy figured The Jackdaw might be back. Now that Scoffy and Bennie are both dead, I figure The Jackdaw is back."

THE statement brought a frown from Inspector Klein. Cardona knew the reason. He spoke before Klein had an opportunity to express himself.

"I know what you're thinking, Inspector," said the detective. "It's going to raise hob if we start going after some unknown bird that we call 'The Jackdaw.' The commissioner put the taboo on my mentioning The Shadow in reports—even though I knew there were cases in which The Shadow figured. Now, if I say there's a crook called The Jackdaw—"

Inspector Klein raised his hands. He tried to curb Cardona's outburst.

"Easy, Joe," he said. "You're getting ahead of yourself. There are no reports of robberies as yet."

"That's just it," returned Cardona grimly. "The other times we came in after The Jackdaw was gone. This trip I want to be ahead of him."

"Excellent," affirmed Klein.

"I've figured it this way," asserted Cardona. "If The Jackdaw is back on the job, he'll be after big game. Here—right on the same page of this afternoon's newspaper—is something that ought to interest him."

Inspector Klein looked at the item which Cardona indicated. Half aloud, he read the words which most impressed him:

Among the gems which Rutherford Casslin will exhibit at his home on Wednesday night is a large diamond of a decided reddish tint. Its value has not been stated; but Mr. Casslin stated that he regards it as the prize of his collection.

"Casslin is a millionaire," explained Cardona. "Lives out on Long Island in a big place he calls 'Five Towers.' I talked to him on the telephone this afternoon."

"About the diamond?"

"Yes. I told him who I was. I asked him about being present at his home on Wednesday night."

"What did he say?"

"I think he's crazy," growled Cardona. "He told me to go back to Bombay; that he was tired of people calling him up and misrepresenting themselves. He wanted to know if I was the same fellow who talked to him in London, and claimed to be from Scotland Yard."

"That's odd," commented Klein. "He must have obtained the diamond in India. Listen, Joe; why don't you go out here this evening and see this millionaire? Get his slant on whatever he suspects; but don't mention anything about The Jackdaw. That ought to pave the way for a visit on Wednesday night."

A shadow fell across the floor as the inspector was speaking. Joe Cardona saw the approaching streak of black; he wheeled in his chair, and looked toward the door. He grinned as he saw a tall, stoop-shouldered janitor, who was carrying a pail and mop. The fellow looked at the detective with dull, listless eyes.

"Hello, Fritz," laughed Cardona. "Cleaning up early again, eh?"

"Yah," returned the janitor.

"Well, I'm not interfering," said Cardona. "I'm on my way right now." He turned to Klein. "I'm all set, Inspector. I'll run out to Casslin's place some time this evening."

"So he can see you're not from Bombay," added Klein, with a short laugh. "That sure is an odd one, Joe, unless some—"

"Unless Casslin is goofy?"

"No." Klein was rising from the desk as he spoke. "Unless there is some Hindu business mixed up with that diamond. I've seen some strange hookups in my time."

"I'll find out the whole story, Inspector."

The two men walked from the room. Klein was pocketing his report as he went. He looked toward the janitor, who was busy with mop and bucket.

"Good night, Fritz," he said.

"Yah" was the janitor's reply.

Footsteps died in the corridor.

IT was then that Fritz ceased his mopping. His tall form seemed to straighten to unusual proportions.

A soft laugh came from his thick lips. In the direct light of the room, Fritz's face took on an artificial expression that neither Cardona nor Klein had noticed. It was more a mask than a face.

Stooping again, this curious janitor shambled from the office. He emitted a friendly "Yah" to a detective whom he passed in the hall. He reached an obscure room, placed mop and bucket upon the floor, and opened the door of a locker.

Folds of black cloth tumbled forth. A cloaklike garment rolled over the janitor's head. Long hands placed a slouch hat upon the head above. With swift, gliding stride, a phantom shape swung away from the locker, and reentered the gloomy corridor.

The metamorphosis was complete. The pretended janitor had become The Shadow.

No one could have traced The Shadow's course from then on. Not even the real Fritz, arriving for janitor duty, saw the lurking shape which waited near the outer door until he had passed. The Shadow, by his remarkable impersonation, had listened from the corridor to the conversation between Detective Cardona and Inspector Klein. He had learned why Joe Cardona had visited Scoffy; he had also discovered why Bennie Lizzit had slain the stool pigeon.

To The Shadow, the information gained was usable for a more direct purpose than an immediate visit to the home of Rutherford Casslin. One hour after his departure from headquarters, The Shadow appeared in an obscure portion of Manhattan. A corner light revealed him only as a passing shade of blackness against a dingy wall.

The Shadow had arrived in a district of cosmopolitan Manhattan where members of a dark-skinned race were wont to be. Hindus are rare in New York, but the spot chosen by The Shadow was one which they frequented. The tall shape was lost in obscurity; it reappeared at a little used doorway, and glided into the side entrance of a small restaurant.

Half an hour passed while The Shadow watched from obscurity. The proprietor of the restaurant was a Hindu, garbed in American attire. Most of his patrons were Americans; but as The Shadow lingered, a dark-skinned individual entered and spoke to the restaurant keeper. After that, he went to a table in a corner of the place and sat down.

The Shadow glided from the unused entrance. Shortly afterward, a second Hindu entered, spied the one seated at the table, and joined him. The men waited until bowls of curried rice had been set before them.

Alone, they were about to speak, when a tall American strolled in and took his seat at a table nearby. One of the Hindus glanced in his direction, then shrugged his shoulders, and started to talk to his companion.

THE Hindus were obviously men of intelligence. The fineness of their Aryan features showed that fact. Their talk was partly English, partly the native tongue familiar to them. It would have been an indecipherable jargon to the average American.

The customer nearby had ordered a dish of Indian food. He seemed quite oblivious to the words which the Hindus were uttering. Nevertheless, his ears were keen, and nothing escaped him. The dialect came within his understanding.

"It can only be the one," a Hindu was declaring. "Its color—red—is all that we need to know. It is the diamond taken from Bishenpur."

"Would Changra of Bombay still seek it?" queried the man's companion.

"No" was the reply. "Once it had left London, and come to New York, the price would be too great for any offer he might make. Changra sells his gems at profit."

"He sought the Bishenpur diamond."

"Yes. The Nizam of Hyderabad would gladly buy it for his vast collection. The Nizam would pay a great price."

"How much would Changra offer for the diamond?"

"One hundred and fifty thousand rupees."

An eager hiss came from the listening Hindu.

"You are going back to India," said the first speaker. "If you should carry with you the Bishenpur diamond, it would mean great gain for each of us."

"Changra would ask no questions?"

"None."

"But the diamond? How can you obtain it?"

"Tippu is watching at the American's castle. Tippu is bold. He will do his utmost to seize it."

The listener nodded in agreement. His dark eyes gleamed at the thought of great gain. The ensuing discussion dealt with the arrangements which he must make upon reaching Bombay.

While the Hindus were still talking, the American finished his meal and arose. He strolled leisurely from the restaurant. The plotting Hindus gave no more thought to him. They had no idea whatever that he had understood their conversation.

NOT far from the restaurant, the tall listener stopped beside a parked coupé. He stepped into the car. Blackened folds of cloth dropped over his shoulders. Black gloves and slouch hat completed his adopted garb.

The coupé moved, guided by an unseen hand. As it rolled from the vicinity where New York's small Hindu population thronged, a soft laugh betrayed the hidden thoughts of the driver of that car.

The Shadow had learned more than Joe Cardona. He had discovered why Rutherford Casslin had regarded the detective's telephone call as a hoax. Possessor of a rare stone which he had brought from India, the American millionaire had refused all offers which had been made for its purchase.

The Shadow had learned of a definite danger which overclouded Rutherford Casslin's possession of the diamond. He had heard the name of a man who was watching the millionaire's Long Island home—Tippu, a vigilant Hindu bent on crime.

The Shadow, like Joe Cardona, was bound for Rutherford Casslin's home. Whether or not The Jackdaw was concerned in this enterprise did not matter. Crime threatened and where crime hovered, there would The Shadow be.

The clock on the dashboard of the coupé showed the hour of nine as The Shadow guided his car through the traffic of Manhattan, headed for an East River bridge.

CHAPTER III
CASSLIN'S CASTLE

THE chimes of a jeweled clock were striking nine. A fashionable throng was gathered in the spacious living room of Rutherford Casslin's home. The group had come to this apartment following a sumptuous dinner.

Rutherford Casslin, a tall, portly man of fifty years, surveyed the group with a self-satisfied air. Most of the men present were ones who had gained prestige and wealth through commercial success. A small group, but a select one, so Casslin decided.

Most of the women were of middle age. There was one exception, Casslin noted, as he smiled beamingly. That was Yvonne Lydell, a beautiful girl in her early twenties. Garforth Lydell, Yvonne's father, was one of Casslin's old friends. Garforth, Casslin remembered, was away from New York at present.

Beside Yvonne was seated a young man, attired in a perfectly fitted Tuxedo. This was Bart Melken, wealthy scion of an old New York family. Melken was Yvonne Lydell's fiance. The pair would make an excellent match, Rutherford Casslin decided.

Only one guest was not seated. Of middle height, but thin to an extreme that made him seem tall, this worthy was standing in a corner of the room. He was a man whose status as a surgeon had gained him high recognition, yet who seemed out of place in this purely social gathering.

Rutherford Casslin had considered long before inviting Doctor Lysander Dubrong to dine here tonight. There was something about the physician's cynical demeanor that made it difficult for Casslin to understand him.

Rutherford Casslin was a domineering, boastful individual. So long as he could hold the center of conversation, he was a perfect host. His guests seemed to sense this; out of courtesy, they listened as Casslin took the floor. The millionaire was about to make an announcement which he regarded as of paramount interest.

"Tonight," declared Casslin, "I have a treat in store for you. This is Monday. I have announced that on Wednesday I shall exhibit certain rare gems which I possess. Those jewels are in a safe-deposit vault—with one exception.

"I refer to the prize of my collection—a beautiful diamond of high value. I brought the stone from India. It is here in my mansion tonight. I am ready to show it to you on this occasion."

A murmur of surprise swept through the throng. Casslin had created the effect that he wanted. He paused to add further remarks.

"Many persons have wondered," he stated, "how I am able to keep valuables in my home with absolutely no fear of burglary. My answer is that this house is itself as strong as any vault.

"This building, which I have called 'Five Towers,' is the modernized replica of a famous English castle. No feudal lord ever possessed a more formidable fortress. Each turret of this castle has walls of solid stone; and one tower, in particular, is especially provided against attack. It is there that I keep any valuables that I bring to my house; it is there that the diamond is now safeguarded."

Casslin stared about him with a proud smile. Seeing interest on the faces of his listeners, he proceeded with a new statement.

"Some of you," he declared, "have seen the arrangement of my stronghold. Others have not. I am going to my tower to procure the diamond. Any who wish may accompany me."

THE invitation was promptly grasped by several of the persons present. There were exceptions, however, and chief among them was Doctor Lysander Dubrong. With a cynical smile upon his thin, dry lips, the physician advanced and extended his hand to Rutherford Casslin.

"Sorry," he explained. "I must forgo the pleasure. I have visited your tower before."

"You are welcome again," returned the millionaire.

"It is after nine o'clock," objected Dubrong. "I have an important appointment in Manhattan."

"You are not remaining to see my diamond?"

"I can wait until Wednesday night."

"Evidently you are not a connoisseur of gems, Doctor Dubrong."

There was criticism in Rutherford Casslin's tone. It was matched by the sharp sarcasm of Dubrong's reply.

"Cold stones," said the physician, "do not

LIMPS SILVEY

LIMPS SILVEY is an underworld character deluxe. Crook he is, without a doubt, and yet he does nothing for which the law can hold him. But, throughout the mesh and web of this tale, Limps Silvey hobbles along, appearing in places where he is least expected to appear—and finally being traced to the clinic of Doctor Dubrong, where the scum of the city come for treatment.

DOCTOR DUBRONG

DOCTOR DUBRONG, a wealthy practicing physician who devotes a great deal of his time to a free clinic treating the poor and downtrodden, placed in the very heart of the toughest section of the city. The doctor's interest in criminals appears noble and philanthropic—until Detective Joe Cardona gets on his trail and observes a lot of queer things which occur there, and sees the connection between the doctor and Limps Silvey.

FARRELL SARBORN, traveler, adventurer, and friend of Bart Melken, who returns from one of his trips just in time to be of help to the weak-willed young man who has become embroiled in The Jackdaw's evil plots. But The Jackdaw proves a more difficult case than problems of the jungle, or of the mountains. Sarborn and Melken learn that crime is different.

FARRELL SARBORN

BART MELKEN, who was not strong enough to resist the temptation of evil when it first came, and who found, day after day, that the grip of evil becomes stronger and stronger with time, harder to escape. A man weak-willed enough to succumb to crime is not strong enough to escape it—not without the help of others stronger than he. Is Sarborn strong enough to save him?

BART MELKEN

impress me. Though they may sparkle, they are mere baubles. The real gems in life are human achievements."

Dubrong was shaking Casslin's hand as he spoke. With a gesture that bordered almost on contempt, the physician swung and walked from the living room. He stopped in an outer hallway.

Alone, he donned his hat and coat, in slow, methodical fashion. He was peering through a curtained doorway, and his gaze was centered upon Bart Melken, the young man of wealth who was engaged to Yvonne Lydell.

So far as the group was concerned, Doctor Dubrong's departure was of no importance. Even Bart Melken, the man Dubrong watched, had given no further thought to the physician. When Dubrong went from the outer hallway, no one noticed his final leave-taking.

Rutherford Casslin had summoned two servants. Husky fellows, attired in uniform, they looked like a pair of bodyguards. Casslin referred to one as "Hubert" to the other as "Hodges." At the millionaire's order, each servant exhibited a loaded revolver.

Casslin's living room was on the second story of the castle. It had two doorways; one at the side, through which Doctor Dubrong had gone; the other at the rear. It was through this opening that the millionaire invited his guests to follow him. Three men and two ladies responded; the others remained in the living room, for they had previously seen the strongroom.

Mrs. Casslin, the millionaire's bejeweled wife, remained in the living room talking to the few who had not followed her husband. Among these persons were Yvonne Lydell and Bart Melken. Speaking to Yvonne, Mrs. Casslin mentioned the magnificent diamond of which Casslin had boasted.

"It is a marvelous stone," said the portly hostess. "These jewels which I wear are merely trifles compared with it. They are worth only a few thousand at the most—"

"Your necklace, Mrs. Casslin?" inquired Yvonne in surprise, as she indicated the string of jewels which the millionaire's wife was wearing.

"They are paste," confided Mrs. Casslin, with a smile. "I would never dream of wearing the real ones. They are in a safe-deposit vault. I do not like to have valuable gems here in the house."

Bart Melken, half a dozen paces away, was listening to Mrs. Casslin's statements. With an attitude of indifference, as though talk of jewels was boring, the young man strolled toward the side windows of the big living room. There, he extracted a cigarette from an ornate case. He drew a lighter from his pocket and flicked it.

THE flame responded and died. It was repeated.

Melken seemed nervous. A third attempt failed. It was only after he had stepped away from the window that Melken managed to obtain a light for his cigarette. At the moment of such accomplishment, his back was toward the window.

No one had been watching the young man at the time of his odd performance. Keen eyes might have taken his flickering work with the lighter as a signal to someone on the ground beyond the window. The few persons present, however, were talking with Mrs. Casslin.

Meanwhile, the guests who had accompanied Rutherford Casslin had reached a gloomy spot in a hallway that paralleled the rear of the living room. They were standing in front of a steel door that was set in the solid wall. A massive lock showed the strength of this formidable barrier

Casslin was talking like a lecturer as he drew a key from his pocket. He turned the lock, and before he opened the door, he finished with a few concluding remarks.

"This," he said, "is the entrance to the rear tower. I alone hold the key. It is my practice to enter here by myself. I entrust the key to one of my servants only while I am in the tower."

Unlocking the door, Casslin revealed the interior of a circular, stone-walled tower that extended upward for thirty feet, a hollow shaft. A narrow circular stairway of iron formed the mode of ascent. The stairway ran about the inner sides of the wall. It had a thin rail of metal.

Casslin pressed a switch. The interior of the turret was lighted with dim illumination. The visitors noted that the steps of the circular stairway were unblocked; one could see between them. The entire shaft showed emptiness.

Casslin handed the key to Hubert. While this servant and Hodges waited below, Casslin led his guests up the steps. The big door clanged behind them. Their footfalls sounded weirdly upon the iron steps.

Casslin's voice came in echoes as the millionaire preceded his friends on the thirty-foot climb. Casslin was pointing out a feature of the tower: tall, slitlike windows at intervals along the stairs.

"These windows," he explained, "were placed here before I made the tower my stronghold. You will observe, however, that they are less than eight inches in width. Moreover, they are strengthened by horizontal bars, set at intervals of six inches."

The guests could observe what Casslin said. The windows were tall, each nearly three feet high, to admit light. They were fitted with glass in iron frames, so that they could easily be opened. The crossbars, however, made it impossible for more than a hand and arm to enter through any opening.

Casslin reached the top of the steps. Here was

another door, of wood, but braced with iron, which he opened with a smaller key. The door swung inward. Casslin pressed a single light switch and conducted his guests into the lighted turret.

THE room was stone-walled and unfurnished. It was about a dozen feet in diameter. It possessed three long, slitted windows, like those on the stairway. They were also barred with crosswise metal rods.

"In old-time castles," explained Casslin, "these served as openings through which archers delivered their shafts. You will notice that three directions are covered. The openings were purposely narrowed, so that if the enemy scaled the wall with ladders, it would be impossible for them to enter.

"This portion of the wall"—he turned to the half which had no opening—"holds the strongbox. It is a small wall safe of a specially designed pattern. I, alone, know the combination."

The guests saw the spot indicated. The front of a small, square safe projected from the wall. Set in solid stone, buttressed by the house itself, this device was capable of withstanding the attack of a dynamiter.

"Now," decided Casslin, "I shall ask you all to retire below. I never permit anyone to be here when I open the wall safe."

The guests filed out through the door. While they were clanking down the circular steps, Casslin shut the barrier. He opened the safe and removed a small metal box. He closed the safe and followed the others who had gone below. He closed the door of the strongroom as he departed.

Hubert and Hodges were waiting outside the lower door. The guests had opened it from the inside; Casslin did the same. He took the key from Hubert, shut the steel door, and proceeded to join his guests who had gone back to the living room. The two servants, holding their revolvers, formed a bodyguard for the millionaire.

The tension was dramatic when Casslin entered the living room and placed the box upon the table. In the light, the small container showed its beauty. The box was inlaid with ivory. Casslin pressed a catch; the lid came open. Incredible gasps came from the onlookers.

Set upon white plush was a diamond of lustrous beauty. The stone sparkled with gorgeous radiance; its size, too, was remarkable. The feature which made the spectators gaze in awe was the coloring of the gem. A distinctly reddish tint seemed to pervade the diamond; and this elusive hue was always present.

"I purchased this diamond in India," lectured Rutherford Casslin. "It is said to have come from the collection of the King of Bishenpur. That monarch owned two of the most magnificent rubies in existence! I suppose that he fancied the diamond because of its reddish tinge.

"Shortly after I bought the diamond, I was approached by a jewel merchant of Bombay, who offered me one hundred and fifty thousand rupees for it. I could have shown a fancy profit above the price I paid, had I disposed of the diamond to Changra, the jewel merchant.

"However, I refused his offer. I would not part with this gem at any price. I am simply mentioning, though, that in India, this jewel would command the equivalent of fifty thousand dollars.

"The offer I had received followed me on my journey from India to England. In London, persistent representatives of the Bombay merchant still tried to buy the gem. They failed. I am keeping the diamond from Bishenpur."

As he concluded his talk, Rutherford Casslin held the jewel between thumb and forefinger. He raised it above the level of his eyes. A pale crimson aura seemed to hover about the Bishenpur diamond. Then, with a dramatic gesture, Casslin replaced the jewel in its case. With a bow that caused the guests to spread apart, he turned to return to his strongroom in the tower.

Yvonne Lydell walked toward the side window, where Bart Melken, cigarette lighter in hand, was having trouble making new bursts of flame. The young man looked up as his fiancée approached. He dropped the lighter into his vest pocket.

Yvonne, as she came from the back of the room, was facing toward the front window. Something made her stare in that direction, instead of looking at her fiancé. Suddenly, the girl gripped Bart Melken's arm.

"Look! Look!" she gasped.

Pressed against the front window was a brownish face. Dark, glittering eyes caught the girl's stare. Then, in a twinkling, the face was gone.

Bart Melken, as he followed the direction of Yvonne's gaze, was too late to see the visage that had been peering in from the outer darkness.

Yvonne's startled gasp faded on her lips as the girl felt Bart Melken's firm and reassuring grip upon her arm.

CHAPTER IV
MURDER STRIKES

"DID you see it, Bart?"

The question came in a whisper from Yvonne Lydell. Bravely, the girl was trying to curb the sudden terror which had caught her in its sway.

"See what?" returned Bart, in a calm undertone.

"The face," whispered Yvonne. "The face at the window."

"No," replied Bart. "It must have been pure imagination on your part."

Although the young man's voice was calm, his

own face had turned ashen. Yvonne did not notice Bart's strained expression. She was staring toward the front windows. Beyond them, she could see the rail of a narrow balcony that ran to the right from the living room, and probably opened upon other windows at the front of the house.

The intruder, whoever he was, had gone. With a slight shudder, Yvonne turned back toward the other guests.

Rutherford Casslin, with Hubert and Hodges beside him, was departing in the direction of the tower. Guests were asking questions about the Bishenpur diamond. Yvonne's suppressed excitement had not been noticed by anyone save Bart Melken.

"Say nothing," prompted the young man. "There is no need to alarm anyone—at least not until after Mr. Casslin has returned from his strongroom."

Yvonne reluctantly nodded her agreement with her fiancée's decision.

Casslin had walked through the rear door, in company with his two servants. He had evidently entered the steel door to the tower, and had gone up, for Hodges had returned, and was standing just within the doorway through which he had come.

Every guest was in the living room. Hodges, as though to make sure that all was well, stayed in the room himself. After a short interval, he turned to go back and join Hubert at the foot of the stairway to the tower.

At that moment, a hoarse, raucous shout came from beyond the door. Hodges stood momentarily startled; some of the men started toward the door before the servant moved. Then Hodges sprang to action. With three men at his heels, he dashed into the hallway.

THE cause of the cry was immediately apparent. Backed against the steel door was Hubert. He was clutching at a man who had pinned him there—a man in rough clothes, who turned a dark face toward those who came rushing into the hallway. At sight of Hodges, Hubert's assailant broke away.

In his hand, the dark-skinned man held a flashing knife. It was dripping with crimson blood, for the fellow had stabbed Hubert before the servant had gained an opportunity to shoot him. Seeing Hodges, the assailant made a move as though intent on flight; then realizing the predicament, leaped suddenly at the advancing rescuer.

The knife gleamed as the dark hand came upward. Hodges, justifying the faith that Rutherford Casslin held in his ability, fired point-blank. The assailant was uttering a wild cry as he sprang forward. It turned to a shriek as Hodges delivered the shot.

The dark-skinned man rolled to the floor. His features showed in the light as he landed on his back. It was plain that the man was a Hindu.

Startled exclamations came from the guests who were with Hodges. All remembered Rutherford Casslin's talk of Hindus who had sought the Bishenpur diamond.

The Hindu was dying. His hands lay loosely at his sides. The knife had fallen a foot away, and the man made no effort to grasp it. One of the guests seized the weapon. Hodges, whose quick action had saved the situation, was turning to his fellow servant, Hubert.

The man at the door had collapsed to the floor. Blood was issuing from his side. His revolver lay beside him. His lips were trembling. He could only gasp a few feeble words.

"The master"—Hubert panted as he paused—"in the tower. The master—look after him. The key—here—the key—"

Hubert's fingers clawed at a pocket in the side of his coat. His effort failed. His body sagged and sank away from the arm that held him. Hubert, like the Hindu, had received a mortal wound.

Worried guests were crowding about. They looked to Hodges for advice. The servant, thrust in a position of importance, showed excellent judgment. He managed to calm the excited men about him.

"Someone call for a doctor," he said. "Mr. Casslin is in the tower. We can inform him what has happened. The key must be in Hubert's pocket."

Hodges stooped over Hubert's body and found the key. One of the guests was trying the steel door. It was locked. Another had gone to make the telephone call.

They could hear Mrs. Casslin in the living room, talking excitedly. A few moments later, the woman appeared in the hallway. She placed her hands to her head in horror as she saw the bodies on the floor; then, with an effort, she managed to ignore the gruesome scene.

"Where is my husband?" she questioned. "Where is Rutherford?"

"In the tower, madam," returned Hodges. "The key was in Hubert's pocket. I have it here."

"He is safe, then!" exclaimed Mrs. Casslin. "He does not know what has happened here. This is terrible! Why did Doctor Dubrong go? Oh, why did he go? If he were only here now!"

"Shall I inform Mr. Casslin what has happened?" questioned Hodges. "Or shall I wait, madam, until he has come down from the tower?"

"Wait a few minutes, Hodges," decided Mrs. Casslin. "He will be back here any moment. He must be safe; the tower door is locked."

One of the guests appeared, to announce that he had called Doctor Dubrong's apartment. There had been no answer. Mrs. Casslin stood in a quandary.

"We must call another physician," she decided.

In his hand the
dark-skinned man
held a flashing knife.

"Yes, we must call another. We must call the police, also—"

"I got the apartment house on the phone," informed the guest. "They said that if Doctor Dubrong returned or called, they would tell him to come here. There was no answer when they rang his apartment. Probably he has not had time to reach there."

Mrs. Casslin was nervously wringing her hands. She looked from one guest to another. She seemed incapable of speech. Her eyes turned toward the steel door.

"What is keeping Rutherford?" she questioned. "He must have put the diamond away by now! Where is he? Where is my husband?"

AT that moment, another servant appeared at the end of the hallway. The uniformed man stopped short as he saw the confusion that existed. His face turned pale. He stared at Hubert's body, then looked toward Mrs. Casslin.

"Where have you been, Gilkins?" questioned Hodges.

"Downstairs," stammered the arrival. "What—what has happened here?"

"Didn't you hear the shot?" questioned Hodges.

"No," returned Gilkins, his face still ashen. "We—we were sitting in the kitchen. The doorbell just rang—I went to answer it."

"Who was there?" questioned Mrs. Casslin excitedly. "Doctor Dubrong?"

"No, madam," returned Gilkins. "There is a man who wishes to speak with Mr. Casslin. He says that he is from detective headquarters. His name is Mr. Cardona—it is important, he says, that he should see Mr. Casslin."

"A detective!" exclaimed Mrs. Casslin. "Tell him to come up at once, Gilkins!"

The servant hurried from the hallway. Mrs. Casslin rested against the wall, pressing her hands to her heart. One of the guests was supporting her.

All the others had come from the living room, including Bart Melken and Yvonne Lydell. They formed a small, silent group, away from the center of the hall where the bodies lay.

Everyone waited in tense silence. Then footsteps sounded, and Gilkins reappeared at the other end of the hallway. As the servant stopped, another man stepped by him. Detective Joe Cardona appeared to view this scene where death had fallen.

The first object that Cardona noted was the gun which Hodges was still holding. Without a word, the detective stepped forward and plucked the weapon from the servant's hand. Hodges yielded the revolver without question.

With precision, Cardona opened the gun and noted its contents. He pocketed the weapon; stooped and picked up the other gun, which was lying beside Hubert's body. He examined that weapon also, and dropped it in another pocket of his coat.

The guest who held the knife moved forward and gave the weapon to Cardona. The detective looked at it, and placed it on a small, narrow table that stood beside the wall. He bent over the Hindu's body, and saw that the man was dead. He made an examination of Hubert's prostrate form. Then he looked at the pale-faced group about him.

"Both men are dead," he asserted. "What has happened here? Has anyone left this place?"

MRS. CASSLIN was too weak to answer. One of the guests, a middle-aged gentleman, stepped forward, and drew a card from his pocket. He handed it to Cardona.

"Ah!" exclaimed the detective, in a respectful tone. "You are Stephen Gloucester, of the State Banking Department?"

"Yes," replied the gentleman, with dignity. "I am a guest here this evening. I observed all that occurred. This servant"—he indicated Hodges—"is in no wise culpable. He is to be commended. His companion"—Gloucester pointed to Hubert's body—"was slain by the Hindu. This man Hodges was forced to shoot the murderer to prevent him from attacking us."

"Where did the Hindu come from?" demanded Cardona.

"I don't know, sir," interposed Hodges, who had gained his tongue now that blame had been lifted from him. "Hubert, here, was standing by this door. He was guarding it while Mr. Casslin was above. I heard Hubert cry for aid. I rushed here from the living room. This is the key to the tower door, sir. It was in Hubert's pocket."

Cardona took the key and nudged his thumb toward the steel door.

"You mean that Rutherford Casslin is in there?" he asked.

Universal nods came from the amazed guests.

"Why hasn't he come out?" demanded Joe.

"I doubt that he heard the shot, sir," began Hodges. "This door is thick; there is another door above."

"Rutherford should be here!" blurted Mrs. Casslin suddenly. "He should not have remained in the tower so long. What is keeping him? What can be keeping him?"

Cardona raised his hand for silence. He motioned to all the guests, and lined them along the hallway. He strode to the living room, saw that no one else was there, and walked back to the steel door. He passed a revolver to Stephen Gloucester.

"I shall ask you, sir," decided Cardona, "to see that no one leaves this hallway. I am going into the tower. I shall ask you to accompany me, Mrs.

Casslin, and you"—he turned to the servant, Hodges—"can come along also."

Cardona opened the steel door with the key that Hodges had given him. The light was on within the tower.

As Hodges and Mrs. Casslin started up the circular stairs, Cardona made sure that no one was under shelter of the spiral. He followed them rapidly. He reached the top of the stairs just behind the two who had gone ahead. The closed door blocked the passage.

"Mr. Casslin is in here, sir," vouchsafed Hodges. "He has the key with him."

Cardona pounded upon the door. There was no response. Mrs. Casslin gave a nervous cry.

"Go down to the bottom of the stairs," Cardona ordered Hodges. "Call that other servant, and tell him to bring an ax."

Hodges clanked down the steps. He called for Gilkins before he reached the bottom, and relayed the order to the other man. Hodges returned at Cardona's call. The detective turned to Mrs. Casslin.

"If you would prefer to go below," he began, "it will be all right."

Mrs. Casslin shook her head bravely.

"Let me stay here," she pleaded. "I know that something has happened—if it has happened, it would be better for me to be here."

Gilkins was coming up the steps. The servant had a large fire ax. Cardona moved Mrs. Casslin and Hodges a short way down the steps and remained with them while he ordered Gilkins to attack the door.

With husky strokes, the servant demolished the barrier. As a huge piece of wood splintered away from the long metal hinge that reinforced it, Gilkins uttered a cry of horror, and stepped back against the wall.

Cardona leaped up the steps, revolver in hand. He jammed his shoulder through the opening, and sprang into the strongroom. Swiftly, boldly, he looked about him to see that the three windows were closed. His eyes fell to the floor beside the inner wall.

There lay the body of Rutherford Casslin. A gaping wound showed that the millionaire had been shot in the back! Sprawled upon the floor, with arms outstretched, Rutherford Casslin exhibited empty hands with spread fingers that rested almost against the base of the wall, just below the closed door of the safe.

Detective Joe Cardona was dumfounded. This tragedy was stunning, through the very circumstances that surrounded it. Rutherford Casslin's empty hands spoke words of their own.

Here, within a tightly locked room, behind slit-like windows braced with crossbars, with a steel door locked below and the key in the pocket of a trusted servant, Rutherford Casslin had been slain.

Empty hands told the motive of this mysterious murder. There was reason for the death of the millionaire. Somehow, in this isolated place, a prize had been plucked from a dead man's hand.

The Bishenpur diamond had been stolen!

CHAPTER V
THE SHADOW SEES

AMAZING though events had been at the home of Rutherford Casslin, the time element had been quite short. The living room clock had been chiming nine when Doctor Dubrong had left. That same clock marked thirty-eight minutes past the hour when Joe Cardona reassembled the guests in the living room, following his finding of Rutherford Casslin's body.

In the space of less than forty minutes, Casslin had exhibited the Bishenpur diamond, Hubert had been slain, Hodges had killed a murderous Hindu, and Casslin's dead body had been found under circumstances which seemed incredible.

The bodies of Hubert and the Hindu still lay where they had fallen. Casslin's body was upstairs in the tower room. The steel door was closed and locked; the key was in Cardona's pocket. The detective, ever alert, was standing at the rear door of the living room. From this position, he could see all within the room, and also keep an eye on the steel door in the hallway.

Word had been sent to Inspector Timothy Klein. The grizzled police officer was coming hither with detectives. In the meantime, Cardona, a lone investigator, was analyzing the strange situation that existed.

The guests were seated about the room. Gilkins and Hodges were standing within the doorway. Mrs. Casslin, alone, seemed on the verge of collapse. She had not seen her husband's body, but she knew that death had struck.

Cardona was in a quandary. He was solicitous for Mrs. Casslin, yet he knew the importance of obtaining statements and proceeding with an investigation. He spoke to Stephen Gloucester.

"Is everyone here?" he questioned.

"Yes," returned Gloucester. "All except Doctor Lysander Dubrong. He left, however, before Mr. Casslin brought the diamond from the strongroom."

"Doctor Dubrong," mused Cardona. "He is the man who has the East Side clinic?"

"I believe so."

An interruption came from Gilkins who was standing by the wall.

"Pardon, sir," said the servant, "I believe I heard the doorbell. Shall I answer it?"

"No, stay here," ordered Cardona. "Would you"—he turned again to Gloucester—"mind answering the door?"

"Not at all," returned Gloucester.

The dignified gentleman went from the living room. A few minutes later, rapid footsteps sounded. Into the room strode Doctor Lysander Dubrong, with Stephen Gloucester behind him. The physician went at once to Mrs. Casslin. The bereaved woman sighed.

"This is Doctor Dubrong," said Gloucester, in an undertone, to Cardona.

Dubrong himself spoke to Cardona a moment later. Standing beside the chair where Mrs. Casslin was resting, the physician made a professional pronouncement.

"Mr. Gloucester has told me what occurred," he said. "We must take Mrs. Casslin to her room at once."

"All right," agreed Cardona. "Mr. Gloucester will aid you."

"There are two maids in the kitchen, sir," volunteered Gilkins. "I do not believe that they know what has happened. You can summon them from this telephone here, sir."

"Call them," ordered Cardona, while Gloucester and Dubrong were aiding Mrs. Casslin from the room. "Tell them to go to Mrs. Casslin's room."

Gilkins went to the telephone. Cardona, half in the hallway, kept throwing occasional glances toward the steel door. Tension seemed to be relaxing.

Yvonne Lydell was seated beside Bart Melken. Unconsciously, the girl found her eyes going toward the window at the front of the room. She suppressed a gasp; Bart's fingers immediately clutched her arm.

For an instant, the girl had fancied that she had caught the gleam of eyes beyond that window.

Sprawled upon the floor, with arms outstretched, Rutherford Casslin exhibited empty hands...

Then the illusion was dispelled. She regained her calm. She heard Bart whisper for her to remain quiet.

Straining her eyes, Yvonne could see the balcony rail beyond the window. The rail seemed to emerge from a haze of darkness, as though a blanketing cloud of black had been removed. Yet Yvonne decided that it could not be a living form.

IN this decision, the girl was wrong. There was someone upon the balcony. Eyes had actually viewed the scene within the room. Yet they were not the eyes that Yvonne had seen before.

Earlier, she had actually observed the peering Hindu. This time, she had caught a momentary glimpse of the eyes of The Shadow!

A tall shape was moving along the balcony. Like a creature of darkness, The Shadow had arrived from the void. He had not started for Five Towers as early as had Joe Cardona. Like the detective, The Shadow had gained his evening's destination only to find that death had already fallen.

A window opened softly in the room that adjoined the living room. A creature of stealth, the black-garbed phantom entered. His footsteps were noiseless; even the swish of his black cloak was not apparent as The Shadow crossed the floor.

The Shadow went by the side entrance of the living room. No one even glimpsed his gliding shape. He arrived at the far end of the hallway. There his gleaming eyes saw the very sight which Joe Cardona was so carefully observing.

Hubert's body on the floor; beyond the dead servant, the form of the dead Hindu, whom The Shadow knew was Tippu. The steel door also came within The Shadow's notice. Then, his cloak blanketing him like a shroud, The Shadow moved away.

Doctor Lysander Dubrong and Stephen Gloucester returned into the living room via the side door. They took chairs, and looked toward Joe Cardona. Neither had noted a gliding shape that had followed them. Beyond the curtained doorway, The Shadow was looking in upon the quiz that was to come.

"Mrs. Casslin?" queried Cardona.

"Resting," replied Dubrong suavely. "I gave her an opiate. The maids are in attendance."

"All right," decided Cardona. "I shall ask you, Mr. Gloucester, to repeat the brief statement which you gave me on arrival. After that, we shall have the testimony of the others present."

Cardona made notes as Gloucester began. The other persons gave their versions; all were corroborations of what Gloucester said. It was Yvonne Lydell who added the only testimony that was remarkable.

As the girl began to speak, Bart Melken's hand grip tightened on her wrist. Nevertheless, the girl kept on. Bart relaxed his hold, and chewed his lips.

"I saw someone on the balcony," stated Yvonne.

"Just as Mr. Casslin left to go back to the tower, I happened to glance in that direction. I saw a dark face and gleaming eyes."

"A Hindu?" asked Cardona quickly.

"I think so," said the girl.

"Why didn't you say something then?" quizzed Cardona.

Bart Melken's grip again tightened on Yvonne's wrist. The detective did not observe the action. Bart was on the other side of the girl. Doctor Lysander Dubrong, however, detected the movement. Nor were his eyes the only ones that made the observation. Peering from the curtain, just beyond the spot where Dubrong was seated, The Shadow also saw.

"I intended to tell Mr. Casslin," announced Yvonne frankly. "However, he had already left the room. I intended to speak to him when he returned, for he had mentioned that a Hindu in Bombay was anxious to obtain his diamond. Then all the excitement happened."

Cardona stared at the girl. He saw no reason to doubt Yvonne's testimony. It had been voluntary. There was a naiveté in Yvonne's expression that added to her simple beauty. Cardona, as he jotted down the point that Yvonne had mentioned, felt that he had gained a valuable bit of evidence, one that would be useful later on.

"Did anyone else see a prowler by the window?" questioned the detective.

There was no reply. Bart Melken did not speak. When Yvonne made no further comment, the young man was relieved. He had not wanted Yvonne to mention that she had seen someone outside the window. However, the girl had omitted the one point that worried Bart the most: the fact that she had spoken to him of the face she had seen.

WHEN his turn for testimony came, Bart merely stated facts which others had mentioned. He gave his own reactions to the hubbub in the hallway. When the statement taking was completed, no mention had been made of anything that constituted suspicious actions on the part of Bart Melken.

Nevertheless, Cardona had been seemingly thorough in his questioning; and he had barely finished before Gilkins again announced that he had heard the doorbell. Stephen Gloucester volunteered to answer the ring. When he returned. Gloucester was accompanied by Inspector Timothy Klein, a trio of detectives, and a police surgeon.

Arrangements were quickly made. Two detectives were dispatched to make a thorough search of the grounds surrounding Five Towers. One was left in charge of the living room, with the guests. Klein, Cardona, and the police surgeon prepared to visit the tower.

It was then that Doctor Dubrong advanced and

stated that he would like to view the body of Rutherford Casslin. Inspector Klein stated that he could accompany the group. They began by examining the bodies of Hubert and the Hindu. Then Joe Cardona unlocked the steel door that led to the tower.

Strange it was that in this house, where death had fallen, a hidden being should be stalking almost within reach of the investigators. The Shadow had moved into a darkened room upon the arrival of Klein and the detectives.

After the two sleuths had been sent out to examine the grounds, he had moved to the far entrance of the hallway, where the bodies lay. Before Cardona had decided to unlock the steel door, The Shadow had departed.

His phantom presence manifested itself outside the castle. A fleeting patch of blackness against cold, gray walls. The Shadow circled the huge building, unseen by the detectives who were inspecting the dry ground with flashlights.

The rear of Casslin's castle was almost black in the gloom of night. The tall turret that housed the dead millionaire's strongroom showed as a massive cylinder with ivied walls. At intervals appeared gloomy rectangles of light, the slitlike windows of the stairway and the three openings in the turret itself. The bars showed plainly against the dim glow.

Within the tower, Joe Cardona was leading the advance up the spiral steps. At each window, the detective stopped to unfasten the ironbound glass frame. Every crossbar came under his careful inspection.

During the ascent within the tower, another climb was taking place outside. The Shadow, blackened against the stones of the tower, was scaling the wall like a human fly. He was not trusting to the ivy; that was not thick enough to support more than twenty pounds of weight. Instead, The Shadow was relying upon flat disks that were pressed to his hands and feet.

Soft, squdgy sounds marked The Shadow's upward progress. Those disks were concave circles of rubber that affixed themselves under pressure. A twist of hand or foot made each disk yield and come free while the others served as supports.

THE SHADOW'S climb was a steady one. When the black-garbed investigator reached the uppermost windows of the tower, his peering eyes saw that Cardona and the others had not yet arrived. Casslin's body still lay alone upon the floor, with arms outstretched toward the wall below the safe.

The Shadow was clinging to the wall like a mammoth bat. His head moved away from the window as the broken door of the tower room opened, and Cardona came into view.

The detective's first action was to open each one of the three windows, and try the crossbars. In performing this action, Cardona came within a foot of The Shadow's head. He did not, however, notice the phantom shape without. The Shadow was motionless upon the wall.

As Cardona went over to Casslin's body, where the police surgeon and Doctor Dubrong were making their examination, The Shadow's head appeared at the lowest point of the central window. The frame was still open; Cardona had left it that way. Words as well as actions were plain to The Shadow.

"What about the windows?" Inspector Klein was inquiring.

"The same as those on the stairs," replied Cardona, in a laconic tone. "The frames are nothing— anyone could jimmy them open and shut them again. But what good would it do?"

The Shadow saw Cardona make a gesture with his hands, to indicate a measurement.

"No one could squeeze through a space that wide," declared the detective. "Those bars are just as solid as if they were part of the wall. That makes a square about six inches each way. This place is like a vault, so far as entering it is concerned."

"What about the diamond?" questioned Klein.

"It's gone," assured Cardona, "unless Casslin put it back in the safe. That's locked—"

"Are you sure?" interposed Doctor Dubrong, looking up from Casslin's body. "I don't see why Casslin would have locked it up while the diamond was out."

Cardona walked over to the safe and tugged at the handle. The door refused to budge.

"Turn the handle farther," suggested Dubrong.

Cardona complied. The firm twist succeeded. The combination knobs had not been turned. The safe came open. The small strongbox was quite empty.

"That proves that the diamond is gone," declared Cardona grimly.

The detective stepped to the window. The Shadow's head wavered away from view. Cardona uttered a shrill whistle. An answering call came from one of the detectives below.

"See anything there?" shouted Cardona.

"Nothing," came the answer.

"All right," ordered Cardona. "Meet us inside."

With Inspector Klein, Cardona completed the examination of Rutherford Casslin's stronghold. Accompanied by the two physicians, the investigators started below.

THE room was again empty, save for Casslin's body. The Shadow's right hand appeared upon the central bar of the window. White fingers emerged from a glove. The Shadow touched the central bar—one which Cardona had so recently tested.

There was no firmness in The Shadow's grip. Cardona's examination had shown that the bar was firm. It was with fingers only that The Shadow acted. His light touch moved along the bar, which was roughened with rust, except at the center, where the fingers encountered smoothness.

The same fingers moved along each of the other bars. With gleaming eyes, The Shadow stared through the opened slit, directly at the back of Rutherford Casslin's prone body, a dozen feet away.

Then the descent began. Slowly, steadily, The Shadow moved downward. The ground detectives had gone within the house. At certain points, a tiny flashlight glimmered, its disk of illumination no larger than a silver dollar.

One hand was free; this, perhaps, accounted partly for The Shadow's slow descent. Rubber suction cups paused in their squdge; occasionally, bits of ivy vine rustled under The Shadow's touch. Once a twig broke free with a snap.

At the bottom of the tower, The Shadow became a thing of night. His flashlight no longer glimmered as his weirdly blackened shape again circled the house. The only sign of The Shadow's presence was a murmured laugh that came in whispered tones.

The eerie sound faded. Silence lay about Five Towers, the castle of death. The Shadow had again entered the house where murder had struck.

The Shadow had seen all that others had seen. The Shadow had learned more. From the outside of the tower, he had peered in to gain a clue to the death of Rutherford Casslin.

CHAPTER VI
CARDONA'S THEORY

THE clock in the Casslin living room was chiming twelve. This midnight hour found a group of four men seated in tense conference. Of the guests who had been present while death had struck thrice, only one remained.

This was Stephen Gloucester. The dignified banking official had volunteered to stay. The other guests had been dismissed following the checking of their testimony.

With Gloucester were Inspector Timothy Klein and Detective Joe Cardona. The fourth member of the group was a new arrival, none other than Police Commissioner Ralph Weston.

A man of dynamic personality, a powerful driver, who forced his subordinates hard along the trail of crime, the police commissioner took an active interest in all cases where mystery lay thick. He had been reached by telephone. He had come here to learn facts.

Joe Cardona, in a careful but monotonous tone, was reading the testimony of all who had been present. Stephen Gloucester was nodding his accord with every statement. When Cardona completed his reading, he laid his sheets aside and looked at the police commissioner.

"Is that all?" snapped Weston.

"All," returned Cardona.

There was a pause. Cardona arose and paced the floor. His footsteps carried him to the hallway at the rear of the living room. He swung back, hands in pockets. and faced the police commissioner.

"I have accounted for everyone," he declared. "You heard the statements, Commissioner. I double-checked them, and they fitted. At the time when Rutherford Casslin left this room to go up to his tower, every guest was here."

"What about the servants?" asked Weston.

"Hubert and Hodges accompanied Casslin to the tower door," explained Cardona. "While Hubert was locking it after Casslin had entered, Hodges came back here."

Another pause. Cardona offered no theory. He was leaving that to Commissioner Weston. The ace detective had an inferiority complex so far as the commissioner was concerned. He preferred to let Weston speak first, and then offer suggestions. Whenever Cardona began with a theory, Weston was sure to shoot holes in it.

While the group was silent, a footstep sounded at the side door of the living room. Doctor Lysander Dubrong, suave of manner and frail of build, entered to join the group.

"Mrs. Casslin is resting well," he announced, in a mild tone. "Very well, indeed."

He drew a pipe from his pocket, filled it with tobacco from a pouch, and applied a match. The heavy aroma of perique became apparent as the physician puffed the strong mixture. Dubrong sat down and looked from one person to another with an almost inquiring air.

COMMISSIONER WESTON, puzzled by the problem which confronted him, swung to the physician and advanced a query. Cardona listened intently.

"You were not here, Doctor Dubrong?" asked Weston.

"At the time of the murder?" returned the physician. "No. I left here shortly after nine o'clock. I had started home, but before I reached Manhattan, I called my apartment. They told me that I was wanted back here. I made good time on the return ride. I called my apartment house from close by the bridge, so I had very little traffic to impede me."

A slight flicker of keen interest showed on Cardona's swarthy face. The detective made no comment, however. He had not obtained this statement from Doctor Dubrong. The physician's exactitude of speaking impressed him.

"It was after your departure, then," observed Weston, "that a few of the guests accompanied Casslin when he went to the tower to obtain the diamond."

"I presume so," smiled Dubrong. "Not having been here, Commissioner, I am unable to state what happened."

"How many persons"—Weston turned to Cardona—"accompanied Casslin on that trip?"

"When he went up to get the diamond?" asked the detective. "Five, I think"—Cardona paused to refer to his notations—"yes, five."

"And the last time," reflected Weston, "Casslin went up alone. Hm-m-m. What puzzles me is this. The Hindu was after that diamond. He didn't have it on his person, however. He was armed only with a knife."

"May I offer a theory?" inquired Doctor Dubrong.

"Certainly," agreed Weston.

"I have seen a few Hindus in New York," asserted the physician. "Perhaps you have heard of my East Side Clinic, where I give free medical attention to characters whom others might regard as hopeless. Hindus have come there."

"Was the dead Hindu ever in your clinic?"

"I do not believe so. I have, however, noticed this fact regarding Hindus who live in New York. Being far from their native land, and few in number, they invariably travel in pairs. Therefore, I suppose that on an enterprise so important as the theft of a valuable diamond, two would work together."

"Remarkable!" exclaimed the commissioner. "What is your opinion on this point, Cardona?"

"I have none, Commissioner," admitted the detective. "The Hindus that I have seen keep away from crime. If they are anything like the Chinese—"

"They are entirely different from the Chinese," interposed Doctor Dubrong, in an authoritative tone. "As I have just mentioned, they travel in pairs. Every time a Hindu has come to my clinic, he has been accompanied by a friend.

"This is a characteristic of the Hindu race—particularly among those who are murderously inclined. I have studied the history of the Thugs of India. With them, murder was a religion; and there were always two—or more—involved."

"But in this case," began the commissioner, "there could not well have been two. Unless one managed to escape while his companion was scuffling with Hubert, the servant."

"That is not my theory at all," returned Dubrong. The physician puffed furiously at his pipe; then laid it on a table, while he leaned forward to impress his point. "I believe there were two but that only one entered the tower. How he passed Hubert is only a matter of conjecture. But let us consider it as follows.

"Two Hindus. One was doubly armed, with revolver as well as knife. Another was peering through the window of this room. Miss Lydell, I understand, caught a glimpse of his face. The first Hindu was somewhere in the house. He managed to follow Casslin into the tower. The other dropped from the balcony and circled the castle.

"The Hindu who slipped by Hubert shot Casslin in the tower room. He took the box that contained the diamond. He tossed it, and his revolver also, through one of the slitted windows, to his companion below."

"Why the revolver?" asked Commissioner Weston.

"You mean why did he rid himself of the revolver as well as the diamond?" Dubrong smiled. "Because the revolver was the instrument of murder. He did not want to have it on his person. Moreover, he knew that it would be unwise to use it below, where the sound of a shot could be heard."

"Logical," decided Weston.

"Then came the attempt at escape," proceeded Dubrong. "The Hindu came down the stairs. He knocked at the door. Hubert opened it. The Hindu leaped upon him, with the knife. He killed Hubert, but Hodges arrived in time to end the assassin's life.

"Thus, Mr. Commissioner, we have the answer. Hindus were seeking the Bishenpur diamond. Hindus were unable to buy it from Rutherford Casslin. Hindus plotted, and Hindus gained the diamond."

As Dubrong arose and picked up his pipe, Commissioner Weston arose also. He extended his hand in congratulation. Doctor Dubrong received it with a smile.

"I congratulate you, Doctor," assured the commissioner. "Your theory is an excellent one. We shall send out a flyer to apprehend all Hindus in New York. Perhaps we shall be able to capture the man who has the Bishenpur diamond."

Doctor Dubrong bowed. His thin lips wore a faint smile. Joe Cardona alone detected the expression. Dubrong prepared to leave. Cardona watched him. After the physician had departed, the ace detective settled back into his chair.

COMMISSIONER WESTON seemed elated. He began to expound upon Dubrong's theory. Klein and Gloucester received his words with nods. Cardona, alone, remained obdurate. The detective was referring to his notes.

"Well, Cardona," said Weston suddenly, "it looks as though we are on a real trail. Doctor Dubrong has acquainted us with some very valuable facts."

Cardona smiled grimly. This was the chance he had been awaiting. His own theory, vague, a few minutes ago, had become strengthened. Placing his notes in his pocket, the detective arose and strode across the room. He pointed to the front window.

"This," he affirmed, "is where Miss Lydell saw the face. I have examined this balcony,

Commissioner. It opens into an adjoining room. I believe, to begin with, that the Hindu who was looking in from here was the same one who entered the hallway by the steel door."

"A minor point," objected Commissioner Weston.

"Not at all," asserted Cardona briskly, "when we follow a theory that only one Hindu was concerned in the affair. Let us go into the rear hallway, Commissioner."

As Cardona strode past the entrance at the side of the living room, he failed to notice a pair of gleaming eyes that watched his progress. The Shadow, stationed in the adjacent gloom, was still upon the scene.

As Cardona walked through the door at the rear of the living room, Weston, Klein, and Gloucester followed with one accord. Hardly had they gone, before a motion occurred at the side door. A shaft of darkness seemed to project itself into the living room. Uncannily, it assumed a living shape.

The Shadow became visible. Clad in his cloak of black, his face concealed by the brim of his slouch hat, the tall master of mystery advanced across the room until he reached the doorway through which the others had gone.

There, with steady gaze, he peered toward the group in the hallway. Joe Cardona and the others were standing beside the steel door that formed the entrance to the tower. Cardona's words were plain as he pointed out significant facts.

"Hubert admitted Casslin to the tower," he explained. "Then Hubert was struck down. Hodges arrived in time to kill the Hindu."

"Exactly what Doctor Dubrong suggested," remarked Weston.

"No," objected Cardona. "Doctor Dubrong omitted a very important point. I have notations here. Mr. Gloucester can support them. Considering every element involved—the face at the window; the locked door, the key in Hubert's pocket—there is only one inference to draw."

"Which is—"

"That the Hindu did not come from the tower. He was trying to *enter* the tower, in pursuit of Rutherford Casslin."

Cardona's voice rang with triumph. Stephen Gloucester nodded in accordance. The police commissioner appeared perplexed. Cardona followed up his point.

"There were two men here," he asserted. "Hubert and Hodges. Both were trusted servants. Hubert fought the Hindu and died. Hodges killed the Hindu. The honesty of both servants cannot be questioned.

"How could the Hindu have followed Casslin? Remember, Hodges was here when Hubert closed the door. No! The Hindu was there"—Cardona was pointing down the hallway—"and as soon as Hodges walked away, he rushed forward to attack Hubert!"

The explanation came like a thunderbolt. Joe Cardona had scored a triumph. He could see Commissioner Weston nodding in reluctant agreement.

"The Hindu wanted the key." Dramatically, Cardona was gesturing to depict the struggle at the door. "That is why he attacked. He stabbed Hubert as they grappled. One more point, Commissioner. Hubert had closed the door. He was naturally facing it. That gave the Hindu the chance to spring at him."

IN simple, emphatic words, Joe Cardona had completely shattered the theory advanced by Doctor Dubrong. There was, however, one point which the detective had not mentioned. Weston was quick to seize upon it.

"Then who," demanded the commissioner, "was the man that killed Rutherford Casslin?"

"Someone in the tower," returned Cardona.

"But how did he get there?" asked Weston.

"Beforehand," smiled Joe Cardona. "Some guests went upstairs with Casslin. No one remembers just how many were in the crowd. Let us suppose that one person managed to remain within the tower, to await Casslin's return. It is gloomy in that tower. He would not have been noticed."

"Then afterward—"

"He must have managed to escape, with gun, diamond, and all. He couldn't have gone out through one of the windows in the tower; he must have managed to come through this door. But the point is this, commissioner. The Hindu was never in the tower. Casslin was killed in the tower. So someone else must have been in the tower."

Weston considered. He turned and strolled slowly back toward the living room, the others pacing with him. Within the living room, The Shadow suddenly moved away with remarkable swiftness. He had glided through the side door before the others entered the room from the rear.

"Cardona," said the commissioner solemnly, "I accept your theory. There is a murderer at large. The Hindu still may have been his accomplice; or possibly the Hindu was working on his own. However, the murderer—the thief—is the man that you must capture.

"I am counting upon you to learn his identity. We must not form opinions too hastily, but it is probable that he is a man of high intelligence, one who could pass himself unobtrusively in good company. Get him, Cardona."

This was Weston's final statement. The commissioner left, accompanied by Stephen Gloucester, whose car had gone into New York. Joe Cardona stood alone with Inspector Timothy Klein.

"Joe," said the inspector warmly, "you put it across great tonight. You're on the right track. The only question is—who are you after?"

Cardona wheeled as he was crossing the living room. He spoke emphatically as he tuned to Klein. "I'll tell you the guy I'm after," he asserted bluntly. "I'm after The Jackdaw!"

"You didn't say that to the commissioner—"

"Of course not. I'll bring that up later. But The Jackdaw pulled this job tonight, and The Jackdaw is the guy I'm going to get. He's keen enough to cover up his tracks. I'm good enough to uncover them."

From his pocket, Joe Cardona pulled a list of the persons who had been present here when Rutherford Casslin had died. One by one, he crossed off the names. The last on the list was that of Bart Melken. Cardona crossed it off with the others.

Then, while Klein's back was turned, Cardona wrote another name at the bottom of the column. It was the name of one who had not been here when the confusion had begun; yet one whose connection with affairs of Rutherford Casslin's might prove to be of considerable consequence.

Cardona was standing beside the curtain when he wrote the name. Inspector Klein did not see the action. Yet there were eyes that did see; eyes that peered from above Cardona's shoulder; eyes that the detective never dreamed were present. They saw the name that Cardona inscribed:

Doctor Lysander Dubrong

JOE CARDONA thrust the list into his pocket. He stepped forward to join Inspector Klein. Together, they walked through the rear door, to take a last look at the hallway and the tower.

Again, The Shadow stepped from the gloom. His tall form basked momentarily in the light of the living room. From hidden lips, lost in the folds of the cloak collar, came a soft, sinister laugh that was no more than an echoed whisper.

The Shadow had heard all. He had listened to Doctor Dubrong's theory—a statement, which, if accepted, would have diverted all suspicion from any persons other than Hindus. He had heard Joe Cardona's theory—shattering facts that broke Doctor Dubrong's findings.

Joe Cardona had learned the part that the Hindu had played. He knew that someone—The Jackdaw— had accomplished the murder of Rutherford Casslin, and had departed with the Bishenpur diamond.

Joe Cardona suspected Doctor Lysander Dubrong. He had reason. The physician's words could well have been calculated to throw the detective off the correct track.

Was Doctor Dubrong The Jackdaw? Or was that mysterious crook some other person who had kept completely from the light?

The Shadow, like Joe Cardona, was confronted with these questions. But The Shadow had gained advantages over the detective.

He—The Shadow—knew that one man here tonight had been working for The Jackdaw. He knew that Bart Melken had played a minor part in crime. Moreover, The Shadow had seen the tower room from the outside of the house.

The soft laugh whispered once again. It showed a glimmering of facts, an inkling of how Rutherford Casslin could have been slain in his tower room without the murderer being caught in his escape. It told, moreover, how the Bishenpur diamond might well have been stolen away.

The Shadow, like Joe Cardona, was on the trail of mysterious crime. The Shadow, master of the darkness, had found an insidious opponent worthy of his steel. From now on, The Shadow's quest would be to find The Jackdaw, that master crook whose subtle ways were the mark of the supercriminal.

The Shadow's laugh faded as the tall form in black merged with the gloom beyond the door of Rutherford Casslin's living room.

CHAPTER VII
THE JACKDAW'S MINIONS

EARLY the next evening, a young man sauntered forth from one of New York's uptown hotels. He hailed a taxicab and entered it. As the vehicle pulled away, a tall figure suddenly emerged from the darkened front of the building. A mysterious passenger stepped into another cab that was parked close by.

"Follow instructions," came a quiet voice from the rear seat.

The taximan looked about in amazement. He had not heard anyone entering his cab. For a moment, he hesitated; then he spied a pair of burning eyes peering at him from the darkness of the vehicle. A ten-dollar bill fluttered into the driver's hand. The argument was clinched.

The driver started his cab, and nodded as he took quiet instructions for every turn. He received no definite information that he was following the cab ahead; the weird passenger merely required that he should obey.

Twenty minutes later, the lead cab pulled up in a decrepit district of the East Side. The passenger in the rear cab gave a signal to stop. The driver obeyed. He waited, expecting further word. It did not come.

When the driver, gaining nerve, peered into the back of the cab, he found it empty. The burning eyes were gone. The unknown passenger had made a silent departure.

The young man who had come from the hotel was walking rather rapidly along a side street not far from the spot where he had left his cab. His eyes were straight ahead; but had he glanced to the rear, he would not have seen the flitting form that followed him. A streak of blackness, changing shape as it glided along the sidewalk, was the only token of an unseen presence.

The young man reached an alleyway, and stopped beneath a streetlamp. His features came in view.

This visitor to a questionable neighborhood was none other than Bart Melken. The young man who had appeared as a fashion plate at Rutherford Casslin's home had chosen a much less desirable district for tonight's journey.

Melken entered the alley. Hardly had he disappeared before a blackened streak appeared beneath the glow that permeated the sidewalk. That patch of darkness was the visible sign of an invisible being. The Shadow was on Bart Melken's trail.

BART MELKEN had been crossed from Joe Cardona's list. The ace detective had not held a single guest for complicity in Rutherford Casslin's murder.

But The Shadow had seen Bart Melken's actions when the young man had urged Yvonne Lydell not to say too much. Only Doctor Lysander Dubrong had also witnessed Melken's signal.

Until now, The Shadow had let Joe Cardona lead the way. That period was ended. The Shadow was working on his own. He was trusting in no subordinate tonight. He knew the worriment that was festering within Bart Melken's mind. Since last night, he had been waiting some step on the young man's part.

In the alleyway, Melken paused before an obscure door. It was the side entrance to what had once been an old hotel, but which was now an apartment building, of a sort. Bart Melken pressed an obscure bell. The door clicked. The young man entered.

The Shadow did not follow. From the other side of the alleyway, he had spotted lights on the third floor. At the rear of the dilapidated building was an old-fashioned fire escape with hanging ladder that was up. A long stick could have reached that pivoted ladder. The Shadow, however, did not resort to so simple a measure.

Pressed against the surface of the wall, he moved his long, supple body upward. The suction cups were not needed for this climb; The Shadow made the ascent by digging into the cracked spaces between the crumbling bricks. His gloved hands gained the fire escape.

The first manifestation of The Shadow as an actual form occurred when his tall figure appeared in the dim light of a third-floor hall. A closing door betokened the fact that Bart Melken had entered an apartment. The Shadow moved silently toward that door.

After a moment's pause, The Shadow moved to the next door. This place had obviously been a hotel once; changed to an apartment, each room of the suite had its own opening on the hallway. A blackened instrument of steel appeared in The Shadow's gloved hand. Keen eyes directed the probing tool. The door unlocked with a muffled click. The Shadow stepped into a dark room.

The adjoining door was open. The sound of voices came from that direction. The Shadow glided to the spot; ensconced in darkness, he could see, as well as hear, what happened in the other room.

BART MELKEN was sitting in an easy chair. Opposite him was another man. Their faces formed a contrast. Bart Melken, handsome of physiognomy, but worried in expression, formed an antithesis of the man before him. The other was a tough-faced, sullen fellow, whose ugly countenance registered nothing but self-confidence.

The sitting room which the two occupied was luxuriously furnished; an odd arrangement in this neighborhood where poverty seemed rampant. The man with the ugly face was one whose identity was well known in the underworld. He was "Bing" Claver, a gang gorilla who had gone into retirement.

Unwanted by the police, unconnected with any racket, Bing Claver, well supplied with cash that he had saved, was the last man whom anyone would regard as a present menace to the law.

Such a character might well have been pleased to receive a visitor of Bart Melken's appearance. This was not the case, however. Bing Claver's growls showed that the hard-boiled gorilla was quite annoyed because Bart Melken had come to his apartment. Bing was expressing himself in this fashion.

"What's the idea?" he was questioning. "There's no use in you coming down here, Melken. You didn't get no orders to show up, did you?"

"I'm worried, Claver," protested the young man, in a troubled tone. "I—I've got to get out of it. That's all. I'm telling you that I've got to quit."

"Telling me?" Bing Claver snorted. "Tell The Jackdaw. That's who you'd better tell."

"I'd tell him," returned Melken nervously, "if I could find him. I've got to see The Jackdaw. That's why I've come to you. I want to know who he is."

"The Jackdaw?" Bing Claver was scoffing. "Say—do you think I know who he is? Find The Jackdaw! Say—you'll be asking me to find The Shadow next!"

"I'm losing my nerve, Bing."

"Pipe down! Guys that go yellow get lead poisoning. I'm one of the guys that doses out the lead pills, too."

"But I can't go any further—"

"Easy!" Bing Claver's growl was steady. "The bulls ain't after you, Melken. What've you got to worry about?"

Bart Melken was a picture of dejection. He licked his lips and stared pleadingly at his ugly tormentor. At last he seemed to gain control of his emotions.

"Here's the trouble, Bing," he stated. "I had to work for The Jackdaw. I was hard up after the gambling houses swindled me. I stole some bonds; how The Jackdaw learned it is more than I know. You were the man who got hold of me, and told me that I would have to work for The Jackdaw, or be exposed.

"I thought I could go through with it. All I had to do was play a minor part; work on the inside at the homes of wealthy friends. There were times in between when I thought those jobs had ended. But always there were new instructions from The Jackdaw; more jobs to do. I stood it until last night.

"I didn't care if Rutherford Casslin lost his diamond. He could afford it. But when murder crept in, I lost my nerve. I didn't think, when I gave those signals with my cigarette lighter, that The Jackdaw intended to kill Casslin."

"Yeah?" There was no sympathy in Bing's growl. "Well, you might have expected some guy would get the bump sooner or later. You've got to stick with The Jackdaw now."

"Who is The Jackdaw?" demanded Melken.

"I told you I don't know," retorted Bing. "I get word from him like you do—over the telephone. He needs me once in a while, too. I'm telling you, Melken, if you go yellow, you'll get yours. If you expect to marry that ritzy jane you're engaged to, you'd better stick with The Jackdaw's racket."

The reference to Yvonne Lydell brought a troubled look to Bart Melken's face. The young society man knew that Bing Claver had made a definite threat.

"I'll—I'll try to go through with it," stammered Melken. "But I'm telling you, Bing—if you have a chance to tell it to The Jackdaw—that I'm likely to lose my nerve on the next job. This Casslin affair was something for which I didn't bargain."

Bing Claver snorted contemptuously. He looked at Bart Melken to make sure that the young man had meant what he said. Bing saw that Bart had spoken the truth.

"All right," growled the gang leader. "I'll put The Jackdaw wise when I hear from him. It won't be so hot for you, though, if you try to slide out of your job. I guess you're getting worried on account of the girl."

"I am," admitted Melken. "She may have suspected something—last night she—"

"What if she did? Who'll she tell?"

"I don't think she will say anything. Her father—Garforth Lydell—is in Florida at present. He is the only one in whom she would confide."

"Don't worry, then."

Bart Melken bobbed in startled fashion as he heard a bell ring. Bing Claver laughed at this sign of nerves. He arose and pressed a button alongside the wall.

"Who is it?" queried Melken anxiously.

"Just Limps Silvey," answered Bing Claver. "He's harmless. A guy that's been hanging around here. Tells me a little about what's going on outside. I don't go out except when I have to."

BING opened the door to the hall. A few moments later, dragging footsteps were heard. A pitiful figure appeared at the door of the room.

A man with a twisted form, frail of build, and faltering of step, hobbled into the room with the aid of a cane. He turned a brownish, leering face toward Bing Claver; then looked with sharp eyes at Bart Melken.

"Just a friend of mine," explained Bing. "That's all, Limps. A guy I've known for a while. Sit down."

"Limps" dropped into a chair.

"Anything new?" growled Bing.

"Nah," rejoined the cripple. "Tings are quiet out on de street, Bing. Some of de guys are talkin' about dat diamond dat a smart bird stole."

"Yeah? Who do they think did it?"

"Dey don't have no idea. But I got one, Bing."

"Who?"

"I'll put you wise later."

"Don't mind this guy," returned Bing, with a nudge toward Bart Melken. "Tell me—what do you know about that job at Casslin's?"

"It ain't nothin' that I know, Bing. It's what I've figured. Dere's only one guy smart enough to get away wid somethin' like dat. De guy I'm thinkin' of is De Jackdaw."

A smart grin spread over Limps Silvey's dirty face. Bing Claver smiled slightly.

"Anything else?" he asked.

"Nothin', Bing," responded Limps.

"Scram, then," ordered Bing.

The cripple arose from his chair and shuffled from the room. Bing Claver looked at Bart Melken.

"This guy Limps don't know much," he said in an undertone. "Sometimes I think, though, that he figures I work for The Jackdaw. It don't hurt if he does. He keeps mum."

The gang leader paused to make a new study of Bart Melken's anxious face. Then, in a gruff manner, he arose and snarled as he made a final statement.

... Through streets and alleys, he kept on the track of Limps Silvey ...

"Keep away from here after this," he ordered. "You got your job; I got mine. See? Just because I hooked you up with The Jackdaw don't mean nothing. I don't know who the guy is. He pays me for what I do—like he paid you. But I'll tell you this"—Bing's voice was harsh—"and you can take it or leave it. Any guy that crosses The Jackdaw don't live long. When you think about this Casslin bird, think about yourself. Maybe The Jackdaw will give you what he gave Casslin. He can do it."

Bart Melken nodded. He recognized the wisdom of the gang leader's words. He detested this ex-gorilla; he had come here only in hope of reaching the unknown master whom both he and Bing Claver served. Realizing, now, that he could learn nothing from the other minion, Bart Melken arose and walked from the room.

AS soon as his visitor was gone, Bing Claver strode back across the well-furnished room to the door beyond which The Shadow had been standing. He was too late, however, to spy that sinister figure which had hovered in the next room.

As though foreseeing Bing Claver's move, The Shadow had chosen a new and quick method of departure. His fingers had raised the half opened sash of the window; his figure had swung clear of the sill. Silently, The Shadow was lowering his tall, lithe form into the blackness of the alleyway.

He was not departing directly downward; instead, he had shifted to the side. Hence Bing Claver, peering into darkness, did not see his mysteriously descending form. Bing was watching for a sign of Bart Melken. It came. A slight flicker of light denoted the opening and the closing of the door below. Bing could hear Melken's footsteps clicking on the stone paving of the alley below.

Bart Melken, however, was not alone as he strode from that darkened area. Behind him, unseen in the gloom, stalked the figure of The Shadow. As Bart reached the entrance of the alley-way, the tall figure lingered. Keen eyes peered through darkness, as though watching for the appearance of another person.

A full minute elapsed. Melken had turned the nearest corner. Then, from the darkness across the street, came a slinking human form. Soft feet took up a shuffling gait. Limps Silvey had been waiting to make sure that Bart Melken had left Bing Claver's.

The Shadow followed. The shuffler was moving at a rapid pace. Evidently he had capped his cane with a rubber tip, for it made no sound as he tapped it against the sidewalk. Limps was not on Melken's trail; he had remained only to assure himself of the young man's departure from the neighborhood.

Indeed, Limps moved so swiftly that his shifty form seemed to elude detection. The Shadow's trailing was a marvelous achievement. Through streets and alleys, he kept on the track of Limps Silvey, until the course ended abruptly in a cul-de-sac where walls were on three sides. There were door-ways here; none showed a trace of Limps Silvey's entrance. The frail hobbler had made a rapid dive into some hideout.

The Shadow glided from the darkened blind alley. His laugh whispered softly as he reached the street. He had, at least, learned the exact neighborhood where Limps belonged, and the sights that he marked along the street outside the blind alley seemed to give The Shadow an inkling of the shuffler's whereabouts.

WHEN The Shadow again appeared, he was back at the improvised apartment house where Bing Claver lived. This time he made his progress upward from the darkness of the alley; the rubber cups squdged as his climbing form neared the opened window of the apartment.

There was a light in the room where The Shadow had been before. A telephone bell was ringing. The Shadow could hear Bing Claver's low growl. Peering from beyond the window, the master investigator saw the gang leader at the telephone.

"Yeah..." Bing's voice was emphatic. "He came here... Like I thought he would... Sure, he's yellow... You're going to use him just the same?... I get you... All right... I'll be ready for the job when you want me..."

The receiver clicked, and Bing turned away from the telephone. He did not see the eyes of The Shadow. Those burning optics had disappeared. Once more, the mysterious phantom of darkness was descending into the darkness of the night.

Later, a shuddering burst of chilling laughter occurred in the darkness of a deserted street. It died as quickly as it had come, but its eerie echoes seemed to cling to darkened walls. A policeman on the street stopped short as he caught the reverberation. He turned and stared to seek the author of the uncanny mockery. He saw no one.

That was the laugh of The Shadow. Departing from his mission to the badlands, it was the weird investigator's challenge to the hordes of evil. Tonight, The Shadow had scored a point in the battle which he now was waging.

He had seen the minions of The Jackdaw. Through them, The Shadow would gain the clue to the murderer himself. He had heard Bing Claver receiving instructions from the chief; had heard the gang leader report the yellowness of Bart Melken.

More crime was in the wind. When it arrived, The Shadow would have his say.

CHAPTER VIII
AT THE CLINIC

THE SHADOW, in his trailing of Bart Melken, had followed a lead which he had gained at Rutherford Casslin's home. He had picked up a definite angle of the case which Detective Joe Cardona had failed to observe.

Yet Cardona's negligence was excusable. The sleuth had found a track of his own, and was determined to follow it with precision. Emphatically, Joe Cardona felt that through Doctor Lysander Dubrong, some answer could be learned regarding Casslin's death.

Casslin had died on a Monday night. The Shadow had trailed Bart Melken on Tuesday evening. Wednesday afternoon found Joe Cardona ready for action. In his office at headquarters, the ace detective was considering his important move.

The Jackdaw had returned. Of that, Joe Cardona was convinced. Despite his natural egotism, Cardona was not blind to his failures. He was positive that there had been an important prelude to the murder of Rutherford Casslin: namely, the deaths of Scoffy and Bennie Lizzit.

Had either of those two been living now, Cardona would have been able to find a direct lead to The Jackdaw. But with Scoffy and Bennie dead, the detective had a more difficult task. Pondering, Cardona was forced to admit that he had played his cards wrong when he had made that visit to Scoffy's hideout. Joe realized that he must have been recognized by someone in the badlands.

The Jackdaw was in back of the trouble. He had eyes in the underworld. Cardona must avoid them. He had failed to escape recognition by night; he knew that he would certainly be spotted by day. Yet the mission which he had in mind was one that could not be entrusted to a stool pigeon.

Smiling grimly, Cardona opened a desk drawer and drew out a package. It was a large bundle; one that completely filled the drawer. Donning his hat and coat, Cardona took the package with him and left the office. Outside of headquarters, he hailed a taxicab and rode for some twenty blocks.

He reached an old house, entered the front door, and ascended to the third floor. In a little room at the rear, he opened the package and drew out an old jacket, a pair of baggy trousers, and a mass of grayish hair, together with a weatherbeaten hat.

Within a few minutes, Cardona had donned these garments. He looked at his reflection in a mirror, and uttered a chuckle. To all intents, Joe Cardona had become a decrepit old man with gray hair and gray beard—a derelict who would pass unnoticed along the East Side.

It was seldom that Cardona resorted to this disguise. He kept the articles at headquarters so that he could don them if emergency demanded such action. To make doubly sure today, he had come to this secluded room, there to put on the garments.

This room was, in a sense, a hideout, a place to which Cardona came on rare occasions when he wanted to remain unnoticed in Manhattan. The room was serving him well at present, for here he had plenty of opportunity to make his disguise effective.

Weather was chilly. Cardona needed an overcoat. He brought one from the closet. It was an old, frayed coat that Cardona had outworn during the previous winter. It was all that the detective needed to complete the part that he intended to play.

Thus, instead of Detective Joe Cardona, a heavy but stoop-shouldered old man came from the obscure house. This odd-looking individual made his way to an elevated station, rode for some distance, and finally alighted in a tawdry district. Joe Cardona was again invading the territory where he had gone to see Scoffy, the stool pigeon.

SHAMBLING beneath the superstructure of the "L," Cardona crossed the thoroughfare and turned into a side street. The buildings here were mournful. One, alone, showed signs of rehabilitation. Above it hung a sign:

EAST SIDE CLINIC

Cardona, peering along the street, saw another man coming from the opposite direction. A frail, twisted figure that hobbled with the aid of a cane, the approaching individual attracted Cardona's immediate interest.

This was Limps Silvey. Cardona did not know the man's identity, but he stared suspiciously at Silvey's brownish, evil face, as they met outside the entrance to the clinic. Limps was a few steps ahead. Cardona let him enter first.

Inside the door, Cardona found a large waiting room. Sprawled on chairs about the place were men and women of all the types that might be found in this district.

Sullen, dejected bums; cripples more hopeless than Limps; women who stared solemnly at the bare walls—these formed the crowd who awaited consultation with Doctor Lysander Dubrong.

Joe Cardona had heard of this clinic. Doctor Dubrong had gained high credit through its institution. Three days every week—sometimes at more frequent intervals—the eminent physician devoted his time to the riffraff of New York.

People had spoken of the work as a noble, philanthropic enterprise. Joe Cardona had considered it in this light until two nights ago. Then, his sudden suspicions of Doctor Dubrong had caused him to gain doubts.

A middle-aged woman was seated at a table in the corner. She was evidently Dubrong's secretary. She saw Joe Cardona as he slid into a chair, and beckoned to him. Carefully feigning his part as an old man, the detective approached.

"You wish an appointment with Doctor Dubrong?" asked the secretary.

Cardona nodded.

"Your name?"

"Michael Gaston."

The woman made a notation.

"You will have to await your turn," she said. "Some of these people have appointments from two days ago. Others are already registered to see Doctor Dubrong."

Cardona nodded dully and resumed his seat. A moment later, the door opened, and another East Sider entered. This was a rheumatic blind man, his body almost doubled. He wore black glasses, and he leaned heavily on a weatherbeaten cane. He seemed to sense where he should go, for he tapped his way to the corner, and mumbled a name to the secretary. He was told to take a chair, which he managed to find after tapping his way along the row of waiting patients.

A clock struck eleven. The secretary arose and went to the front door. She latched it, so that no new patients could enter. Then, referring to her list, she singled out Limps Silvey. The cripple, evidently one who had an appointment from Monday, arose and hobbled to a door which the woman opened. Cardona caught a glimpse of a gloomy anteroom with a door beyond. Then the opening closed behind Limps Silvey.

Cardona heard a voice beside him. One patient was talking to another. The words were informative.

"Dat was Limps Silvey," the speaker growled. "Foist on de list. Wisht I was foist. Gets my goat sittin' around dis joint."

Cardona remembered the name. Limps Silvey. Probably the cripple was a regular patient at Doctor Dubrong's clinic. There was something about Limps Silvey's shrewd stare that Cardona had not liked.

THE first patient had been ushered in at the stroke of eleven. Ten minutes later, a buzzer sounded. Evidently Limps had been sent out through another door, for the woman secretary picked another patient from the list. Fifteen minutes elapsed. The buzzer sounded again.

Thus proceeded the affairs of the East Side Clinic. Patient after patient was ushered through the little anteroom to see Doctor Lysander Dubrong. At last only Joe Cardona and the blind man remained. While they were waiting, the clock struck one.

"I am sorry," said the secretary. "The clinic hours are ended. You two will be the first appointments on Friday. That is, unless Doctor Dubrong is willing to remain a while longer—a practice which he seldom follows."

At that moment, the buzzer sounded twice. With a gesture that indicated the patients should remain, the secretary went through the anteroom. She returned a minute later.

"Doctor Dubrong will see one of you," she announced. "It is your turn, Mr. Gaston."

Joe Cardona arose and moved toward the anteroom. He entered, and the door closed behind him. The blind man remained seated in his chair. The secretary approached him.

"I am sorry," she said, "you will have to return on Friday. You must leave now."

The blind man gripped his cane. He arose and stood in his bent attitude.

"All right, lady," he said. "I can come back Friday. Never mind the door; I can open it. I find my way very well."

As he spoke, the blind man edged toward the door. Seeing that he had found the knob, the secretary turned and went toward her desk. There was a door in the corner just beyond the desk. The woman opened it and stepped into a small closet to obtain her hat and coat. She heard the outer door open and bang shut. She thought the blind man had gone.

In this surmise, the secretary was wrong. The moment that she had turned, the blind man had gazed after her. He had opened the door, and let it shut at just the psychological moment. In fact, while the door was automatically closing, the blind man had moved with surprising swiftness.

Across the waiting room, with long, noiseless stride, he had reached the door to the anteroom. There, his ways had been those of stealth. Silently, he had gained that gloomy entrance to Doctor Dubrong's consultation room.

He stood within a widened chamber that was lighted by a single bulb in the ceiling. Stretching his form to an amazing height, he thrust a long-fingered hand toward the incandescent. The light went out as he twisted it. The windowless anteroom was in darkness.

Simultaneously, the blind man slid his large, gogglelike black glasses to his forehead. His eyes, previously hidden, seemed to blaze in the darkness. Edging toward the inner door, this remarkable intruder softly turned the knob. He opened the door the fraction of an inch. Peering through the space, he could see the interior of the consultation room.

Doctor Lysander Dubrong was seated at a desk. Opposite him was the bearded old man who had entered as the final patient. Doctor Dubrong was speaking; the bearded patient was listening attentively.

Neither man sensed the presence of a watching eye. The pretended blind man in the anteroom was peering unobserved. His keen eyes glistened; his sharp ears heard.

Joe Cardona was not the only surreptitious visitor to Doctor Dubrong's East Side Clinic. The detective, as well as the physician, was under observation at this moment.

The fake blind man who had gained secret access to the anteroom was also in disguise. He was The Shadow. By day, as well as night, The Shadow could move unrecognized!

CHAPTER IX
THE CONSULTATION

JOE CARDONA was sitting away from the light. In this procedure, the detective was acting with method. He was confident that he looked the part that he was playing; that Doctor Dubrong could suspect nothing if he did not have the opportunity to observe his consultant too closely.

The physician had asked Cardona's name. He was writing down the one which Cardona gave him: Michael Gaston. Meanwhile, the detective was noting the setup of the consultation room. It looked like a well-equipped office. Three small, but strongly locked lockers formed a rather odd feature, inasmuch as they were firmly fixed to the corner in which they were located. Cardona, however, gave them no more than a passing notice.

"What is your trouble?"

Dubrong's brusque question made Joe Cardona immediately alert. The detective had an answer.

"No trouble of mine, Doctor," he grumbled. "It's my brother. He is very sick."

"Why didn't you bring him here?"

"Too sick. My brother Howard. He is in bed; he cannot move his arms. I wanted a doctor to come and see him. He said 'no.' I came to ask you what to do."

"This does not come within the range of my clinic," declared Doctor Dubrong. "I can recommend a physician; in fact, I can arrange for one to visit your brother, if that would be satisfactory."

"Tell me what doctor to see," urged Cardona. "I will go to see him. My brother Howard is very sick."

"Obviously," remarked Dubrong, staring hard at Cardona, "a paralytic patient could not well come to this clinic. I try to take care of all deserving patients. Sometimes I am able to give advice which, if followed, will clear up the difficulty without the necessity of a physician's visit.

"You mean my brother Howard—"

"I mean that his case can be handled to perfect satisfaction if you will merely follow the advice that I shall give you now. After that, you will not worry about him any longer."

Joe Cardona was puzzled. He had expected Dubrong to recommend a visiting physician for the mythical brother; this odd statement that indicated an immediate cure for paralysis was something that the detective could not understand.

Doctor Dubrong had risen from his chair. He was pacing back and forth on the other side of the desk. His hands were behind his back. His eyes wore a distant gaze; his lips a thin, suave smile.

"The trouble in this case," decided Doctor Dubrong, "is a very peculiar one. I can define it in a single word." He paused; then added: "Whiskers."

Cardona was staring as the physician gazed in his direction. Dubrong's smile persisted. His eyes were glittering shrewdly.

"Whiskers," he repeated. "They are very uncomfortable, particularly to those who are unaccustomed to wearing them. More than that, they can be responsible for strange mental delusions. They can make a normal man imagine that he has a paralytic brother. Do you agree with me, Mr. Cardona?"

THE end of the statement came so suavely that Joe Cardona was caught almost unaware of it. His own name, as uttered by Dubrong, seemed to re-echo in his mind. While the detective sat stolidly in his chair, Dubrong offered a suggestion.

"You came here for a consultation," he declared. "I made a special effort to give you one. I would prefer, however, that we conduct our talk face to face. Unless, Cardona, you would prefer that I also put on some masquerading makeup."

Realizing that he was discovered, Cardona's first impulse was to bluff it through. Then he realized that such a plan would be folly. Dubrong had unquestionably recognized his visitor's true identity. Sullenly, Joe Cardona removed his hat, his wig, and his false beard to reveal his own swarthy visage.

"That is better," commented Dubrong, resuming his chair. "Now, Cardona, we are in a position to discuss the purpose of your unexpected visit."

There was a tinge of sarcasm in the physician's voice. Before Cardona could make a response, Dubrong continued, resuming his ironical tone.

"I make a study of human beings," declared Dubrong. "Many types come into this consulting room. I have been approached by thieves, by murderers, by gangsters; but never before by a disguised detective.

"A man possessed of less penetration than myself might well be annoyed by such a visit. We met two nights ago, upon a scene where murder had fallen. At that time, I provided you with an excellent theory regarding the death of Rutherford Casslin. I notice that the newspapers have emphasized the murderous qualities of the Hindu whom I picked as the killer.

"To have you come here now would indicate doubt on your part—at least it would indicate such to a suspicious-minded person. But to me, Cardona, the truth is apparent. Realizing that I must have been observant in my clinic, you chose it as a spot to make some observations of your own.

"I quite admire your friendliness in not informing me that you intended to make this visit. It shows consideration on your part. You thought, probably, that I might not like to have you here. On the contrary, you are quite welcome. If that beard is not troublesome to you, I would suggest that you wear it and come here regularly. If you are interested in underworld types, you will find a parade of them in my waiting room, and I doubt that any will be keen enough to penetrate your really excellent disguise.

"Indeed, it nearly baffled me. As you sat there, however, I noticed it and realized who you must be. I saw that you intended to remove the beard and reveal yourself, although you were hesitating for fear I might misunderstand your motive in coming here. That is why I suggested, myself, that you should unmask."

Joe Cardona clenched his fists. He would have liked to throttle this suave man who talked in such artful, purring tones of veiled sarcasm. Not content with merely unmasking Cardona, Dubrong had also saved the detective the trouble of making an excuse. Dubrong was gloating over his ability at detecting Cardona's ruse.

The physician had ceased speaking. His eyes were inquiring now.

CARDONA felt his partially formed suspicions crystallizing into a definite opinion. He realized that he was no match at wits with Doctor Lysander Dubrong.

"Well," he growled, "I thought maybe one of those Hindu mugs might be coming in here. I was a little worried about you, Doctor. That was all. Guess I shouldn't have been. You probably look out for yourself down here."

"Of course," smiled the physician. He opened a desk drawer and brought out a snub-nosed revolver. "I always have this with me. Would you like to see the license?"

"No," returned Cardona. "I figured you might carry a gun, Doctor. Thought I'd better make sure, though, that things were all right. I didn't like to come brashing in here just out of a clear sky. Maybe some of your patients would have lit out if they saw a detective."

"Another token of your consideration," commended Dubrong, with a wan smile. "Well, Cardona, if there is any way in which I can be of service to you, be sure and advise me. How are you progressing with the Casslin case?"

"No results yet," said Cardona. "We found out that the dead Hindu is named Tippu, but we haven't located anybody who seems to know much about him."

"I shall bear that name in mind," returned Dubrong sagely. "There are many persons in the underworld who may make remarks to a physician that they would not make to a detective. Well"—Dubrong was glancing at his watch—"I must be leaving. I would suggest that you resume your effective disguise, and allow me to usher you out as I would any other patient."

With a sour smile, Cardona picked up his false beard and donned it, together with wig and hat. Doctor Dubrong nodded approvingly, but still maintained his sophisticated smile. The physician arose and accompanied the detective to a doorway at the rear of the office. They went through a little entry, and came to another door, through which Cardona passed alone. Doctor Dubrong locked the door after the detective had gone.

Returning to his office, the physician locked the door of the entry, and began to chuckle. He seemed highly pleased with his unmasking of Joe Cardona. He did not reckon, however, that he, in turn, was unmasking himself. The peering eyes of The Shadow had never moved from beyond the anteroom door.

Seated at his desk, the physician remained a while in thought. His face showed peculiar changes; yet it was impossible to gain an exact trail of his thoughts through the flickering expressions. At last, under sudden impulse, Dubrong ended his reverie. He arose and came directly to the anteroom.

The Shadow edged into the deep side of the little room. When Doctor Dubrong opened the door from the consulting room, a shaft of light came through, but it did not reveal the silent, motionless form that was against the wall.

Even in his guise of a pretended blind man, The Shadow had donned his habitual color: black. Somber as ever, he had taken the guise of darkness as easily as a chameleon gains the color of its surroundings.

Moreover, Dubrong noticed something which engaged his entire attention. He saw that the light was out. He chuckled as he stared toward the ceiling, and mechanically opened the door beyond. He thought that this had simply been a ruse on Cardona's part, while the detective was in the entry. Dubrong clicked the wall switch. The light did not come on. Finding that he could not quite reach the extinguished bulb, the physician continued through to the waiting room.

The Shadow moved swiftly then. He gained the

consulting room, and looked about him. He could
hear Dubrong returning with a chair, to tighten the
light. The Shadow noted the lockers in the corner.
He moved in that direction.

Crouched in the corner, he softly tried each
locker. Two were open; the third was closed. Its
lock was strong and of the most modern pattern.
The light, flicking from the anteroom, was a signal
that Doctor Dubrong had readjusted the turned-out
bulb. The Shadow arose and crossed the consulting
room. He could hear the physician carrying the
chair to the waiting room.

THERE were two doors at the back of the consulting room. Cardona had gone through the one at
left. The Shadow slipped to the one at the right. It
opened into a large closet, where coats were hanging.
The Shadow moved to the rear and remained there,
his tall form hidden by the garments.

A few minutes later, Doctor Dubrong arrived.
The physician took one of the coats, lifted a hat
from a hook at the side of the closet, and closed the
door. The dull slam of the other rear door
announced his departure from his consulting room.

Shortly afterward, The Shadow reappeared. The
removal of his heavy glasses showed a hawklike
countenance that was dulled by puffy, masklike
cheeks, which even the closest scrutiny would not
have shown as artificial. He went back to the
closed locker, but made no attempt now to pick its
ponderous lock.

Instead, The Shadow produced a tiny flashlight.
Stooping, he turned its beams upward through the
overhanging slits that marked the front of the
locker. His keen eyes saw within. A soft laugh
came from motionless lips.

The flashlight went out. The Shadow returned to
the closet. Beyond the coats, he made another
inspection, which, like the visit to the locker,
brought a soft laugh in whispered tones. Pressing
his fingers along the edge, he was rewarded by a
clicking sound. The rear of the closet slid away.
The Shadow entered a smaller closet. He smoothly
opened the door beyond. The sliding panel closed
behind him.

In his character of a bespectacled blind man, The
Shadow now stood in the small ground-floor parlor
of a deserted house. On his right was a doorway to
the street. It was locked, but it opened easily to the
pick which The Shadow applied. A short pause;
then the stooped-shouldered blind man emerged
upon the sidewalk. He fumbled as he locked the
door behind him. He moved away, tapping lightly
with his cane as he advanced.

From the lips beneath the black spectacles came
a soft, barely audible laugh; the third which The
Shadow had uttered since his arrival in Doctor

Dubrong's East Side Clinic. There was significance
in that laugh. It was caused by The Shadow's
present surroundings.

The spot where the pretended blind man had
emerged was not upon a side thoroughfare. It was
in a blind alley; one which The Shadow, by day,
recognized as a place that he had visited by night.

The secret exit from Doctor Dubrong's consulting room had brought The Shadow into the very
cul-de-sac where Limps Silvey had disappeared
upon the previous night!

<h2 style="text-align:center">CHAPTER X
MELKEN FINDS A FRIEND</h2>

EVENING had come to Manhattan. Bart Melken,
seated at a desk in the corner of his sumptuous
hotel room, was staring dully from the window.
The twinkling lights of the great city; the distant
glow of the Rialto; these were discouraging rather
than alluring to the young man who served as The
Jackdaw's minion.

Since his protest to Bing Claver, Melken had
been despondent. He had made the appeal to the
gang leader, hoping that it might reach The
Jackdaw. He was sure, now, that if it had, there
would be small comfort in the fact.

Bart Melken knew that he was deep in The
Jackdaw's toils. There was no retreating; but he felt
the need of aid. The murder of Rutherford Casslin
had brought him face to face with desperate facts.

Crime was not distasteful to Bart Melken; the
penalty was what he feared. Capable though The
Jackdaw might be, there was always chance of a
slip. When that time arrived, Bart felt sure, he, and
not The Jackdaw, would be the scapegoat.

The telephone bell rang. It was only a few feet
from the spot where Melken sat. The ringing
startled the young man. With trembling hand, he
lifted the receiver of the telephone. He feared that
this might be a message from The Jackdaw—a
stern order giving him another task to perform for
the crook who dealt in subtle theft, with murder as
a sideline. Bart knew The Jackdaw's voice, a
strained, faraway method of talking. He sighed in
relief as he recognized other tones.

"Hello, Bart," a friendly voice was saying.
"How have you been since I saw you last."

"Who is calling?" stammered Bart Melken.

"Farrell Sarborn," came the reply. "Just landed
back in New York yesterday. Called you last
night—there was no answer."

"Farrell Sarborn!" The exclamation came from
Melken with a note of alleviation. "Where are you,
Farrell? Stopping here in town?"

"Apartment up on Seventy-eighth Street,"
returned the speaker at the other end. "Come up

and see the place. I picked up a few oddities when I was in South America."

Bart Melken repeated the address as Sarborn gave it to him. He agreed to come and see his friend at once. Leaving the apartment, Melken went down to the lobby, arrived on the street, and hailed a taxicab.

ONCE again, the young man was followed. It was not The Shadow who trailed him tonight, however. A young man, seated in the lobby, had strolled out to a coupé immediately after Melken's departure. He drove in pursuit of the taxi which Melken had hailed.

This young man was Harry Vincent, an agent of The Shadow. Just as Cliff Marsland served as watchdog in the underworld, so did Harry Vincent take up trails in the fashionable districts. Each of these subordinates served The Shadow well. Since The Shadow had trailed Melken to his meeting with Bing Claver, other duties had concerned The Shadow. To Harry Vincent remained the work of keeping The Shadow posted on Melken's future actions.

The taxicab stopped at a small apartment building on Seventy-eighth Street. Bart Melken alighted, paid the driver, and entered the lobby. He found a bell which was beside the card bearing Farrell Sarborn's name. The door clicked. Bart Melken entered.

Immediately afterward, Harry Vincent stepped into the same lobby. He saw the depressed button, not yet released by a closing door. He knew the apartment to which Bart Melken had gone. He went away to report his finding to The Shadow.

On the third floor, Bart Melken spied an opened door. Framed there was the figure of Farrell Sarborn. Tall and thin in his shirtsleeves, Sarborn was smiling a friendly greeting as he extended his hand to Melken.

A few minutes later, the two men were seated in Sarborn's living room, and a squat, greasy-faced servant was bringing them drinks upon a tray. Sarborn indicated the fellow with a nudge of his thumb.

"This is Jalon," he said. "Brought him along from Caracas. Needed a servant, and he speaks English. Used to work in the States. Wanted to come back."

Bart Melken nodded. He was accustomed to Farrell Sarborn's brisk, phraselike way of speaking. Melken was not a man with many friends, although he had numerous acquaintances. He was accustomed, however, to consider Farrell Sarborn as a real friend.

Although Sarborn was not of the elite, he could take his place in any company. The man had money, and was a traveler. A few months ago, he had started out for South America. His return had

been quite unexpected. To Bart Melken, it was a most propitious event.

For though Bart had never said a word to anyone regarding the hold which The Jackdaw held over him, he had always felt that if the crisis came, he could confide in Farrell Sarborn.

The traveler was truly a man of the world; his keen, poker face showed that trait. He was at least a dozen years older than Bart Melken; that, too, gave Bart a greater reliance on his friend's judgment.

Bart Melken felt that a crisis was impending now. He did not intend to speak of it in detail, even to Farrell Sarborn, but he saw in the traveler's presence an opportunity to gain a companion who might serve him well when trouble arrived.

"What have you been doing?" questioned Sarborn, in a friendly tone. "You aren't married yet?"

"Not yet," returned Bart. "I've just been hanging around New York. I see Yvonne quite often, of course. Tonight happens to be an exception."

"A wonderful girl, Yvonne," observed Sarborn. "You're very lucky to be marrying her. I hope you've been keeping out of mischief."

"I have," said Bart dully.

Sarborn's eyes became keen. The traveler sipped from a glass, and stared at his companion. Bart Melken felt a bit uneasy. He tried to curb his restlessness.

"What have you been doing, Farrell?" he questioned, when his friend made no comment. "Seeing much of South America?"

Sarborn chuckled.

"South America," he declared, "is responsible for my being in this apartment. If I hadn't been there, I probably would be living at the Ritz. As it is, I have to keep a place where my pets can stay."

"Your pets?"

"Yes." Sarborn arose and beckoned. Melken followed him into an unfurnished room. There, in a long, wide cage, Melken observed a dozen green plumaged birds that were sitting solemnly on perches.

"Parakeets," remarked Sarborn. "I made quite a study of them, and brought these along with me."

"Do they chatter much?" asked Melken.

"Not these," returned Sarborn, "but there's the baby that does—when he feels in the mood."

Melken turned toward the corner of the room. There, perched upon a metal bar set in the front of a deep windowsill, was one of the most beautiful birds that he had ever seen. Its plumage was of a vivid red; the size of the bird was also remarkable. It measured nearly three feet from head to tail.

"A great scarlet macaw," explained Sarborn. "A rare species for one to find in captivity. This bird is worth more than the whole cageload of parakeets."

"Does the macaw talk?"

"Yes. When coaxed. I have trained him."

SARBORN approached the bird. He reached up and scratched the macaw's head. The big bird began to ruffle its throat feathers and open its bill, but no sound came. Sarborn continued the treatment. He nodded to Melken, and motioned him toward the door.

"Bustle up toward the bird," he ordered. "Make out that you are threatening it. Stop short, though, before you arrive too close."

The macaw was watching Melken as it moved its bill. The young man followed Sarborn's instructions. As he made a fierce advance, a shrill warning came from the scarlet macaw.

"Keep away! Keep away!"

Melken stopped suddenly as he heard the high falsetto cry. Sarborn, still scratching the macaw's head, laughed at his friend's surprise. He gave another order.

"Be more affable," he said. "Then stroll away and pretend that you are going out the door."

Melken followed instructions. As he hesitated at the door, another call came from the macaw's trembling beak.

"Come back!" shrilled the bird. "Come back!"

"Remarkable!" exclaimed Melken, as the cry died. "The bird seems to have almost human intelligence."

"It is observant," admitted Sarborn. "More than that, it has an aptitude for remembering things that it hears. It only chooses words that appeal to it, however. Try some."

"New York," suggested Melken.

"Repeat it," ordered Sarborn. "Emphasize the name."

"New York—New York—"

"New York!" screamed the macaw. "New York!"

Melken laughed. Sarborn ceased stroking the bird's head. The macaw kept ruffling its throat, but gave no further cry. Melken approached, scratched the bird's head; there was no response.

"It will only take its cues from me," explained Sarborn. "Speaking of birds—here are some interesting eggs. I brought a small collection with me from South America."

Sarborn pointed to a glass case in the corner. There, Melken saw a variety of eggs of different sizes. He remarked upon a large, blotched egg that was about three inches in length.

"What species of egg is that?" he questioned.

"A condor's egg," replied Sarborn. "The condor is one of the largest of all birds. They can fly to greater altitudes than the eagle."

"It must be difficult to obtain their eggs."

"No. They have no marked nesting habits. The eggs are found upon rocks, in the mountains. Such eggs are not particularly rare."

A slight sound came from a covered box in the corner. Melken looked in that direction. Sarborn reached over and raised the lid of the box. A small monkey poked its head into view.

"Are you raising monkeys, too?" laughed Melken, as he saw the little creature scramble up to Sarborn's arms.

"No," replied Sarborn. "I started to, but gave it up. I'm going to get rid of this little beast later on. Affectionate, but a nuisance. Just a common species. South American monkey. Called a sapajou."

The monkey had seized Sarborn's necktie. It was starting to climb up it, hand over hand. Sarborn wrested the sapajou free, and dropped it back into the box. He closed the lid and strolled back to the living room.

"Well," he remarked, "you've seen the menagerie. Wouldn't do at the Ritz. Better here. Guess I'll get rid of the whole shebang. All except the macaw."

"How long are you going to be in town?" questioned Melken anxiously.

AGAIN, Sarborn looked quizzically at his friend. He seemed to sense the worriment that was present in Melken's mind.

"Quite a while," said Sarborn. "Why?"

"Thought we might get together occasionally," returned Melken. "I've been nervous during the past few days."

"Why?"

"The trouble out at Casslin's house. You must have read about it in the newspapers."

"The murder of the millionaire?"

"Yes."

"You were there?"

"Yes."

"Hm-m-m." Sarborn was shaking his head. "Very mysterious affair. Read about it in the newspapers. None of the guests were implicated, were they?"

"No," answered Melken, "but I'm worried just the same. Farrell, there were some other robberies a few months ago—robberies that took place at houses where I had been. This was the first one where a murder occurred."

"You think—"

"I don't know what to think. I'm worried. If there's one crook in back of all these robberies, there's no telling what may happen next."

"Why should it concern you?" Sarborn asked.

"Here's why." Melken's tone became serious. "It's going to look as though someone might be on the inside of some of these crimes. It's also going to be tough for anyone who might observe too much."

"You mean something might be planted on you?"

"Not on me," broke in Melken hastily. "That is—not necessarily on me. On someone, though, and I might be the person."

"Or," added Sarborn calmly, "someone might decide that you knew too much and give the orders to bump you off?"

"I don't know," responded Melken. "I only know that I've been terribly worried since Casslin was killed. I've had a feeling that there is a menace hanging over me. We're old friends, Farrell. You're the only man to whom I can talk about this."

Sarborn arose and clapped his friend on the shoulder. His action seemed to given Melken encouragement. There was a firmness in Sarborn's manner that aroused confidence.

"Don't worry, old top," volunteered Sarborn. "If you have any idea whatever that trouble is brewing, let me know. If you're uneasy, maybe you can arrange for me to be with you. I've faced everything. Anacondas to orangutans. I like trouble."

Bart Melken nodded. Under this persuasion, he was ready to talk further.

"At Casslin's," he said seriously, "Yvonne saw a face at the window. She told me about it. That was just before the murder. She told the police afterward; but I didn't say that she had spoken to me when she saw the face.

"That's what has me worried, Farrell. I'll be looking for danger signs from now on. I won't be able to keep myself from doing so. If—if I begin to look like I'm—well, a menace to some crooks—they may decide to put me on the spot."

"Don't worry, Bart," reassured Sarborn. "This hunch of yours is interesting. I think we'd better stick around together a bit."

Bart Melken shook hands warmly. He felt the value of this friendship. When he left Sarborn's apartment, a while later, he decided that he had accomplished something.

Melken, like Cardona and The Shadow, was out to learn the identity of The Jackdaw. His purpose was not guided by any dislike of crime; it was merely inspired by a desire for self-preservation; to escape a bargain that was proving one-sided.

Wrapped in thought as he departed, Bart Melken did not notice the peering eyes that watched him as he crossed the street in front of Farrell Sarborn's apartment. He did not know that once again he was under the surveillance of The Shadow.

CHAPTER XI
THE JACKDAW ORDERS

TWO days had passed since Bart Melken's visit to his friend, Farrell Sarborn. Those two days had been anxious ones for Melken. The Jackdaw's minion knew well that he would soon receive another order to play his part in crime.

There were hours, in the late afternoon, when Melken made it a practice to remain alone in his hotel room. That was part of The Jackdaw's bargain. Today, with afternoon waning, Melken was in the room. Today, more than ever before, he sensed impending orders from his chief.

Accounts in the newspapers had given no new findings on the murder of Rutherford Casslin. That, at least, was satisfactory to Bart Melken. He was sure that Joe Cardona was making no progress that would lead him to The Jackdaw.

The position was a singular one. Bart was anxious that no one else would learn The Jackdaw's identity. He was anxious, also, that he could learn it. His scheme was simply to meet The Jackdaw on an equal basis, for the first time, and thus be able to make terms that would result in his own freedom.

To date, Bart had gained no inkling whatever regarding The Jackdaw's identity. That fact, as much as any other, made him dread the power of his task-making chief. With Farrell Sarborn as an ally, there was some chance that Bart Melken might gain a helpful clue.

As for The Shadow, Bart Melken had no idea whatever that his mysterious presence had appeared. He figured only himself, the police, and The Jackdaw. Yet The Shadow's part, so far as Bart was concerned, was more important than that of any other.

This very room in which Bart Melken sat had been fitted, during his absence, with a dictograph. In an adjoining hotel room, a young man was on duty. Harry Vincent, agent of The Shadow, was not only watching for any who might visit Bart Melken; he was also keeping tabs on Bart's end of telephone conversations.

The telephone bell rang while Bart was deep in thought. Yvonne Lydell was on the wire. Bart was relieved to hear her voice. He conducted a leisurely conversation.

"Tonight?" he questioned. "Certainly. I can meet you at Winchendon's... Yes, about half past nine is the time I expect to arrive there. I can take you home afterward. Very well. Has your father returned from Florida? ... Ah, next week... That is later than he expected... Very well, Yvonne. I shall met you at Winchendon's."

Melken hung up the telephone. He strolled back and forth across the room. The bell began to ring again. Bart hesitated; then answered the summons. He paled as he heard the voice over the wire.

It was The Jackdaw.

THERE was an effect about The Jackdaw's voice that had always placed Melken on the defensive.

The Jackdaw seldom asked questions. He dealt in statements, and gave his orders. He seemed to have plans for crime already mapped. Moreover, his direct way of talking invariably gave Melken the impression that The Jackdaw knew much about him.

"Tonight," came The Jackdaw's oddly pitched voice, "you are going to an affair at the home of Silas Winchendon."

"Yes," stammered Melken. "I'll be at Winchendon's."

"The signal will be required," ordered The Jackdaw. "Wait until all the guests are assembled in Winchendon's living room. Signal near the French doors at the side. Retire, and act as the other guests."

"What time?" queried Melken.

"Any time after ten o'clock," came The Jackdaw's final command.

"But—but wait a moment," began Melken. "I'm not—not sure about tonight. If—"

A click came over the wire. The Jackdaw had ended the conversation. Melken knew the answer. He would have to go through with the game or take the consequences.

Melken paced the room. He was muttering to himself, but his words had no meaning.

Harry Vincent, in the other room, had noted down the few facts that he had gleaned from Melken's talk with The Jackdaw. They were sufficient only to reveal that Melken had some important duty to perform at Winchendon's this night.

Minutes passed; Melken, with a sigh of resignation, went to the telephone. His hand was trembling as it lifted the receiver. The Jackdaw's minion was losing his nerve; he was afraid that he would fail in the task placed before him.

Melken was choosing the only way out; he was reverting to his half-formed plan of counting on his friend, Farrell Sarborn, as a protector. He gave the operator the number of Sarborn's apartment.

When he heard his friend's easy, cheery voice, Melken felt a return of confidence. He began a conversation that kept Harry Vincent busy recording it.

"This is Bart Melken," began The Jackdaw's minion. "Listen, Farrell, I'm still feeling nervous. More so than ever. I have to go out tonight—to a party at Silas Winchendon's home. I—I'd like to get out of it."

Sarborn's reply was to the effect that such should be an easy matter. Melken quickly changed his tack.

"The trouble, Farrell," he said, "is that Yvonne will be there. She'll wonder why I didn't come. I've promised to take her home, afterward. I—I tell you what I'd like to do. I'd like to take you along. I might be able to arrange it by calling Mrs. Winchendon. But there would have to be some good reason."

Sarborn put a question over the wire. It was a query regarding the type of party that was to be held.

"A swanky affair," explained Melken, "but a very quiet one. The Winchendons like to have interesting people. They always invite guests who offer something unusual by way of diversion."

As Bart Melken paused, he heard Farrell Sarborn offer a suggestion. The idea caused a gleam to appear upon Bart's pallid face.

"Great!" he exclaimed. "By Jove, that would be just the ticket! If you could give them a short talk on the bird life of South America, and bring the big macaw with you, they'd fall for it to perfection. You will be the lion of the evening, Farrell!"

A pause; then Melken added:

"Certainly! I'll call Mrs. Winchendon at once. Unless you hear from me to the contrary, you'll know that it has been arranged. I'll stop for you in a cab. This is important to me, Farrell"—Melken's tone became sober—"and you'll never regret helping me out. I'll tell you more about the situation later on. Thanks, old fellow."

Melken hung up; then made another call, to the home of Silas Winchendon. As he had anticipated, the young man had no difficulty in arranging for Farrell Sarborn to appear as an invited guest. His description of the remarkable scarlet macaw aroused Mrs. Winchendon's interest to such an extent that it appeared that she was inviting the bird rather than its master.

A CURIOUS elation governed Bart Melken when he had completed his arrangements. He knew that trouble was in the air. No specified orders had been given by The Jackdaw other than a necessary signal. What the shrewd crook plotted was more than Bart could decide.

The presence of Farrell Sarborn, however, would be of vital value. That was the cause of Melken's elation. He felt that with his friend there, he would be able to show nerve enough to either give the signal or completely ignore it. All that he needed was surety that would enable him to make a decision one way or the other.

At heart, Bart Melken was a weakling. Susceptible to persons of stronger will, he had hitherto followed The Jackdaw like an unprotesting lamb. Now, with the sense that he could depend upon the strong personality of Farrell Sarborn, Bart had gained synthetic courage. He had lost his fear of consequences whether he might continue his unliked work or whether he might choose to defy The Jackdaw's orders.

As Bart Melken rested in an easy chair, he never once supposed that through his telephone calls he had paved the way to startling consequences. The words that he had uttered had been recorded. Already, Harry Vincent, seated in the adjoining room, was completing an exact report to The Shadow.

It was nearly five o'clock—Melken's last call had been completed shortly before the hour—when Harry Vincent appeared in the lobby of Melken's hotel. The Shadow's agent hailed a cab, and rolled to a huge skyscraper—the Badger Building. He rode by elevator to a high floor, and entered an office which bore the legend:

RUTLEDGE MANN INVESTMENTS

In an inner room, Harry came face to face with a lethargic, chubby-faced individual, who was seated at a desk beside the window. This was Rutledge Mann, who served as a contact man and special investigator for The Shadow. Harry gave Mann the sealed envelope which contained his report. He left the office shortly afterward.

Ten minutes later, Mann left the Badger Building, and rode by cab to Twenty-third Street. Here, he entered a dilapidated building, and ascended a flight of dingy stairs. He stopped in front of an office which bore a name upon its central panel of unwashed glass:

B. JONAS

Mann dropped the envelope through the mail chute. He stared a few moments at the door, with its frosted front that made it impossible to see within. Every sign told of desertion. Cobwebs were apparent on the glass panel. To all appearances, no one had been in that office for many months.

Yet Mann knew that the letter which he had dropped would be delivered; for this mail chute was the collection box where The Shadow received such messages as the one which Mann had brought.

No one approached that door after Mann had left. Yet the message in the mail chute was gained by the recipient for whom it was intended. The proof of this took place in a silent, mysterious room, somewhere in the maze that is Manhattan.

A CLICK resounded amid total blackness. A bluish light came on; its rays were concentrated by an opaque shade so they spread uncanny illumination upon the polished surface of a corner table.

Appearing beneath the light were two white hands that moved like detached creatures creeping into life from oblivion. Between them, they held the envelope which had come from Harry Vincent through the agency of Rutledge Mann.

The hands of The Shadow! One token told of their identity. This was a gleaming gem that flashed mysteriously from the long third finger of the left hand. That jewel, unmatched in all the world, was The Shadow's girasol—a fire opal of shimmering splendor. The strange stone emitted sparks that seemed to come from a living coal.

Harry Vincent's report tumbled from the envelope. It was written in ink; it was prepared in simple code. To The Shadow, its wording was plain. Thus did the master learn all that Bart Melken had said over the telephone that afternoon.

Strangely, the blue-inked words began to fade as promptly as The Shadow read them. An invisible hand seemed to be obliterating them from view. That was due to the special type of ink that The Shadow and his agents used in their private correspondence. Writing disappeared shortly after it contacted with the open air.

Melken's conversations had been somewhat obscure in certain details—particularly the one which he had conducted with The Jackdaw. To The Shadow, however, the gaps were easy ones to fill. The report gave the super sleuth the vital facts that he wished to know.

Crime was due to strike tonight, at the home of Silas Winchendon. Bart Melken, nervous and disturbed, had called upon a friend to be close at hand—without revealing facts to that friend. Orders had come from Melken's superior—and The Shadow knew the name under which that hidden crook masqueraded.

The Jackdaw planned to follow his success at Rutherford Casslin's with another well-laid scheme of crime. Although his purpose was not mentioned, The Shadow seemed to sense the type of robbery that the crook had planned.

The whispered laugh that echoed from the darkness revealed The Shadow's hidden thoughts. The black-garbed master was already formulating a method of offsetting The Jackdaw's efforts.

Tonight, The Jackdaw's cleverness would be met by The Shadow's skill. The meeting ground would be the home of Silas Winchendon. A mighty struggle was in the making; what its outcome would be, only The Shadow could foresee.

The light clicked out. A weird, chilling laugh broke the silence of the gloom. Reverberations died. Silence returned.

The Shadow had departed from that room of blackness. He had left his mysterious sanctum to issue forth in battle against crime.

CHAPTER XII
CARDONA PERSISTS

WHILE The Shadow, in his sanctum, was studying reports that were bringing him closer to The Jackdaw's trail, Joe Cardona, in his office at headquarters, was gloomily considering the situation that he faced.

Ever since he had been forced to take Doctor

Lysander Dubrong's bitter gibes, Cardona had been seeking a comeback. He had realized fully that Dubrong was too clever for him. In that realization, however, Joe had reached a definite and startling conclusion.

The detective was sure that someone had spotted him while he had been in Doctor Dubrong's waiting room; that the physician had known the identity of his bewhiskered patient all during the clinic hours.

In proof of this, Cardona cited to himself the fact that Dubrong had departed from usual procedure by letting a patient into the consulting room after the one o'clock deadline. Cardona, therefore, had tried to figure who had tipped off Dubrong to the fact that a detective was close by.

In his two-hour waiting period at the clinic, Cardona had studied the patients there. One, only, had aroused his keen suspicion. That was the man whom he had encountered at the outer door, the shuffling cripple called Limps Silvey.

Was there collusion between Limps and Dubrong? Cardona had determined to find that out. He had, accordingly, put stool pigeons watching Limps. So far, their findings had been meager.

Limps had appeared only at intervals. He had revisited the East Side Clinic; he had been seen wandering about the streets at night. He had also shown a proclivity for passing out of sight in a hurry.

With another evening arriving, Joe Cardona was angry at this lack of action. He wanted to get close on Limps Silvey's trail. He was positive that the frail, twisted man served Dubrong in some important capacity.

The telephone began to ring. Cardona picked up the instrument. He recognized the voice of one of his stool pigeons. The words came in an eager, whining tone.

"I'm wise to this guy Limps," the stool was saying. "He's been duckin' us cute until just now. I'll tell you where he is—he's sneakin' in an' out from Bing Claver's joint. He's there now, an' I think he's goin' to stay a while."

"O.K.," ordered Cardona briskly. "Stick there until I show up."

DUSK had settled. Cardona scorned disguise. He felt that he could trail Limps Silvey under cover of night.

He started out from headquarters. A while later, he appeared by the decadent alley where the side entrance to Bing Claver's apartment was located.

It was darkening; the stool pigeons sneaked out and whispered as they saw the detective. Joe heard their words. Apparently, Limps Silvey had suddenly dropped his usual crafty tactics. Off his guard, the stools had trailed him. Joe dismissed the stools and took up watch alone.

Usually stolid, Joe Cardona was anxious tonight. He had cause to be. The blind lead on the Casslin murder—nothing had developed from the Hindu theory—had brought criticism from Police Commissioner Weston.

Cardona had been forced to keep silent on the point concerning The Jackdaw. Had he brought in the idea of an anonymous crook, a masquerader in the underworld, Weston would have been enraged. The commissioner branded all such unknown characters as myths.

Yet Cardona was sure that The Jackdaw existed. He had a real hunch that the king of thieves had slain Rutherford Casslin. Clues had failed at the millionaire's mansion. The dead body in the tower was still an unexplained mystery. The answer lay in uncovering The Jackdaw himself.

Cardona was relying upon one basic fact. Scoffy had told him that The Jackdaw had henchmen among gangsters. One of these, Bennie Lizzit, had been slain with Scoffy himself. Where gunmen were employed, there was usually a leader. Now, for the first time, Cardona had an inkling of who the gang chief might be: Bing Claver.

This was a real achievement. Bing Claver, a dominating gorilla who had apparently retired from crime, was just the type of gangster whom The Jackdaw might choose to command his crew of torpedoes. Limps Silvey would also be an excellent go-between. Cardona saw the link he wanted: a possible hookup between Doctor Lysander Dubrong and Bing Claver.

Long minutes passed while Cardona waited in reflection. Suddenly, the detective became alert. He saw a shaft of light in the alleyway; then a slinking figure coming in his direction. He recognized Limps, and eased back into the cover of a deserted doorway, as he watched the shuffling man approach.

Apparently, Limps had no idea that anyone was watching him. The frail hobbler turned along the street, and Cardona took up his trail. The detective, his overcoat up around his neck, was watching closely every time that Limps threw a sidelong glance.

So concerned was Cardona in watching the man ahead that he never thought to look in back. Thus he had no idea that he, too, was being followed. It would have gained Cardona nothing, however, to have glanced backward. He would not have caught even a glimpse of the one who was on his trail.

For the third member of this trio that was advancing along a dilapidated street was one who moved with the silence of the growing night itself. No sign of his form was visible; only an occasional patch of sidewalk blackness betokened his strange presence.

The Shadow, fresh from his sanctum, had come to this section of the underworld. Unseen, unsuspected, he was watching the pursuit ahead: Joe Cardona on the trail of Limps Silvey.

SHUFFLING down another thoroughfare, Limps stopped in front of a dilapidated store. He looked craftily about him. Joe Cardona was almost caught flat-footed; but he leaned back against a wall. Limps must have missed him; for the cripple showed no concern. He hobbled into the store.

Joe Cardona approached and looked through a grimy window. He crouched against the wall, and suppressed a chuckle. He was in luck. He had seen Limps Silvey.

The shuffler had gone into the store to telephone; and the coin box, although secluded in the store itself, was within three feet of the window. Moreover, a pane was broken from the window and Joe, as he listened, could hear the clicking of the dial as Limps rang up a number.

As before, Cardona was intent upon his objective. He gave no thought to anything else about him. He did not sense the presence of The Shadow, as the black-garbed follower came closer. Stationed but a few feet away, pressed beside a projection of the building, The Shadow, like Cardona, was listening in on Limps Silvey.

The cripple's voice was a husky one; although lowered, it could plainly be heard. Limps had obtained his number. He was talking.

"All gettin' ready for tonight," Limps was saying. "I'm goin' to duck out of town, see? ... Yeah—after I look over the lay... An' if it's all right, I'm just goin' to lose myself. But if it ain't all right, I'll give you the tip... I'll tell you where I'll be... Yeah, out in Corona... When it comes ten o'clock, I'll be hangin' out at the Derry Café, near the "L" station... Ring up there, when you're ready to go... You can tell me what you're plannin' then—which job you're goin' to grab tonight... O.K.—here's the number"—Limps paused to consult a crumpled sheet of paper—"Seabright 0664... Got it? O.K..."

Limps shuffled away from the telephone. He came from the store, and headed for the corner after a glance in both directions. Cardona paused; then started in pursuit.

At the corner, he glimpsed Limps beneath a streetlamp, halfway down the block. The twisted man was hobbling away with remarkable swiftness.

For a moment, Cardona was tempted to halt his quarry. His fist tightened on his pocket revolver. At that moment, Limps slid into an alleyway. Cardona started forward at a quick pace. He reached the spot where the man had disappeared.

Peering down the alleyway, Joe could see no sign of Limps. The narrow path ran between houses to another street. There were lights above, in house windows. To his chagrin, Cardona realized that Limps had given him the slip.

Standing on the sidewalk, Cardona considered what to do next. He thought of going back to Bing Claver's. He paused as he contemplated.

It would be a mistake to talk to Bing. If the gang leader planned an expedition tonight, particularly one in The Jackdaw's service, a challenging visit from a detective would amount to nothing more than a warning.

It was obvious that mobsters planned a foray; their destination was not known, but it would be mentioned to Limps Silvey over the telephone at the number in Corona. That was the place to be stationed. Cardona saw opportunities ahead.

Nevertheless, he was wise enough to figure on more than one trail. Nearly half an hour had elapsed since he had left the alleyway by Bing's apartment. Cardona decided it would be worth while to take another look back there.

SWINGING on his heel, the detective headed back the way that he had come. This time there was no sinister presence bringing up the rear. The Shadow had disappeared with the same promptitude as Limps Silvey.

When Cardona reached Bing Claver's alley, he noted that the side of the rickety apartment building was black. The upstairs lights—Cardona had observed them previously—had been extinguished.

A stool pigeon shuffled out of the darkness. The man whined a message in a low voice as he stood beside Cardona. The detective grunted as he heard it.

"Seen Bing Claver," informed the stool. "He come out just after Limps scrammed. Don't know where he went, though. Kinda afraid to follow Bing, I was."

"All right," growled Cardona. "Beat it. Call me up if you spot either one of them."

Joe Cardona, as he stalked away, still found himself wondering what had become of Limps Silvey. The detective decided that no one, no matter how clever, could have trailed that quick-moving hobbler. In this surmise, Cardona was in error.

Limps Silvey was being trailed, by one who moved with silence as well as swiftness. At that moment, Limps, heading for the darkness of a blind alley, did not realize that anyone was close at hand. Even Limps, clever though he was, did not spy the obscure form of The Shadow.

With noiseless cane, Limps slipped into the darkness. Keen eyes followed him; keen ears heard the soft closing of a door. A whispered laugh followed. The Shadow was standing by the entrance to the cul-de-sac where he had trailed Limps before. This time he had spotted the door which Limps had used. The cripple had entered through the secret way to Doctor Lysander Dubrong's consulting room.

Swiftly, The Shadow glided from the spot. His silent strides carried him on a roundabout course beyond the alley where Bing Claver lived. Suddenly, The Shadow stopped; under the projecting top of a battered brick wall, he peered keenly as he heard footsteps on the other side of the street.

Through the gloom loomed Joe Cardona. The detective was pounding his way back to headquarters. His steady gait, his bent shoulders, both were tokens of his lack of success. The Shadow knew that Joe Cardona had learned nothing more.

Yet Joe Cardona was not defeated. Out of this evening's effort, he had gained one thing which might prove vital to the plans that lay ahead. He had learned the number where Limps Silvey would be expecting a telephone call. It was one bet that the detective could play

That Cardona would stake much on that chance was certain. The Shadow knew Cardona's only possible plan. As the detective's footsteps faded, a soft laugh began to rise; clipped abruptly during its crescendo, it dwindled to a sobbing sigh of merriment that was suppressed beneath the overhanging wall.

There was a presagement in The Shadow's laugh; a foreknowledge of the events that were to come. The Shadow knew the part that Limps Silvey was playing in the approaching drama.

He had made a study of The Jackdaw's minions. All were scheduled for work this night. The Shadow's challenge, however, reached beyond the underlings. The Jackdaw himself was the game The Shadow sought.

CHAPTER XIII
AT WINCHENDON'S

IT was after nine o'clock when Bart Melken and Farrell Sarborn arrived by taxicab at Silas Winchendon's Long Island home. Both men entered, dressed in faultless evening clothes. Mrs. Winchendon, a plump, middle-aged woman, greeted them.

One of the servants had received a tall, cylindrical package at the door. Mrs. Winchendon indicated it with an interested gesture.

"The macaw's cage?" she questioned.

"Yes," smiled Melken. "The bird is in there. Mr. Sarborn will bring him out when you are ready."

The servant took the cage into a small room. Mrs. Winchendon led the two guests to the living room. She stopped a moment, just outside the door.

"We have another treat tonight," she remarked. "Mr. Cranston—Lamont Cranston, the famous globetrotter. He has been telling us of his experiences in the Orient. It was so fortunate—he just chanced to call up Mr. Winchendon—"

Mrs. Winchendon ceased speaking. They were already at the door of the living room.

Bart Melken spied Yvonne Lydell among the guests who were listening to a quiet, convincing-toned speaker who was standing near the end of the living room.

Lamont Cranston was a man of whom Bart Melken had heard. Farrell Sarborn had known of him also, and the two studied the speaker with interest. Tall, impressive in his well-tailored evening clothes, Cranston had the appearance of a man who knew the world.

His face seemed immobile in expression. His chiseled features were almost masklike. His aquiline nose gave him a hawkish look, which was accentuated by a pair of keen, penetrating eyes.

Cranston, as everyone knew, was a multimillionaire who traveled when and where he chose. He maintained a large mansion in New Jersey. He had a habit of setting forth at most unexpected times on journeys that included the most distant places.

From the vastnesses of Siberia, to the depths of darkest Africa, Lamont Cranston had traveled. His ways carried him to bypaths that ordinary travelers dreaded. His present discourse on his journey to India concerned the little-known summits of the Himalaya Mountains.

CRANSTON concluded speaking a few minutes after Melken and Sarborn entered. A murmur of admiration came from the listeners who had heard his remarkable discourse. Mrs. Winchendon drew Farrell Sarborn and Bart Melken forward. She introduced Sarborn first.

"Mr. Sarborn is a traveler also," she said to Cranston. "He has just returned from a trip to South America."

"I am scarcely a traveler," put forth Sarborn, as he shook hands with Cranston. "My journeys have been trivial compared with yours. I can merely claim some slight distinction as a student of certain districts where I have been."

"That is much to your credit," observed Cranston. "I, myself, have often neglected interesting surroundings due to my desire to arrive at another destination. It is a fault, I assure you—a fault which I must commend you for not possessing."

There was no flattery in the millionaire's tone; his words were given with the quiet positiveness of a simple statement. This was pleasing to Farrell Sarborn. It seemed to place the new guest at his ease.

Bart Melken was looking about him. He was

studying the people in the living room. He had come to a prompt realization that in this throng alone was sufficient pelf to arouse The Jackdaw's cupidity.

Mrs. Winchendon was adorned with large and expensive gems. So were other of the guests. Indeed, when viewed from the standpoint of personal ornamentation, the living room was fairly glittering.

Melken noticed the French doors on the opposite side of the room. He also noted several curtained doorways.

It was possible that one of these might lead to a hidden spot where The Jackdaw intended to make a foray, but Bart could not imagine any haul that would exceed that of the jewelry. The Jackdaw, Bart knew well, had a penchant for precious stones.

"I regret," Sarborn was saying to Cranston, "that I failed to hear your talk on India. I have often intended to travel there."

"I shall be pleased to discuss India at any time," returned Cranston. "In the meantime, I am anxious to hear your observations on South America."

As the men parted, Cranston's keen eyes turned in the direction of Bart Melken. The pale-faced young man had crossed the living room to join Yvonne Lydell. Cranston saw his gaze go again to the French windows.

There was a contrast between the man and the girl. Melken now had no claim to handsomeness. His pallor, his furtive expression, were damaging to his appearance. Yvonne Lydell, tall and slender, was a perfect blonde, whose beautiful face showed a vivacity that made her fiancé's gloominess more noticeable.

Mrs. Winchendon was introducing Sarborn to the other guests. Melken's friend was well received. Silas Winchendon, a big, heavy man, seemed pleased to meet another visitor who had a reputation as a traveler.

It was quite a while before the arrangements were finished for Sarborn to speak to the gathering. At last, Sarborn beckoned to a servant. The covered cage was brought into the room. Sarborn smiled as he heard buzzing conversation end.

"IT is my pleasure," announced Sarborn, "to discuss the avifauna of South America. I must admit that my knowledge of the birds of that continent is somewhat restricted. I have been more interested in the birds themselves than in a study of the various species.

"In South America, I obtained one bird that is rarely brought to the United States. I refer to the great scarlet macaw. I was fortunate enough to acquire an excellent specimen; and the bird has shown a remarkable response to its captivity."

Removing the top of the cage, Sarborn dipped his arm within and brought out the three-foot macaw on his hand. He carried the bird to a chair back, and let it perch there.

Exclamations of admiration greeted the appearance of the macaw. The brilliant plumage was something that few of the guests had ever seen before.

The macaw, blinking in the light, kept moving its beak and ruffling its throat feathers so furiously that all the observers laughed. Lamont Cranston, lighting a cigarette beside the nearer of the French windows, looked up and studied the bird curiously.

"I have trained the macaw to speak," explained Sarborn, "but he is as wise as an owl, and requires considerable coaxing. Let me demonstrate."

He scratched the macaw's head. The bird kept up its beak motion. Suddenly, it spoke in high falsetto:

"Hello! Hello, there!"

Everyone laughed at the shrill sound. Sarborn, his head bent close toward the bird, looked up and smiled. He raised his hand for silence.

"This bird," he said, "has a remarkable proclivity for remembering words that it hears. For instance, suppose someone is introduced to it—"

Mrs. Winchendon stepped forward.

"This is Mrs. Winchendon," said Sarborn, to the macaw. "Mrs. Winchendon. Would you remember her?"

He was scratching the bird's head and looking toward it as he spoke. The macaw's trembling beak became more furious.

"Winchendon!" shrilled the scarlet bird. "Winchendon!"

Sarborn began some new experiments, much like those he had shown to Melken. To further demonstrate the bird's intelligence, he stepped away and stood at arm's length, while he made a noise like a kitten mewing.

"Cats! Cats!" screamed the bird.

"It is odd," remarked Sarborn, when the macaw had become silent, "how this bird has managed to actually associate sounds with words that it has heard concerning them. The reference to cats was a surprising accomplishment. On the boat, coming up from South America, we had a joke of pointing out other ships and saying, 'Pirates.' In the harbor of Port-au-Prince, the macaw fairly screamed 'Pirates! Pirates!' every time we had it on deck and it saw the shipping of the harbor."

"Pirates!" shrilled the macaw.

A clock was chiming ten. Bart Melken, who had been standing across the room, strolled near a French window and began to fumble with his cigarette lighter. Only Lamont Cranston observed the action.

CRANSTON'S position was so taken that he could see from the other French window, although he did not appear to glance in that direction. While Sarborn was still coaxing the macaw, Cranston's keen eye again turned toward the darkness outside.

A tiny speck of light glimmered beyond. It went out. It reappeared. That was all. Cranston strolled toward the spot where Farrell Sarborn had the macaw.

"Can the bird tell my name?" he asked. "I think it heard you give it."

"We'll try," replied Sarborn. He scratched the macaw's head, then shrugged his shoulders.

"I'm afraid you have stepped too close to it," he said. "Just step back a few paces, Mr. Cranston."

"Cranston!" screamed the macaw, the moment the millionaire obeyed.

"It heard your name again, then," laughed Sarborn. "I did not realize that I was mentioning it."

Cranston had joined in the general laughter. He was retiring toward one of the curtained doorways. As Sarborn again turned his attention to the macaw, all eyes were on the bird. Cranston's keen gaze observed that fact.

With a slight sidewise motion, the millionaire eased through the curtained doorway, so unobtrusively that not a single person witnessed his departure. In the darkness of a hallway he lifted folded garments from beneath a chair.

Cloth rustled over shoulders. A black slouch hat settled upon the millionaire's head. With swift, silent motion, Lamont Cranston gained a window at the end of the hallway. The sash rose noiselessly. A dark form passed over the sill.

Lamont Cranston had become The Shadow.

CHAPTER XIV
THE CALL

TEN o'clock had been the time that Bart Melken was awaiting. There was another man who was watchful for that hour. Joe Cardona, huddled in a corner of the Derry Cafe, in Corona, was hoping that Limps Silvey would appear.

Outside, Joe had a squad of men in readiness. They were far enough away not to attract attention. They had two cars; they were anxious for the word to go. Joe had told them that important work might be afoot tonight.

Where was Limps Silvey? Joe Cardona began to wonder if he was the victim of a stall. Had the crafty hobbler seen him in the darkness, and made a fake call? Joe did not know. He had nothing to do but wait.

The telephone bell began to ring. The coin box was situated in an obscure corner of the restaurant, not far from the spot where Cardona was located. Joe waited, then realized that it might be the call for Limps.

Under sudden impulse, Cardona arose and approached the telephone. He raised the receiver. He heard an unfamiliar voice. It asked a single question.

"That you, Limps?"

"Yeah," responded Joe, in an attempt to imitate Limps Silvey's husky tones.

"Scram, then," came the voice over the wire. "We've picked our lay. It's O.K. We're on the ground now. Bing decided to go ahead with the Winchendon job."

"Which one?" inquired Cardona huskily.

"I didn't say which one," came the voice. "I said Winchendon. You know—the place you looked over. Old Silas Winchendon's house. We're busting in there. That's why you'd better scram. It's only a few miles from where you are now."

"O.K."

Joe Cardona hung up the receiver. He had the dope he wanted. He had been studying society news in an effort to pick places which might lure The Jackdaw. He had seen a mention of a party at Winchendon's; he had paid little attention to it, because it had not appeared to be more than a mere formal gathering.

Cardona did know, however, that the Winchendons lived in Copperwood, near Long Island Sound. It was not far there from Corona; but the speaker on the telephone had mentioned that the gang was already there.

Joe considered quickly. He realized that a rapid swoop would be more effective than a delayed telephone call. He hurried out to the street.

"Stay here to grab Limps Silvey," ordered Joe. "We're hopping out to stop a job."

Rounding a corner close by, Joe leaped into the first of two parked cars. The automobiles were filled with detectives. Joe gave his next order.

"Head for Copperwood," he barked. "The Winchendon house. I can locate it when we get there."

The motor thrummed. The first car shot away. The second followed. Joe Cardona gave instructions as they rode along. It was a mad chase; a broad, good road lay ahead. It was not until they made a turn at Cardona's order that trouble was encountered.

JOE knew the way to Copperwood. He had picked a good shortcut. Barring signs blocked it, half a mile from the spot that they had left the main road. There was no passing. The signs marked a fallen bridge.

Joe Cardona fumed as he gave the order to turn around. The cars headed back to the main road. Five good minutes had been lost through this misadventure. More would be gone because the longer route must be taken. Joe Cardona regretted that he had not called Silas Winchendon by telephone.

It was too late to do so now. The only hope was to make all speed. Crime lay ahead. Word had been gained through a fortunate break. Now, mischance seemed destined to ruin Cardona's opportunity to net The Jackdaw's hordes.

Meanwhile, Silas Winchendon's mansion lay silent amid the grounds that surrounded it. Cars were parked in the driveway; others were on the sloping street that ran by the side of the house more than fifty yards away.

IT was in one of these cars—a coupé—that a young man was seated. Harry Vincent, agent of The Shadow, was peering into darkness. He had been here long, had Harry. He had been watching the lights in the French windows that indicated Silas Winchendon's living room.

He had noticed something else. Creeping figures had shown dimly beyond the low hedge that lined the sidewalk. Mumbled voices had come to Harry's ears. In response, he had flicked the dashlight twice. That sudden glimmer, on and off, on and off, had been a signal to The Shadow.

Harry was sure that it had not been observed. The men in the darkness were under cover of the hedge. Now, however, since they had advanced farther across the lawn, Harry had become worried. Had The Shadow seen the signal?

Yielding to an impulse, Harry Vincent repeated the signal. On went the light; off again. On; then off. Twice in quick succession. Harry knew that The Shadow was alert; indeed, he had seen tokens of miraculous ability on the part of his mysterious chief. In the tenseness of the moment, however, Harry was overanxious to play his part.

Harry had been ordered here by instructions received from Burbank. Harry knew, from his own report, that The Shadow must have picked the Winchendon home as a danger spot tonight. It had been Harry's duty to remain huddled in his own car, lined with others that were presumably empty.

The mobsters, rather than attract attention, had not made a close inspection of these vehicles. Harry had locked his doors from the inside; with windows up, he had been protected. At the first sign of figures beyond the hedge, he had lowered the windows. Thus he had also heard the invaders, as they spoke in low whispers.

Harry felt more at ease after he had given the second pair of light signals. The men who were approaching the house had evidently reached the flat, stone veranda by the French windows. Their forms were lost beyond patches of shrubbery. Harry could not hear a sound.

He had warned The Shadow. He awaited only a definite sign that would either send him on his way, or bring him to some new duty. It was while Harry counted on such a result—an expected ending to his night's work—that the unexpected happened.

A SLIGHT sound came from the left side of the car. As Harry turned in that direction, the jab of cold steel came suddenly against the side of his neck. A flashlight glimmered, its glare lowered toward the floor of the coupé. A voice growled an order.

"Shut up and don't budge," came the command. "It'll be curtains for you, bimbo. Put up them dukes."

Harry raised his arms. It was too late to reach for his automatic, which was ready in a side pocket of the car. An ugly snarl came from the man who had surprised him.

"Blinking your light, eh?" questioned the mobster, as he extinguished his flashlight. "Well, I'm wise to you. Don't think you can get away with something now you're in the dark. I'm watching. What are you—a dick or something?"

Harry made no reply. His situation was a serious one. Fear, however, was not the emotion that swept The Shadow's agent. Harry was chagrined because he had shown stupidity; he was alarmed because he had caused a slip-up in The Shadow's plans.

The mobster who now controlled him had evidently caught the glimmer of the second signal, and had doubled back around the hedge. He had trapped Harry Vincent with neither sound nor trouble. Yet Harry still possessed a temporary safety. He knew that this man would not dare to fire while his companions were still waiting for the attack.

A critical stage, however, might be approaching. If gunplay burst loose around the Winchendon mansion, the gangster's logical course would be to shoot his prisoner. In anticipation of this danger, Harry let his right hand creep over toward the pocket in the door. It was a desperate chance; yet he wanted to have his automatic ready if the mobster should choose to fire at him.

Harry's left shoulder hunched unconsciously. The gangster growled; he flashed his light simultaneously. The glare, confined entirely to the car, revealed Harry's hand; it also showed the butt of the automatic. The muzzle of the gangster's revolver jabbed more firmly. Harry could imagine the finger trembling on the trigger.

"One inch, bimbo," came the snarl, "and it'll be curtains. Make a grab for that rod if you want—I'm going to snuff you out anyway in a minute. This is where you—"

The sentence ended abruptly. A gargling gasp coughed from the gangster's lips. His body slumped. The revolver barrel flopped away from Harry's neck. The flashlight tumbled to the floor of the coupé. Harry reached down and extinguished it.

Staring through the window, Harry saw nothing

but blackness where the mobster had been. Yet in the back of his head, he held the impression of a dull, thudding sound that he had heard. Solid blackness seemed to move before Harry's eyes. He realized then that a living presence was outside the window.

The Shadow had come to the coupé. He must have seen the second signal as well as the first that Harry Vincent had given. Rising like a specter from the darkness, the black-garbed master of the night had struck down the gangster who had held Harry Vincent in his power.

CHAPTER XV
THE SHADOW RETURNS

THE tones of a whispered voice came to Harry Vincent's ears. From the darkness, The Shadow was issuing a command.

"Let the car roll" were the monotoned words, "as soon as trouble begins inside the house. Start the motor at the bottom of the slope."

"Right," whispered Harry.

He saw The Shadow's purpose. It would be a mistake for Harry to slide away now. The other mobsters thought that their companion had taken care of him.

What if they should investigate? Perhaps another gangster would come from the crew. Harry could visualize The Shadow disposing of such investigators one by one. He realized, a moment later, that The Shadow could not depend upon such a plan. Trouble was due within the house. The Shadow must return to prevent it.

Something was going on in the darkness. Straining his eyes, Harry could see a figure moving on the street. A grayish cloth seemed to be coming up over arms and shoulders.

Harry suddenly knew what it meant. The Shadow was peeling a sweater from the stunned gangster's body.

The sweater seemed to move away. Harry caught a flash of what appeared to be a checkered cap. Staring through the rear window, he saw cap and sweater settling into place. It dawned on him that The Shadow had taken off his hat; that over his cloak he had drawn the mobster's sweater; that on his head he wore the stunned man's cap!

Harry could see a crouching figure hurrying across the lawn. It disappeared beyond the shrubbery. The Shadow had taken the place of the growling gangster!

That was the last that Harry Vincent saw. Up by the house, however, there were those who noted the arrival of the sweatered figure. Bing Claver, crouched on the stones beside the veranda, hissed a warning.

"Did you get him?"

"Knocked him cold." The growl was a perfect imitation of the stunned gangster. "But he may come to. I didn't want to plug him. I'm going back."

"All right, Cady," agreed Bing. "Give him the works as soon as we pile into the place. Then come up with us."

THE sweatered form moved away. It took a circuitous path alongside the house. That was natural, for the opening in the hedge was farther back. Thus did The Shadow come into the midst of Bing Claver and his mobsters, to lull them into thinking that Cady, the stunned gangster, had fulfilled his mission.

Bing Claver and his mob were in readiness. Scattered, they would have been a difficult problem for The Shadow at this moment. The master fighter preferred to meet them in a massed attack. Behind a bush, he doffed the sweater and the cap. His black hat settled on his head.

Silently, The Shadow crept to the opened window of the little hallway. He glided over the ledge— inward as easily as he came outward.

One minute after The Shadow's return, Lamont Cranston appeared just beyond the curtains. His form was still unseen within the living room. His sharp eyes, however, could spy what was going on. The macaw was still giving its performance under Farrell Sarborn's supervision,

Over by the farther French window was Bart Melken. The young man who served The Jackdaw was still fidgeting with his cigarette lighter. He flipped it; the flame appeared, and went out an instant later, as Melken dropped the cap upon it. Then, with twitching lips, Melken suddenly moved away to the shelter of the wall.

There was a moment's pause. One of the French doors seemed to tremble. It hesitated. The macaw, its eyes staring across the room, uttered a shrill and unexpected cry.

"Robbers!" shrieked the bird. "Robbers!"

Some of Winchendon's guests began to laugh. They stopped short as they saw Farrell Sarborn's startled face. The man who owned the macaw was staring in the same direction as the bird. His lips seemed to phrase a silent warning; his arms suddenly spread.

People turned toward the outer side of the room. At that instant, the French doors crashed. In from the outer darkness sprang Bing Claver, two mobsters at his heels. All wore caps and handkerchiefs over their eyes.

"Up with your dukes!" came Bing Claver's shout.

Guests obeyed spontaneously. The flash of revolvers dimmed the shine of jewels. This entire throng was at the mercy of the invaders from the underworld. The Jackdaw's minions had arrived tonight. Unaccompanied by their chief, they were springing a massed attack.

Bing Claver advanced. His gun arm lowered. The presence of two henchmen at his heels was sufficient. As he gestured with his revolver, guests backed up against the wall. Women were too frightened to scream.

Bing Claver sneered. He had nearly reached the center of the clearing room. A straight path lay between the curtained doorway and the French windows, where two mobsters stood in readiness. Bing was midway on that path. Not one of the helpless guests intervened.

As his eyes swept around the room, Bing stopped and stared at the farther curtain. He saw it tremble. Up came his revolver.

The motion was too late. A terrific roar re-echoed from the curtain. Bing Claver staggered and sprawled headlong.

THE SHADOW'S shot had been delivered with a purpose. The Shadow had foreseen the way that Bing would work. He had waited until the room had cleared. He had fired at Bing in action. His deed had attracted the attention of the gangsters by the windows.

Up came their revolvers. While they were rising, The Shadow's automatics spoke again. Two massive weapons, looming through the curtains, unloosed a burst of lead. One gangster tumbled into the living room. The other, screaming, staggered to the veranda.

The other pair of French windows burst inward. With the crash of glass came the roar of The Shadow's weapons. The guests were dropping for cover as revolvers were firing back their answer to The Shadow's message. Hasty mobsmen, behind their fellows, were shooting wildly at the only targets they could see—bursting shafts of flame from the curtains.

Bullets zimmed against the walls, all close by the doorway. One whistled through the upper section of the curtain; The Shadow's guns were roaring from a point lower down. The Shadow was attracting fire as well as giving it. The guests were safe throughout this conflict.

Five mobsmen had fallen in the skirmish, Bing Claver in that number. The Shadow, his form vague behind the curtain, had given the leaden hail to the ones in advance. Now, overwhelmed by the onslaught, the others of the tribe were leaping away for safety. The French windows were cleared quickly of mobsmen.

While guests were trembling, Farrell Sarborn jumped into action. He dashed to the nearest window and grabbed a gun that was lying on the floor. He fired a deluge of shots wildly in the air. Other emboldened guests joined him. At the same time, shots barked from the little window of the hallway.

Then came volleys from the lawn. Shouts arose; the sounds of a fierce conflict were breaking loose. Guests staggered in from the doors, wondering what new danger had arisen.

The sounds of police whistles gave the answer. Joe Cardona and his detectives had arrived.

Farrell Sarborn, striding back across the room, stopped short as he saw Bing Claver rising to his knees. The gang leader, critically wounded, was uttering oaths as he reached for his revolver, which had fallen beneath his body.

Sarborn held an empty gun—one that he had plucked from a dead gangster. He flung it at Bing's head and missed. Bing did not see the weapon. He was swinging his revolver, ready to shoot anyone. Sarborn leaped for the chair where the macaw was perched. He sent the scarlet bird flapping wildly as he used the chair as a club to meet Bing Claver.

A shot came from beyond the curtain. Bing's arm dropped. The gang leader wavered. That bullet marked his finish. As Bing was on the verge of toppling, the chair came hurtling from Sarborn's hands. It crashed against the gang leader's head and shoulders. Bing Claver collapsed upon the floor.

This was the dramatic finish to the wild invasion. It left Farrell Sarborn standing in the center of the room, with Bing Claver's inert form stretched at his feet. It brought all attention there for a long instant of suspense.

Then came a shout from the French windows. Into the living room entered a swarthy man, his coat thrown back to show his badge, his right hand gripping a smoking revolver. Detective Joe Cardona had arrived with his squad of underlings.

ORDER returned where chaos had held sway. Guests began to congratulate each other. Farrell Sarborn, because of his timely actions, was surrounded by a handshaking throng. Among them was Lamont Cranston. The millionaire, calmer even than Sarborn, was convincing in his congratulations.

The detectives had wiped out the fleeing mobsters. One dick was wounded; none of the others had been touched. The remnants of Bing Claver's gang had rushed directly into the arms of the men who represented the law.

Calming guests began to tell their stories. All, apparently, had been in the living room when the attack had occurred. All recalled that shots had come from beyond the curtain. Recollections were vague; the sight of falling mobsters had attracted most attention. No one seemed to have any idea of how the counterattack had been launched against the invading mobsters.

With the crash of glass came the roar of The Shadow's weapons ...

So far as Winchendon and his guests were concerned, the police could have the credit, along with the cool hands who had acted well—when Farrell Sarborn had shown the way.

But to Joe Cardona, as he viewed the dead and riddled body of Bing Claver, this affair was filled with mystery. The detective was convinced that Bing was the chief of The Jackdaw's minions; that the supercrook had ordered this attack.

The Jackdaw himself was missing, and so was the mysterious fighter who had driven back the evil horde. This, to Joe Cardona, was proof of a new and startling conflict that was in the making. He knew that another and more powerful hand had entered in the game.

He, Joe Cardona, was but an outsider in the clash. The Jackdaw—whoever he might be—was opposed by an enemy whose skill had proven greater than the crook's.

The fight lay between The Jackdaw and The Shadow.

CHAPTER XVI
CARDONA LEARNS

DAYS had passed since the affray at Silas Winchendon's. Newspapers and tabloids alike had told their tale of gangland's invasion of the Four Hundred. Sensational incidents had seized the news. Among them, the scarlet macaw's scream of "Robbers! Robbers!" had commanded interest.

Yet to Joe Cardona, ace detective, all angles of the case were trivial excepting one. Cardona knew what others did not know. Behind the frustrated assault at Winchendon's lay a menace that had not yet been uncovered: the menace of The Jackdaw.

Heralded as the ace who had brought destruction to hordes of the underworld, Cardona basked in a glory of publicity that offset his failure to uncover the murderer of Rutherford Casslin. Joe had met gangland's latest thrust. That fact had crowded out his previous failure.

Cardona knew, however, that the menace had not been ended. The most important enemy who had died at Winchendon's was Bing Claver. To all appearances, the ex-gorilla had been inspired to higher efforts in the field of crime—and had failed. Joe Cardona appreciated, nevertheless, that Bing had been nothing more than a mere underling.

The ace detective realized that a new combat was afoot. The Jackdaw would surely know that the police had not arrived in time to obstruct the mobsters whom he had launched on a drive of wholesale robbery. The Jackdaw, if he intended to persist with his baffling ways of crime, must manage to evade The Shadow.

Oddly, the defeat of The Jackdaw's gangsters had broken the chain which Cardona had been following. Bing Claver was dead. He, alone of the rowdies who had fallen, could have told Cardona facts that the ace detective wanted. Those of Bing's outfit who still lived, persistently stated that they were working for Bing. They denied all connection with any other master.

Had this defeat ended The Jackdaw's power? Had the unknown crook scampered for cover?

These were questions that Joe Cardona sought to answer; and he realized their importance. The hunch that Joe held was that the threat of The Jackdaw still remained.

IN studying past crimes which he attributed to The Jackdaw, Cardona saw that the crook was rising to his zenith. The theft of the Bishenpur diamond had been a master stroke of crime. The huge gem was still missing. The Jackdaw had simply failed to add to the collection of valuables of which the diamond was evidently intended as a nucleus.

Previous robberies, from The Jackdaw's former activities, totaled a large amount, as Cardona summed them up. Yet it was obvious that until now The Jackdaw had operated only in a small way. His murder of Rutherford Casslin appeared to be the beginning of a new and greater era in his mad career.

Stealth at Casslin's—a lone hand working startling crime. Violence at Winchendon's—a mob attack launched under a lieutenant's command. These events showed The Jackdaw's versatility. Gangless, he now had but two choices. One was to retire; the other was to resort to craft once more. Cardona decided that The Jackdaw would choose the latter course.

It was imperative that Joe should flag The Jackdaw. The detective was determined to end the crook's mad career; he wanted also to solve the murder of Rutherford Casslin and regain the Bishenpur diamond. But Joe found himself balked.

Limps Silvey had disappeared. Stools had thought that they had seen him once or twice. They had not managed to follow him. This brought Cardona back to a consideration of Doctor Lysander Dubrong. He decided to match wits with the physician.

Joe's first step was to visit the neighborhood of the East Side Clinic. He went there on a night when he had made certain that Dubrong was at his Park Avenue residence. He found that the house directly in back of the clinic was vacant.

On the second floor, Joe made a discovery. The floor here—so Joe figured—was lower than the ceiling of Dubrong's consulting room. The wall was crumbling. It offered opportunity. Joe put a competent man to work. A hole was drilled through to Dubrong's consulting room.

A perfect job, Joe was positive that the physician would not observe this well-made peephole. To make certain, the detective sent a stool pigeon into Dubrong's clinic. The stool got by with the visit. He reported to Cardona that the hole could not be seen.

It was then that Cardona decided to visit Doctor Dubrong and pave the way to the result he wanted. One evening found the detective at the large apartment house on Park Avenue where the physician lived. Cardona inquired for Dubrong. He was sent upstairs to the doctor's apartment.

DUBRONG'S sumptuous abode proved a striking contrast to the plainness of his East Side Clinic. Joe Cardona was impressed by the extravagance of the furnishings. He knew that Dubrong was a wealthy man; but thick rugs, paneled walls, and magnificent furniture proved more than the detective had expected.

Dubrong received Cardona in his study. The suave physician seemed pleased to see the detective.

"Congratulations, Cardona!" he exclaimed. "Your handling of that affair at Winchendon's was excellent. How are you making out with the Casslin case?"

"No results," returned Cardona.

"Indeed." Dubrong's tone seemed disappointed. "I thought that you might have gained some results. Ah, well—I am afraid that you have let the bird escape. I am still convinced that the Hindu dropped the stolen diamond from the window."

"To another Hindu?"

"Of course. Cardona, I doubt that the Bishenpur diamond will ever be reclaimed."

"I'm not so sure of that." Cardona stared squarely at the physician. "I've learned something, Doctor Dubrong—something that may surprise you. There is a supercrook at work. These gangsters who were killed at Winchendon's were unquestionably in his employ."

"Ah! That is remarkable!"

"Besides that, I have a hunch that the same crook was in back of Casslin's murder."

"You do?" Dubrong arched his eyebrows. "Have you any idea as to his identity?"

"Not as yet. I have stool pigeons in the underworld. They have brought me unusual reports. They are talking about a crook whom they call The Jackdaw."

"A jewel thief?"

"Yes. Wherever gangsters meet, this talk of The Jackdaw has begun to buzz. Whenever a mob is wiped out—as we cleaned up Bing Claver's outfit—other gangsters begin to look into the matter. They want to know who the big shots are; they want to find out if there was any double-crossing.

"This case seemed to have them buffaloed, until—well, I received my first detailed report today—somebody wised up to a big boy in back of the jewel-stealing game. The Jackdaw—that's what they call him—and I'm going to find out who he is."

"Could I be of aid to you?"

"Yes," replied Cardona. "That is why I have come to see you. Did you ever have, among your patients at the clinic, a man called Limps Silvey?"

"Let me see," mused Dubrong. "The name sounds familiar. I should have to look him up in my records."

"Limps Silvey," declared Cardona, "had some minor connection with Bing Claver. In fact, by intercepting a message for Limps, I learned of the trouble impending at Winchendon's. There was only one unfortunate consequence. Limps disappeared after that."

"Naturally," laughed Dubrong.

"Hardly," returned Cardona. "After all, I had nothing on the fellow. I did not intend to arrest him. I expect him to be back in town."

"You will arrest him then?"

"No. I shall leave him entirely alone. I want to watch him; but I don't intend to put stools on the job. I am pretty sure, from what I have heard, that Limps Silvey was one of your patients. He is apt to show up at your clinic. If he does, you can aid me by questioning him."

"I am not a police official," protested Dubrong. "I am willing to give you advice—to tell you what I may chance to learn—but to aid in an arrest—"

"I am not asking you that."

"It would defeat the purpose of my clinic. You must understand that."

"Get me straight, Doctor." Cardona's tone was earnest. "I don't want to arrest Limps Silvey. I give you my word that he will be entirely immune. The Jackdaw is the man that I am after. I think Limps may know who he is."

"Ah!" An idea came to Dubrong. "You want to use this Limps Silvey as a stool pigeon?"

"If I can get him. Fellows of his type are easily gained. Perhaps, through overtures on your part—"

"Leave that to me." Dubrong smiled wisely as he interrupted. "If this man Silvey was one of my patients—and I believe he was—he will come back. If he is afraid to show himself at the clinic, he may call up for advice. I have had men do that on various pretexts. I can let him come to my clinic, then, with a guaranty of no trouble for him?"

"No trouble."

"And if he appears to be worried, I can advise him to see you, promising him that he will be immune from arrest?"

"That's right."

"I shall bear this in mind, Cardona."

The detective smiled grimly as he left the physician's apartment. Cardona felt that he had scored a triumph. By dealing cagily with Dubrong, Cardona had paved a way to immediate results.

CARDONA was positive that Limps Silvey was hiding out somewhere in Manhattan. He was also sure that the cripple was connected with Dubrong. Cardona's subtle statement—purely fictitious— that the underworld was buzzing with talk of The Jackdaw, was calculated to arouse Dubrong's interest in what was happening in the badlands.

To cap this, Cardona had followed with talk of his policy concerning Limps Silvey. His statement that he wanted the cripple as a stool was the climax of the plan.

As matters now stood, Dubrong would consider it imperative for Limps to visit underworld hangouts, to learn what was being said there. Moreover, it would be safe for Limps to visit Dubrong at any time.

Hunches were Joe Cardona's specialty. He had one now. He was positive that if he remained constantly at the peephole which he had prepared above Doctor Dubrong's consulting room, he would eventually overhear an interview between Limps Silvey and Dubrong. What was more, Cardona had another hunch that the meeting might take place this very night.

Accordingly, the sleuth made his plans. After an hour's stay at headquarters, he wended his way to the neighborhood of the East Side Clinic. Muffled, he entered the house in the cul-de-sac. He went upstairs and sprawled out, his head beside the peephole.

Two hours went by. Joe Cardona waited patiently. He was determined in his vigil. Then came a glimmer of light. Joe quickly raised his head and peered into the room below. It was empty. Joe wondered how the light had been turned on.

A door opened. It was the door of the closet. The detective realized that the light switch must have been sprung in there. Out from the closet stepped the figure of Limps Silvey.

Lysander Dubrong must be coming here. Joe Cardona stared, wondering when and how the physician would arrive. The shades of the consulting room were lowered. Limps Silvey was staring about him, grinning. Suddenly his expression seemed to change. He placed his cane beside the closed locker in the corner. Standing upright, he rubbed his hands across his face, then seized a towel and began to mop his countenance.

Joe Cardona suppressed a gasp as the man chanced to turn so that the light fully revealed his face. No longer a cripple, no longer a sordid denizen of the underworld. Out of that mopping was coming another face that Joe Cardona recognized.

Limps Silvey had needed no hideout. Limps Silvey was a myth; a clever character created by a cunning brain. His makeup off, his real identity was revealed.

The man who had worn the disguise of Limps Silvey was Doctor Lysander Dubrong. The physician and his satellite were one and the same!

Clothes, cane, and makeup were going in the locker. The transformation was completed. Suave and debonair, a smile upon his thin lips, Doctor Dubrong strolled through the rear exit of his consulting room, turning out the light as he departed.

IN darkness, Joe Cardona smiled to himself. There was no need for action now. It was merely a case of waiting and watching. The scene had shifted from the East Side to Park Avenue. The job was to trail Doctor Dubrong himself.

Bing Claver had served The Jackdaw. Limps Silvey had been connected with Bing Claver. Limps Silvey, Joe had suspected, was working for Doctor Lysander Dubrong. The subtlety of it all now came to the detective.

The Jackdaw's mob was wiped out. The Jackdaw's next action, so Joe had believed, could be traced only through Limps Silvey, for the detective had considered Doctor Dubrong was too wise to offer a trail of his own.

But now, as matters stood, Dubrong had become the single bet. Joe Cardona's task was simplified. Once more, the detective had a hunch—one that he regarded as a surety.

Traveling the underworld as Limps Silvey, Doctor Dubrong had tonight learned that The Jackdaw rumors were lacking. That would give him confidence. Another thrust would soon be delivered by The Jackdaw. Once again, Joe Cardona would be present.

The detective intended, from now on, to keep close tabs on Doctor Lysander Dubrong, the man who played the part of his own accomplice!

CHAPTER XVII
THE NEXT NIGHT

ON the evening following Joe Cardona's detection of the double part played by Lysander Dubrong, Farrell Sarborn was seated in his apartment, reading the afternoon newspaper. It was early; Sarborn had just dined.

Someone rang the outside bell. Sarborn motioned his servant Jalon to answer it. The greasy-faced fellow talked through the little telephone that connected with the lobby.

"It is Mr. Melken," he reported to his master.

"Tell him to come up," ordered Sarborn.

A few minutes later, Bart Melken arrived. He shook hands with his friend, then sprawled himself in a large chair and stared unsteadily. Sarborn did not seem to notice Melken's uneasiness.

"I see," remarked Sarborn, tapping the newspaper, "that your prospective father-in-law has returned to New York."

"Yes," blurted Melken. "Garforth Lydell is back."

"You don't appear to be pleased about it," decided Sarborn, looking at his friend. "What's the matter, Bart? You look pale tonight."

"I don't feel well."

"Talk to the macaw," laughed Sarborn. He arose and opened the door of the next room. "Maybe he can cheer you up."

He brought out the scarlet bird and perched it on the back of the chair. The macaw ruffled its throat, but made no utterance. It looked about wisely.

"Don't be trivial, Farrell," pleaded Melken. "I've got to go up to Lydell's house. I promised Yvonne I'd be there tonight. I don't want to go."

"Why not? Has all this publicity about old Lydell's big banking deals given you stage fright?"

"I'm worried, Farrell—"

Melken's pleading tones ended as the bell rang. Sarborn, on his feet, answered the summons himself. He spoke in a pleased manner, clicked the button to let the visitor enter, and turned to Melken.

"Lamont Cranston," said Sarborn. "He dropped up here twice. I thought he might be in tonight. A wonderful chap—and very interesting."

"He was dumb enough out at Winchendon's," retorted Melken. "As near as I can figure it, no one ever found out just which sofa he dived behind when the mob came in."

"You weren't so brisk yourself," returned Sarborn. "I didn't do much, either, until somebody plugged a few of those rowdies. Cranston is a retiring sort of a chap, but he's had plenty of adventures. Even at that, with all his travels, he was quite impressed with my small collection of eggs."

Sarborn opened the door. A few moments later, Cranston appeared within the room. He shook hands with Sarborn and Melken.

"We have a visitor, I see," remarked Cranston, indicating the macaw.

Sarborn nodded as he picked up the bird and took it into the other room. Cranston followed him. Sarborn put the macaw on the window perch. Cranston had stopped beside the box which contained the little monkey.

"Cute fellow," he remarked. "Can I look at him?"

"Certainly," returned Sarborn.

Cranston brought the sapajou from its crate. He carried the monkey in his arms as he strolled toward the window. The little creature was staring all about it. Cranston made a movement with his gold watch chain. The monkey seized it.

BEFORE Cranston could grab the sapajou, it leaped from his arms and tried to pull away the watch chain. Cranston broke the beast's hold; the sapajou jumped up the side of the wall toward the macaw's perch. Sarborn grabbed it.

"If those two get together," he exclaimed, "there'll be a battle. This little beast is a nuisance. Cute, but troublesome. I'm going to get rid of him."

He dropped the monkey back into its box. Cranston lighted a cigarette. His gaze fell admiringly upon the glass case, with its collection of eggs. Chancing to look back toward the macaw, he observed that the bird was fluttering furiously. Sarborn noted it also. He took the scarlet bird from its perch.

"You wouldn't think a macaw had nerves," he laughed, "but I believe this one has. It was scared when the monkey came after it. I'll take it out into the other room with us."

Cranston preceded Sarborn into the living room. Sarborn closed the door of the room where he kept his pets. He perched the macaw on the back of a chair. He picked up the newspaper that he had been reading, and placed it on a table.

Lamont Cranston's keen eyes observed a one-column portrait that adorned the page. It was a photograph of Garforth Lydell, who had just returned to New York. Headlines spoke of large banking transactions which would proceed now that Lydell had come back to the city.

Cranston chatted a while with Sarborn and Melken. He arranged a later appointment with Sarborn, on some evening when they could study a series of remarkable photographs of India, which Cranston had brought back with him. Mentioning that he was going to the Cobalt Club, Cranston added:

"If you intend to be about after midnight, Sarborn, perhaps we can get together then. I intend to call my home from the club. I can instruct Stanley, my chauffeur, to bring in the photographs. It is possible that I might be able to drop in here prior to midnight."

"Very well," agreed Sarborn. "I intend to be about. I shall expect to hear from you later tonight."

Sarborn walked to the elevator with his guest. He came back to his apartment while the automatic lift was descending. He found Bart Melken pacing nervously.

"What's the matter, Bart?" inquired Sarborn.

"I'm worrying about tonight," confessed Melken. "I'm going up to Lydell's—and I'm afraid of the consequences."

"What consequences?"

Melken gulped at Sarborn's question. He faced the other man squarely.

"Suppose, Farrell," he said, "that I should tell you something startling—almost incriminating—"

"Regarding whom?"

"I don't know. Except that it concerns me. Would you preserve silence regarding the matter?"

"Certainly," returned Sarborn, "if it would prove of any aid to you, Bart."

"All right." Melken was pondering. He was trying to veil the truth, yet tell enough to convey the situation to Sarborn. "I'll talk to you, Farrell. It's about a telephone call that I received this afternoon."

"Where?"

"At my hotel."

"From whom?"

"I don't know."

Sarborn smiled. He was scratching the macaw's head. He shrugged his shoulders in deprecatory fashion.

"Anonymous messages," he declared, "should never be taken seriously."

"But this one"—Melken caught himself. He had been about to say that it was not the first—"this one was serious, Farrell. It was from—well, from a man who means business."

"Sit down," urged Sarborn. "Light a cigarette, calm yourself, and talk to me. Something is worrying you, that's certain. Let's get at the root of it."

As though to insure privacy, Farrell Sarborn went to the hall door and opened it. He glanced along the corridor. He saw no one. He closed the door and returned.

IT was then that a figure appeared in the hallway. From the gloom at the head of a flight of stairs, the form of The Shadow appeared. Evidently the black-garbed investigator had been expecting some action such as this. He knew now that the door would not be reopened immediately. He glided along the hall.

Stopped by the door, The Shadow drew a disk-like object from his pocket and placed it firmly against the door. Two tubes projected from the plate, like the connections of a stethoscope. These passed beneath the slouch hat which The Shadow wore. Equipped with this device that magnified sound, The Shadow could overhear the conversation within Sarborn's apartment.

Beyond the door, Bart Melken was starting the plea that he had promised. He was telling Farrell Sarborn the burdens that were on his mind.

"A phone call this afternoon," he declared. "It came from—from someone who called himself The Jackdaw. He—he threatened me unless I promised to do his bidding."

"Threatened you with what?"

"With death, if necessary. Specifically, though, he threatened to load me with false accusations—to name me as responsible, in part, for certain crimes."

"Which were?"

"The murder of Rutherford Casslin and the attempted raid at Silas Winchendon's home."

"You should not worry about such futile threats."

"They are serious, Farrell. Do you remember that mob leader who was killed at Winchendon's? Well, I knew him—I met him some time ago, when I was in what looked like a jam. Bing Claver helped me out of it.

"Since then—well, crimes have hit at places where I have been. I have been afraid that I would be implicated"—Melken paused—"falsely implicated."

As he made the hasty addition, Melken looked hastily at Sarborn to see if his friend had noted it. Sarborn's expression was entirely sympathetic. Melken was encouraged.

"I had feared," he said, "that I might someday be called upon to commit crime. After Bing was killed, I thought that I might be safe. I knew that Bing served a big shot whom he called The Jackdaw. I heard from the man himself today."

"What did he demand?"

"Cooperation in a crime."

"When?"

"Tonight."

"Where?"

"At Lydell's."

"You mean he wants you to aid him there?"

"Yes. To rob Lydell."

"To rob Lydell!"

As he made this exclamation, Farrell Sarborn showed intense surprise. He ceased scratching the macaw's head. A puzzled look came upon his face as he stared at Melken.

"You read the newspaper," declared Melken soberly.

"About Lydell?"

"Yes. That he has arranged banking negotiations."

"What has that to do with robbery?"

"Plenty. Lydell arrived in town today. This is a Saturday; tomorrow is Sunday; Monday happens to be a holiday. Yet a large banking transaction has been promised—immediately."

"Yes, I read that."

"Garforth Lydell's methods are well known. He works quickly and effectively. It is obvious to anyone who understands his ways that Lydell must have hundreds of thousands of dollars in negotiable securities tucked away in his vault at home. That is where he does business. He will probably talk with bankers between now and Tuesday."

"And you think The Jackdaw knows?"

"The Jackdaw does know. That is where I figure. I am to open the door of Lydell's vault, so that The Jackdaw may enter."

Farrell Sarborn stared in astonishment. Bart Melken hastened with a specific explanation.

"THERE are two doors to the vault room," he said. "One opens into Lydell's library, the other, into a disused hallway. The Jackdaw's orders are that I shall open the door from the library; in the vault room, I can unbar the other door, which is kept barred on the inside.

"It should be simple for me to do this. Lydell keeps his keys in his desk. I may be able to obtain them. Once I have opened the door from the library, I can unbar the other door, then go out the way I came, and lock the library door behind me. That will leave the opening that The Jackdaw wants. He will have all the time in the world to crack the vault. It is an old contrivance with steel doors guarding its room; Lydell considers it sufficiently protected, however."

"Suppose," said Sarborn reflectively, "that you should pretend inability to go through with this?"

"It would not suffice," responded Melken. "The Jackdaw will not take excuses."

Nervously, the young man glanced at his watch. He shook his head as he noted the hour.

"I'm due there now, Farrell!" he exclaimed. "Due there at once! I've got to go through with this job."

"Stay here—"

"I can't!" Melken's tone was excited. "I've told you this, Farrell, so you can help me later. When this job is done, I'll be free of The Jackdaw. He told me so, today, when he talked to me over the telephone. I'm going through with it, Farrell. I only want to know that I can count on you if trouble comes. I want to come back here when this is finished."

"Take me along with you," Sarborn asked, pleadingly.

"Impossible! Yvonne and her father expect me alone. I must manage to deceive them. I'll be away before the loss is discovered. After that, I can talk about an alibi—"

Melken was turning toward the door. Sarborn threw out an arm to restrain him. The delay was only momentary, but in that interval, The Shadow, beyond the barrier, glided away, the listening disk clutched in his black-gloved hand.

When Bart Melken broke free from Farrell Sarborn in the hallway, The Shadow was no longer in sight. He was watching, though, from the stairway. He saw Melken stride toward the elevator. Farrell Sarborn, shaking his head solemnly, stepped back into the apartment.

THE elevator door opened; Melken entered, closed the door, and descended. The Shadow crept forward. At the door of the apartment, he again employed his sound-detecting disk.

Within the apartment, Farrell Sarborn had lighted a cigarette. He was pacing slowly back and forth. He glanced at his watch, then called his servant, Jalon.

"Bring my hat and coat," he ordered. "I am going out."

While the servant followed the command, Sarborn opened a table drawer. From it, he brought forth a loaded revolver, which he dropped in his side pocket. Jalon returned with the outer garments. Sarborn donned hat and overcoat.

"If anyone calls," he said to Jalon, "tell them that I am busy. You understand? Do not let them come up here"—he paused—"unless Mr. Cranston should call. I do not expect him, however, until nearly midnight. You can admit Mr. Cranston—no one else, however."

Jalon grunted his understanding of the instructions. Farrell Sarborn strode to the door. Simultaneously, The Shadow glided away from his listening post.

When Farrell Sarborn strode out into the hallway, The Shadow was already on the stairs. His tall form was descending; he would arrive at the bottom by the time Sarborn had reached the first floor in the elevator.

The Shadow had divined Farrell Sarborn's destination. Sarborn, like Melken, had chosen one definite place: the home of Garforth Lydell. Sarborn had realized, more fully than Melken had supposed, the power which The Jackdaw wielded over his friend.

Sarborn had openly accompanied Melken to Winchendon's; that had been when Melken had volunteered no specific facts. Now, with Melken's fullest fears asserted, Sarborn was secretly on his way to join the young man at Garforth Lydell's.

CHAPTER XVIII
THE INTERLUDE

WHEN Farrell Sarborn strode from the elevator, the eyes of The Shadow were upon him. Sequestered in the darkness of the stairway, the keen-visioned observer watched Bart Melken's friend make his departure.

The Shadow made no motion for a short while. Then, like a spectral shape, he glided forth from his spot of hiding, and moved easily toward the door. His form seemed to shroud the light; it cast a long splotch through the narrow glass panels, upon the tiled floor of the lobby.

The Shadow's gloved hand rested on the knob of the door. It paused there as the outer door swung open, and a man entered the lobby. In the dim light, The Shadow recognized the new arrival. It was Doctor Lysander Dubrong.

The physician's face seemed sallow in the yellow light. Dubrong was wearing a serious, worried expression. His suave smile was absent. The Shadow watched him run his finger along the line of push buttons to the one which The Shadow knew belonged to Farrell Sarborn.

Dubrong was holding the little receiver to his ear. His eyes were upon the mouthpiece by the name board.

The Shadow was not only observant, his keen ears could hear the conversation which Dubrong was conducting with Jalon, in the apartment above.

"Hello... Mr. Sarborn..." Dubrong paused. "I want to talk with Mr. Sarborn... What's that? Who am I? ... Let me talk to Mr. Sarborn... What? Am I Mr. Cranston?" The flicker of the suave smile returned to Dubrong's thin lips. "Yes... I am Mr. Cranston... I must see Mr. Sarborn..."

The Shadow sidled into darkness as the door began to click. Dubrong with surprising agility, leaped from the name board and pushed open the door. He strode directly past the spot where The Shadow was standing. The door came directly in front of the black-cloaked watcher.

While the door was closing, The Shadow spied a new entrant into the lobby. A squat man had arrived there just as Dubrong sprang past the door. The way was blocked to him.

The Shadow, peering from the edge of the door, again recognized a face. This man was a second-class detective from headquarters; he had evidently been detailed to watch the movements of Doctor Dubrong.

The dick looked at the name board. He saw the pressed button, with the name of Farrell Sarborn. He paused for a few moments, then turned and hurried from the lobby. A soft laugh came from The Shadow. He knew that the trailer was hastening to report to Joe Cardona.

DUBRONG had gone above, using the elevator which was waiting when he entered. The Shadow followed on his trail, using the stairway. As he neared the top, he heard the sound of excited voices. Doctor Dubrong was arguing with Jalon.

"Get out of my way!" ordered the physician. "I want to see your master—not you."

"He is not here," returned Jalon, blocking the door to the apartment.

"Where is Bart Melken?" demanded Dubrong.

"He is not here," retorted Jalon.

"He came here—from his hotel" was Dubrong's savage response. "I learned that when I called there. Where is he?"

"He has left."

"I'm going to find out—from your master."

"He has left, also."

Dubrong shot a vicious punch into the servant's body. As Jalon doubled up, The Shadow saw Dubrong stride past his blocker. He could hear angry shouts as Jalon followed. The two men came staggering forth, locked in a furious grasp.

It appeared an unequal struggle, the frail physician against the squat, thick-formed South American servant. Dubrong, however, showed marked skill in combat. He twisted free, delivered another punch, and sent the squat man staggering. He headed for the elevator this time. He had evidently assured himself that neither Sarborn nor Melken was in the apartment.

Jalon, however, was not satisfied. Like a tiger, the servant sprang after the departing physician. A knife blade flashed as Jalon leaped toward the open door of the elevator.

The Shadow sprang suddenly forth from his spot of obscurity. Dubrong did not see him; the physician was in the elevator. Jalon did not see him; the servant was intent upon stopping Dubrong.

As The Shadow made his swift approach, a shot resounded. It came from the elevator. Jalon, already pounding into the car to grapple with the man who appeared an enemy to his master, collapsed with suddenness.

Dubrong must have pulled a revolver and delivered a quick but certain shot. The elevator door clanged shut. The car began its descent as The Shadow reached the closed door.

Doctor Dubrong was making a getaway. His shot had mortally wounded Farrell Sarborn's servant. There was no need for The Shadow's presence here. Swiftly, the black-clad intervener swung toward the stairway.

The elevator stopped at the ground floor before The Shadow had sufficient time to make the descent. Its door slid open, and Doctor Dubrong leaped forth with the wild fury of a madman. He dashed from the apartment building, pocketing his revolver as he ran. He had used the weapon that he had shown Joe Cardona, that day in the consulting room at the clinic.

A MOTOR sounded as The Shadow arrived at the bottom of the stairs. When the tall pursuer had reached the street, the taillight of Dubrong's car was rounding the corner. The Shadow paused just beyond the sphere of light outside of the apartment. He turned quickly as he sidled back into darkness.

A stocky man was striding up the street. It was Joe Cardona.

Whatever thought The Shadow might have held regarding a pursuit of Doctor Dubrong was ended at the sight of the detective. As Cardona entered the lobby, The Shadow moved across the street to the side of a parked coupé. There, he flung his cloak and hat into the car. Visible now, he returned, a figure in evening clothes. His face came into light as he opened the outer door of the lobby. The Shadow bore the features of Lamont Cranston.

Joe Cardona, studying the nameplates on the board, swung around as Cranston entered. The detective recognized the arrival. Not only did he remember Cranston, from the affray at Winchendon's, he knew also that the millionaire was a friend of the police commissioner's.

"Mr. Cranston!" exclaimed the detective. "How do you happen to be here?"

"Dropping in to see a friend of mine," remarked Cranston quietly. "Farrell Sarborn—perhaps you remember him at Winchendon's. He was the man who owned the macaw."

"Say!" Cardona pointed to the name on the board. "That's the place I'm going, too. I want to find doc—a fellow who came here to Sarborn's place for no good reason. I don't want to ring Sarborn's bell. Do you know anyone else here?"

Cranston shook his head. Cardona seemed perplexed. The millionaire made a slight smile.

"Why not," he suggested, "break the glass panel in the door?"

"I couldn't wedge through there," returned Cardona.

"You could reach in and turn the knob," remarked Cranston.

Joe Cardona grunted. The plan was simple enough. The detective pulled a revolver from his pocket, and delivered a stroke with the butt. He shattered the glass, reached through, and turned the knob.

"Coming up?" he questioned.

"Very well," returned Cranston.

WHEN the pair stepped from the elevator on the third floor, Cardona uttered a surprised exclamation. Bathed in light from the doorway of Sarborn's apartment lay the dead form of Jalon, the servant. The man had managed to crawl that far before he died.

Joe gripped his revolver. He heard Lamont Cranston remark that the dead man was Sarborn's servant. Joe nodded and motioned to Cranston to accompany him. They entered the apartment. They saw at once that the place was empty.

"I know the man who got this fellow!" exclaimed Cardona. "I'll tell you who it was. Doctor Lysander Dubrong—the man who has the East Side Clinic. He came up here ten minutes ago."

"Doctor Dubrong!" uttered Cranston, in a tone of incredulity. "That must be impossible! He is a man of high reputation."

"I know him for what he is," growled Cardona. "The question now is where he's gone. He's made a getaway."

"Maybe the macaw knows," suggested Cranston.

"The macaw?" asked Cardona.

"Yes," returned Cranston, "the scarlet bird, there on the chair."

Cardona stared at the macaw. The bird was perched as calmly as ever, the only challenge in its bearing being the motion of its beak.

"At Winchendon's," remarked Cranston, "the macaw had a remarkable ability to utter names that it had heard. Perhaps Sarborn, before he left, stated where he was going. Perhaps Dubrong has followed him there."

"How do you make the bird talk?" asked Cardona.

Cranston was lighting a cigarette. Holding it between his lips, he approached and scratched the macaw's head. The bird ruffed its throat feathers and wagged its beak. Suddenly, its shrill cry sounded.

"Lydell!" screamed the macaw. "Lydell! Lydell!"

Cranston removed the cigarette from his lips as he stepped away from the chair.

"That sounded plain enough," he told Cardona. "It was a name, all right."

"Lydell," repeated Cardona.

"Lydell!" shrilled the scarlet macaw.

Cranston had spied the newspaper on the table. He picked it up and pointed to the news paragraph beside the picture.

"Look at that," he said.

"Garforth Lydell!" exclaimed Cardona. "Say"— he was reading the paragraph—"he lives less than a dozen blocks from here. That's where I'm going—to Lydell's."

Cardona leaped to the telephone. He turned to Cranston before raising the receiver.

"I'm calling police headquarters before I start," he informed the millionaire. "I don't want to lose any time. I've got a man outside, Mr. Cranston. Detective Sergeant Markham. You'll do me a favor if you'll go down and tell him to come up. I'm hopping for Lydell's. You can stay here—"

Cranston was nodding as Cardona spoke. With no further delay, the millionaire turned and strode from the apartment. He took the elevator to the ground floor. At the outer door, he stood and made a beckoning gesture with his arms. Detective Sergeant Markham came hurrying from a car parked down the street. Like Cardona, Markham also remembered Lamont Cranston.

"Cardona wants you up at Sarborn's apartment," informed Cranston. "Right away, Markham. Third floor. Tell him I shall return here shortly. I have an appointment at the Cobalt Club which I must keep."

Markham nodded. There was no mention of

murder up above. He went into the apartment building as Cranston departed. Markham saw no reason why the millionaire should remain.

Cranston reached his coupé. There, he quickly donned his masking cloak and hat. It was The Shadow who drove away from the front of the apartment house. His hands, as they were manipulating the wheel, were drawing on their black gloves.

Bart Melken had gone to Garforth Lydell's. Farrell Sarborn had followed him. Doctor Lysander Dubrong had taken up the trail. Detective Joe Cardona was on his way. Besides these, there was another who would arrive before Cardona.

The Shadow, too, was traveling to the focal point where crime was due to strike. The Shadow's laugh was echoing as the coupé turned uptown at the nearest avenue.

Tonight, The Shadow would meet The Jackdaw. The elusive bird of crime would come face to face with the avenger who had crossed his path before. The Shadow knew.

He was out to snare The Jackdaw in the act of crime.

CHAPTER XIX
THE JACKDAW ARRIVES

GARFORTH LYDELL'S home was an old-fashioned brownstone mansion in the Nineties. The house had a central hall; on the right, as one entered, was a living room. Connected to it was a smaller room, Garforth Lydell's study.

On the left of the hallway lay the library. At the rear of this room was a steel door that led to the vault. An old pantry had been transformed into the vault room, and its other side was blocked with another door of steel. This second door was the one which was permanently barred on the inside.

Two men were seated in the study, the room most remote from the vault.

One was Bart Melken; the other was Garforth Lydell himself. The banker was a man of fifty years. His iron-gray hair alone betrayed his age. Physically, he was in the pink of condition.

Bart Melken, nervous and pale-faced, seemed a weakling compared to his intended father-in-law. Garforth Lydell, although not a large man, showed action and power in every mood or gesture.

The two were talking about Lydell's trip. Melken was questioning Lydell about conditions in Florida. The banker made an open-handed gesture.

"Don't ask me about Florida," he said. "I was only there part of the time that I was away."

"Where else were you?" queried Melken in surprise.

"Cuba," returned Lydell. "The Bahamas. Even Puerto Rico."

"On business?"

"Pleasure. I was incognito." Lydell smiled. "In fact, I came north—well, let us say a few days ago—in order to attend to a few matters here. I didn't want to appear in New York as returned from Florida until I was ready to swing the big deal that I intend to handle over the weekend."

"It involves a large sum?"

"Millions, Bart. Actual securities will be handled to the extent of half a million. They are in my vault—here at the house."

"Do you think they are safe in your vault?"

"Perfectly. I would trust them there even if they were my own. It happens, however, that they belong to other people."

"You are responsible for them, though."

"Yes, in a sense. I should not like to have them stolen. Nevertheless, they were fairly thrust upon me. I am keeping them at the risk of the owners."

"That seems unbelievable."

"Not in the affairs of the large corporations involved. To them, securities—to a certain amount of course—are merely certificates. It is surprising how lax some people are about handling them.

"Tonight, Bart"—Lydell was chuckling as he spoke—"I could rob my own vault with one-hundred-percent profit. I mentioned that to Yvonne at dinner. She was horrified."

"Where is Yvonne?" asked Bart. "I expected to find her downstairs when I arrived."

"She had a slight headache," declared Garforth Lydell. "She told me to call her when you arrived. I forgot about it, when we began to talk together. I shall call her now."

The banker arose and clapped his prospective son-in-law on the shoulder. He seemed to have a fatherly interest in Bart Melken.

"You'll have to entertain yourself for fifteen or twenty minutes," said Lydell. "I'm going upstairs to unpack a trunk. After that, I'll call Yvonne. I think it is best not to disturb her for a little while."

Garforth Lydell was smiling as he left the study. Bart Melken stared after him. This was one of the first real talks he had ever had with Lydell. The banker had always been cordial, but rather formal in the past.

NOW, as Bart reviewed the year that he had been engaged to Yvonne, he could see that Lydell had been watching him more closely than he had supposed. It was just after his engagement to Yvonne, Bart recalled, that he had landed in the trouble that had caused him to appeal to Bing Claver.

Thus Bart's acquaintance with Garforth Lydell had begun almost simultaneously with his term of service to The Jackdaw. The coincidence was something that Bart had never appreciated before tonight. Strained and nervous, the young man began to wonder.

Bart's mind was in that hectic state where delusions come to prominence. Thoughts flashed through his brain—thoughts that were names. Garforth Lydell—Bing Claver—The Jackdaw—the last name kept thrumming through Bart's mental activities.

The Jackdaw!

That mysterious chieftain had imposed a special task for tonight. Bart was to pave the way for an impressive theft—the stealing of half a million dollars in securities. Valuables in the custody of Garforth Lydell; securities which the banker had said were not his own.

Would it hurt Lydell if these were stolen? No—the banker had stated that the loss would not be his own. The thought was a salve to Bart Melken's conscience. Mechanically, he arose from the chair in which he was seated, and took the one beyond Garforth Lydell's desk. He opened the central drawer, finding it unlocked.

Directly before his eyes, Bart Melken saw a key. He recognized it as the key that would unlock the door in the library; the steel door to the vault. Either chance or design had favored Bart tonight. Hastily, the young man removed the key.

There were no servants in the house. Two had been on duty while Yvonne had been living here alone, during her widowed father's absence. Garforth Lydell had had the key in his possession; he had left it in this drawer, apparently through force of habit or perhaps forgetfulness.

Alone, on the ground floor of the house, Bart Melken had the opportunity he wished. It was his chance to clear the way for The Jackdaw's final haul, to relieve himself of servitude to the clever supercrook.

Key in hand, Bart Melken hurried from the study. He went across the hall, after passing through the living room. He paused momentarily at the foot of the stairs. There was no sound from above. Garforth Lydell might just as well be outside the house as here.

Bart Melken entered the library. He stopped there for a moment. As he did, a pair of eyes were focused upon him from the window. A face showed there, against the pane. Bart Melken did not see it. He would have recognized it if he had. It was the face of his friend, Farrell Sarborn.

Bart reached the steel door. He unlocked it with a trembling hand. As he did, an action occurred far behind him—at the front door of the house. That portal opened; into the hallway stepped a slender, skulking figure—Doctor Lysander Dubrong.

The physician advanced to the doorway of the library. Peering craftily, he saw Bart Melken unlocking the steel door. A suave smile registered

itself upon the doctor's lips. Dubrong moved back to the front door, and slipped out into the darkness.

Farrell Sarborn's face was no longer at the side window. It had disappeared when Melken had approached the steel door. Thus neither Sarborn nor Dubrong had seen the other.

The steel door was open. Stepping down two paces, Bart Melken found himself beside the disused door that was barred on the inside. The bar grated as Bart manipulated it. It came clear. The door was free upon its hinges.

The way was open to The Jackdaw.

BART backed toward the library. He stood there trembling, ready to depart. As he turned, the sound of a footfall frightened him. He swung to face the last person whom he had expected to encounter: Yvonne Lydell.

"Bart!" The girl's word was a low and startled whisper. "Bart!"

Melken stood aghast.

"What are you doing?" Yvonne's question was breathless. "What are you doing—here in the vault?"

"It's all right, Yvonne!" Bart's words were husky. "You—you must not say anything. You—your father is—"

"Bart!" gasped Yvonne. The girl's eyes were wide. "Bart! You have opened the other door—"

The sentence ended. Yvonne was staring beyond her fiancé. Instinctively, Bart Melken turned in that direction. He saw the cause of Yvonne Lydell's horror.

The farther door had opened. Its grating hinges had attracted the girl's notice. Framed in the doorway stood a man, his face obscured by a mask. In his hand, he clutched a shining revolver.

Yvonne Lydell was speechless. She did not know the might of this arrival. Bart Melken, too, found his throat dry and incapable of utterance.

For the first time, The Jackdaw's minion was face to face with his crime-dealing chief.

The Jackdaw had arrived!

CHAPTER XX
THE SHADOW'S TASK

THE JACKDAW swung his revolver toward the man and the girl at the library door. His gesture was a potent threat. Bart Melken backed away. Yvonne Lydell, however, retained her ground. She did not fear the menace of this masked intruder.

"Yvonne!" Bart Melken gasped the girl's name. "Yvonne! Be quiet!"

The urgent words—a recognition of The Jackdaw's cold-blooded deeds—worked opposite to Melken's intention. The order for silence gave Yvonne the ray of hope that she desired. Wildly, the girl began to scream.

Bart Melken saw The Jackdaw's finger on the trigger. With the first display of courage that he had ever shown in his life, he flung himself into the path of fire. His hurtling body met The Jackdaw with full force. The two men struggled.

A burst of flame. Bart Melken staggered. His body began to sag. Yvonne, gaining action as well as words, was backing across the library. She realized that the shot had been meant for her.

As The Jackdaw's shot resounded, the unlatched front door burst open, and a stocky man dashed across the hallway to the library. The detective had heard the shot. He saw the girl. He did not look toward the windows at the side, where one was slightly open. He thought only of the menace that must lie ahead.

Drawing his revolver, Cardona flung the girl aside and stopped short at the door. His gun hand was but half raised. Before him, he saw the glistening muzzle of the revolver that The Jackdaw held.

Joe Cardona was face to face with death. He half dropped to the floor, swinging his revolver upward in a futile gesture.

Then came the second shot in this strange conflict. It came from the spot where it might be least expected. A terrific roar sounded from the partly opened window of the library. It was the cannonade of a huge automatic, that an unseen hand had thrust through the opening.

The Jackdaw saw that shot. He saw the eyes above the gun that fired it—the burning eyes of The Shadow. The black-clad warrior was framed within the window, his outline a shady shape, his black-gloved hand thrust free.

The Shadow's bullet found its mark in The Jackdaw's shoulder. The crook's trigger finger made a clutch. The revolver fired a futile, hopeless shot. The Jackdaw's arm was sagging as his hand tried to retain its aim.

IN quick staccato came the third shot of the fray. Joe Cardona's gun had reached the level. The detective, last to fire, was the only one to repeat. Again and again he delivered bullets into The Jackdaw's crumpling frame. The crook's body sprawled riddled on the floor. The Jackdaw's pouring blood mingled with that of his fellow henchman, Bart Melken.

Cardona had killed The Jackdaw—but he had gained the opportunity only through The Shadow's intervention. Joe had not seen the mysterious fighter fire. He had merely followed the opportunity that had arrived.

It was The Shadow's shot, however, that had done the work. But for it, Joe Cardona would have been slaughtered in his tracks.

The detective stood motionless. Before he could advance, Yvonne Lydell had sprung past him. The girl was kneeling by the bodies on the floor, neglectful of the blood that spread upon the floor. It was not Bart Melken's form that she sought. Her hands were upon the shoulders of The Jackdaw.

"Father!" she moaned. "I feared this! Oh, father, I should have known tonight—when you told me—told me that you could rob yourself—"

"Your father?" The question came from Joe Cardona. The detective was stepping forward.

"My father," gasped Yvonne. "My father—Garforth Lydell!"

Joe Cardona shook his head.

"You're wrong, lady," he declared. "I'll tell you who this man is." He reached down and seized the mask that The Jackdaw wore. "This is Doctor Lysander Dubrong!"

As he spoke, Cardona plucked away the mask. His action turned The Jackdaw's head upon its side. Yvonne Lydell, staring, saw that the face was not that of her father. Joe Cardona, open-mouthed, saw that it was not Lysander Dubrong!

The face on the floor was the countenance of Farrell Sarborn. He—Farrell Sarborn—was The Jackdaw!

The echoes of a rising laugh crept through the library. A quick crescendo, those chilling tones ended in an abrupt pause, while whispered reverberations came in lulling gasps. This was The Shadow's pronouncement. He had not spoken the true name of The Jackdaw. But The Shadow knew the identity of the dead man on the floor.

Before Cardona could stare back toward the living room, a noise interrupted him from the open door through which The Jackdaw had come. A man was standing there, a man who had entered the hallway from an outside door. The newcomer was Doctor Lysander Dubrong.

A moment later, an excited voice sounded from the library. Turning in bewilderment, Joe Cardona found himself staring at Garforth Lydell. At sight of the banker, Yvonne leaped to her feet, and threw herself into her father's arms.

Then, while she sobbed, the girl turned and pointed to Bart Melken's dead form. In a choking voice, she uttered words of pity for the man who had saved her life.

"Poor Bart!" sobbed Yvonne. "Poor Bart!"

"Do not say that," came a dry-voiced tone. All turned to face Doctor Dubrong. "Say rather that Bart Melken at last deserves a word of praise. He has performed the only deed of courage in all his life."

As if in answer came a sighing whisper from the closing window of the library. The strange, vague sound was a laugh. Yet it carried no tone of mirth or mockery. It was, rather, a knell; a weird note that carried unworded corroboration of what Doctor Lysander Dubrong had said.

It was the parting token of The Shadow, the hidden fighter, who had brought an end to The Jackdaw, following Bart Melken's sacrifice.

CHAPTER XXI
THE JACKDAW'S NEST

A GROUP of men were assembled in Farrell Sarborn's apartment. Joe Cardona was there. With him had come Doctor Lysander Dubrong and Garforth Lydell. Lamont Cranston had just arrived; returning—as he said—from the Cobalt Club, he was surprised to find the trio that had arrived.

Besides these, another man had come upon the scene. Police Commissioner Ralph Weston had hurried hither in response to a call from Detective Joe Cardona.

The first man to speak was Garforth Lydell.

"Amazing!" exclaimed the banker. "To think that Bart Melken was working for this crook, who called himself the—"

"The Jackdaw," interposed Joe Cardona.

"The Jackdaw," repeated Lydell. "It was odd that my daughter should take seriously my statement that I could rob myself tonight. No wonder she thought that I lay dead and masked upon the floor of the vault!"

Joe Cardona turned to Doctor Dubrong.

"I owe you an apology," said the detective. "I suspected you—"

"No apology from you, Cardona," returned Dubrong dryly. "I am the one who must give an explanation. I must tell you why I played the part I did.

"I knew Bart Melken's father—who died years ago. Naturally, I took an interest in the young man without his knowledge. I saw, some months ago, that he was becoming restless. I also noticed that robberies had taken place where he had been.

"Through my East Side Clinic, I heard rumors of a high-class crook called The Jackdaw. To learn more, I adopted the mythical character of Limps Silvey. I toadied—in that disguise—to different gang leaders, and finally picked Bing Claver as the one who was in The Jackdaw's employ.

"Bing, like Bart, received his instructions by telephone. I had no direct foreknowledge that Rutherford Casslin was to be murdered. The Jackdaw did that job alone. I thought that all was safe at the time I left Casslin's home.

"When I returned to the castle, I realized that Bart Melken was implicated in murder. I put forth the Hindu theory merely to protect him—my friend's son—while I could continue my efforts to track The Jackdaw."

"As Limps Silvey, I learned facts concerning Bing Claver's proposed attack at Winchendon's. I knew Cardona's stools were trailing me. I deliberately drew you, Cardona, on my track so that I could make that pretended telephone call. It was I who called you at the restaurant in Corona. I wanted you and your men to get to Winchendon's.

"Your tip-off came in time," acknowledged Cardona, as the physician paused. "It wasn't your fault that the road was blocked. You did your part—and fooled me into the bargain."

"I again adopted the guise of Limps Silvey," resumed Dubrong with a smile, "when you told me that there were rumors of The Jackdaw. I found out that your statement was incorrect. I began to watch Bart Melken. He seemed to be The Jackdaw's only aide.

"WHEN I read in the newspaper that Garforth Lydell had returned, I suddenly sensed where The Jackdaw might be planning to make a final stroke. I went to Melken's hotel. I learned that he had come here, to Sarborn's apartment. Both men were gone. Sarborn's servant tried to kill me. I killed him. I hurried to prevent crime at Lydell's.

"I went around the house; but I picked the wrong way. I was late arriving at the door to the hallway— too late to hurry in until you had slain The Jackdaw, Cardona."

"While I was upstairs," interposed Garforth Lydell. "Upstairs, unpacking—knowing nothing until I heard muffled shots from far below. Had I known that Yvonne had risen to go downstairs and find Bart Melken—"

"Bart did a good deed," broke in Dubrong. "I am not sorry that he died as he did. It was a worthwhile way to end a misspent life."

Commissioner Weston was staring hard. These revelations were unquestionably correct. Yet he could not yet fully accept the theory of The Jackdaw.

"What about Casslin?" he demanded. "Where is The Bishenpur diamond?"

"Perhaps I can answer that," remarked Lamont Cranston quietly.

All turned to the millionaire. His statement was unexpected. No one had figured Cranston as one with an active knowledge of these affairs.

"I do not claim to be a detective." There was a tinge of calm irony in Cranston's steady voice. "Yet I noticed, out at Winchendon's, that Farrell Sarborn was a faker."

"A faker?" questioned Weston.

"Yes," replied Cranston, "a faker. Sometimes fakers prove to be crooks. This bird of his"—the millionaire pointed to the scarlet macaw, still perched upon a chair back—"was an impossible performer.

"Macaws, first of all, have a penchant for screaming. They can never be cured of the habit. Secondly, they are poor talkers. Yet here is a phenomenal macaw: one that never screams; one that speaks with almost human intelligence. Both are impossible factors, especially in a scarlet macaw, one of the most difficult species to train at all."

"But this bird may be unusual," exclaimed Weston.

"It is unusual," declared Cranston, with a faint smile. "It is dumb."

"Dumb!" cried Cardona.

"Most certainly," explained Cranston. "Look at it now. Watch its moving beak, its ruffling throat. It is trying to scream—trying constantly—and it cannot do so."

"It spoke for Sarborn," protested Weston.

"Sarborn spoke for it," retorted Cranston. "He was always close beside it, scratching its head, looking toward it. The simplest possible feat of ventriloquism is to imitate the falsetto cry of a parrot. The bird's constant habit of trying to scream made Sarborn's ventriloquism even more effective. He kept the people just far enough away to make the illusion perfect."

The listeners found themselves nodding.

"Sarborn was a mimic," added Cranston. "He gave a perfect imitation of a kitten's mew at Winchendon's. I realized then that he was a ventriloquist. I saw nothing in his game outside of trickery." Cranston's knowing smile and slight sarcastic tone remained unnoticed. "Now, however, that you are seeking facts, I am able to supply them. I was at Winchendon's. Bart Melken evidently failed to give a proper signal—so Sarborn gave one instead. The macaw's cry of 'Robbers'."

"When I was playing the part of Limps," recalled Dubrong, "I remember hearing the end of a telephone call in which Bing Claver mentioned the word 'Robbers'."

"A wise guy," decided Joe Cardona. "Sarborn had no more use for Bing, once the game was up. He played the hero act at the end of the big fight. I fell for it."

"But Casslin's death!" blurted Weston. "You spoke of that, Cranston. How does the macaw explain it?"

"Just an idea," returned Cranston. "Let us see if it is correct. One pet played well for Sarborn. Maybe another was trained to do its work. I read about Casslin's odd, barred tower. I noticed something, here at Sarborn's, that has given me a potent thought."

HE led the way to the other room. He opened the crate in the corner, and brought out the little monkey. In the corner, Cranston spied a coil of string. He gave an end of the twine to the monkey.

"This," said Cranston, "is a sapajou—the most intelligent species of monkeys found in South America. Look up there—that bar over the window frame—ostensibly the macaw's perch."

Cranston released the sapajou. The little creature clambered up the wall, carrying the end of the string. It took the cord over the bar, and brought it down the wall to Cranston. The string formed a loop over the perch.

"I see it!" cried Cardona. "Sarborn was outside by Casslin's tower. When he got the signal that the diamond was downstairs, he sent the monkey up with a rope. Then he climbed up the rope himself."

"How could he have gotten the diamond?" questioned Weston. "I see how he killed Casslin—he thrust a revolver between the bars and fired. But the diamond—"

Cranston, holding the sapajou under one arm, placed his gold watch upon the seat of a chair. He drew the monkey in back of the upright rods in the chair back. When he released his hold, the sapajou wriggled between, picked up the watch, and brought it back through the rods.

"He sent the monkey in for it!" shouted Cardona. "In for the diamond! That explains it all. I'm going to look at the ivy on that tower; at those bars. From the outside, this time."

Commissioner Weston was no longer skeptical. He thrust out his hand to Lamont Cranston.

"You'd make a good detective," he commended. "After you squander those millions of yours, come around for a job on the force. Wait—wait a moment. What about the diamond?"

"The Bishenpur diamond?" queried Cranston. "Ah, yes. There must be a clue to it. Let us see—perhaps The Jackdaw—"

His smile broadened. Everyone seemed breathless. This keen-minded investigator had made another strike.

"The Jackdaw," repeated Cranston. "The thieving bird—the bird that even steals eggs from other bird nests. The Bishenpur diamond was The Jackdaw's egg. Farrell Sarborn, strangely enough, was a collector of birds' eggs—"

He waved his hand as he spoke. All turned toward the glass case that contained Sarborn's collection of eggs. Joe Cardona, suddenly impulsed, yanked out his revolver and shattered the glass.

"A condor's egg," remarked Cranston, picking out the largest ovoid in the group. "Very heavy—now that I am examining it for the first time. Look—it has a seam. It is not an egg at all. It is a thin metal container."

With a twist of his hands, he wrenched the egg apart. In one half, he exhibited a gorgeous, glittering gem, that shone with ruddy tint.

It was the Bishenpur diamond!

CARDONA was breaking open another, smaller egg. He found some gems within it. He was exulting. Here were the fruits of former robberies—the other eggs from The Jackdaw's nest!

Lamont Cranston retained his smile as more and more gems put in their appearance when new eggs were broken. The final mystery was solved; The Jackdaw's spoils had been recovered.

It was not until afterward that Joe Cardona suddenly gained a hunch. It was when the group had gone downstairs, when Cranston, at the door of the apartment building, was about to enter his coupé.

Joe Cardona stepped forward to the millionaire. He put a question as Cranston took the wheel of the car. The millionaire smiled as he heard it.

"The macaw," remarked Cardona. "You said that Sarborn talked for it. You proved it, right enough. But I just remember that when I came up to Sarborn's, it was the macaw that told me where Farrell Sarborn had gone—to Lydell's—"

Cranston had started the motor. He became solemn as he leaned to the window of the car.

"Remarkable, wasn't it?" he questioned. "The macaw did talk once—when it had a right to talk."

The coupé rolled away. Joe Cardona stood bewildered on the curb. His hazy senses cleared. He began to build up facts. They all referred to Lamont Cranston.

The mysterious fighter out at Winchendon's— the macaw that spoke even when its master was not present—the timely bullet that had downed The Jackdaw in Garforth Lydell's vault. All went back to that significant point, the time when the macaw had spoken for Joe Cardona—when Lamont Cranston had stood beside the bird, coaxing it.

He—Cranston—had provided the macaw's falsetto. He was in the open at that time; he had been under cover during the more important episodes which Cardona now remembered.

Throughout this case, the might of a powerful fighter had manifested itself. Well did Cardona know the only one whom it could have been: The Shadow.

Joe realized now that while he, Cardona, had been following the wrong trail, doing no more than interfere with Doctor Dubrong's desperate efforts to aid the law, The Shadow had been closing a net about the real criminal—Farrell Sarborn.

It was The Shadow who had trapped The Jackdaw. It was The Shadow who, had ended the crook's career of crime. It was The Shadow who had played the part of Lamont Cranston.

As he stood on the curb, staring after the tiny taillight of the millionaire's coupé, Joe Cardona fancied that he heard the faint echo of a weird, unearthly mirth. It was the laughter that had sounded at Garforth Lydell's. Its tones were creepier than ever now.

Echoes of the past, the sinister mockery dispelled itself with the night breeze.

Thus ended the laugh of The Shadow!

THE END

INTERLUDE by Will Murray

Once again, we explore The Shadow's radio roots, this time on the occasion of the 80th anniversary of the Man of Mystery's broadcasting debut. Our two selections reflect The Shadow transitioning from a scolding narrator of stories plucked from the pages of Street & Smith's *Detective Story Magazine* to a full-blown dramatic character.

Walter Gibson told the story of The Shadow's origins to many interviewers over many years. He was not a part of the legend at the very beginning.

"I had been planning a weird and mysterious character with magical ways of getting out of problems," he related. "At the same time, Frank Blackwell, editor of *Detective Story Magazine*, was looking for a writer to bring to life a sinister radio voice then featured on *The Detective Story Hour*."

From its 1931 debut, *The Shadow Magazine* eclipsed *Detective Story* and its spinoff broadcast. *The Detective Story Program* soon gave way to a new series called *The Blue Coal Radio Revue*, with The Shadow performing narration duties.

"Blue Coal, who had a mystery program, wanted to have The Shadow as an announcer," Gibson recalled. "He just announced the program in a weird voice. And Street & Smith had tried that for a while."

The pressure to bring the authentic Shadow to the airwaves grew irresistible. The sponsor nevertheless resisted to the bitter end. "For a year or so we used an announcer called The Shadow on the radio show to boost the magazine," Gibson explained. "Then we told them they'd have to use adaptations from the stories for the radio scripts."

As Gibson often explained, his concepts had to be rethought and tailored for the young medium:

Lamont Cranston was the name I'd given The Shadow. That was one of the characters in which he appeared. He was a master of disguise. In the magazine he appeared in various forms. But in this, we took Lamont Cranston because we were able then to focus it on that one type of story. And we put Margo Lane in.... Police Commissioner Weston, we kept. Joe Cardona, the inspector. And

Shrevvie the cab driver. So we made them as running characters in every one of the stories. If we'd gone into the 20 or 30 other characters I had, it would have confused listeners, because they only had half an hour and you couldn't stop and explain who these people were.

As with the pulp magazine, the radio Shadow was a suspense vehicle, although individual storylines ranged from crime stories or science fiction to outright horror. Gibson often observed that The Shadow was perfect for radio's theatre of the imagination:

> Of course, he was ghostly in his own right. That was one of the things where he was ideally suited to radio. In the magazines, I had to describe actions he took. He would blend with darkness. He would fade from sight. In radio, when the right moment came, suddenly his voice came in. He talked from an echo chamber. And the people would be amazed. "Shadow, where are you? We can't see you!" Well, neither could the listening audience. That was the beauty of it! That was made to order.

The Shadow aired once a week on Sunday afternoon. "That was the witching hour for most of the old Shadow fans," Gibson recalled. "Of course, the time varied at different places. It was recorded and the records were used later in other areas, and in other seasons, because the sponsor was a coal company. But the basic program was in the winter.

"There were a good many hands in it," he added. "The men that played the part of The Shadow on radio were terrific. The first was Orson Welles. There had been a Shadow voice before—different people. It was a set idea that they tried out in order to get the actual dramatizations. Orson Welles was playing with the Mercury Theatre. This was in 1937, or thereabouts, when it started. And they took the cast from the Mercury Theatre and did the *Shadow* broadcasts on Sundays. Orson Welles played the part of Lamont Cranston. Later, a man named Bret Morrison played the part."

The Shadow provided the 22-year-old Orson Welles with his first significant national exposure:

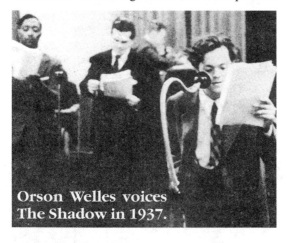

Orson Welles voices The Shadow in 1937.

Don't forget radio was in its infancy. There were only a couple of dramatic shows existing. Maybe all of a sudden another dramatic show would jump up. Nobody knew how long it was going to last. Most of the radio actors that came in were thinking the same way. So if a fellow had a chance to play The Shadow for so many weeks, fine. He was available and played it. Then he might go on, and go completely away from it. Orson Welles only did it as a sideline. Orson Welles happened be in New York with the Mercury Theatre.... They were doing nicely with it. But the actors wanted extra work, so they decided to do something on radio.

Well, of course people of that ability naturally could get on the radio immediately. But it just happened that The Shadow came along then. So Orson Welles was the first Shadow in the dramatic series. The two men after that, Johnstone and Morrison, were the ones that did most of the Shadows.

As prolific as he was, Gibson did not involve himself in scripting *The Shadow* beyond pounding out a few audition scripts in 1934 and conferring with scriptwriter Edward Hale Bierstadt before the start of the 1937 season:

> Now, I could have gotten in on it pretty easy, but in radio those days you had to be right there. All the writers were in New York, just as movie writers were in Hollywood. They would write the scripts. They would have to come in on the day the show played and immediately make changes, do what the director wanted and so forth. Well, I was used to writing up in Maine during the Summer and down in Florida during the Winter and so forth. I was too busy with The Shadows. After all, two a month, I couldn't bother with a radio story every week. It didn't pay any better money, either.

Realistically, Gibson didn't need to pitch in, having already produced over 100 Shadow novels that were perfectly suited to adapting. Yet in most instances, the radio producers chose to brainstorm original ideas—even if many were byproducts of what Gibson had established as the essence of The Shadow.

Gibson's editor, John L. Nanovic, was drafted to liase between Street & Smith's interests and the series' producers. "So John acted as coordinator on all the radio programs. He and I would suggest which ones would be good for them to use. And they'd read the stories and adapt them as they saw fit. That was announced. That was one of the important things. That was why Street & Smith said to go ahead, because every time they said, 'This story comes from *The Shadow Magazine.*'"

The Crime Clinic holds the distinction of having been one of the rare Shadow novels to be adapted for radio. It aired as "The Red Macaw" on October 3, 1937 as the second Shadow episode starring Orson Welles, with Margot Lane substituting for agent Harry Vincent from the original story.

Commissioner Ralph Weston and the Cobalt Club were carried over from the novel as well.

Submitted to editor John L. Nanovic on March 24, 1933, as "The Jackdaw," the novel was published in the December 1, 1933 issue of *The Shadow Magazine*. At 30 minutes running time, "The Red Macaw" was a distillation of Gibson's pulp novel, and the resemblance between the two is largely limited to its avian villain. Jackdaws are typically black and are related to crows and ravens, while macaws are tropical parrots.

Cards of Death was written during the summer of 1937 at Gibson's Gray, Maine summer home, around the time he met with Bierstadt to discuss the new Shadow program. So *Cards of Death* has a radio connection as well. Published in the May 1, 1938 issue, its cover featured The Shadow poised at an MBS microphone, to tie in with the new radio ratings smash that the character had engendered.

For this occasion, Gibson resurected his mythical radio station WNX, over which The Shadow had broadcast coded instructions to his agents in other novels. This was a device Gibson had introduced in the earliest Shadow novels which was carried over into the *Shadow* radio broadcasts during the final 1934-35 CBS season as an audience participation gimmick.

Walter B. Gibson

While Gibson was only tangentially involved with the show, inasmuch as he had developed the core characters, he was always associated with it in the public mind, then and now. Over the years, he was subjected to audience opinions of all stripes.

"They have different reactions," Walter once said. "In the old days, the women used to say, 'Oh, you're the man that scares all my children.' They were very much against that. But today, there are women who heard *The Shadow* when they were children. And they used to say how they used to stay in on Sunday afternoons just for that. There was a stronger male audience. I'm sure of that. Many of the old Shadow buffs of course read the magazine. I did the magazine, and the stories were adapted from that. So we're always running into various reactions."

Despite those objections, The Shadow on radio was nowhere near as violent as he was in the pulps, where he brandished twin .45 automatics and used them lavishly to punish criminals.

"Yes, there was a certain amount [of violence], but not too much," he acknowledged. "It was always very carefully handled. We saw to it. Well, there might be some shooting. Shots, and so forth. But there was never anything brutal brought in. We stayed away from torture, or anything of that sort. Oddly, those things dated back to way before the comic books. If they showed anything about a man climbing a cliff in a comic, or a pulp magazine, next thing a whole bunch of kids would be out climbing cliffs and the fire department would be around bringing them down with ladders! So there was a great taboo on all that. Because we knew we had juvenile readers."

In the 1940s, Gibson did work in the radio medium, scripting or plotting *Nick Carter, Master Detective, Chick Carter, The Avenger* and *Blackstone, the Magic Detective*. He found it a fascinating but demanding field.

When he was alive, Gibson felt strongly that The Shadow, whether in print or over the air, remained just as vital as he had been in his heyday.

"Oh, I think it holds [up]. I feel definitely so. All good stories and all suspense things are timeless. There just seem to be trends, that's all."

But he also readily acknowledged that the broadcast version of his character was not the true Shadow.

"The Shadow radio had a lot of trouble with its limitations," Gibson once observed. "They couldn't run some of the better Shadow things, because they couldn't have The Shadow play any other part than Cranston, or the listener wouldn't have been able to follow it. You find most of the people that remember the radio show remember it in a general way, whereas the people who read remember the stories, remember it specifically."

Walter was once asked if he felt that The Shadow had taken on a life of its own and if he hadn't sometimes felt that Lamont Cranston had eclipsed his creator. His response was classic Walter Gibson.

"Well, yes, to quite a degree. When I did the magazine stories, I used the name Maxwell Grant. I didn't even use my own name on it, because they wanted a name that could be identified with it. They always thought someday I was going to quit, or wear out. And they wanted to keep on with it. But I didn't. I outlasted them. Street & Smith had been going 75 years when I came in to work for them. And they said, "Well, we've been here 75 years. We'll be here a good long time." Well, I'm still around, and they aren't!" •

A Complete Book-length Novel from the Private Annals
of The Shadow, as told to

Maxwell Grant

*One by one, these little paste-
boards turn up, dealt by a fiendish
murderer. Will The Shadow be
able to hold the winning hand in*

CARDS OF DEATH

CHAPTER I
DEATH STALKS

THERE were half a dozen passengers aboard the South-bound plane, as it waited for the takeoff. Outside the windows lay the broad stretch of Newark Airport, dull, barren except for the hangars that squatted against the muggy sky.

Afternoon was well advanced, and dusk was due early, because of the overcast sky. Flight, however, would not be difficult at low altitude. Passengers felt apprehensive; as they watched the lines of automobiles streaming along the Skyway with headlamps already lighted; but the pilot did not share their worry.

Propellers were spinning; there was a call of "All aboard!" That cry came like a cue to a messenger in uniform, who stood near the ship. Hurriedly, he advanced to the closing door, extended an envelope.

"For Mr. Balcray," the messenger told the stewardess. "Elwood Balcray. He's aboard."

The stewardess looked annoyed. She had seen the messenger standing there gawking at the plane. She wondered why he had waited, and the messenger knew it. He muttered something about orders to hold the message until the last minute.

The stewardess summoned Elwood Balcray. He appeared at the door—a stoop-shouldered, long-faced man, with sharply nervous eyes. The messenger handed him the envelope, with the question:

"Any answer, sir?"

Balcray opened the yellow envelope, amid the increasing *whir*

of propellers. Impatiently, the plane dispatcher stood ready to signal the plane's departure. He wasn't noting Balcray closely; nor was the stewardess.

The one person who saw the horror that swept Balcray's face was the messenger. Moreover, he spied the cause.

The object that Balcray had drawn from the envelope was a card. It looked like a playing card; but it was longer, narrower than those in most packs. Furthermore, it differed from any such card that the messenger had ever seen.

Instead of spots, the card had long rods, six of them, in diagonal rows of three each. Those crossed rods formed an elongated letter X within the borders of the card.

"Any answer, Mr. Balcray?"

The messenger's question brought a response from Balcray's lips. The action seemed mechanical; the man's voice was a hoarse whisper.

"No answer"—Balcray was forcing the words, as his eyes stared glassily—"there can be no answer—to this!"

The messenger turned away. The door went shut; the dispatcher gave his signal. It was then that Balcray's horror took a frantic swing. He realized that he was cut off from the world; isolated aboard the plane. Still clutching the curious card, he pounced toward the stewardess.

"I've got to leave this ship!" Balcray's shout was wild. "Let me off! Open that door—I've got to get out!"

The *whir* of the propellers had become a roar. The plane was rolling along the runway. Balcray's grapple for the door was a dangerous move; by the time he succeeded, it would be suicidal.

Valiantly, the stewardess fought him away from the door; other passengers rallied to help her.

Though Balcray was battling like a madman, they overcame him. Gripped by half a dozen hands, he was shoved along the aisle, clear to the front of the plane, where the rescue squad plopped him into a seat.

Balcray subsided with a groan, the cardboard card crumpled in his tight-clutched hand. He was at the most distant spot from the door he wanted; and the route was blocked. With frenzy useless, Balcray had changed in an instant to a pitiful, hopeless figure.

NONE of the ground crew saw that short-lived struggle. Door and windows had moved beyond their view. They were watching the plane as it gathered speed along the runway. Swift ships of this type, though speedy in the air, required a long takeoff. A half-second more and the plane would be rising in the air.

At that instant, the swerve came.

The plane gave a telltale wobble to the right, as the wheel on that side crumpled. There was a lurchy swoop, as though wings sought to clutch the air. A slew to the right; the ship was off the runway. The tip of the right wing clipped the ground.

The crackup was immediate.

Propellers chewed the turf, as the plane's nose hit. Sleek, silvery metal crackled into junk. Flames spurted; the rising blaze licked the twisting fuselage. Sirens wailed the alarm; running men followed the fire apparatus that sped to the spot of the catastrophe.

Prompt work extinguished the blaze. From the debris, men dragged the stewardess, scarcely injured. Then came passengers, four of them, to be placed in an arriving ambulance. After that, two more, who needed no aid.

Like the pilots, those passengers were dead. They had been at the front of the cabin, where the shock was worst. Life had been crushed from them.

One of the dead passengers was Elwood Balcray. His fist, jammed, clawlike, hard against his chest, still gripped the curious card with its design of six crossed rods.

Elwood Balcray had recognized the threat of that strange card. It had proven his warrant of doom.

Two hours passed. Deep dusk had gripped Manhattan, when a short, pompous man strode into the lobby of the Sheffield Apartments. It wasn't a pretentious place, the Sheffield, but it was exclusive; therefore, it suited this pompous resident.

He stopped at the desk for mail. The clerk handed

him an envelope addressed to Sylvester Lysand. The pompous man opened it; he halted, stock-still.

"Is anything the matter, Mr. Lysand?"

The clerk's question was a logical one. He had seen Lysand's face. It carried the same expression of horror that Elwood Balcray had shown, two hours before.

Lysand gave no answer.

The clerk looked downward, saw the object that projected from a frozen hand. Like the messenger at the airport, the clerk was astonished.

Lysand was holding what seemed to be a playing card, except that its design was unusual. Set in its ornamental design were six spots shaped like ancient goblets. Lysand's eyes were riveted on those printed cups.

The clerk repeated his anxious question. Lysand did not hear it. He turned, as though lost in a trance, and walked toward the elevators.

There were two of those cars; only one was in use. The operator was jerking at a lever; as Lysand arrived, he called to the clerk:

"Jammed again. Better send Joe up with the other car."

The clerk beckoned to an attendant who was seated near the desk. The fellow opened the door of the little-used elevator; Lysand and two other passengers went aboard. Joe's elevator had scarcely started, before the man who had suggested it left his own car and walked out through a side door of the lobby.

New bewilderment gripped the clerk. The man who had just left wasn't the regular operator. Who he was—how he happened to be here—were riddles. Unfortunately, too, the clerk did not get a good look at the stranger's face; something that he was to regret greatly, later.

For the present, the clerk had less than half a minute to think it over. A rumbling sound quivered the building. It came from the shaft where Joe's elevator had gone up. The clerk stared in that direction. The dial above the elevator door showed that the car was at the fifth floor; but it was quivering at that mark.

As the clerk gaped, horrified, he saw the dial take a long sweep toward the bottom. With it came the rumble, louder than before, accompanied by a terrific clatter.

The door shook as the plunging elevator whizzed past the ground floor. There was a terrific crash from the basement; with it, shrieks that faded.

The palsied clerk suddenly gained control of his muscles; leaping out from the desk, he dashed to the street, where he shouted the ill tidings to the first policeman that he saw.

TEN minutes later, a cluster of firemen had reached the basement of the Sheffield Apartments. They were hacking through the elevator door, where few groans answered them. The barrier gave; they dragged out Joe, the operator, limp but alive.

The passengers were extricated from the wreckage. One still lived; he went to the hospital along with Joe. But the other two were dead; and one of them was Sylvester Lysand. Like Elwood Balcray, he had been crushed to death.

Lysand's hands had a dying clutch. The object the rescuers pried from those stilled fingers was the six-spotted card that had come in the envelope.

Again, doom had been predicted; and death had stalked along its trail.

Both events had seemed like accidents, but the link of those fatal cards proved them otherwise. Some master hand had arranged those thrusts, to strike down the victims that he wanted. Ruthless, that invisible murderer had sacrificed others along with Balcray and Lysand, the chosen victims.

Was death's toll finished?

Only the murderer, himself, could give the answer. His reply might be another stroke: the massacre of other innocent persons, along with a third victim. How long the chain would last, no one could tell.

Yet, with all its suddenness, death would not come without its warning. Like a venomous rattlesnake, the hidden killer gave his signals before he struck.

Cards of doom were the tokens that told each victim that death was due!

CHAPTER II
THE THIRD CARD

SOON after the elevator crash at the Sheffield, a man checked out of a pretentious New York hotel. He was a jolly, broad-faced individual, who looked brawny despite his stout build. When he asked for his bill, he stated his name. It was Hastings Keever.

Although Keever had been a guest at the hotel for only a few days, the bill ran close to two hundred dollars. Keever paid it from a fat bankroll that his pudgy fist could scarcely circle. Going out through the lobby, he peeled more notes from the roll, to tip bellboys, porter and doorman.

It was the doorman who politely closed the door of Keever's cab, expressing the hope that the departing guest would soon return. That brought a smile from Keever.

They knew him well at that hotel; and Keever was glad of it. It was an asset to be established there. For Hastings Keever was a man who made money by spending money. He was a promoter who could talk wealthy men into big deals.

Precarious though his business was, Keever had

done well with it. Luck and good judgment traveled with him. Enough of Keever's deals came through to give him a good reputation. Satisfied clients produced more. Whenever Keever fluked, he always had an explanation.

Keever had told the cab driver to take him to the Pennsylvania Station. He altered that order, as the cab rolled southward on Seventh Avenue. The new address that Keever gave was twenty blocks farther south, near the heart of Greenwich Village.

The cab reached a gloomy street; stopped before an old-fashioned building that had once been a private residence. Paying off the driver, Keever alighted, suitcase in one hand, an evening news-paper in the other.

He entered the old house; its lighted lobby showed that it had been converted into an apartment. A box marked "3B" carried the name of Hastings Keever.

Few of the promoter's clients knew that he maintained this small apartment in the Village. It served Keever as a residence only during those intervals between his big promotion deals.

There was no elevator in the place. Keever went up two flights of narrow stairs, puffing as he reached the third floor. The stairs brought him to the center of a lengthwise hall; his apartment was a dozen feet toward the front.

Unlocking the door, Keever turned on the lights. He placed his bag in a corner of the little living room; stretched himself in a comfortable chair.

AS his puffy breaths subsided, Keever spread the newspaper. His eyes centered on the most conspicuous headline: a report of a plane crash at Newark Airport. Keever seldom traveled by air; the news scarcely interested him, until he saw the names of the victims.

That list brought the pudgy man bolt upright. His pointing finger jabbed the line that carried the name of Elwood Balcray, wealthy real estate operator.

Again Keever's breaths were long drawn; this time through a tautness of his nerves. The genial smile went from his lips, to be replaced by an anxious twitch. His beady eyes showed a trace of terror.

Gripping the chair arms, Keever regained composure. He forced a smile, as he muttered:

"Maybe it *was* an accident. Yes, just an accident—like the newspaper says it was—"

Keever's eyes showed lingering doubt, despite his words. Those eyes also glimmered with an idea. Turning the pages of the newspaper, Keever found the radio programs. He noted that news reports were almost due from Station WNX.

There was a radio set in the corner. Keever thumbed the dial; paced his little living room while he listened to the finish of a musical program. There was a lull, then the announcer for the news reports. Keever was intent, expecting further details regarding the plane crash. Instead:

"Flash!" The announcer's voice was brisk. "*Two persons were killed, two others injured, in a fall of an elevator at the Sheffield Apartments—*"

"The Sheffield!" Keever's tone was gaspy again. "That's where—"

He was about to mention a man's name. It proved unnecessary. The news broadcaster was stating that very name across the air. The brisk tone drilled through Keever's ears:

"*Sylvester Lysand, killed in the fall, was a direc-tor of the Triton National Bank. Well-known in financial circles, Mr. Lysand—*"

Keever snapped off the radio without changing the dial. His beady eyes were hunted.

"Balcray—Lysand, both of them!" he muttered. "It couldn't be coincidence. It's *his* work! Legrec is back of it!"

Keever shot a wild look toward the door; he took a few steps in that direction. Pausing, he shook his head; mopped his forehead with a crumpled hand-kerchief. He wanted safety; he figured he might find it, if he remained in this isolated apartment.

There was a telephone on a table in the corner. Keever pounded to it; crouched as he lifted the receiver and dialed a number. His pudgy fingers succeeding in that task, he calmed as he lifted the telephone from the table.

An instant later, Keever was riveted, too terrified to quiver.

On the spot where the telephone had rested lay a narrow card that spoke its promise of doom!

THAT card resembled those that Balcray and Lysand had received, even to the fact that it was a six spot. But instead of rods or cups, it had rounded spots, resembling coins. One at the top; beneath it a pair, side by side; below, another pair, with a last spot at the bottom.

Keever counted them, all six. His hands relaxed; the telephone dropped from his grasp, to hit the carpet with a dull thump.

"Six"—Keever's tone was the barest whisper. "Six of money—"

His awed tone faded. There was a clicking sound from the telephone receiver; a voice questioning across the wire. Keever did not hear it. His beady eyes were shut; his lips were twitching, voiceless, as his body swayed.

There was another sound that Keever did not hear: the slight scrape of a key in the lock of the apartment door.

While the voice repeated from the telephone receiver, the door opened. A man was standing there, watching Keever; but the angle of the door cut off all light from the watcher's face.

Keever became conscious of the repeating voice from the telephone receiver. He stooped to pick up the telephone. The man at the door stepped quickly into the living room. With back turned, he closed the door, loud enough for Keever to hear it.

Hands dropping the telephone, Keever sprang about. He saw the man inside the doorway; recognized him as he turned around. An instant later, before Keever could make a move, the man was driving for him.

Shoving his thick hands upward to ward off the attack, Keever found his voice, to half shout the name that he had uttered before:

"Legrec!"

If Keever intended more words, they never came. His voice produced a rattly gargle, as fingers clutched his throat. Though he outbulked his opponent, Keever was helpless. Iron fingers whipped his body back and forth like a mongoose lashing a huge snake.

The only expression that came over Keever's face was the bulge of his eyes as they fixed on his enemy's face. There was sight in that stare; but it soon faded. Keever's eyes glazed as his efforts ended. Choking fingers relaxed; Keever collapsed to the floor.

Again death had followed the delivery of a dooming card. This time, the sender of the token had supplied murder in person.

AS coolly as he had slain Keever, the man called Legrec completed other tasks. He had an intuitive skill at keeping his face from the light; for he had revealed it only during those moments of Keever's recognition.

While choking Keever, Legrec had kept his shoulders hunched, turning so that they partially obscured his face. His features were darkish as he stooped beside the telephone, to replace the receiver upon the hook.

That done, Legrec put the telephone on its table, setting it slightly to one side, so that a portion of the death card projected from beneath it. Hand half across his chin, Legrec moved to the corner and hovered over Keever's suitcase.

Finding nothing in the bag that interested him, Legrec sidled along the wall. He reached for the light switch, pressed it, to plunge the room in darkness.

Seconds passed; softly, the murderer opened the door. The fresh air from the hallway was a contrast to the stuffiness of Keever's living room; but that was not why Legrec waited.

He was a calculator, this killer. Death delivered, he chose to linger, to make sure that no sounds of the struggle had been heard. The hallway, like the apartment, was pitch-black; for Legrec had extinguished its lights preparatory to his invasion of Keever's abode.

That was another reason why the murderer waited. If anyone had observed the dousing of the lights; Legrec would soon learn it. He had measures, too, for anyone who might approach this scene too early.

At that moment, Legrec doubted that his precautions would prove necessary. He was to change that opinion within the next few minutes.

Legrec, the master killer, was due for a foray in the dark, against a being whose ways of vengeance were as skillful as Legrec's own modes of murder.

CHAPTER III
DEEDS IN THE DARK

EYES were looking upward from the street in front of the old house. They were weird eyes, like living beings in themselves; for their owner was invisible. He was a shape in the darkness where he stood; and the thick gloom beneath a building wall completely shrouded him.

Only one human watcher could have blended with darkness in that supernal fashion.

The unseen observer was The Shadow.

Master investigator who hunted men of crime, The Shadow frequently looked into the affairs of persons who passed muster with the law. For some reason, he had decided to have an interview with Hastings Keever; and had chosen the Village apartment as the place for it.

Agents of The Shadow had witnessed Keever's return to that abode, and had notified their chief. During the brief interim, however, no one had spotted the arrival of Legrec.

From his vantage point, The Shadow held an angled view of Keever's apartment, situated at the side of the house. He had seen the lights go out, but doubted that it signified Keever's departure.

The promoter had not come to his apartment within the last few days. Chances were that his visit there would not be a short one.

There were various reasons why those lights could have gone out; and on this occasion, The Shadow rejected the correct one. The Shadow had labeled Keever as a gilt-edged crook, whose tricky promotion methods were unsuspected by the law. It followed that Keever would avoid alliances with criminals of a dangerous sort.

Therefore, the extinguishing of the lights seemed to be Keever's own action. The sudden darkness merely spurred The Shadow's plan to pay the man a visit.

Blackness moved from blackness. The trickling glow of a streetlamp showed the outline of a cloaked form, with slouch hat above shrouded shoulders. That fleeting trace was gone; the lights of the little lobby showed it next.

Even there, The Shadow was too obscured to be identified. Only a gliding streak of blackness silhouetted against the wall; then the sight had vanished.

The inside stairway furnished the sort of gloom that The Shadow liked. He was a spectral figure as he neared the third floor. A turn of the stairs produced a flicker from a tiny flashlight; but that blink was not repeated.

The Shadow had discovered that the third floor hall was as dark as Keever's apartment.

That was something that he had not noted from the street; for the hallway's only window was at the back of the building, opening above the roof of a garage, one floor below.

Having discovered the third floor darkness, The Shadow adopted new tactics. He approached through utter darkness, actually picking his way by touch alone.

SOMETHING creaked in the hallway. The Shadow located the sound, some six feet distant. He knew at once that someone was present; whether Keever or another, the sound did not tell. One fact, though, was certain. That mover in the darkness had spotted the blink that The Shadow had given his flashlight, while still on the stairs.

Instantly, The Shadow scented that the person was moving away from Keever's apartment. Lurking, he would wait for proof that The Shadow was bound there. That was why The Shadow chose the very destination that the foe suspected. But in his shift toward the apartment, The Shadow did not make the sounds that Legrec expected.

Absolute silence marked The Shadow's course. When he reached the door, he sensed that no one was close. Moreover, The Shadow's probing hand found something much to his choice.

Legrec, seeking a silent course of his own, had left the door of the apartment open.

It was obvious to The Shadow that he had passed the lurking man; that his adversary, whoever he might be, was somewhere near the stairs, still in listening attitude. Once inside the living room, The Shadow rose silently; found that there was no transom above the door.

With consummate skill, The Shadow closed that door; not the slightest sound betrayed the fact that he had shut it.

The Shadow had scored one on Legrec. In the hallway, the killer still awaited The Shadow's passage. He would be there, later, after The Shadow had finished a quick survey of Keever's apartment.

The tiny flashlight blinked guardedly from the folds of the cloak. The Shadow found Keever's body. He saw the telephone; the card that edged from beneath it. That identified Keever's killer.

The Shadow had heard of these tokens of Legrec.

The newspaper lay beside the radio. There, The Shadow saw a chart that listed stations according to Keever's dial. Legrec had left the radio as Keever had tuned it. The Shadow knew that the dead man had listened to WNX.

That gave The Shadow a partial sequence of Keever's own thoughts. The promoter had been interested in the affairs of someone who had died when the plane crashed.

While coming here by taxi, The Shadow had been listening to the radio news. He had heard the flash from WNX. He recognized the possible link between two previous deaths. There was a chance—a strong one—that both concerned Keever.

That happened to be something for future study. Right now, The Shadow was thinking of a murderer.

Gautier Legrec!

Such was the name of a celebrated international crook, almost unknown in annals of American crime, but whose death tokens were famed in foreign lands. A killer extraordinary, who used hidden methods of assassination but who could supply quick strokes, in person, when occasion called.

He was canny, Legrec. When he staged crime, it broke suddenly, leaving the police at a loss. While they still hunted for Legrec, and guessed where he might be, Legrec was gone.

Such swift vanishes explained why The Shadow had never before crossed Legrec's actual trail. Though The Shadow moved everywhere to strike down crime, he had never been in any foreign capitals at the times when Legrec had bobbed up in those cities.

There was much, therefore, that The Shadow had to learn about Legrec; but circumstances had suddenly reversed the situation. For once, The Shadow was where Legrec happened to be.

The supercrook, lurking outside Keever's apartment, was within The Shadow's immediate reach!

THERE were no more blinks from The Shadow's flashlight. A gloved hand gripped the doorknob; silently, the barrier opened.

A few seconds later, The Shadow was creeping through the dark hall, moving foot by foot toward the stairway where Legrec still lurked.

A creak answered The Shadow's advance. Grimly, The Shadow analyzed its cause. It did not mean that Legrec had heard a sound denoting The Shadow's presence. Legrec had simply guessed that the black-cloaked hunter had arrived. To a smart crook like Legrec, absence of telltale sounds meant The Shadow.

The stairs offered a sure outlet; but Legrec wasn't using them. The Shadow heard the creaks continue, back along the hall. There was the scrape of a rising window; but the darkness was sufficient to hide the man himself.

Timing his actions, The Shadow made sure of the moment when Legrec dropped to the roof below. With a sweeping stride, The Shadow reached the window itself.

Below lay darkness; beyond that stretch, the city's lights showed an expanse of the garage roof. In choosing that outlet, Legrec had trapped himself. He was safe, so long as he remained in the darkened fringe. He could not risk a trip beyond it.

To any hunter but The Shadow, that would have brought elation. From this window, he held absolute control. Mere vigil would bring success, even if it meant a wait until daybreak. No window lay below for Legrec to enter. Every portion of the roof edge was light enough to betray a man who moved there.

It was that very situation that made The Shadow understand why Legrec had chosen the window as an outlet.

The crook *wanted* The Shadow to stay at that hallway window. Why?

There was only one answer. Something, apart from either The Shadow or Legrec, would reverse the situation. It was The Shadow—not Legrec—who would meet disaster before this game of hide-and-seek had ended, provided that The Shadow kept up the vigil, as Legrec hoped.

Through The Shadow's mind flashed recollections of those previous murders; one camouflaged as an airplane crash, the other as an elevator fall.

Some similar catastrophe was planned to cover the fact that Legrec had strangled Keever!

THE SHADOW moved back from the window. He didn't have to stay there, to deceive Legrec. Lurking in the shelter of the house wall, the criminal was taking it for granted that The Shadow was watching from above.

Reaching the door of "3C," The Shadow listened. That was the apartment just in back of Keever's, the nearest trouble spot to where the dead man lay.

Hearing nothing, The Shadow used a tiny picklike instrument to probe the door's lock. The pointed metal encountered a plug of wadded paper.

With a plierlike instrument, The Shadow pulled the wadding loose. Through the keyhole he caught the flicker of faint light, like a wavering flame. The sound of a faint hiss came from the empty apartment; with it, the odor of gas.

Legrec had prepared for Keever's return. He had turned on the gas in the next apartment, and had left the pilot light aglow. At this very moment, the lurking crook was huddled in safety, waiting for results.

There might be time for The Shadow to use a scant few minutes, to circle around and invade Legrec's hiding place from an unexpected direction. That prospect, however, was not the reason why The Shadow made a swift dive for the stairway. He was considering the chance that perhaps those few minutes did not remain to him.

The Shadow's speed was wise. He reached the stairs, took them with a downward stride, caring nothing for the sounds he made. Before he reached the second floor, the clatter of his descent was drowned by noise above.

There was a choking roar; a mammoth sigh, as though the whole third floor had drawn in a mighty breath. Prompt upon that titanic cough came a terrific blast that shook the whole building.

Walls buckled against the strain; then crashed inward. Partitions shattered; there was a smashing roar as the roof collapsed. Keever's apartment, like the whole third floor, was buried under tons of debris.

Fissures opened in the second floor ceiling, as The Shadow sped beneath it. He was on the first floor when chunks of masonry clattered through. Reaching the sidewalk, The Shadow pressed against the front wall, while stones from the cornice pounded near him.

Crashes ended. Faces appeared at windows of the lower floors. Apartment dwellers saw that they could descend in safety; but they did not spy The Shadow. He was gone, through a space below the battered windows along the side of the apartment, picking his way along a stone-strewn path, to reach Legrec.

Scaling a corner of the garage in the rear, The Shadow looked across the edge. Flames from the third floor of the apartment house threw a glare upon the space where Legrec had lurked. Only wreckage lay there—too far from the house wall to have buried the killer beneath it.

The murderer had fled quickly to safety before The Shadow could reach him, leaving no trace of his course. Nevertheless, a sinister laugh throbbed from the cloaked pursuer.

The Shadow still knew a way whereby he might find Legrec, before this night was ended.

CHAPTER IV
LINKED TRAILS

"LEGREC!"

The name came in a whisper from a girl's strained lips. It seemed mysterious, that name, as Eleanor Margale uttered it. Her voice was like an echo, in that alcove beside the hallway stairs.

The echo of a dying man's cry!

Eleanor stared about her. The scene was somber, yet very real. She was in her uncle's home; there, beside her, was the telephone that she had answered only a short while ago.

In response to her queries across the wire had come nothing but that one word: "Legrec!"

Who had called; and why?

Eleanor could not answer either question. The receiver had clicked shortly after she had heard the voice. Since then, she had been standing here gripped by one horrible impression.

Whoever had screamed that lone name, had been face to face with doom. Only total despair could have produced the tone that Eleanor had heard.

More than temporary strain was shown on Eleanor's face. She was a girl of marked beauty; her well-formed features and dark eyes were exquisite, outlined against her brunette hair. But even the soft light of the hallway betrayed the thinness of her cheeks; the lines that wrinkled her otherwise attractive forehead.

Some long-nourished worry was responsible. The girl's nerves were ready for a break.

Eleanor realized that fact, herself, when she stared at the big grandfather's clock. She couldn't believe, at first, that she had been standing here for twenty minutes. For a moment, she felt terrified; then her wits returned.

This was the time when something must be done. That voice over the wire was proof, at last, that matters were wrong in this household. Steadily, Eleanor reviewed events that had come before tonight.

HER uncle, Thomas Margale, had always been eccentric; but in a harmless way. He seemed to live in spurts; first seeking money, then spending it. Oddly, that energy had worked to his advantage, for he had acquired a large store of wealth. It was a well-known fact that Thomas Margale was worth several million dollars.

Six months ago, Eleanor believed that her uncle had outlived his thirst for wealth. He had gone abroad, for a longer trip than ever before. He had seemed in fine spirits when he returned from his vacation on the French Riviera.

A few short weeks had changed his mood—much to the concern of both Eleanor and Nordham, the personal servant who always traveled with Thomas Margale.

Ill health had been Margale's first worry. He had summoned physicians; they had found nothing wrong with him. Eleanor remembered that the verdict had angered her uncle. Since then, he had refused to see all doctors, but he would not admit that he was well again.

Margale had decided that he would cure his illness by forgetting it; and he had chosen business enterprises as the right way to occupy his mind. With that policy, Margale had become secretive. He secluded himself in his downstairs study, days at a time, visited only by Nordham, who carried in meals.

There had been visitors to the house; Eleanor had never met them. Her uncle insisted that she remain upstairs. He had not even allowed Nordham to answer the door when those visitors were expected. That task had been left to another servant, who had later been discharged.

Since then, Thomas Margale had received occasional telephone calls. Nordham answered them; but names were never mentioned over the wire. Eleanor knew that because she had questioned Nordham, only to find that the servant was as puzzled as herself.

Tonight's call produced new mystery. Eleanor was confident that the man on the wire had sought to reach her uncle. It chanced that Thomas Margale had gone out for a walk, taking Nordham with him. That was the only reason why Eleanor had answered the telephone.

Legrec. The name was French; it might link with her uncle's last trip to France. There was no way to find a clue in the study; not only was it locked, but Eleanor's uncle kept all documents in a big safe.

The thought of prying into such matters did not trouble Eleanor. It was time, she felt, that something should be done about Margale's affairs.

Eleanor, herself, was entitled to

some consideration. Her uncle had kept her almost a prisoner in this forgotten mansion, behind its big wall. Outside was a secluded Manhattan avenue; but Eleanor could see little of it, even from her upstairs room.

ELEANOR was tapping the telephone table. She suddenly observed the drawer, remembered that her uncle made calls from here, as well as from his study. She opened the drawer, plucked out the papers that she found there.

None were important, until Eleanor discovered a scrawled sheet in her uncle's handwriting. All that it bore was an address on Twentieth Street, with a telephone number.

Hurriedly replacing the papers, Eleanor dialed the number. There was a response from the operator, stating that the telephone had been disconnected. That proved that the mystery call had not come from that telephone; but the fact merely centered Eleanor's interest upon the address.

The girl started to close the table drawer. She left it, not quite shut, when she heard the front door open. Moving to the stairway, she halted there, just as a stocky, middle-aged man entered. The arrival was Nordham; Eleanor was relieved when she saw that her uncle was not with the servant.

"Where is Uncle Thomas?" questioned Eleanor.

"He went to the club, Miss Margale," replied the servant. "I left him there, an hour ago; but I supposed that he would be back by this time. I really believe"—Nordham's tone was a pleased one—"that your uncle is feeling better, Miss Margale."

"I hope he is," assured Eleanor. Then, briskly: "When he returns, Nordham, tell him that I have gone out."

Nordham looked troubled.

"I know he won't like it," added Eleanor, "but I'll leave it to you to humor him, Nordham."

"I shall do my best, Miss Margale."

Eleanor hurried up to her room; she gathered hat and coat. Coming back to the head of the stairs, she saw Nordham in the hall below. The servant gave a gesture, waving her back to her room. Instead, Eleanor remained out of sight at the top of the stairs.

Again the front door had opened. From between the banister rails, Eleanor saw her uncle. Despite Nordham's good report, Eleanor could not feel that his condition had improved.

Tall, thin of build, Thomas Margale looked spry for a man of sixty; but he offset that by his low crouch, the faltering way in which he relied on his big cane. His face was haggard, sharp pointed like a vulture's, and as gray in hue as the thin hair that topped it.

His eyes, at least, were active, but they had an ugly, suspicious glare that Eleanor had never noticed until recently. She sensed, from the fierceness of his gaze, that he was looking for her. His words proved that she was right.

"Where is Eleanor?" demanded Margale, in a savage, high-keyed rasp. "Has she gone out, against my orders?"

"Miss Eleanor is upstairs, sir," returned Nordham, mildly. "Shall I summon her to the study?"

"To the study?" snarled Margale. "Bah! Do you think I would be fool enough to allow anyone in there? Nordham"—the gray-haired man had stopped by the telephone table, and was wagging his cane—"Nordham, the girl has tricked us! I tell you, she has gone out!"

ELEANOR waited no longer. Since her uncle chose to think that she was missing, he could find her gone. She hurried away from the front stairs, headed down a rear flight toward the kitchen.

There was a side door to the house, but it was always locked. The best route would be the back door.

As Eleanor descended the back way, she heard footsteps pounding up the front stairs. She thought they must be Nordham's, until she heard her uncle, shouting from above:

"She's gone, Nordham! I told you she was gone! You must find her, at once, wherever she is! Bring her back here, Nordham!"

There was a response from the servant, Eleanor could hear the muffled tone, as Nordham called upstairs from the front hall. He was promising that he would do as Margale ordered.

No servants were in the kitchen. Eleanor hurried through the back door, reached the gate in the rear wall. She breathed better in the darkness of the rear street.

There was an apartment house half a block away, taxicabs in front of it. Making for the nearest one, Eleanor stepped into it and gave the address that she had seen upon the paper scrawled with her uncle's handwriting.

As she rode, Eleanor promised herself that she would soon return to her uncle's mansion. Not because he wanted her there, but on account of Nordham. The servant was too good a friend; she could not let him be blamed for her temporary flight.

An hour from now, Margale's rage would be abated; and Nordham would be a buffer, if needed. Meanwhile, Eleanor was determined to complete this trip, even though it might lead to nothing. It was, at least, her only clue to the mysterious Legrec—who might be the person responsible for her uncle's strange behavior.

Legrec! It was strange how the name repeated itself in Eleanor's mind. Stranger, though, would be the experiences that she would encounter through trying to find the man himself.

In seeking her present quest, Eleanor Margale had linked herself with a trail that promised doom to anyone who crossed it!

CHAPTER V
SNARE OF STEEL

THE house on Twentieth Street looked old and deserted. Remembering that the telephone had been disconnected, Eleanor supposed that it must be empty. The cabby thought the same; he waited, expecting that his passenger would go elsewhere.

Instead, Eleanor suddenly dismissed the cab. She waited until it had turned the corner; then, after a quick look along the street, Eleanor approached a basement door that stood half-hidden beneath the high front steps.

It had occurred to her that an empty house could furnish more evidence than an occupied one; particularly if the former tenants had left some of their belongings.

She realized that entering the place might be a form of burglary; but that did not worry her, since her purpose was not a criminal one. Eleanor's chief concern was the basement door. She wondered if she could manage to force it open.

It occurred to her to try the knob. The door swung inward, almost at touch. The house was unlocked!

Inside, with the door closed, Eleanor encountered a new handicap. She had not foreseen that she might need a flashlight; hence she was forced to rely on a few matches that she had brought with her.

It took her some time to pick her way through the basement. None of the rooms were furnished, but a stairway gave a route to the floor above.

Matters were better on the ground floor. A street lamp furnished a vague light through dusty windows. By that glow, Eleanor saw vacant rooms. They spoke of complete desertion, but the emptiness gave Eleanor confidence. She decided that she could search further, without chance of interruption.

Again a stairway. Eleanor ascended to the second floor, pausing whenever a step creaked. Those sounds were magnified within the empty walls; the girl gave a relieved sigh when she reached the hall above.

Then, in a flash, her nerves were taut again.

Eleanor had thought that she heard a sound from far below, like the thrusting of a rusted bolt.

Could someone have locked the door by which she entered?

Eleanor listened; she fancied creaks coming upward, like the echoes of her own tread. She pictured someone creeping from basement to first floor.

Flight was Eleanor's first instinct. Reason intervened. If those sounds were real, they meant that her path was cut off. If imaginary, there was no cause for alarm. In either event, her lone policy was to remain where she was, until she learned more.

A truck rolled along the front street. Its rumble gave Eleanor comfort, until she realized that the noise might have drowned other sounds. A hush returned, so deep that Eleanor could hear the ticking of her tiny wristwatch. There was no sound from the hallway below. Eleanor smiled at her own fears.

Lighting another match, she found the door of a second floor room. Faint light from windows showed new vacancy.

Following the hall, Eleanor found more doors, all open, their rooms deserted. She passed a narrow rear stairway, reached the end of the hall.

There, Eleanor encountered the first closed door. It was unlike the others, for its knob was brass. The metal reflected the gleam of a dying match. With darkness, Eleanor decided to learn what lay beyond that barrier.

She tried the knob; it yielded. A moment later, the girl halted in alarm. Light filtered through the open space. The glow, though mild, did not come from a window.

The room, itself, was lighted!

PEERING inward, Eleanor saw a squarish room. It was oak paneled; furnished like a study. She saw a desk patterned of that same rich wood. There were chairs; a couch in the corner.

The rear of the room had a small reading nook, that projected deep between the ends of two bookcases.

The ceiling of the nook was low. There was a table in the tiny space, set with a chessboard; on each side were chairs, as if awaiting absent players.

There was no one in the room. Eleanor entered, closing the door softly behind her. Curiosity had replaced her dread. There was nothing ominous about this cozy room, with its tasteful decorations. It was amazing, though, to find such a place in an otherwise unfurnished house.

Something else, too, was cause for perplexity; although it did not strike Eleanor at first. As she looked about the room, she observed that it had no windows.

A feeling of oppressiveness seized Eleanor. She wanted to get away from the scene, but her natural curiosity would not let her. There, on the desk, was the telephone with the very number that she had tried to call.

Perhaps, in that desk, as in the telephone table at her uncle's home, she might find some clue more valuable than the one that brought her here.

A link, perhaps, to Legrec!

Eleanor tried the desk drawers. They were locked. She looked toward the nook, saw a drawer in the chess table. She went there; the drawer clattered when she opened it. Its only contents were the discarded chessmen of an old set.

Mechanically, Eleanor pushed the drawer shut. She heard the muffled roll of the chess pieces; next, she was conscious of a sound from another quarter. Alarmed, she turned toward the door that she had entered.

Eleanor was no longer alone.

Within the portal, the girl saw a curious being, whose very appearance gave her a tingle of alarm. He was slender, crouchy like her uncle; but his almost crablike pose made it impossible to gauge his height.

His slippers and smoking jacket marked him as the owner of this isolated room; but Eleanor scarcely noted the man's attire. It was his face that held her gaze.

That countenance was smooth as parchment, so dry, that it seemed but a mask fitted over a face beneath. Lips had a dry smile; eyes were sharp, unblinking. The broad, smooth forehead was topped by a shock of pure white hair, so plentiful that it might have been a wig.

Eleanor could not account for the mingled impressions that seized her. They seemed to be produced by the varied expressions in the eyes that watched her. One moment, they were fierce; an instant later, kindly.

THE girl tried to speak. Her voice was a stammer. Those sharp eyes ferreted out her thoughts. Dried lips crackled a harsh question:

"Why have you come here?"

Eleanor suppressed an answer.

"You seek someone"—the dry voice chuckled—"but you are afraid to speak his name. Ah! I am right!"

The crouched shoulders straightened partially. The shock-haired man advanced, raising one clawish hand in friendly gesture. His voice, his manner, had taken on a kindliness. Eleanor's bravery returned.

"Yes," she admitted, "I am looking for someone. A man who is called Legrec—"

Eleanor paused. This time, *her* eyes had the keenness. The old man's gaze was dulled. He shook his head, almost piteously.

"Legrec?" he questioned, sadly. "No. I have never heard that name." Then, with a proud gleam in his eyes, he pointed toward himself, to ask: "You know who I am?"

Eleanor shook her head. Dried lips crackled a half-pleased laugh. As if talking to himself, the old man added:

"You have never heard of Rupert Roban!"

He reached the chess table, seated himself there. With a wave, he invited Eleanor to take the chair opposite.

The girl sat down, wondering if the old man's name was really Rupert Roban; if so, just why she should have heard of him.

"I can trust you?"

Roban tilted his head as he spoke the question. Eleanor nodded. Chances were that the old man was a half-crazed recluse. Her best course was to humor him.

"Very well," smiled Roban. "I am a counterfeiter, and a clever one. Too clever to copy money, because my very skill would betray me. That is why I followed the advice of"—he paused, his eyes gleaming shrewdly—"of a man whose name I have sworn not to reveal.

"I manufacture bonds, instead of money. Why not? The market is always good. Particularly when one has a friend who knows how to dispose of them."

Roban arose, but gestured for Eleanor to remain seated. He stepped out into the room, began to tap the walls. Eleanor heard metal ring beneath his knuckles.

"They look like oak," chortled Roban. "Actually, they are steel. Would your friend Legrec"—he spoke the name with emphasis—"think of such a clever plan? Watch!"

Spryly, he stepped to the door, pressed a spot along the wall. A steel barrier slithered shut on the room side of the wooden door. It made another panel to the room, closing the only visible exit.

"That is not all." Roban approached the little nook. "It happens that I have removed my equipment; otherwise, you would see it there"—he pointed to the chess table. "This little space"—he stepped into the nook—"is an elevator, contrived to sink into the floor, between thick walls below.

"There, I could bury all evidence where it would never be found. Moreover, when this tiny alcove sinks it gives me a new exit. Above the steel ceiling"—Roban pointed a bony finger upward—"is a trapdoor to the roof. I can leave through it while invaders storm this room."

He eyed Eleanor as though expecting comment. The girl spoke humoring words.

"It is very clever," she agreed. "I am glad, however, that you have removed your equipment—"

Roban clucked an interruption: "My equipment, yes. But not all evidence."

Puzzled, Eleanor looked at the chessboard. She pointed to the chessmen, as she questioned:

"You mean these?"

"I mean you!" Roban screeched the words. "You are evidence! You can speak! That is why you came here: to learn all you could. So I told you everything"—his laugh was maddened—"because you never shall repeat it!"

BEFORE Eleanor could reach her feet, Roban seized the chess table and flung it from the nook. The girl sprang from her chair while the table was clattering; but the crazed man was too swift for her.

Seizing the other chair, Roban swung it viciously. Eleanor warded off the blow, but sprawled to the inner wall of the alcove doing so.

Hurling the chair out into the room, Roban grabbed the one that Eleanor had used; he made another fierce sweep, as the girl tried to rise.

Eleanor put her arms before her eyes

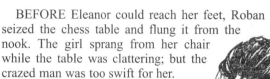

He grabbed the chair, made another fierce sweep as the girl tried to rise.

as the chair swished past. When she peered over her elbow, Roban was gone from the nook carrying the last chair with him. He whipped a pair of books from a bookcase, shoved his hand deep against the wall.

A steel door slid across the mouth of the little alcove, drowning Roban's shrill laugh. Frantically, Eleanor reached the barrier, to beat against it. Her pounding was useless. If Roban heard it, the sound merely sped him to his next deed.

Eleanor heard a muffled *click*. The floor began to sink, carrying walls and ceiling with it. There were four walls—not merely three—for the new barrier was descending with the others.

Rupert Roban was making good his boast. He was burying the evidence that might betray him, caring little that his deed was another human's doom!

CHAPTER VI
VANISHED EVIDENCE

TERRIFIED by her plight, Eleanor Margale was no longer thinking of Rupert Roban, the crazed man from whom she could expect no aid. Roban, in his turn, had forgotten Eleanor. As soon as the sealed nook had begun its downward glide, the white-haired inventor had flung himself to hands and knees.

In the middle of his study, he was fondly gathering the scattered chessmen, packing them away in a box that he drew from the desk. He muttered gleefully, while the faint rumble of a mechanism marked Eleanor's journey to the thick-walled space below.

The rumble ceased. Roban noted it as he placed the last chessman in the box. Pushing the sliding cover into place, he came to his feet. His eyes were raised upward, as he turned to look at the ceiling above the alcove.

New walls were visible; the top of the secret elevator had formed another floor. There was a new ceiling, too; but it was higher than the other. In it was the trapdoor that Roban had mentioned.

Clutching the box of chessmen with one hand, Roban reached for a bookcase to draw its shelves into the alcove, where they would serve him as a ladder. His gaze came downward, and stopped.

The amazement on Roban's face was similar to Eleanor's expression when the old man had first stepped into the study.

Like the girl whom he had sentenced to doom, Roban was faced by an unexpected intruder.

A being in black stood in the new-formed alcove. Roban saw a cloaked form, burning eyes beneath the brim of a slouch hat. He spied the yawning muzzle of an automatic, that bulged a threat of prompt disaster.

Like others steeped in crime, Roban recognized that figure. The counterfeiter pronounced himself a deep-dyed crook, as he gulped the name:
"The Shadow!"

A SINISTER, taunting laugh whispered its answer. Roban edged backward, whining a plea.

"I've done nothing! Nothing, I tell you, in all the years that I have been away—"

"Until you met Hastings Keever," interposed The Shadow. "That much might be true, Roban."

Wild alarm showed in Roban's eyes. It faded, a moment later. His gaze became shrewd.

"Keever never talked," sneered the counterfeiter. "He would never talk—not even to you, The Shadow."

"Keever is dead!"

Surprise spread over Roban's dryish face, evidenced chiefly by the dropping of his jaw. It meant nothing, for the shock-haired crook could counterfeit emotions as cleverly as bonds.

The Shadow watched the old man's expression. Roban's teeth clicked shut; his lips tightened. He changed the subject, speaking through gritted teeth.

"You were always clever," he told The Shadow. "Yet you never found me, through all these years. It took a blunderer like Keever to bring you here.

"Since Keever is dead"—Roban's lips relaxed, his tone became glib—"we have no quarrel. This room"—the old man shrugged—"was merely a device that I designed to while away my time.

"I thought it proof against intruders, but I was wrong. You have done me a service, by demonstrating that my upper exit was a weak spot, that could be used for entrance also. Fancy it!" Roban chuckled heartily. "I bring down the ceiling—and with it comes The Shadow!"

THE SHADOW was eyeing Roban steadily. The old man was playing his best game: that of a crazed inventor. It worked with others, but not with The Shadow. Roban was hiding something deeper than whatever deal he had made with Keever.

"Look!" Roban stepped across the room. "This is my regular entrance." He pressed the switch; the front panel glided open. "The way is clear, when you choose to use it.

"Meanwhile"—Roban came back, placed the box of chessmen on the table—"shall we match our wits in a friendly contest? A game of chess—there, in the little nook where I always play?"

Roban's smile faded when The Shadow did not answer. The schemer had overplayed his hand. His mention of the nook was the very clue The Shadow awaited. It gave away the spot that Roban wanted his visitor to ignore.

Stepping straight toward Roban, The Shadow thrust his automatic closer. He hissed the command:

"Press the other switch!"

Roban hesitated; crafty though his eyes were, they gave his thoughts away, with their dart toward the bookcase.

The Shadow moved backward; he shot a sidelong glance to the right spot. He reached into the space, felt two switches. He pressed one.

There was no motion from the alcove. The Shadow threw the other switch. Machinery rumbled. Stepping to the center of the study, The Shadow kept Roban covered while he watched the elevator rise.

Roban's fingers clawed the box of chessmen. He knew that the front of the sealed room was open, thanks to the switch that The Shadow had pressed first. He expected to hear Eleanor's voice, denouncing him; instead, there was silence, until the original alcove came into place.

Then Roban heard The Shadow's laugh, grim and mirthless. It threatened ill to Roban; the old man saw why, when The Shadow stepped into the nook. On the floor lay Eleanor; the girl was motionless.

"She can't be dead!" insisted Roban. "She was unhurt when I trapped her! No, no—she can't be dead!"

Roban was thinking of his own hide, when he screeched those words; but his tone was filled with remorse. It broke into sobs of relief, when The Shadow raised Eleanor's head and Roban saw the girl's eyes open.

For once, Roban's emotion seemed sincere. The counterfeiter's face was buried in his scrawny hands. For the moment, The Shadow forgot Roban, because of Eleanor. It was the break that Roban wanted.

With a sudden twisting leap, the crook sprang for the door; he yanked it open, started to dive for the hallway. The Shadow aimed an automatic, to cut off Roban's flight. One bullet, sizzling past that shock of white hair, would be enough to frighten Roban into a prompt halt.

ROBAN'S high-cackled shout, given as he dived, was the cause that changed The Shadow's plan. With a quick sweep, The Shadow whipped Eleanor from the tiny elevator, pushed her to safety past the desk in the corner. Wheeling, he reached the edge of the door through which Roban had gone.

From the door edge, The Shadow's automatic tongued its answer.

Guns spurted from the hallway: a response to Roban's command. It was lucky that The Shadow had recognized the cry's significance. For the first time in his curious career of crime, Roban was provided with a crew of gunmen. Through overzeal, he had given the fact away.

Whining slugs slammed the steel walls of Roban's study. The counterfeiter was below that line of fire, continuing his dive down the back stairs. Marksmen were snarling their anger, because The Shadow had been too quick for them. They were due for another demonstration of his speed.

From the door edge, The Shadow's automatic tongued its answer. He wasn't taking pot shots, like the thugs in the front hallway. Revolver spurts were his targets; his bullets winged the foemen who used those telltale guns.

There were howls as the .45 slugs hit home. Clipped gunmen staggered for the front stairway, went thudding downward, with their pals scrambling after them. The Shadow reached the hallway; his laugh was a fierce, strident challenge to all comers.

Downstairs, crooks were rallying for new battle. The Shadow could hear Roban's high-screamed call.

Stepping back into the study, The Shadow pressed the switch to send the alcove downward. He knew that Roban would hear the rumble, telling that the exit to the roof had opened.

Beckoning to Eleanor, The Shadow moved out to the hallway. The girl had recovered; she followed. Blinking a flashlight, The Shadow led the way down the back stairs. The rear of the first floor was deserted. Roban and his band had hurried out to cut off the route across the roof.

The Shadow handed Eleanor his flashlight, whispering a quick order:

"Through to the rear street—four flashes of the light—take the cab that comes from the corner."

Eleanor was away. Behind her, she heard The Shadow's laugh tone eerily from darkness. Shouts answered from the roof; then gunfire. Crooks had taken The Shadow's bait. They were shooting, hopelessly, into the lower darkness, making themselves new targets for The Shadow.

Meanwhile, Eleanor's flight was covered.

The girl reached the next street. She paused to blink the flashlight; before her finger pressed it, she saw a cab parked near by. Mistaking it for the one

There were howls as the .45 slugs hit home.

mentioned by The Shadow, Eleanor started toward it.

A stocky man sprang out to seize her. Eleanor tried to wrench away, then recognized his voice. The man was Nordham; he hurried her into the cab.

The servant told the cabby to get started; the fellow hesitated, until he heard Eleanor's assurance:

"It's all right, driver. This man is my friend."

RIDING back to the mansion, Eleanor whispered her story to Nordham, in a low tone that the cabby could not hear. The servant gasped bewilderment, when he heard it.

"It was fortunate that I followed you promptly," he declared. "I saw your cab drive away; this man's cab was next in line. I asked where you had gone. He had heard you say 'Twentieth Street'; so we rode along there. We were coming back when we heard the gunfire."

Eleanor nodded gratefully; then questioned in worried tone:

"What does it all mean, Nordham? What connection is there between my uncle and this madman, Roban? And who can Legrec be?"

"I don't know, Miss Margale," replied Nordham. "I, too, have puzzled over your uncle's strange behavior. What is most important is that he learn nothing of tonight's occurrence."

Eleanor agreed. She and Nordham decided to tell her uncle that she had come back alone, by cab; that the servant had met her at the corner. That settled, they rode along in silence. All the while, Eleanor was wondering how The Shadow had fared in final battle.

It happened that The Shadow, in another cab, was thinking about Eleanor at that moment. Crooks had scattered before his devastating fire, and Roban had escaped with them. Departing, The Shadow had found his own cab, still at the corner.

The driver, Moe Shrevnitz—one of The Shadow's own agents—had seen no flashlight signal; but he remembered that a cruising cab had paused, apparently to pick up a passenger. That satisfied The Shadow regarding Eleanor's safety.

It told him nothing, however, of the girl's identity; how she had crossed the trail that The Shadow had hoped would lead him to Legrec. She was a new mystery in the case.

Though The Shadow had saved Eleanor Margale from doom, the girl remained the very factor that Rupert Roban had termed her.

Eleanor Margale was vanished evidence.

CHAPTER VII
THE LAW'S LEAD

EARLY the next evening, a contented man was seated at a table in the grillroom of the exclusive Cobalt Club. He had finished a hearty meal; he was chuckling over the headlines of the latest newspapers.

The pleased man was Ralph Weston, New York City's police commissioner. Usually, his mustached military face was dour when crime was on the rampage. Not so tonight.

It happened that the newspapers had little to say regarding crime. They carried reports of accidents, yesterday: an airplane crash, an elevator fall, an explosion in Greenwich Village. The only account that involved the police was the story of a gunfight on Twentieth Street.

There, the law had invaded an old house, to find a steel-walled room that looked like a pillbox. Apparently it was the hideout of some jittery mob leader, who had fled when attacked by rivals. A trapdoor in the ceiling proved how the unknown big shot had escaped.

Weston concentrated on the accident reports. He folded the newspaper, reached into his pocket and drew out a telegram. He read the message on the yellow paper, put it away again.

A streak of blackness stretched across the table; for the moment, it formed a hawkish silhouette. The shaded image slid away as Weston looked up, to see a tall personage standing beside him. There was something placid in the face that Weston recognized; with it, a leisurely air.

Eyes gazing mildly from each side of an aquiline nose added to the masklike expression of those features. The commissioner, however, was familiar with that countenance. The arrival was his friend and fellow club member, Lamont Cranston.

"Sit down, Cranston," invited Weston. "Tell me"—his tone became serious—"what do you think of this wave of recent accidents?"

"Quite extraordinary." Cranston's reply was quiet, even-toned. "But purely from the standpoint of coincidence."

Weston turned his head to suppress a smile. Cranston had simply repeated the newspaper theory. His glance averted, the commissioner failed to observe the momentary glow that came to Cranston's eyes.

They were the eyes of The Shadow.

The guise of Cranston was simply one that The Shadow chose on certain occasions, particularly when he wanted to learn what the police were about. There was a real Cranston, a millionaire globetrotter, who was at present trekking across the South African veldt. When the actual Cranston was faraway, The Shadow doubled for him.

There was a reason for The Shadow's revealing gaze. He had seen the telegram that Weston had stowed away. Though he had gained no chance to read the message, The Shadow connected it with the accidents that the commissioner had mentioned.

"CURIOUS, those accidents," observed The Shadow. His eyes, like his tone, had become Cranston's. "I wonder—"

He paused, slowly shaking his head. Weston became alert, put a quick question:

"You wonder if anything lay in back of them?"

A nod from Cranston. Weston inquired why. Pointing to the newspaper, The Shadow remarked:

"That trouble on Twentieth Street, happening so soon afterward. There might be a connection, Commissioner."

"You are miles wide, Cranston," laughed Weston. "That gun fray was a horse of a different sort. Tell me, though"—Weston's tone was brisk— "what gave you the idea in the first place? Something must have inspired it."

A solemn expression set itself upon Cranston's lips, as he spoke:

"I knew all three men, quite well. Balcray, Lysand, Keever—it seems incredible that those friends should have perished, separately, within the space of a few hours."

It never occurred to Weston that Cranston had totally reversed his original statement. Everything that The Shadow said had been based upon his observation of the commissioner. He knew that Weston had a habit of forgetting casual statements, when he heard more pointed ones.

"You're the man I've wanted to talk to, Cranston!" asserted Weston, eagerly. "Someone acquainted with all three of those victims."

Cranston seemed disinterested. He was rising from the table. The commissioner gripped his arm.

"Don't you understand?" insisted Weston. "Those deaths *were* crimes, perpetrated by the same murderer. They are linked; but we have to learn why those victims were chosen."

Cranston showed bewilderment. "But the newspapers say nothing, Commissioner—"

"Because they know nothing!" snapped Weston. "Cranston, we are on the trail of a supercriminal; one whose arrival we anticipated. We were watching for something, and we found it. For once"—the commissioner's smile showed grim satisfaction—"we managed to keep that detail from the newspapers."

There was interest in Cranston's eyes: the sort that generally inspired Weston to further statements. On this occasion, however, Weston suddenly dropped the subject.

"Where can I reach you later?" he questioned, abruptly. "Say, in about an hour? Will you be back here, at the club?"

"I can call here."

"Very well. There is someone—rather, there is something—that I shall want to talk to you about. I am expecting more information that will aid our discussion."

STROLLING out through the foyer of the club, Lamont Cranston encountered a stocky-built man who entered. He nodded, as he recognized the arrival's swarthy face. The man was Inspector Joe Cardona, Weston's ace investigator.

Cardona was coming to hold conference with the commissioner; but he was not the person that Weston had begun to mention. The Shadow had already linked another party with the case: someone who had sent the commissioner that precious telegram.

An hour's interval did not annoy The Shadow. He needed it to build up the bluff that he had made to Weston. Except for Keever, The Shadow had been totally unacquainted with the men who had died in yesterday's so-called accidents.

Today, however, The Shadow's agents had been on the job, gathering all available data that concerned the three dead men. There would be reports, accessible to The Shadow when he needed them. From those, The Shadow could gain enough information to establish his pretext.

Meanwhile, Cardona had joined Weston in the grill-room. The ace pulled a sheaf of papers from his pocket, thwacked them on the table.

"No luck," gruffed the inspector. "We can't hook up those three deaths, so far as the victims were concerned. All we know is that Legrec staged them."

"Which is quite enough," assured Weston.

"I don't see it that way, Commissioner," returned Cardona, bluntly. "Here's the original flyer, that came in weeks ago, from England. Scotland Yard tipped us off that Gautier Legrec was supposed to have headed here. But they gave us no description of the fellow."

"Except his habit of placing death cards with his victims."

"That's his method, Commissioner. It doesn't give us a line on Legrec himself. As far as I know, nobody knows much about Legrec."

"No one except Alan Rigby."

For a moment, Cardona looked enthused, then his expression faded.

"Rigby could help us," he admitted. "I remember him from a few years back, before this Legrec business ever started. He's an ace in his line—the best of private investigators. I used to wonder what had become of Rigby, until I learned that he was chasing Legrec.

"But where is Rigby? Scotland Yard said that Legrec had started for New York. That meant that Rigby ought to have followed. But he didn't. We've been expecting him on every boat, and he hasn't shown up yet."

WITH a smile, Weston produced the telegram. Cardona eyed the paper with interest; but Weston paused before unfolding it.

"Had it occurred to you, Cardona," questioned the commissioner, "that Legrec might have foreseen trouble in entering the United States?"

"It hadn't," admitted Cardona, "but it makes sense."

"Very well. May I remark, also, that Legrec is a Frenchman?"

"His name sounds French, but it may be phony."

"At least, Cardona, you will concede that Legrec is conversant with the French language; that he could probably pass himself as a Frenchman?"

"I'll grant that, Commissioner."

Weston spread the telegram, handed it to Cardona with the comment:

"That is why Legrec may have entered the United States by way of Montreal. That city has a large French population. Legrec could find Montreal an ideal stopping place. In fact, he probably did stay over at that city."

Cardona was reading the telegram. He finished it, and exclaimed with new enthusiasm:

"So that's where Rigby chased Legrec! Hot on the trail again; but Legrec slipped him. So Rigby sent this wire, telling you he'd be in from Montreal some time tonight!"

"Early this evening," corrected Weston. "To be precise, Cardona, Rigby will arrive at Grand Central Station in exactly thirty-five minutes. That is why I summoned you: so that we both can meet him."

Cardona needed no further urging. He was reaching for his hat. Weston copied the inspector's move. Together, they started to the street, where the commissioner's official car awaited.

Though The Shadow was not present to learn it, the reason for the law's knowledge was explained. Thanks to word from Scotland Yard, plus the services of Alan Rigby, the authorities had gained their start along the trail of Gautier Legrec.

CHAPTER VIII
THE SHADOW'S DETOUR

THOSE minutes that preceded Rigby's arrival were important to The Shadow. He was in his sanctum, a hidden black-walled room, reviewing reports that his agents had supplied.

New facts pieced with The Shadow's theories, producing new insight into the ways of Gautier Legrec.

First, the murders themselves formed a paradox. They showed a curious conflict of methods.

Legrec had sent each victim a death card. The Shadow had gathered that from his talk with Weston. Agents had also established the fact, by inquiries at the airport and the Sheffield Apartments.

Though the matter had slipped past the newspaper reporters, a messenger at the airport had seen Elwood Balcray holding a strange card. The clerk at the Sheffield had observed a similar token in the possession of Sylvester Lysand. The Shadow, himself, had spied a death card close to the body of Hastings Keever.

The law had needed none of those testimonies; for the police, themselves, had found the actual cards. Commissioner Weston probably regarded the clues as lucky ones; but there, The Shadow's opinion differed.

Legrec had wanted those death cards to be discovered.

Why, then, had he tried to camouflage the murders as accidents? The two policies did not fit. Behind it lay some purpose, to which The Shadow saw a plausible answer, one that he intended to reserve for his own investigation.

Oddly, luck had been with Legrec; for The Shadow saw where the plotter had nearly failed.

Some helper had loosened the wheel of the southbound plane, but the crash had not been wanted during the takeoff. Legrec had expected it to happen when the ship landed at Washington. A sharp descent on a difficult field would have meant a complete crack-up.

Balcray would have died only a short while before the fall of Lysand's elevator, which had probably been fixed with greased cables. Keever, therefore, would have known nothing of those previous deaths.

The explosion in the Greenwich Village apartment house had been designed as the only measure to dispose of Keever. Legrec had been forced to make a special visit, because the plane had crashed too soon.

The whole case proved that Keever had known who Balcray and Lysand were, even though they might have known nothing about Keever.

Had Balcray and Lysand been innocent men, Legrec would not have needed to hide their deaths from Keever, himself a crook. It followed, therefore, that Balcray and Lysand were tools of Legrec. He had disposed of them because he needed their services no longer.

Knowing Balcray and Lysand for what they were, Keever had naturally become a problem, for he had inferred that he was slated for a similar fate.

Who, actually, was Gautier Legrec?

Was he an existing personage in his own right, or was he a crook who merely assumed that name?

CONSIDERING the latter probability, The Shadow had found one candidate who might be the master crook. That man was Rupert Roban. The old counterfeiter's absence during the past few years was a factor that made him eligible.

There could be others. To list them, The Shadow

studied reports concerning Balcray, Lysand and Keever. Legrec, whoever he was, had certainly known those three.

Agents had done well with their reports. Beneath a bluish light, The Shadow penned names that he found mentioned. One by one, he eliminated them, until only one remained.

That name glared in bluish ink.

It was the name of Thomas Margale.

One of The Shadow's agents was a newspaper reporter named Clyde Burke. He had learned that Elwood Balcray had made previous trips to Florida, to dispose of property there. Some of that real estate had been Balcray's. The rest had belonged to Thomas Margale.

Another agent was Rutledge Mann, an insurance broker. Checking on Sylvester Lysand, Mann had learned that the bank director had arranged certain loans at the Triton National. Among them were short-term loans advanced to Thomas Margale. The amounts were large; but all had been repaid.

A third agent, Harry Vincent, had visited the hotel where Hastings Keever had stopped a few days before his death. Posing as a relative of Keever's, Harry had been given a list of telephone calls that the promoter had made. Two of those calls bore the number listed under the name of Thomas Margale.

The Shadow had reports on Margale. The millionaire had been abroad frequently during the past few years. He could have been almost anywhere during those periods.

Moreover, Thomas Margale had a niece named Eleanor. From among a sheaf of clippings, The Shadow drew one that had been cut from the society columns of a New York newspaper.

There was a whispered laugh from hidden lips, as eyes studied that printed portrait.

The Shadow had learned the identity of the girl whom he had rescued the night before.

While he still noted Eleanor's picture, The Shadow was conscious of a tiny light that glowed from the wall beyond his table. His hand stretched forward to pluck up earphones. A methodical voice responded:

"Burbank speaking."

"Report!" whispered The Shadow.

"A call from Commissioner Weston, at the Cobalt Club," informed The Shadow's contact man. "He wants Lamont Cranston to come immediately to the Weatherly Arms Apartments. Top floor."

"Report received!"

The bluish light clicked off. There was a *swish* of The Shadow's cloak. The sanctum was empty.

SOON afterward, The Shadow was riding in his taxi along a side street near Times Square. The cab passed the police commissioner's car; a short distance onward The Shadow saw two signs, spaced sixty feet apart.

The first bore the name: "WEATHERLY ARMS"; the next read "HOTEL WEATHERLY."

Of the two, the hotel was the older. Its success had caused its owners to erect the newer apartment house next door, and to give it a similar name.

That coincidence meant little to The Shadow, as he started to slide his cloak from his shoulders, so that he could leave the cab as Lamont Cranston. A moment later, The Shadow had changed his immediate plan.

A man was pacing near the entrance of the Hotel Weatherly, looking toward The Shadow's cab. That man was Harry Vincent. The agent had come here as a matter of mere routine, in case The Shadow needed him; but the fact that he had gone to the hotel instead of the Weatherly Arms was proof that Harry had some message.

The Shadow whispered to the driver. The cab glided ahead. It looked empty when it stopped at the hotel entrance. Harry boarded it; heard a whisper in the darkness. As the cab slowly rounded the block, the agent reported.

"Tough customer went into the Weatherly Hotel," stated Harry. "He looked a lot like Mort Fadler, the triggerman."

The Shadow knew the name. Mort was classed as a specialist in murder.

"Looked like he was going to the twentieth floor," added Harry, tersely. "The elevator only made one stop before the top."

The cab had reached the rear street. An alleyway past a deserted theater offered a quick route through to the hotel. The Shadow decided to postpone his visit to the Weatherly Arms, while he looked into the matter of Mort Fadler.

With an order for Harry to remain on duty, The Shadow alighted in the darkness. The cab continued its circuit to the front street.

When The Shadow entered the rear of the hotel lobby, he was no longer wearing cloak and hat. They were folded across his arm, so bundled that they looked like ordinary garments. He took an elevator to the twentieth floor.

FROM a hallway window, The Shadow observed the top of the Weatherly Arms. The apartment house was about the same height as the hotel, but it was topped by a duplex penthouse. That two-story structure was set back from the edge; its lower floor opened to a roof promenade that extended in this direction.

There were lights in the lower half of the penthouse, but they were dulled by thick curtains. All seemed quiet there.

Craning from his window, The Shadow looked

along the row of rooms on this side of the hotel. As he watched, he saw a flicker come from one. It seemed like the blink of a flashlight. Counting to that window, The Shadow stepped back into the little hall. There, he donned his hat and cloak.

Moving to the door that corresponded to the window where he had spotted the flash, The Shadow produced a pick. He was about to probe the lock when an elevator door clanged open. The Shadow glided from sight as a bellboy, loaded with luggage, conducted two guests to a room at the other end of the hall.

While he waited for the bellboy's departure, The Shadow watched the space beneath the door that he had chosen to open. He saw another flicker from the flashlight. Though the delay was troublesome, The Shadow had at least gained positive proof that he had picked the room where Mort Fadler lurked.

That delay was to produce a chain of consequences. Below the hotel, near a rear corner of the building, two men were looking upward. One seeing the flashlight's reflection gave the other a nudge in the darkness.

"Looks like Mort's there," growled one. "We're not so dumb, after all."

"Who said we were?" demanded the other. "If Mort's up there, though, what's keeping us here?"

The two moved into the hotel, their destination the same floor, the very room, where The Shadow was seeking a silent meeting with Mort Fadler.

CHAPTER IX
SWIFT MINUTES

THE penthouse atop the Weatherly Arms was less gloomy than its windows indicated. Inside, three men were seated in a living room. Weston and Cardona were two, the third was Alan Rigby.

The celebrated investigator was of average height. His deep-lined face and well-grayed temples showed him close to middle age. He had a nervous energy, though, that gave him a youthful mood. His speech, slightly English in its accent, was rapid.

"It was well that I came by Montreal," snapped Rigby. "Even though I did not find Legrec, he did not find me."

Weston started a question; Rigby answered it before it came.

"I meant exactly that," said the investigator. "Legrec is out to get me.

The bounder is anxious to amend his previous failures."

The clatter of a cocktail shaker sounded from a pantry. Rigby called out:

"Hurry in here, Clyston, with those drinks!" Then, when a dapper man in shirtsleeves appeared, Rigby introduced him: "This is Clyston—my secretary, batman, and what-have-you. Like myself, he is eager to trap Legrec."

"We'll catch up with the blighter someday," commented Clyston, with a grin. "I'm looking forward to it!"

"And I'm looking forward to a cocktail," reminded Rigby.

Clyston's grin widened. He handled the shaker with increased speed, as he approached a table where glasses were set upon a tray.

"When I decided to come by Montreal," Rigby told Weston, "I sent Clyston directly to New York. I told him to rent a suitable apartment—if possible, a penthouse.

"He chose this one. I like its location. But I can't say that the arrangements quite suit me. Tell me, Clyston"—Rigby turned to the secretary—"why did you take a duplex, when we require only one floor?"

The secretary was busy pouring the cocktails. He hesitated a moment before he replied:

"The floor above us is locked off, sir. Some tenant had an unexpired lease. His furniture is stored there and no one uses the place."

"I would have preferred the upper apartment," returned Rigby. "What use is a penthouse without a roof, where one can stroll and enjoy the night air?"

"We have a promenade of our own, Mr. Rigby," explained Clyston, eagerly.

"Really? That's jolly! This place is frightfully stuffy. Let us have our drinks on the promenade, Clyston."

OBLIGINGLY, Clyston set aside the cocktail shaker. He put on vest and coat, crossed the room, and opened the French windows. A pleasant breeze swept through the stuffy living room.

Rigby was filling his pipe from a tobacco jar; he paused to gesture his guests outside.

Commissioner Weston started ahead; but Joe Cardona paused to lay three cards upon the table. They were the death tokens that the inspector had found with the dead men.

"Legrec's souvenirs," nodded

Rigby. "A whim of his, to place them with his victims. They are tarots."

"Tarots?" The word was unfamiliar to Cardona.

"Ancient playing cards," interpreted Rigby. "Originally used for telling fortunes. Each tarot has a special significance; that is why they are sometimes termed the Book of Thoth."

Cardona picked up the six spot with the crossed rods, mentioning that it had been delivered to Balcray.

"Six of rods," stated Rigby. "Its meaning is 'failure'."

Cardona indicated the card with the cuplike spots, that Lysand had received.

"Six of cups," defined Rigby. "Its significance is a bit more subtle. It stands for insuperable obstacles. That could mean 'disaster'."

"What about this one with the six coins?" queried Cardona. "We found it in Keever's apartment."

"Six of money," declared Rigby. "It symbolizes complete ruin."

Gathering the cards, Cardona pocketed them. He was about to ask another question, when Rigby intervened. The investigator was glancing at his watch, when he inquired:

"What is keeping that chap Cranston? The friend that the commissioner mentioned while we were riding here? If he can tell us important facts regarding those three victims, his testimony may prove vital."

Cardona surmised that Cranston would arrive in a short while, and said so. Rigby curbed his impatience.

"We shall wait until he joins us," decided the investigator. "Since those murders constitute our first evidence of Legrec's operations, we must consider them as a starting point. Come, Inspector, let us join the commissioner on that delightfully cool promenade."

RIGBY lighted his pipe. Cardona walked ahead of him, out through the French windows toward a table near a parapet, where Weston was already seated. Cardona sat down opposite the commissioner, leaving a chair for Rigby.

Clyston was arriving with the tray. He set it on a chair; tendered a glass to Weston, another to Cardona. The secretary picked up a third glass, started to set it on the table, at the same time moving the chair intended for Rigby.

Cardona remembered that action afterward.

At that particular moment, Clyston could easily have been mistaken for the owner of the penthouse. His motion almost indicated that he intended to take his place in the empty chair. Rigby had not yet appeared from the living room.

Something whimpered in the air, its momentary sizzle followed by an impact. Cardona caught a dull, sighing echo that came from beyond the penthouse terrace. Springing to his feet, Cardona upset the cocktail glass as he grabbed the table edge.

A moment later, Joe was staring across the parapet toward the windows of the adjacent hotel.

There was a shout from the opening to the penthouse living room. Rigby's voice:

"Down! Down! Both of you!"

Weston was the first to turn; he saw Rigby's gestures; dropped to the shelter of the parapet. Cardona copied the move, an instant later. Rigby, coming in a long dash, went to hands and knees and scrambled up to join them.

There was good reason for Rigby's excited order.

A silent form had slumped without a murmur. Clyston was lying on the floor beside the table, his arms outspread. His face was staring straight upward; below the face, Cardona saw a splotch of blood spreading itself on the man's light-gray vest, just above his heart.

"A silencer!" gulped Cardona. "On a gun—from one of those hotel windows! Some sharpshooter—"

Joe was drawing a revolver. Rigby stopped him before he could poke his head above the parapet.

"Legrec's work," grated Rigby. "Careful, Inspector, or we may share Clyston's fate. Poor Clyston—the assassin may have mistaken him for me."

Something projected from Clyston's vest. It was the white edge of a card, forced up from the upper breast pocket by the impact of the bullet. Rigby drew the object into full view.

The card was another tarot—but with seven symbols instead of six. They represented swords; two groups of three, curved like scimitars, with a straight blade between them.

"Seven of swords!" muttered Rigby. "It signifies an enemy's success. Legrec's success—through another of his hired assassins!"

As Rigby spoke, the eyes of his huddled companions were fixed upon that telltale tarot. The card was stained with Clyston's life blood. Through the center was a hole drilled by the death-dealing bullet.

Legrec had struck again, leaving another of his sinister souvenirs as a token of defiance to the law!

CHAPTER X
THE MAN IN THE ROOM

THE door of the hotel room shoved inward. The Shadow sprang across the threshold, moments late. Delay in the corridor had prevented him from picking the lock in time to stop a killer's thrust.

There was the window; outlined against it the sweatered figure of the murderer, Mort Fadler. Something gleamed in dim light. It was the barrel of the killer's rifle.

Cardona caught a dull sighing echo that came from beyond the penthouse terrace. A moment later Joe was staring across the parapet …

Beyond, The Shadow saw the parapet of the penthouse promenade; the glow from the opened French windows made a background. No one was in sight; but The Shadow knew why. Men had ducked below the parapet for safety.

The sigh of Fadler's gun had come just as the room door yielded to The Shadow's operations. But the killer hadn't heard the door swing inward. Swishing through the darkness, The Shadow had a seemingly sure chance to grab the murderer.

A chance event warned Fadler.

From the hotel corridor came the *clang* of an

elevator door. The sound was audible, and the murderer heard it. Realizing that the door of the room must also be open, Fadler spun from the window. Dim corridor lights enabled him to see the shape of blackness that was sweeping in upon him.

The killer swung his overweighted rifle. A hard stroke and a lucky one, descending straight for The Shadow's head.

Up sped a warding hand. The rifle barrel clashed the steel of an automatic. The Shadow had stopped Mort's stroke; an instant later, the cloaked fighter tugged his automatic trigger.

Driven down by the rifle blow, the automatic muzzle was off aim. The gun blast scorched past Mort's ear. The killer grappled with The Shadow.

Again the automatic tongued. A chance bob of Mort's head saved him from that bullet. Moreover, it gave him a momentary advantage. He managed to drive the butt of the rifle against The Shadow's neck.

The savage jolt was like an electric shock. The Shadow went limp, lost his grip on Mort. Dropping the rifle, the killer clamped brawny hands on his adversary's shoulders, gave The Shadow a heave toward the window.

There was a long instant during which The Shadow saw what lay below.

Twenty stories to the blackened ground. At intervals were ledges—dark streaks—each three feet wide. Good enough for a grip, if a climber approached them; but not for a falling person.

A jolt against one of those ledges would jar a man so swiftly that he would hardly have a chance to stop his plunge. Only the greatest of luck could save anyone who went from this high window.

Mort Fadler knew it. He exerted every effort to pitch The Shadow downward.

The Shadow's head and shoulders went through the window. His head tilted downward; his slouch hat fell, skimming the building wall as it scaled toward the depths. Mort made a fierce snatch at The Shadow's hands, trying to pry them from the windowsill.

There were shouts from the corridor. The gunfire had been heard. Those cries seemed far distant to The Shadow, like faint voices from a dream. They meant nothing to Mort Fadler. He was on the verge of the greatest triumph of his murderous career.

DOOM to The Shadow!

That was Mort's aim. His lips spat a victorious snarl as he broke the hold of The Shadow's left hand. He grabbed for The Shadow's right wrist, wrenched it hard.

His clutch loosened, The Shadow took a backward twist, half out through the window. His gun was gone; he couldn't thrust his numbed fists past Mort's shoving forearms. But that last instant brought a spasm to The Shadow.

His strength was back; it still might serve him, although he was on the very brink of oblivion.

The Shadow flayed one arm wide. It came up above Mort's shoulder, swooped over the killer's head. The folds of a cloak sleeve entangled across the killer's eyes. Mort tried to shake it away; unwisely, he let one arm go low.

The Shadow's other hand thrust through. The second sleeve bagged Mort's head. Savagely, Mort used one hand to rip at the black cloth. The Shadow dropped inside the windowsill; twisted half away. More of the cloak enveloped Mort.

Grips were even. The pair were a swaying mass of blackness against the dimness of the window. Hands were gripping through the folds of the twisted cloak. If one fighter gained a throat clutch, the battle would be over.

Those shouts from the corridor had loudened. Two men were on the threshold: the same pair that had viewed Mort's blinking flashlight from the ground. They had flashlights of their own. They used them.

The beam showed a chaos of blackness, which the arriving men mistook for a turning figure. They ducked away, snapping off their lights. They saw the shape heave upward at the window, poise there, as if ready for an outward plunge.

They didn't realize that a fighter had gone suddenly helpless in the grip of a foeman. From within the doorway, the two arrivals opened fire with revolvers. There was a rip of cloth; they didn't hear it, for the sound was drowned by the echoes of the guns.

The fighter swayed across the windowsill, went through the space beyond, the sweep of cloth spreading behind it. So rapid was the dive of that cloaked form, that it deceived the men who had fired the clipping shot.

"It was Mort!" shouted one. "We got him! He took a dive out through the—"

"Hold it," interrupted the other. "I think he plopped inside, here in the room!"

A flashlight glittered. Oddly, it proved that both speakers were right. A diving form *had* gone through that window; but another still remained within the room.

BEFORE the flashlight could outline the crouched fighter, he was driving toward the doorway. He fell upon the man who held the light, wrenched it from the fellow's hand. Two figures wrestled; a third sprang into the battle.

Snarls, oaths were frequent during the fray that followed. Neither of the two fresh fighters dared use a gun as a bludgeon, for fear of slugging his own pal. It was a barehanded battle; two squatly, husky men against a wiry foe who offset them, although he could not wrench away.

Back and forth across the room they went, hitting chairs and tables. At times, the wiry man was almost clear; but always, a lucky grab halted his escape. Guns were forgotten; fists, clawing fingers were the only weapons, except when chairs were slung.

Minutes passed while the struggle raged. There was tumult from the corridor; the pounding of feet.

"Hold him!" panted one of the blocky fighters. "We've got help coming!"

"We've got him!" shouted the other. "We've got Mort Fadler! Give us some light!"

They thought they had Mort Fadler, but they had no one. With a last desperate heave, the man from the window was away, breaking for the door. One of the blocky men made a wild dive, and had the luck to grab a passing ankle.

There was a sprawl in the darkness: two men bounding for the spot where a body thumped.

An instant later, the lights came on.

On the threshold stood Joe Cardona, holding a revolver; behind him were Commissioner Weston and Alan Rigby. The three were backed by a squad of hotel employees.

Cardona was gazing toward the floor; he saw two husky men throw themselves upon the prone form of a prisoner, smothering the captive's last effort to rise. Cardona recognized that pair; they were headquarters detectives.

"They've got the killer!" shouted Weston.

"It's Mort Fadler," panted one of the dicks. "We got a tip-off that he was coming up here."

Joe Cardona thrust forward; he brushed the detectives aside. Looking at the senseless prisoner, the ace shook his head. He tilted the face up into the light.

It was Commissioner Weston who supplied the rest, in a tone that he blurted from mechanical lips: "My word! It's Cranston!"

CHAPTER XI
THE LAW GAINS FACTS

COMMISSIONER WESTON was overwhelmed by the circumstances. He knew that this room had contained a killer; for it was on a direct line with the penthouse terrace. But the last person he would have considered as a murderer was his friend Lamont Cranston.

It did look black for Cranston. Though the headquarters detectives admitted they had come to seek Mort Fadler, they swore that Cranston was the only man they had encountered. If the death shot had been fired from this room, they said, Cranston was the man who had dispatched it.

There was no question about the death shot. On the floor beside the window lay the rifle, with its silencer: grim evidence that Cranston was the murderer. Joe Cardona picked up the weapon, handed it to Weston.

The commissioner gave a helpless shrug. His duty to the law compelled him to arrest his friend on a murder charge. Weston was about to give that order to Cardona, when Rigby intervened.

"Odd circumstances, Commissioner," remarked Rigby. "You tell this friend of yours where to meet you. Instead of coming to the penthouse, he heads here. It looks as though he surely intended murder; and then expected to drop in on us, to view the scene."

"Yeah," supplied one of the detectives. "And he sent that false tip-off, so we would think it was Mort Fadler."

"A good theory," commended Rigby, nodding toward the dick. "But it does not apply to this instance. Commissioner, I advise you not to arrest

Cranston. Revive him and hear his story, first."

Weston gave a thankful gulp. Rigby had provided a way out of the dilemma. Cardona was willing to let matters go as Rigby suggested. He told the detectives to get water; to bring Cranston to consciousness as soon as possible. Nevertheless, Cardona was blunt, when he asked Rigby:

"Why don't you think that Cranston is responsible?"

"Because we are dealing with Legrec," replied Rigby, with a meditative gaze. "It would be like him to hire an assassin of Fadler's sort, then have the law trap the fellow."

The killer clamped brawny hands on his adversary's shoulders, gave The Shadow a heave toward the window.

1. Acting on information received from one of his agents, The Shadow, in the guise of Lamont Cranston, enters a hotel through the side entrance and takes an elevator to the twentieth floor, trailing a suspicious-looking character. . . .

2. Leaving the elevator, he seeks a dark corner and changes to black cloak and hat; then, in his own identity of The Shadow, he seeks out the room where his criminal quarry had taken to cover. . . .

3. Picking the lock silently, The Shadow crosses the threshold of the room too late, for the criminal—a notorious gunman—had caused death on the terrace of an apartment penthouse directly opposite the hotel. In the gloom of the room, The Shadow and the killer fight a battle to the death—with an unexpected interruption by the law that brings an amazing showdown. . . .

19TH FLOOR

"You mean Legrec double-crosses his own bunch?"

"Certainly! For the simple reason that he can always hire others. That is his cleverest ability."

"But what about the new ones? Don't they think they'll get theirs, the same way?

"Never!" Rigby was emphatic. "Legrec makes every man believe that he is privileged. He has such an amazing power of persuasion that they believe him. None know that they have been tricked, until their turns arrive."

There was a stir from Cranston. He was propping himself up from the floor, staring in dazed fashion. Weston spoke; apparently, Cranston did not hear him. In trancelike fashion, he found his feet and walked mechanically toward the window.

There, he stopped to stare downward. The detectives, returning with the water, made a quick grab to hold the prisoner. Cranston never noticed them. He was looking into the deep blackness that lay between the hotel and the apartment house.

The Shadow's daze was feigned. He was looking for something of his own: the hat that had fallen first; the cloak that had gone later, draped over Mort Fadler. He saw a trace of deep blackness, that clotted the shaded strip of a wall ledge.

It was the cloak. It had caught there, when Mort's body took a bounce. Probably the hat had halted somewhere else along the route to the ground. Evidence connecting Cranston with The Shadow was safely out of sight. Those garments could be secretly regained later.

All was set for the story that The Shadow wanted to tell.

TURNING from the window, Cranston looked toward Weston with a weary, reproving smile.

"Hello, Commissioner," he said, in slow, even tone. "Why weren't you here?"

"Why wasn't I here?"

"Yes." Cranston's nod was slow. "On the top floor of the Weatherly, as your message stated."

"I said the Weatherly Arms!" ejaculated Weston. "It's next door. This is the Hotel Weatherly."

Understanding dawned on Cranston's hawkish features; then puzzlement replaced it.

"No wonder I was puzzled," declared the commissioner's friend. "That's why I walked into this open room. It was the only place where I supposed you could be. Only, I found someone else instead."

There was grimness in Cranston's voice, despite its monotone. Eagerly, Weston asked to hear more. Cranston stroked his forehead slowly; he began to recall what had happened.

"A chap tried to club me," he remembered. "He had a gun, or something, but I managed to get it away from him. We wound up by the window; he wanted to pitch me out.

"We were at even grips, when a lot of shooting started. I was on the floor; the other chap was gone, through the window. I thought that the shots were meant for me. I went after the men who fired them."

There was a pause, while Cranston stood with hand pressed hard against his forehead. It was Joe Cardona who broke the silence, as he snapped to the detectives:

"Get downstairs, you stupes!! That's where you'll find Mort Fadler—down in the courtyard! Don't you saps know a fight when you see one?"

The dicks muttered to each other, nodding. They recalled that they had seen a lot of commotion at the window. They hurried out to the elevator. At the end of a few minutes, hollow shouts came up from the courtyard.

Cardona answered them from the window. The dicks had found the smashed body of Mort Fadler.

Cardona picked up the death gun, tenderly. He put a question:

"You didn't have a hold on this, did you, Mr. Cranston?"

There was a shake of Cranston's head.

"That's fine," declared Cardona. "We'll get the fingerprints. If Mort's are the only ones on it—as I'll bet they will be—that will put the goods on him."

"One moment," reminded Weston. "You and I have handled the gun, Inspector."

"But our mitts don't count," returned Cardona. "There're three people who couldn't have used this gun, Commissioner. You, myself and Mr. Rigby."

THE group left the hotel room. While Cardona attended to business, Weston and Cranston joined Rigby in a trip up to the penthouse. They formed a solemn group in the living room, while a police surgeon examined Clyston's body.

The secretary's dead form was removed on a stretcher. Rigby suggested that they go outside, since the terrace would certainly be a safe place, with Mort Fadler dead.

They were seated there—Weston, Rigby, Cranston—when Cardona arrived. The detective ace handed a scribbled report to the commissioner. It brought a smile from Weston.

"The case is cleared," announced the commissioner. "Fadler's fingerprints were the only ones on the gun, except"—the commissioner smiled—"except yours and mine, Cardona."

Then, turning to The Shadow, Weston added: "I owe you an apology, Cranston."

"An apology?" queried Cranston. "For what?"

"For suspecting you of murder," replied Weston. "I was actually going to arrest you, when Rigby intervened."

Cranston's lips framed a smile that denoted

surprise. For the first time, apparently, he began to realize that he had been suspected as the killer. Then:

"Tell me about Clyston," remarked The Shadow. "Just why was Fadler sent to murder him?"

"Plain enough." It was Rigby who gave answer. "Clyston took this penthouse in my name. Legrec must have learned it. He left the rest to Fadler, giving tonight as the time.

"I have learned that Clyston sent his suit out to be pressed, with orders to deliver it to this apartment. That must have been when the death card was placed in the vest pocket.

"Legrec always leaves much to his hirelings, when he is confident that complications are absent. This time, Legrec slipped. All along, Clyston was mistaken for me."

The Shadow's smile showed no change. It was a fixed one; the sort that fitted the lips of Cranston. But behind that smile, a keen brain was considering another theory.

Three of Legrec's previous victims had actually been tools of the master crook. Could Clyston— Rigby's own man—be another person bought over by Legrec?

If so, there had been no mistake by either Legrec or Fadler. Assuming that Clyston's usefulness had ended, Legrec would have ordered the man's death.

To make it appear as a mistake, with no one to tell the real fact, Legrec had sent that tip-off to the law. Knowing the sort that Fadler was, Legrec had foreseen that the killer would prefer death to capture.

The theory was sound. Mentally, The Shadow accepted it. A moment later, he heard Rigby's voice:

"You knew the victims, Mr. Cranston. The ones who died in supposed accidents. Tell us about them."

IN quiet fashion, The Shadow gave sketches of Balcray, Lysand, and Keever. He remarked that Balcray had sold considerable real estate in Florida; that Lysand had much to do with loans at the Triton National. He added that Keever had been engaged in his usual promotion work.

That was all. The Shadow left further conclusions to the others. He refrained from mentioning the name of Thomas Margale. That was a lead that The Shadow chose to follow on his own.

Both Weston and Cardona seemed disappointed because Cranston's facts went no further. It was Rigby who seemed to catch an inkling of what the statements could produce.

"There is a link between those three men," declared Rigby. "The link is a person; and his name"—Rigby paused, emphatically—"is Gautier Legrec!"

Rigby's tone pleased The Shadow. It meant that more facts were due—facts which The Shadow wanted, along with the law.

Alan Rigby arose, gave a long sweep of his arm to invite the others into the penthouse living room. The investigator's face was stern; his eyes grim in their gaze.

A trail of murder stretched from the past. A grueling search lay ahead. A double quest, for the law and The Shadow—that hunt for Gautier Legrec. And Alan Rigby, who knew more about Legrec than any other living man, was ready to guide the quest.

Though he did not show it, The Shadow was gripped with eagerness as he strolled into the penthouse.

The time had come when The Shadow was to gain new and needed links to Gautier Legrec.

CHAPTER XII
THE BLAZED TRAIL

IN the quiet of the penthouse, Alan Rigby began a methodical procedure. His trunks had come from the station. He opened them; assembled a variety of objects that made him seem more like a lecturer than a crime investigator.

Rigby set up a portable motion picture projector, with a screen against the wall in front of it. In addition, he had half a dozen cloth rolls that looked like charts, which he arranged on the wall, above the screen.

There were scrapbooks on the table; chairs were stacked with wooden boxes that bore labels. All these were exhibits that pertained to the notorious Gautier Legrec.

The projector chattered. There were flickers from the screen. A picture focused there. Rigby spoke:

"Budapest. Five years ago. The scene is outside the Oriental Bazaar, shortly after Legrec raided there."

The street was flowing into the camera. Clusters of bystanders were pressed aside by a policeman, to allow a close-up of a huddled figure that looked like a Turk.

"One of Legrec's workers," supplied Rigby. "Shot by the police as he attempted to flee with others. We shall see a picture of another henchman, in a moment."

The film shifted to the actual scene of crime: a bazaar booth that had been wrecked by an explosion. Other dead figures appeared: men in varied costumes. The camera concentrated upon a second Turk, whose face was turned up into the light.

"The assassin who threw the bomb," explained Rigby. "Not a Turk, but an Algerian, in disguise. He miscalculated the time element and perished with his victims. The raid followed. Unfortunately, among the innocent persons slain was this man—"

A close-up showed a bloody face tilted askew above crushed shoulders. This victim was unquestionably a Turk; despite the rigidity wrought by death, his features marked him as a man of importance.

"Ali Ras," identified Rigby. "Owner of the jewel bazaar. He ignored threats from Legrec. This was the result."

The camera moved to the dead man's hand. There, clutched by long fingers that lay near a tasseled fez, was a tarot. It did not show plainly in the film; Rigby halted the reel. Turning on the nearest lamp, he held the actual card in view.

Unlike the tarots that had been found on recent victims, this card bore a picture. It showed a square-shaped tower tumbling into ruins; a man plunging headlong amid the crashing stones.

"An *atout*," defined Rigby. "In the tarot pack, it corresponds to a court card of an ordinary deck. It carries many symbolisms; but one is most significant. Termed the 'Castle of Plutus', the card bears a warning to misers.

"That apparently applied to Ali Ras, one of the wealthiest of Ottoman merchants. He was noted for the hoards of money that he had stowed away. In this case, Legrec evidently began with tactics resembling those of a racketeer. When such methods failed, he turned to murder and robbery."

Cardona studied the card from Budapest; he noted the descriptive word, "*La Torre*," beneath the tumbling castle. The tarot passed to Weston; next to Cranston.

"THAT tarot," resumed Rigby, "was but the first of many that I have discovered along Legrec's trail. In Cairo, an Egyptian official was found dead, clutching this card." He produced a tarot showing a demon, above the wording, "*Il Daivolo*," and added: "The murdered man was beside his rifled strongbox."

The next card that Rigby produced was the picture of a hanging man suspended by his feet. It was called "*L'Appeso*," which Rigby translated as the "Hanged Man," stroking his chin when he noted the tarot.

"Sterling Craythorn was an Australian adventurer," recalled Rigby. "He won a million francs in one evening, at Monte Carlo, in most mysterious fashion. Oddly, Craythorn was found dead, off the suicide leap. Usually, losers are the ones who take that plunge.

"Perhaps he jumped because his money had mysteriously vanished. More probably, he was tossed to his death. There is no question who gained Craythorn's profits. One of his pockets disgorged this token from Legrec. The card symbolizes a martyr to a cause."

Rigby's face was stern, its lines deep. He turned to the projector, flashed pictures of Cairo and Monte Carlo. The Shadow pondered on a point that had apparently eluded Rigby.

The deaths of the Turkish merchant and the Egyptian official fitted with Rigby's suppositions. Legrec had slain those men in order to obtain wealth which they rightfully possessed.

But the Australian adventurer marked a departure.

How had the Australian cracked the bank at Monte Carlo? Probably through use of some system that had beaten the roulette table. Where had he acquired that method?

From Legrec!

The case was a link that The Shadow wanted. The very name, Legrec, was a French term for "swindler," or "gambler," the murderer's constant use of tarots also smacked of a gamester's ways.

With the Monte Carlo incident, The Shadow could see the beginning of new tactics on the part of Legrec. The master crook had started using dupes to aid his schemes.

The Australian, Craythorn, could easily have been working under Legrec's supervision. He was the "front" for the master criminal's clean-up at the gambling casino. Instead of a percentage of the profits, the Australian had received death.

Ironically, Legrec had placed the card that branded his murdered dupe as a fool.

Since then, Legrec had worked through other dupes. Balcray, Lysand, Keever, finally Clyston—all had participated in some game, here in New York.

It would be useless to search for coming crime. Legrec had probably completed his present scheme. These deaths of dupes were merely the clean-up men who knew too much; persons who would want a share of the spoils that Legrec intended to keep entirely as his own.

There could, however, still be a trail to Legrec.

RIGBY had finished with the motion pictures. Facing his audience of three, he spoke in recollective tone.

"The police quizzed all foreigners in Budapest," he stated, "myself among them. Learning that I was a crime investigator, they asked my assistance. Clues indicated that Legrec had gone to Istanbul. The authorities there requested that I come.

"I uncovered a dead spy of Legrec's. New evidence pointed to Cairo. I arrived in Egypt too late to save the victimized official. After many months, chance information brought me to Monte Carlo.

"Craythorn, the Australian, made his big winnings just after I arrived there. He was murdered; Legrec was gone with the spoils. On a long chance, I went to Australia, thinking that Legrec, always daring, would try to acquire property that belonged to the dead adventurer."

Rigby drew down a rolled wall map. It showed the world, with lines that marked Rigby's own travels. He ran his forefinger eastward, to the island of Ceylon.

"I was waylaid there by murderous Singhalese," he recounted. "Legrec's work; but I managed to escape before he sent payment for my capture. Afterward, Australia—again, Legrec was gone."

Rigby started to pull down a roll that showed the outline of a man's face. It was the wrong one; he drew down another, instead. The Shadow's eyes became keenly interested.

The face, huge in size, reminded him of some one that he had seen recently: Rupert Roban, the counterfeiter.

There were points that spoiled the exact resemblance. Where Roban's chin was sharp, that of the outlined portrait had a roundishness. The forehead bulged, like Roban's, but the incorrect chin gave a wrong comparison between the lower and upper portions of the face.

The hair was shocky, like Roban's; but grayish, rather than white. The eyes were almost perfect; but they displayed only one of Roban's moods. They were fixed in a cold stare that seemed to threaten eyes that met it.

The portrait showed the face as pale; it lacked the ancient hue of Roban's parchment skin. Withal, Roban could have been identified from it, particularly when Rigby explained the chart's limitations.

"This is a pieced portrait of Legrec," declared the investigator. "I have checked statement after statement, made by persons who claimed that they had seen him. I started to show you one of my earlier charts; its details were bad.

"In fact, I discarded portrait after portrait, keeping only my lists of details. None was satisfactory, until I obtained new information in London. Legrec had begun a swindle there, then dropped it.

"Descriptions of him tallied with some of my old details. They provided new items, from which I constructed the final portrait. I feel confident that I have cleared two important points."

Pausing, Rigby stepped back to survey the picture. Meeting the ugly glare of the huge painted eyes, Rigby added:

"First, that Legrec, despite his name, is *not* a Frenchman. Second, that his crop of hair is real, even though it appears to be a wig. I am positive that, somewhere, we may find a criminal who closely resembles that portrait; that when we discover him, we shall have met Legrec."

RIGBY'S discourse was finished. He invited an inspection of his scrapbooks and the boxes that contained bits of evidence pertaining to Legrec.

Cranston joined the others in studying that material. Rigby's records proved varied, even though they lacked completeness.

Among them was a wisp of almost whitish hair, believed to be Legrec's; a photograph taken on shipboard, which showed a hunched figure, face turned away, that could have been Legrec. There were signatures in scrawly handwriting; possible aliases used by Legrec.

Before leaving, Commissioner Weston granted a request made by Rigby. The investigator wanted two plainclothesmen at hand, in case he needed them.

The request pleased Weston, for the murder of Clyston indicated that another death thrust might be coming from Legrec. Weston was glad that Rigby was the sort of man who would accept the law's protection.

Lamont Cranston was meditative when he and the commissioner reached the street. Weston saw his friend stare upward to the lighted lower floor of the two-story penthouse, with the darkened space above it.

Weston smiled. For once, he had seen Cranston impressed. Those details recounted by Alan Rigby had certainly been effective.

Commissioner Weston would have been personally impressed, had he gone with Lamont Cranston. Soon after his departure, Cranston entered a waiting cab. There, he became The Shadow. His course took him to his hidden sanctum.

Beneath the bluish light, a long-fingered hand held a pen. A weird laugh whispered from the darkness above. The Shadow was thinking of Rupert Roban. He dismissed that name from mind. Roban, a known criminal, who resembled Rigby's portrait of the supposed Legrec, was a man that the law could seek.

Instead of Roban's name, The Shadow wrote another; one that he had previously inscribed. The name of a man who had not even been mentioned in connection with this case.

"Thomas Margale."

The bluish light clicked off. Darkness marked the beginning of The Shadow's own investigation.

To learn the purposes of Legrec, The Shadow chose to solve the unknown factor.

That factor was Thomas Margale.

CHAPTER XIII
THE BLIND TRAIL

UPON leaving his sanctum, The Shadow went directly to the neighborhood of Margale's mansion. The hour was late; the huge mansion loomed dark beyond the wall that surrounded it.

Clad in black, The Shadow formed a gliding, evanescent shape, as he skirted that outer wall. The shelter offered perfect opportunities for concealment. There wasn't a chance that watching eyes from within the house could spy The Shadow.

Nevertheless, The Shadow avoided direct entry to the grounds. The side gate, like the front one, was obviously one of the spots that would be under observation. The easiest method of access, from The Shadow's standpoint, was to scale the wall itself.

The Shadow managed that with upward glide. For a few seconds, he took on the semblance of a human beetle, as he found crevices for fingers and toes. Then his gloved hands gripped the wall top, probed there momentarily. Finally, The Shadow rolled flat upon the ledge itself.

His new location gave him an admirable view of the mansion, as well as a prospect of the surrounding streets. Crawling along the wall, The Shadow remained in blackness, stretching flat at places where an ordinary creeper might have been noted from the house.

All the while, he was taking in the details of the mansion: its big windows and formidable doors. Yet, in those intervals when he paused to view the street, his brief glances were sufficient to tell him that no lurkers were about.

The Shadow's ears were also keen. Catching the distant pound of footsteps, The Shadow waited, watching a corner of the wall. A bulky man came into sight; he was clad in blue uniform. The arrival was the patrolman who regularly covered this beat.

Pacing slowly past, the officer looked upward toward the wall edge. Though this was part of his regular procedure, he was not lax in its performance. The patrolman's eyes were sharp enough to spot any ordinary lurker flattened on that wall. It was The Shadow's uncanny ability to merge with blackness that enabled him to remain undetected.

The officer continued along his beat.

Again The Shadow was in motion, timing his progress to the fade of the patrolman's footsteps. Then, again he flattened. The sound that he heard this time was almost indistinguishable, yet The Shadow sensed it; not only that, he knew what to expect.

THE SHADOW was watching that wall corner, expecting new figures to come around it. He was not disappointed. Close to the shelter of the wall, two sweater-clad men crept into sight. They stopped on the sidewalk, just below The Shadow.

"Hold it," gruffed one, his voice well muffled, "until we lamp the harness bull!"

The reference to the patrolman brought a suppressed guffaw from the other hoodlum.

"Him?" demanded the fellow. "He's clear around the next corner! We ain't runnin' no risk. All we gotta do is case the place and make sure nobody else ain't near here."

"Who else would be around?"

"How do I know?" Again, a chortle sounded. Then: "The Shadow, maybe."

That reference didn't please the thug who heard it. He said so with a growl, remarking that wise guys weren't smart when they kidded about The Shadow. Perhaps his companion was somewhat convinced, for he suggested that they move along.

The hoodlums hadn't gone more than a dozen paces, before something plopped in the gloom behind them. That landing, however, was noiseless—the sort that only The Shadow could perform.

From then on, the skulking men were followed by a spectral shape that they didn't know was near. Close to the wall, The Shadow was stalking the very men who had come to look for lurkers.

There was no question that this pair served Legrec; but, like others who worked for the master crook, they wouldn't know facts concerning him. However, The Shadow recognized that they might offer a worthwhile trail.

This was smart business on Legrec's part, having outside watchers on the job, instead of utilizing spy measures from within the house itself. These hoodlums, if accosted, would not be connected with events inside the Margale mansion.

Finishing their patrol, the thugs headed for an avenue and came to a small lunchroom that was open all night.

Following at a considerable distance, The Shadow had no opportunity to observe their faces. Reaching the lunchroom, only one man entered; the other remained near a darkened wall, on watch.

That again prevented The Shadow from identifying them, but he was very close when the first thug came out from the lunchroom.

"I made the phone call," the fellow told his companion. "It's all O.K., except there's a place where we've got to stop off."

"What for?" demanded the other.

"You'll find out" was the reply. "It ain't far, though, so let's hoof it."

THE pair moved eastward. They came to a

dingy neighborhood. The first thug picked out a house number; the place looked empty, but the door proved to be unlocked. The pair entered.

They had hardly reached an inside stairway, leading upward, before the outer door opened again, without their knowledge. This time, it was The Shadow who entered.

Trailing the thugs, The Shadow heard the hollow echoes of their muffled footsteps: proof in itself that the house was empty. Finally, the crooks reached the third floor and entered a room.

Listening outside the door, The Shadow soon sensed a definite silence.

That was when he eased the door inward, to make his own entry in the pitch-black gloom. A moment later, The Shadow's flashlight cleaved the blackness.

The room was empty, as he had suddenly supposed, and The Shadow saw the reason. There was a door on the far side, filling a crude entry that had been cut through to the next house.

The thugs had used that route, and they had barred the door behind them. The Shadow learned that when he tried the door itself.

The flashlight showed that the room contained a broken-down cot, a few chairs, and other items of furniture. There was a small trunk in one corner; before examining it, The Shadow went to the windows.

They were shaded with battered blinds. Extinguishing his flashlight, The Shadow pushed a rumpled blind aside and looked out to a rear fire escape. He noted that the window was closed and nailed tight shut, but it wouldn't be difficult to jimmy it in a hurry.

Satisfied that there would be no intrusion from the fire escape, The Shadow went to examine the trunk. He had to pry it open, but he had the necessary tools and kept the process muffled.

The moment that he raised the trunk lid, The Shadow knew what this place was. The trunk tray contained a few old letters, addressed in scrawly writing to Mort Fadler. This was a hideout that the dead triggerman had kept for emergency purposes.

HARD upon that discovery, The Shadow stiffened, his only motion the flick of his thumb to extinguish the flashlight. A new sound had reached him, one that came with no advance notice. In busying himself with opening the trunk, The Shadow had failed to hear an intruder's approach.

The present sound was the slight squeak of hinges from the very door that The Shadow had entered.

Instantaneously, The Shadow recognized the fullness of Legrec's scheme. Though the pair of hoodlums didn't know it, they had been sent on very special duty tonight. Their real purpose had not been an inspection tour.

They had been sent by Legrec to lure The Shadow, if he happened to be watching Margalc's mansion!

The thugs had managed that duty. They had brought The Shadow along a blind trail. By bolting the other door, as ordered, they had automatically changed the old hideout into a trap.

The Shadow had fallen for the subtle snare designed by Legrec. Between The Shadow and the one door that offered an immediate path of departure, was a hidden challenger.

The total darkness served the other man as well as it did The Shadow. The end of this blind trail promised blind battle!

CHAPTER XIV
THE SHADOW'S HUNCH

LEGREC!

The name flashed instantly to The Shadow's brain, so clearly that it seemed a spoken word. There was good reason for The Shadow to receive such a vivid impression of that name.

This was the sort of snare that Legrec would visit in person. It was a place where; with one well-delivered bullet, he could forever rid himself of the menace known as The Shadow.

Identifying the man at the doorway as Legrec, The Shadow saw the advantage that the challenger held.

It was impossible for The Shadow exactly to locate his opponent. On the contrary, there was every reason for Legrec to suppose that The Shadow would be close by the trunk.

Once a duel in the dark began, Legrec would hold the odds. But there was still a way whereby The Shadow might forestall that duel until conditions were more nearly equal.

Coolly, he calculated the thoughts that Legrec would hold. The crook couldn't be positive that The Shadow was at the trunk, unless he heard some betraying sound.

Silence would therefore make Legrec guess; and the longer it persisted, the better. For Legrec would begin to reason that The Shadow was not beside the trunk. He would credit The Shadow with an unrestrained desire to get away from that danger spot.

Hearing nothing, Legrec would eventually decide that he had chosen the wrong moment for entry.

It was certain that Legrec would regard himself capable of detecting a sound on this occasion. This room was small; in its cramped space, Legrec would be able to hear noises of a sort that he had failed to discern at Keever's apartment.

It was a case where conditions were reversed, bringing them to Legrec's advantage. But The Shadow, despite death's imminence, was doing his best to outguess Legrec.

There was a creak of a floorboard. The Shadow's tactics were bringing a reward. His opponent was on the move, coming toward the corner where the trunk was located.

That was The Shadow's chance to shift. He did not take it. Footsteps, vague in their approach, might be Legrec's method of luring The Shadow into making a revealing sound.

The footsteps, however, did not halt, as The Shadow logically expected. Instead, they were creeping closer, almost to a point where The Shadow could accurately locate them.

That was when The Shadow gained a sudden hunch.

Silently, he slid a drawn automatic beneath his cloak. Slowly extending his arms, he waited. His adversary was near, low-drawn breathing furnished a giveaway that footsteps had not revealed. The Shadow was ready for a spring.

Despite the fact that he knew a gun must be aimed straight toward him; that a quick trigger finger was ready for a rapid tug, The Shadow had willingly placed away his own gun.

His hunch had suggested possible circumstances, wherein a silent thrust would be preferable to shots in the dark.

A squeak from the floor. From the way it stilled, The Shadow knew that it meant a final step. A gun was probing through the darkness, ready to press against The Shadow's ribs, when once its muzzle found him.

But The Shadow was shifting without moving his feet. He was close to the floor itself.

LIKE an arrow, The Shadow drove. His gloved hands hooked a pair of hips, taking them with a clutch like that of grappling irons.

At that instant, a revolver spoke, its roar sounding like a cannon directly in The Shadow's car.

With the roar came a tongue of flame that seared the brim of The Shadow's hat. Head shifted to the right, The Shadow had allowed for that shot, which his adversary had considered to be a point-blank stab.

An instant later, The Shadow was hoisting upward, flinging his opponent over his shoulder. Headlong, a figure hit the raised lid of the trunk, carrying it backward with a crash. There was the thud of a revolver striking the wall.

With whippet speed, The Shadow twisted, pounding upon the sprawled man. One hand on the fellow's throat, The Shadow flicked his flashlight with the other.

The Shadow's hunch was right. The attacker was not Gautier Legrec. That was something that his own motions had betrayed. Nevertheless, The Shadow was gripped by one of the most startling surprises in all his long career.

The half-stunned man upon the floor was Inspector Joe Cardona!

WISELY had The Shadow refrained from shooting it out with an unknown assailant. That was a policy that he had long since adopted. In this case, convinced though he was that the foeman must be one of Legrec's tools, The Shadow had followed his regular procedure. As a reward, he had won a triumph over Gautier Legrec.

Somehow, the master crook had guessed that Joe Cardona would find Mort Fadler's hideout. Therewith, Legrec had seen an opportunity to throw the ace inspector into conflict with The Shadow. Staying out of the affair himself, Legrec had nothing to lose but much to gain. He had hoped to rid himself of at least one investigator who might later harass him.

There wasn't time for The Shadow to consider more details. Footsteps were hammering the stairs, indicating that Cardona had brought a squad along with him, but had first come up to make a lone inspection of the premises.

Cardona's gunshot had served as the summons. Explanations wouldn't help if detectives found their leader groggy, with The Shadow hovering about him. They would open battle with The Shadow before Cardona would be able to halt them.

Springing across the room, The Shadow reached the windows. Using the same jimmy that he had employed with the trunk, he ripped open one window, then the other. Rolling through the second window, he closed both sashes from the fire escape.

There wasn't time to get below. The Shadow swung over the edge of the metal platform, took a grip beneath it. Thanks to the open slats, he found a perfect security. His fingers clutched through at one end of the platform, his toes pressed between at the other end.

THE police squad reached the room. Lights appeared; detectives were dragging Cardona to his feet. Joe wasn't quite able to tell what had happened, but the detectives saw the windows and yanked them open.

Wisely, The Shadow had taken time to jimmy both windows. The fact that both were loose made the detectives overlook the nails that had previously held them. One window tight, the other loose, would have been a telltale situation.

As it was, the headquarters men were satisfied when they flicked flashlights down the steps of the fire escape. Others sent up beams from below; but the few on the ground couldn't distinguish The Shadow's outline at that height, anymore than the men at the window could spot him through the slats of the platform.

The detectives in the room decided to smash the bolted door that led into the next house. Recuperating from his groggy condition, Cardona directed the work. He took it for granted that his recent opponent had used that route.

MEANWHILE, The Shadow squeezed out from beneath the platform and made a silent descent of the fire escape. Detectives were absent when he reached the bottom. He supposed that they had gone indoors. Therein, The Shadow was mistaken.

Reaching the next street, he came suddenly upon two detectives. Whipping from sight, he moved rapidly toward the street, disregarding a lighted section, because it was past a parked car. At that instant, The Shadow spotted the motion of a car across the street.

As The Shadow dived back, guns roared. In that car were the two hoodlums who had lured him along the trail. They were just starting their own getaway, when they spied The Shadow. Their attempt to drop him had been a foolish effort.

From his new position, The Shadow had an excellent chance to clip the thugs as they wheeled past. All that saved them was the sudden arrival of the detectives. As luck had it, the dicks chose The Shadow's own location as a place from which to fire.

Rather than run into complications, The Shadow whisked along the curb, dropping beside another parked car. He was leaving the battle to the headquarters men, who didn't even see him go.

But in their hurry, the detectives were useless as marksmen. Their shots whizzed wide of the swift-moving car, for already its occupants realized that they had failed in their hasty thrust against The Shadow.

By the time the detectives had chased the fleeing car past the next corner, The Shadow was on his way in the opposite direction. As he reached enshrouding blackness, his hidden lips phrased a grim low laugh.

The law had gained nothing from this latest episode. Joe Cardona would discount the fray at Mort's hideout, figuring he had met up with some pal of the dead triggerman. In turn, The Shadow had made no progress with his investigation of affairs at the Margale mansion.

That matter, however, was one that he could manage on the morrow, but from a different starting point. The Shadow did not intend to resume investigation from the outside.

Instead, he was planning a new measure to off-set Legrec; one whereby The Shadow could gain facts from within the house itself.

CHAPTER XV
HARRY SEEKS TROUBLE

AT dusk, the next evening, Eleanor Margale heard a rap at the door of her second floor room. A servant was summoning her downstairs with the word that her uncle wished to see her.

The servant took the back way to the kitchen. Eleanor went down the front stairs, to get another surprise.

Nordham was standing there. That was logical enough, for he was the only one of all the servants who had recently been allowed in the front hallway. But Nordham was not disengaged. Instead, he was close to the front door, peering through the panes of a tiny window at one side of it.

Eleanor approached. Nordham heard her; turned with a start.

"What is the trouble?" undertoned the girl.

Nordham gestured nervously toward the little window.

"The house is watched," he whispered. "I'm sure of it, Miss Margale!"

"But why?"

"Because of the young man who came this afternoon."

"What young man?"

Eleanor was utterly perplexed. Nordham explained. The young man's name was Harry Vincent. Why he had come here was a mystery. At present, he was with Thomas Margale, in the study.

"That's why your uncle wanted you," Nordham told Eleanor. "Since there is a guest, he intends to dine in the dining room; and he expects you, also, Miss Margale. To help entertain Mr. Vincent."

Eleanor was relieved. She had expected some aftermath regarding her adventure of a few nights ago. As yet, her uncle had not quizzed her on that subject.

A voice came from the study. It was querulous; Thomas Margale was demanding to know how soon dinner would be ready. Nordham went to the kitchen, while Eleanor turned to face her uncle.

The girl's relief increased at sight of Harry Vincent.

For a long while, Eleanor had worried over the problem of her uncle's visitors. She had always doubted that they would be the sort of persons that she would care to meet. Harry, however, was a pleasant surprise.

He was a clean-cut young man, likable at first sight. Even though his purpose here was unexplained, Eleanor was glad that he had come.

THEY dined in a big, musty dining room. Thomas Margale left the task of entertaining Harry to his niece. While they chatted, he kept up a steady glower, that Eleanor noted. It was plain that Margale was not pleased by Harry's presence.

The crab-faced millionaire began to take it out on Nordham, who was serving the dinner. Nothing was to Margale's liking. He became almost violent over the matter of the salad dressing.

In fact, Margale's actions so disturbed Eleanor that she forgot all about Harry. Her uncle had half risen from the table; was shaking his fist at Nordham. Eleanor was about to intervene, when the argument ended. An instant later, she had remembered that Harry was present.

The reason was something that flipped the table beside her and took a short bounce into her lap. It was a wadded note. Eleanor gave a quick look at Harry; then nodded. She kept that message for later inspection.

It was after dinner, when her uncle and the visitor had gone into the study, that Eleanor found a chance to read the note. Its wording was terse:

> Must see you privately. Be in the library. Make sure no one can overhear us.
>
> V.

That was a tall order, considering her uncle's present mood. Eleanor doubted that the interview could be conducted without interference. Then she thought of Nordham. The servant had proven a real ally, in the past. This was a chance to use him again.

Finding Nordham, Eleanor showed him the note. It made the servant shake his head.

"The library would be impossible, Miss Margale," he said. "Your uncle might decide to go in there at any time."

"But Mr. Vincent is depending upon me—"

"To meet him in the library," nodded Nordham. "But you must talk with him elsewhere. I would suggest the little smoking room just behind the library."

Eleanor smiled. The suggestion was a good one. The smoking room had two doors: one from the library, the other from the little-used passage that led to the side door of the house. They would have to enter from the library, for the passage door was always locked. Eleanor mentioned that to Nordham.

"Quite so, Miss Margale," said the servant. "I shall remain in the library, arranging the books. If your uncle comes, I can warn you."

"Good," agreed Eleanor. "I'll depend on you, Nordham."

MEANWHILE, matters were progressing in Margale's study. Secluded with the crabby millionaire, Harry had resumed a conversation that he had started before dinner.

As an agent of The Shadow, Harry was here with the definite purpose of finding out unusual facts that might concern Thomas Margale. He had a perfect smoke-screen for that task. The Shadow had provided Harry with a legitimate purpose for the visit.

The Shadow had learned that Margale was the administrator of a fifty-thousand-dollar trust fund that belonged to Eleanor. That sum was too small to figure in any twisted schemes that might concern Margale at present. But it was the very wedge that The Shadow had needed.

There were other trustees besides Margale. They had not heard from the millionaire for months. Through a prominent physician, The Shadow had stirred those trustees with an inquiry regarding Margale's mental condition.

Like others who knew Margale, the trustees had heard rumors about Margale. They had dismissed them as idle talk, until the physician questioned them. Thereupon, they had agreed that someone should visit Margale. Harry had been introduced as an excellent man for the job.

Whatever Margale's actual condition, he was shrewd enough to see what lay behind Harry's visit, especially when Harry repeated that he had come at the request of Eleanor's trustees. The matter reached a showdown.

"They think I'm crazy, do they?" sneered Margale, from behind his desk. His eyes gleamed fiercely, as much like a vulture's as his profile. "What would they say, Mr. Vincent, if I told them that the trust fund had shown a ten percent increase since last year?"

"They would be pleased, Mr. Margale," assured Harry. "You understand, this is not an inquiry—"

Margale ended the statement with a fierce gesture. He turned toward a bulky safe; then swung about again. From the desk, he produced a metal box.

Soon, Margale had spread the contents on the desk. Here were the stocks that made up the trust fund; with them, tabulated figures. Harry went over them in detail. Margale was right; Eleanor's fund was in order and had shown the stated increase.

Politely, Harry arose with a thank you. He was turning toward the door when Margale stopped him.

"Tell them something else," stormed the millionaire. "Tell them that you found out nothing about my affairs! I saw your face, Vincent, when I turned back from the safe. You wanted to see what was in there, didn't you?" Ugly shrewdness was on Margale's lips. "And you didn't manage it.

"You're not the first who has tried that game, Vincent. Perhaps"—Margale's eyes fastened on Harry's with a beady stare—"perhaps you've been prying into the affairs of others beside myself."

Harry shook his head. Margale's lips twitched, as though the millionaire doubted his own suspicions.

"Certain things have happened recently," reminded Margale, narrowly—"certain things that were unfortunate—let us say coincidental—regarding certain persons."

Harry knew the persons meant: Balcray, Lysand and Keever. He was prepared for some significant remark concerning those three; and The Shadow's orders were to draw Margale along that path. Harry handled it well.

"If you mean the trustees of Miss Margale's estate," he said, innocently, "I can assure you that they are merely worried."

"Those simpletons?" Margale tilted his head for a deep-gargled laugh. "Bah! I never think of them, except when they remind me of their presence. I refer to others!"

MARGALE halted. Harry's gaze was blank. Twitching lips compressed, Margale arose from his desk and crouched over his big cane, as he pressed a buzzer.

Nordham appeared. Crisply, Margale instructed the servant:

"Mr. Vincent is leaving. Perhaps he may wish to speak with my niece. If so, he may be permitted." Margale swung to Harry. "Perhaps you may care to call again.

"You will be welcome, Mr. Vincent. Very welcome! In fact"—Margale's tone took on a bitterness—"another visit would be pleasant. I might induce you to state the names of those persons whose affairs actually interest you!"

Margale's whole face was ablaze. He was standing without the aid of his cane; apparently, he did not realize it, until Nordham spoke in alarm. Realizing his own position, Margale let his knees give way. Nordham caught him; helped him into a chair.

"My medicine"—Margale was panting—"my medicine, Nordham! No, no, not those pills! The tonic that I brought from France!"

"But you said, sir—"

"I said nothing!" Margale was huddled, pitifully, his eyes wide and staring. "Bring that bottle, Nordham!"

The servant brought a bottle from a small cabinet; he poured out a milkish liquid into a cordial glass. Margale swallowed the tonic with one gulp. He sank back into his chair.

Nordham conducted Harry toward the door. When they were almost there, Margale called. His voice was weary; it had a surprising mildness.

"Good evening, Mr. Vincent" were his words. "I trust that you will pardon any undue remarks that I have made. I am not myself; I am actually an ill man.

"But this trust fund"—he gestured toward the box—"is in the best of condition. Like my own affairs"—a satisfied smile came on the tired lips—"it prospers. Remember that, Vincent."

Nordham was holding the door open; his face was toward Harry. The visitor saw a motion of the servant's lips, caught their undertone:

"See Miss Eleanor, sir. Before he changes his mind—"

The advice was good. Harry stepped from the study. The door closed behind him, for Nordham was humoring Margale further. With the closing of that door came silence.

Harry was alone in the big front hall, his interview with Thomas Margale finished. He was ready for the rest of his mission: a talk with Eleanor.

With all his nerve, Harry could not repress a long breath of relief. He felt that the dangerous part of his task had been finished.

Therein, Harry Vincent was mistaken. The menace within this gloomy mansion was deeper than he supposed.

The Shadow had sent Harry here to seek out trouble. Harry was to find it.

CHAPTER XVI
THE VANISHED GUEST

INSTEAD of crossing the big front hall, Harry Vincent went toward the outer door. Beside the little window from which Nordham had previously peered, Harry produced a flashlight. He blinked it through the pane.

Harry was flashing news to an outside watcher, stating that all had gone well. Moreover, he was adding the number of minutes that he intended to remain: a quarter-hour in all.

This was one of The Shadow's precautions, having contact ready. But Harry was convinced that it would no longer be needed; therefore, it was better that the outside man should report to The Shadow.

Harry based his opinion on the fact that he had cut short Margale's quiz. Matters, as Harry saw them, had not gone beyond the safety limit. That was why Harry was using a privilege that The Shadow always granted his agents: that of relying on their own judgment.

Occasionally, such judgment erred; but not often, with a man like Harry. Tonight, however, Harry's guesses were very, very wide. He had hit a bad snag without realizing it.

Entering the library, Harry found Eleanor waiting there. The girl had just greeted him with a whisper, when they heard the door of Margale's study open. Eleanor pointed quickly to the open door of the little smoking room. Harry told her to wait.

"Your uncle gave me permission for this interview," he told Eleanor. "We can wait and see what happens."

Nordham appeared. The servant tiptoed to the spot where Harry and Eleanor stood.

"He's likely to change again, sir," Nordham told Harry. "I managed to stop that tantrum of his—but I know Mr. Margale. He'll rage again, soon."

"He will," agreed Eleanor, soberly. "Tell me, Nordham; do you think he will become angry if he believes that Mr. Vincent is still here?"

"It's best to take no chances."

Nordham's words were serious. They brought prompt decision. Eleanor motioned Harry into the smoking room, while Nordham nodded at her orders. The girl was telling the servant to keep close watch on her uncle; to inform them immediately if his wild mood returned.

IN the smoking room, with the door tight closed, Eleanor asked Harry:

"What can I tell you, Mr. Vincent?"

The tone carried trust. It told that Eleanor felt she could rely upon this outside friend. Harry wasted no time.

"Tell me everything that concerns your uncle," he replied. "Who his friends are, what they are, and, particularly, any matters that have directly concerned you."

There was significance in the final words. Eleanor caught it. She knew that Harry was testing her, by a subtle reference to her adventure in the house on Twentieth Street. Intuitively, the girl divined that Harry must have come from the black-cloaked rescuer who had saved her life.

"I know nothing about my uncle's friends," Eleanor admitted, ruefully, "except that certain visitors came here frequently, until about a week ago. My uncle was always mysterious regarding them; I never saw them, nor did Nordham."

"And then—"

Harry inserted the words; but not as a question. Eleanor understood. She poured the whole story of the episode that had taken her to Roban's, with all that had happened afterward. When she finished, she awaited questions. Harry put some.

"The voice over the telephone," asked Harry—"you are sure that you had never heard it before?"

"Never!" replied Eleanor. "I am positive."

"And the paper in the drawer of the telephone table. You say it was in your uncle's handwriting?"

"I think so. It looked like his."

"You have examined the paper since?"

Eleanor shook her head. Her expression was troubled.

"No," she replied, "because it was gone after I returned that night."

Harry considered. He recalled an important question that The Shadow wanted answered.

"How were you found so promptly?" he asked. "The cab had, of course, come for you."

"Yes," nodded Eleanor. "Nordham brought it. The driver of his cab had heard me give the destination to my driver."

"But your uncle gave Nordham no instructions?"

"Only to bring me back here. I was still in the house and heard the order. When Nordham told me the same thing, later, I knew that he spoke the truth."

The fact impressed Harry. He was here to learn if anyone in the household—specifically, a person like Nordham—was in Margale's confidence. Eleanor's statement proved definitely that Margale was not using Nordham as a secret aide in any of his hidden transactions.

Harry's conclusion was that Margale had known Eleanor's destination, and had been in a bad dilemma. He certainly would not have wanted her to go to Roban's; and he could not risk sending Nordham there.

That left one logical inference. Knowing that Eleanor had been gone only a few minutes, Margale had hoped that Nordham would overtake her before she traveled far.

HARRY was groping for another question, when a cautious rap sounded against the door from the library.

It was Nordham; his face was worried.

"I've been in and out of the study, Miss Margale," informed the servant. "I just suspected that your uncle has been using the telephone. Something has come over him. He's very suspicious. Asking to see you."

"Where is he now?"

"Pacing the study, as if he were coming out here any moment. He'll soon want to talk to you."

Eleanor decided that she would see her uncle immediately. It offered a chance to learn more facts for Harry. He nodded, when Eleanor suggested that he remain in the smoking room.

"Nordham can go into the study with me," said Eleanor. "If wise; I can signal for him to leave. He can then tell you whether it is best to stay or go."

Eleanor left with Nordham. Harry remained in the smoking room, with the door slightly ajar. He listened, as he glanced at his watch. His fifteen minutes were two-thirds gone.

Though Harry strained, he could hear nothing. Sounds were absent from the front of the mansion. Somehow, the hush was maddening, particularly when Harry imagined peculiar, indefinite noises that had no exact location.

A distant scrape; sounds that resembled a peculiar creep—they couldn't come from the study, for its door was closed. Were they upstairs somewhere? Were other servants, practically unmentioned by Eleanor, persons who needed to be watched?

A peculiar—oppressiveness seized Harry. He closed the door; turned about to pace the silence of the smoking room. Oddly, those sounds became more apparent as he turned. Before that fact had drilled his wits, Harry had a visible explanation.

With a quick intake of his breath, he sped his hand to his hip, hoping to draw an automatic. The move was hopelessly late.

A trio of masked men swooped upon Harry, so suddenly that they might have come from nowhere. They had his gun hand pinned in back of him; they were choking him as he struggled.

His eyes bulging, Harry saw the answer to their arrival.

They had come through the back door of the smoking room. The scraping noise had been the turning of the door's lock. The creepings, seemingly distant, had been their sneak behind Harry's very back!

That understanding was Harry's last impression, except for a wave of blackish spots that came when an implement thudded the back of his head. A few seconds later, The Shadow's agent was a limp prisoner in the hands of his captors.

The masked men shouldered Harry out through the door. They locked it behind them. There was a slight thud beyond, as the side door of the house went shut.

THE departure was a timely one. Two minutes later, Eleanor Margale opened the door from the library. Thinking that Harry was still in the smoking room, she whispered:

"It's all right—my uncle has calmed. Nordham is with him—"

Eleanor stopped, puzzled by the silence. She stared all about the room. Her lips trembled; she couldn't believe that Harry could have lost his nerve and gone without word. Suddenly, the girl spied an object beneath a chair.

A moment later, she was holding the automatic that Harry had failed to pull. It had slipped from his grasping hand, to leave his pocket during the struggle. Hurried captors had overlooked the gun.

Grimly, Eleanor turned toward the library. From the determination on her face, her purpose was plain. She was going to the study, to demand an explanation from her uncle.

Eleanor had no doubt regarding the evidence that she had found. It told of the foul play that had come to Harry. But it was more than a clue, that gun. It was something that she could use as a threat of her own.

In the doorway, Eleanor hesitated. Like Harry, she thought that she had heard sounds. She recognized their source more swiftly: that rear door from the passage!

Eleanor turned, aiming the automatic, her finger on the trigger. A driving figure launched upon her; a hand took the gun in one swift clutch. The weapon was literally plucked from Eleanor's hand; before she could scream, she was half smothered in a suppressing grasp.

Cloth folds bagged Eleanor's head. Choking, she heard the library door go shut. Pressure relaxed; Eleanor stared into burning eyes. Panting, wondering, she recognized the intruder who had stopped her effort at gunfire.

Eleanor's captor was The Shadow!

HIDDEN lips spoke reassurance. With the first words, Eleanor realized that The Shadow knew about Harry's visit; that he, too, was concerned over the young man's disappearance.

Eagerly, Eleanor repeated all that she had told before, finishing with the last few minutes, wherein she had visited the study.

The Shadow had a new question. It concerned Thomas Margale.

"Nordham brought word that your uncle asked to see you," he reminded. "Just what did your uncle have to say?"

"Nothing important," replied Eleanor. Then, indignantly: "It was a sham—to bring me in there, with Nordham. My uncle was seated at his desk, in one of his glum moods. He sneered, as he often does, when he asked me what I wanted."

"And you told him—"

"That I understood he wanted to talk with me. He decided that he did. He asked why I was not satisfied with his management of my affairs. When I gave no answer, he muttered to himself, until he seemed to tire. He seemed half asleep when I left the study."

There was silence; then The Shadow's tone:

"Say nothing to your uncle. Tell Nordham that Vincent must have left. By forgetting all that has happened—for the present, at least—you will be in no danger."

The Shadow pointed toward the library door. Eleanor nodded. Though the instructions puzzled her, she was willing to obey. As she entered the library, she heard a whispered laugh; it faded vaguely.

That strange mirth was prophetic. It gave Eleanor full confidence. She turned, to speak a last word to The Shadow. Her eyes showed bewilderment. The cloaked visitant had already departed.

Only the whispered tone of The Shadow seemed to linger in that room where dim floor lamps glowed.

Another visitor to the Margale mansion had vanished into the outer night.

CHAPTER XVII
THE MADDENED MESSAGE

SCANT minutes had passed between the time of Harry's capture and The Shadow's arrival at the mansion; but that period had been long enough for the raiders to manage a quick getaway.

Summoned to Margale's to remove a man who had begun to learn too much, the snatchers had apparently worked in accordance with a clockwork plan.

Harry realized that, himself, when he regained a brief spell of consciousness. He sensed motion; decided that he was riding inside a truck. About him, he could hear the mutters of his captors; occasionally, a flashlight glimmered.

One light flickered toward Harry's face. He shut his eyes, faking a stupor. Chances were that if his captors knew he had come to life, they would favor him with another knockout blow.

Any attempt at escape was hopeless, for the present. Harry's arms and legs were bound; the chafing cords were too tight to be slipped. Shifting his shoulders a trifle, Harry managed to prop his aching head in a spot where it thumped less. That was the extent of his effort.

The truck came to a stop. Men hauled Harry to a darkened street; shoved him into a touring car. Pushed to the floor by the rear seat, Harry could do nothing more than count the turns that the car made at corners, particularly because a grimy lap robe was stretched across his head and shoulders.

That car might have been anywhere on Manhattan Island, when it stopped. The chance had arrived, though, for Harry to take bearings and locate where he was. So Harry thought; but his captors had different ideas.

As they hauled him up from the floor, one man held a flashlight in Harry's eyes; another shoved a hard fist against the prisoner's jaw.

It was blotto, again, for Harry.

The punch could not have left him groggy for many minutes; but it was long enough for Harry to lose all track of where the carriers took him. When he again noted his surroundings, he was lying on an old couch, in a dimly lighted room.

There was considerable furniture about; all the chairs were adorned with dust covers. The place looked like a storeroom; and the effect was ghostly.

What light there was trickled from a transom, to show the shrouded furniture in outlandish shapes.

From somewhere, Harry could hear the murmur of street traffic; but it sounded very different. Half groggy, he arose from the couch and tried to find a window. A breeze guided him toward one wall; there, he encountered a Venetian blind.

The slats of the blind were closed, but the window beyond them was open. Faint lines of light showed between the slats, and Harry pried the blind with his fingers, thinking that he could force a gap. He failed, and the reason astonished him.

The blind was made of steel. Those slats were as strong a barrier as iron bars!

While Harry leaned against the wall beside the window, he heard the turning of a key. Light flooded from the hallway, when the door opened. A pair of huskies saw Harry, advanced with growls. They shoved their prisoner through a narrow hallway, sent him sprawling into another room.

From hands and knees, Harry looked up to see an elderly man crouched above a desk that was lighted by a single lamp. Seldom in all his experience had he seen so evil a face.

The old man had a yellowish smooth-drawn countenance, with glittering eyes. Above his withered features was a mass of white hair.

Harry recognized the fellow from a description furnished by The Shadow; later, by Eleanor Margale.

The man was Rupert Roban.

A PLEASED cackle issued from Roban's lips. It was the murderous tone that Eleanor had mentioned. Something in its lingering note gave Harry an added impression; but whether it was better or worse, the prisoner could not guess.

It signified simply that Harry was one person whose life Roban intended to preserve; but the malice in the old man's eyes betokened lack of mercy. Life, in Roban's power, might prove far less desirable than death.

"Your name"—Roban's eyes took on a false friendliness, as his cackle softened—"is Harry Vincent. Am I correct?"

There was no use denying it. Harry nodded.

"You are searching for a man named Legrec." Roban was leaning forward, to watch the effect of his words. "Am I again correct?"

Harry moved his lips slowly, as though trying to pronounce a name that he had not understood. Roban's laugh was a scoffing one.

"Legrec," he repeated. "Gautier Legrec. Suppose"—his lips pursed wisely—"suppose that I told you that you had found Legrec. Would that please you?"

"Legrec"—Harry pretended to catch the name—"is that your name?"

Withery lips showed a slow smile.

"I call myself Legrec," declared Roban. "How long I shall choose to do so, is another question."

Harry considered the statement. Roban had denied that he was Legrec, the time that Eleanor had invaded his stronghold. That, however, had been at a place different from this one, under circumstances that Roban had not liked.

Perhaps Roban had feared that Eleanor might escape him, hence had taken no chances in declaring a double identity. Certainly, on that occasion, Roban had been ready to abandon one headquarters to seek another one. His position had lacked complete security.

Here, he was complete master. Not only was his isolated stronghold unknown; it was peopled with henchmen of the sort who had carried Harry hither.

Still, Harry was not certain of Roban's reason for declaring himself Legrec, until the old man demanded:

"Who sent you where you went tonight?"

That explained it! Roban wanted Harry to betray himself. Mention of the name Legrec had been the test. Those shrewd eyes of Roban's had a searching power that never lessened. In part, at least, Roban had delved into Harry's thoughts.

Coolly, Harry explained his pretended mission at the Margale mansion. Roban listened in a cunning manner that was worthy of Legrec. When Harry finished, Roban jabbed:

"Suppose I set you free? Where would you go?"

"Back to my hotel," supplied Harry. Then, with a forced smile: "To sleep off this nightmare."

Roban bounced to his feet, pointed a bony finger across the desk.

"You lie!" he shrilled. "I can tell exactly what you would do. You would report to The Shadow!"

Harry tried to look puzzled. It wasn't a good effort.

"Who is he?" demanded Roban. "The man you call The Shadow?"

"Never heard of him," insisted Harry.

"Again you lie!" Roban spat the words. "Again, I give you an opportunity. Who is The Shadow?"

Silence seemed the best answer. Harry used it.

"You cannot deceive Legrec," sneered Roban. "Time will come when you will babble all I wish to hear. You will know the power of Legrec!"

THE old man rattled his clawish knuckles on the desk. It was a signal for others to enter. With a valiant effort, Harry came to his feet, took a lunge in Roban's direction.

Like a whippet, the shocky-haired crook twisted away. He whisked a revolver from his pocket, had it against Harry's ribs when a pair of rowdies entered.

"He tried to deceive Legrec," sneered the old

man. "I shall show you the treatment that I have provided for his sort."

While the thugs held Harry, Roban produced a cone of the type used for administering ether. He clapped it upon Harry's face and turned on a supply of gas.

Harry whiffed an overwhelming odor; he tried to struggle away. The men beside him clamped him to the floor.

Harry expected his senses to leave him. Instead, the room seemed to revolve, while Roban's voice pitched higher amid the basso rumbles of the hoodlums who gripped Harry.

The air crackled. Voices seemed to ring out a hideous chant; a name that thrummed through Harry's brain:

"Legrec—Legrec—Legrec—Legrec—Legrec—"

The gas cone was off. Harry saw faces that looked unreal. Roban's yellowish countenance was tinged with a demonish red, like the face of a tormenting devil. The thugs seemed tusky monsters as they leered.

All objects in the room were distorted. The desk, the chairs, even the walls appeared to swell, then dwindle. At moments, Harry huddled, fearing that the ceiling would swoop down and crush him. At other instants, it looked as faraway as the sky.

Detached phrases wafted upon Harry's ears. They were in hoarse voices, spoken by Legrec's grinning helpers.

"It's knocked him loco, Legrec!"

"Like you said it would!"

"How long will it keep him goofy?" another asked.

Those voices became incoherent, but Harry could hear Roban's tone; it seemed shrilled to a treble.

"The effect of hashish," spoke Roban. "The drug called *bhang*. He will remember what Legrec wishes him to remember"—it seemed to Harry that there was a long pause; then a hideous laugh— "and no more! Later, he will talk. Perhaps another treatment—"

The words became hazy, babbly. Harry felt himself tugged from the room. The hallway was undergoing kaleidoscopic changes, twisting its shape, so that Harry could not hold his footing. The thugs jostled him along, gibing their ugly laughs close to his ears.

After a journey that was mentally prolonged, Harry reached the room where he had first been. They shoved him on the couch. Seconds seemed minutes until the door slammed. The grating of the key was a long-drawn wail.

HARRY'S hands fumbled for his pockets. His fingers found an envelope, tore the front from it. Vaguely, he remembered that it bore his address. Finding a pencil, Harry clutched it and began to scrawl a message.

The words that he wrote were a cipher in themselves. They made but little sense; except in snatches:

Prison—Leg—Roban says he—*bhang*—talk later—hours—loco—window—

Though he held the paper toward the light, Harry could not see the words he scrawled. Each motion of his pencil took a huge labor from his hand; his fingers numbed, so much that he could not even add his initials.

To himself, Harry muttered:

"Name on envelope have to do—got to send this. Right away—got to, right away—"

He was off the couch, reeling in slow-motion fashion toward the window. Harry's forehead thumped the metal blind. He fingered the slats; somehow, he couldn't remember why he had come there, until he sensed the crinkle of the envelope.

Harry's fingers clawed the slats. That touch, connected with the envelope front, reminded him of a mail box. He dug his fingernails deep; wedged the sheet of paper through.

"Going somewhere," muttered Harry. "It's— going—even if I'm—not—"

A last dig of the fingernails. The envelope was through, fluttering in the air outside the window. Harry's knees caved; his fingers rattled from the metal blind. A few moments later, Harry had folded on the floor.

In his last moment of effort against the drug supplied by Legrec, Harry Vincent had dispatched his maddened message to The Shadow!

CHAPTER XVIII
TWO MEN AGREE

WHILE schemes of Legrec were faring well, Alan Rigby was seated morosely in his penthouse living room. On the table before him lay bulky report sheets supplied by the police. From them, Rigby had gathered nothing upon which to work.

A telephone bell jangled. Rigby eyed the telephone with worried air; paced to an outer door, to beckon in a plainclothesman who was standing by the elevator.

"Somebody's on the wire," informed Rigby. "You'd better answer it. Legrec is nervy enough to call here. If he does, I'd like to have someone check his voice beside myself."

"The phone rang?" The dick was surprised. "I didn't hear it, outside the door."

"There it is again." Rigby smiled as the call was repeated. "Answer it, as I told you."

The plainclothesman lifted the receiver, gruffed a "Hello." His serious look changed to a grin.

"It's from downstairs," he told Rigby. "Mr. Cranston wants to see you, the doorman says."

"Tell him to come up," ordered Rigby. Then, when the dick had done so: "Do you know Mr. Cranston when you see him?"

The plainclothesman nodded.

"Very well," decided Rigby. "Make sure it is Cranston, before you usher him in here. Mistakes can prove costly, when one is dealing with Legrec."

It was Cranston who appeared from the elevator. The headquarters man admitted the commissioner's friend, then took his post outside the living room door.

Rigby shook hands, motioned the visitor to a chair. Scanning Cranston's usually impassive face, Rigby commented:

"Something is troubling you, old chap."

Cranston nodded. He looked toward the door. Rigby smiled.

"You can speak. The good old watchdog can't hear a thing that is said here. But if you prefer—"

He gestured his hand toward the penthouse

terrace, inviting Cranston to accompany him there.

"Where Clyston was slain?" Cranston's tone was troubled. "Surely, it is not safe out there. Unless you have another guard posted."

"There is one," assured Rigby. "But he is in the hotel next door. In the very room, in fact, from which Mort Fadler sniped poor Clyston. The terrace is quite safe, I assure you. But I must leave word that we have gone there."

WHILE Cranston was strolling out through the French window, Rigby went to the anteroom to talk with the man who guarded the elevator. Returning, he stopped in the pantry for several minutes. When he joined Cranston, Rigby was carrying a tray with bottles, seltzer and ice.

Cranston was seated at the little table, his hat on a chair beside him. He shook his head at Rigby's offer of a drink.

"I'm badly worried," he confessed. Then, abruptly: "Tell me, Rigby; wouldn't this fellow Legrec have a hideout somewhere?"

"He certainly must have," returned Rigby, "if he is still in New York. But we have not been able to prove that he has remained here."

"I feel positive"—Cranston's tone was slow, but emphatic—"that Legrec is still about."

Rigby showed immediate interest to hear more.

"I have come to you," explained Cranston, "because the matter still lacks certainty; moreover, it is somewhat personal. To put it briefly, a friend of mine has disappeared."

"You think Legrec is responsible?"

"Yes. Because, tonight, that friend—whose name is Harry Vincent—went to see a man named Thomas Margale."

Rigby tried to recall the name. He shook his head. It wasn't mentioned in any of the police reports.

"Vincent chanced to call me," explained Cranston, "because he knew that I was acquainted with Legrec's three victims: Balcray, Lysand, and Keever. I had asked Vincent, among others, to look for anyone who knew all three.

"From the message that Vincent left at the Cobalt Club, it appears that Thomas Margale, who is reputedly a man of much wealth, was a friend of the three dead men."

Rigby's eagerness increased, then faded.

"What sort of a chap is this Vincent?" he quizzed. "How did he learn these facts about Margale?"

"Vincent is reliable," assured Cranston. "The rest, I cannot state. However, there is another important fact. I was to hear from Vincent by eight-thirty. It is now nine o'clock, but there has been no word from him."

Rigby poured himself a drink. He paced beside the table, weighing all that Cranston had said. He remarked aloud that the matter had interest, even though its threads were flimsy. Then, with finality.

"I see your inference, Cranston," declared Rigby. "Margale *could* be Legrec. For that matter"— Rigby's tone was hopeless—"anyone *might* be Legrec. But to have the law invade Margale's home"—the investigator shook his head—"such a step would be unwise, on such slight evidence."

"That is why I came to you," observed Cranston.

"In hope that I would go there?" questioned Rigby. "That would be even worse. Legrec would know me in an instant."

"That is not my plan." Cranston's tone was calm. "I intend to call on Thomas Margale myself."

An enthused look came to Rigby's face.

"Excellent!" he decided. "But if Margale does not expect you—"

"He will expect me. I shall telephone him first. From here, if you will permit me."

RIGBY invited Cranston indoors. Consulting the telephone book, Cranston found Margale's number then dialed it.

"Hello." Cranston's voice was level. "Mr. Margale's residence?... My name? Lamont Cranston... Yes, I would like to talk with Mr. Margale..."

Lowering the telephone, Cranston added, to Rigby: "It was some servant who answered. A solemn-voiced fellow."

A long pause followed; then:

"Hello." Cranston was brisk this time. "Mr. Margale? My name is Cranston—a friend of Mr. Vincent... What's that? You say Vincent has left... Yes, so I understood; but there is a matter he wanted me to discuss with you...

"No. It would be impossible over the telephone. But I can be at your house in fifteen minutes... A half hour would be much better? Very well..."

Hanging up, Cranston dialed another number. This time he called the Cobalt Club, to leave a message for Commissioner Weston. It was to the effect that the commissioner could reach him within an hour at Rigby's penthouse.

Rigby was pleased by the second call. It meant that Weston would be waiting when Cranston returned. He promised, however, to make no mention of the Margale visit until Cranston had time to return.

One point, though, troubled Rigby.

"If something has happened to Vincent," he remarked, "you may be walking into similar trouble, Cranston. Therefore, we should take precautions."

"What would you suggest?" was Cranston's question.

"That I send my outside man along to Margale's," returned Rigby. "I mean the detective that the commissioner furnished. Not with you, of course"—he added that, as Cranston started an objection—"but after you have started."

"You will have him remain outside there?"

"Yes. Ready at your call."

"That would be quite agreeable."

THERE was a smile on Cranston's lips when he stood in the little anteroom, waiting for the elevator. The stationed detective observed it, and wondered what it meant.

He would have liked a view of Rigby's face, also; for he knew that Cranston had conferred with the investigator. But Rigby had remained in the penthouse, to make some notes.

The elevator was a long while coming up. Cranston's faint smile had vanished, leaving his face inscrutable. At last, the elevator door slid open; the hawk-faced visitor stepped aboard.

The Shadow was embarked upon new adventure: a journey that was to bring swifter consequences than Harry's visit to the Margale mansion.

The elevator operator halted at the eighteenth floor. A lanky man stepped aboard; with him was a square-built companion. Despite their attire, neither looked the sort who lived at the Weatherly Arms. They were rough characters, more like the elevator operator.

The car halted again at the sixteenth. Another tough-faced passenger joined the group. He shifted to a corner, to avoid the closing door. An instant later, he had swung about. His coat front was open, showing a sweater instead of a vest. His fist had a revolver, tugged from his hip.

The gun muzzle poked for Cranston; hard lips grated the order:

"Up with the mitts, mug!"

There would be no shooting on that elevator. The Shadow was confident of that, from the moment the first toughs had stepped into the car.

Gunshots would echo up and down the shaft. Under the circumstances, The Shadow could play the part he preferred: that of Cranston.

The hawklike face lost its impassive air. Cranston seemed bewildered; so greatly, that the thugs who flanked him let half-drawn guns slide back into their pockets.

The elevator operator was with the band. He pulled the lever, but the elevator did not descend. Instead, it went up; when it reached the level of Rigby's penthouse, it continued higher.

The car stopped at the very top of the shaft. The operator opened the door to let the passengers step out into the second floor of the duplex penthouse!

This was Clyston's secret: the reason why Rigby's servant had been assassinated. Clyston had been in league with Legrec. He had rented the duplex, with its top floor cut off, so that there would be a secret apartment above Rigby's own!

CROOKS shoved Cranston along a passage, into a room where a lamplight glowed. There, The Shadow saw the triumphant figure of Rupert Roban bowed above his desk.

With cackled laugh, the counterfeiter spoke one word:

"Listen!"

He pressed a switch. There were three seconds of silence, then Rigby's voice, conversing over a telephone.

"Yes, Cranston was here, Commissioner... I expect him back within an hour..."

Roban cut off the switch.

"I hear all that passes below," he sneered. "Because I am Legrec! Tell me, since you are Vincent's friend—do you know The Shadow?"

Cranston's face showed perfect ignorance. It passed Roban's scrutiny. His look became contemptuous.

"We shall not waste time with questions," he declared. "If you have anything to say, it can come later."

Crooks threw a quick grip on the prisoner. Roban pressed the conical appliance to The Shadow's disguised face. The tall form of Cranston swayed almost immediately. Roban held the cone in place a half minute longer.

"Enough!" he decided. "Take him away. Legrec commands!"

Ready hands drew the tottering form along the passage, gave the new prisoner an unceremonious shove into a small room that resembled Harry's prison. The thugs saw Cranston miss the couch and roll heavily to the floor. They laughed as they locked the door.

Whether they would have scoffed more, or less, had they known their captive was The Shadow was an unanswered question. For the present, the guise of Cranston had served its part.

Even Legrec did not know that in capturing Lamont Cranston, he had taken The Shadow!

CHAPTER XIX
MURDER AT THE MANSION

THE electric clock on Rigby's mantel had passed the hour of ten. Commissioner Weston showed anxiety; so did Joe Cardona, who was with him. Their concern was caused by Rigby's recent statements.

The investigator had told them the details of Cranston's visit.

"You shouldn't have let him go there alone!" stormed Weston. "It was folly, Rigby! Folly! What if Legrec is behind affairs at Margale's?"

"We discussed that," admitted Rigby. "But Cranston insisted. After all, it was his plan. He was eager—"

"So eager that he left his hat out there on the chair," interrupted Weston. "Proof that he was not himself; for Cranston is methodical."

"But I sent the man you posted here," reminded Rigby. "He is probably on duty at Margale's home."

"We shall learn that soon enough," decided Weston. "Come! We are starting there at once."

The group left the penthouse. The same operator was on the elevator; but the man's face told nothing. Perhaps he had a lurking hope that there would be orders to snatch one of these passengers; for he detested all of them.

Three, however, were apparently too large an order for Legrec. The trip to the ground floor was made without incident.

It took the commissioner's big car a scant eight minutes to reach Margale's neighborhood. A wailing siren cleared the way; but it ceased its shrieks near Margale's, much to Rigby's relief. The investigator expressed that fact to Weston.

"We must be cautious, Commissioner," warned Rigby. "The house may be watched by others than your own man. Let us be conservative in our approach."

Weston spoke through the speaking tube. The big car halted.

"We are only a block from the house," stated Weston. "What would you suggest next?"

"That two of us—Cardona and myself—go on foot," replied Rigby. "One of us can approach the front; the other, the back." He turned to Cardona. "Does that suit you, Inspector?"

Cardona nodded.

The two alighted. Soon, they were on the silent sidewalk by Margale's wall. They halted at a side gate. Rigby tried it, shook his head. The gate was locked.

"Suppose you take the front," whispered Rigby. "Your man is there; he will report more readily to you. I can try the back gate, if there is one."

They separated. Cardona kept close to the wall until he reached the front corner. He saw the plain-clothesman across the street, sneaked over and talked to him.

No one had been in or out of the mansion during all the while that the headquarters man had been there. No one, at least, who had used the front way.

"Stay here," ordered Cardona. "I'll go back and see how Rigby's making out. If you hear a whistle, bust in through the front."

GOING back along the avenue, Cardona saw a figure waiting for him. It was Rigby, near the locked side gate. He had been to the back, had found another gate there, but it had been bolted from inside.

The two agreed that direct approach would be best. They went to the front, summoned the headquarters dick. All three went through the unlocked front gate; they followed the walk to the big door of the house.

There was something formidable about that mansion; its setting annoyed Cardona. It wasn't sensible, a place like this, squatting in the middle of Manhattan. Anything might happen in an old, forgotten house.

A swell place for Legrec to use as a hideout, particularly for the type of crook he was supposed to be. Posing as a millionaire—yes, that would be Legrec's style. The idea gripped Cardona more and more, as he considered it.

In fact, that growing impression was to explain some of the ace inspector's later actions.

All the while that Cardona pondered, Rigby was ringing the front doorbell. Its tingle was audible from somewhere deep in the house. It gave the impression that the place was abandoned, although dim lights showed at a few windows, including the panes at the sides of the wide front door.

Cardona peered through one of those tiny windows, Rigby through the other. Loose-draped curtains, though thin, made it impossible to see what lay inside.

Rigby resumed his pressure on the bell button.

That tingle could be heard on the second floor, where Eleanor Margale was in bed, trying vainly to sleep.

It was odd, thought Eleanor, that Nordham did not answer. The other servants had retired; but Nordham should be about, for her uncle was still in the study.

Turning on a reading lamp, Eleanor found slippers and dressing gown. Holding the flimsy robe close about her, she stole out through the hallway. The bell was louder, when she heard it here; yet its ring might fail to penetrate into her uncle's study.

Perhaps Nordham was in there, trying to calm another of her uncle's violent moods.

At the top of the stairs, Eleanor hesitated. Who could the person be, who was keeping up the constant summons? Dread gripped her; then, like an echo from a distant past, she remembered whispered words in the unforgettable tones of The Shadow:

"You will be in no danger—"

The words were true; but Eleanor was soon to experience stark terror.

HALFWAY down the stairs, she stopped again. There was something in the hallway—a blocky shape that looked grotesquely human. For a moment, Eleanor laughed at her qualms. The thing didn't move; it might be a rug, scruffed out of shape.

She reached the bottom of the stairs. She saw the object more plainly.

The girl's taut nerves gave way.

Eleanor's shriek was louder than the incessant doorbell. It carried beyond the barrier, for there was a sudden pounding there.

Eleanor's own cries freed her from a terrible paralysis that had gripped her. Though she could not repress her screams, she was able to seek aid.

Whoever was beyond that front door was a friend, in Eleanor's distraught opinion. With a hurried dash, Eleanor ran wide of the thing on the floor and approached the door itself. Her cries had finished; but shudders quailed her as she fumbled with the bolts.

Moments seemed endless, before Eleanor realized that her task was done. She dropped back, gasping aloud that the door was open.

Cardona and Rigby did not hear that faint summons. They had listened, though, to the unlocking of the door. With the finish of such sounds, they grabbed the latch together. The door went inward; they crossed the threshold.

The scene that met them was one of the most surprising that Cardona had ever encountered. Joe saw a girl, beautiful even in her horrified pose, clad in nightgown and disarrayed robe. She was pointing to the floor; with a brave effort, she uttered a name:

"Nordham! It's Nordham—dead!"

Together, Cardona and Rigby reached that shape on the floor. It was huddled; but a face was staring upward from above a contorted neck. Dead features glared, as if in dying hope of vengeance.

They rolled the body sideward. A knife handle gleamed in the dim light. The blade itself was buried in the center of a crimson blotch that covered the dead man's shirtfront.

From the victim's attire, Cardona could see that he was a servant, probably the one who should have answered the door.

Flowing blood told that murder had been recent. That centered Cardona's attention on the knife, for he knew that the thrust must have been swift, straight to the heart. But Rigby noted something else, and pointed it out to rivet Cardona's gaze.

Pinned to the bloodstained shirtfront, by the blade of the knife itself, was the token of the murderer who had so speedily killed this latest victim.

The object was a tarot: another of those death cards that were dealt by the insidious hand of Gautier Legrec!

CHAPTER XX
THE RIDDLE UNRAVELS

THE chimes of the old grandfather's clock were the first sounds that broke the silence of that hallway. The *clang* of the half-hour notes roused Rigby from his rigid pose. Cardona heard Rigby's low-phrased words:

"The three of swords—it symbolizes hatred!"

A short-clipped sound came with the clock's final chime, but from another direction. Both men caught it; so did Eleanor. The girl's voice warned them, as they stared upward.

"Look out!" called Eleanor. "From the study!"

A door had opened. On the threshold stood Thomas Margale; his eyes were glaring, white. The gritting of his teeth was audible; in his hand he held an old-fashioned revolver, that he seemed intent to raise.

"Legrec!"

Cardona spouted the name for Rigby's benefit. Both lunged forward from beside Nordham's body. Their mutual action brought the result they needed. Each man veered, as he drove for the study door, forcing Margale to a choice.

Before the fuming millionaire could decide, both men had gripped him. Margale fought hard to keep his gun; he tugged the trigger while he battled. His shots, however, did no harm. Between them, Cardona and Rigby had forced the gun muzzle to the floor.

For a long half minute, Cardona was impressed by Margale's strength. It was when the struggle seemed to be turning in his favor, that the millionaire gave out. His collapse was complete. Gun gone, he crumpled to the floor, to lie moaning above the bullet holes that he had driven through the woodwork.

When Commissioner Weston arrived, they had Margale plumped in the chair behind his study desk. All fight was out of him; he was a weary, weeping prisoner. Weston could hardly believe it, when he heard reports of the battle. Margale appeared to be anything but a fighter.

Bluntly, Cardona accused the millionaire of murdering Nordham. In whiny tone, Margale pleaded innocence. Leaving Weston to quiz him, the ace stalked about the house, accompanied by Rigby.

They found the side door locked, with no key. The back door was bolted from the inside. There wasn't a servant anywhere nearer than the third floor. Those that they rounded up were huddled in beds, terrified by the sounds of gunfire.

"There's no one could have murdered Nordham," decided Cardona, "except Margale. That is, counting out the girl. It wasn't her work."

"Someone may have gone out," argued Rigby. "We must take that into consideration, Inspector."

Cardona agreed. After all, a passkey could have been used at the side door. But it would have taken a rapid worker to finish Nordham and make a departure in the brief minutes allowed.

As Cardona put it, only Legrec could have managed it, and Thomas Margale happened to be Joe's only choice for the identity of Gautier Legrec.

BY the time Cardona and Rigby had returned to the study, Margale's shattered nerves had steadied. He pleaded for a dose of his medicine; it was in the cabinet. When Eleanor assured Cardona that her uncle took it regularly, the dosage was allowed.

The milkish liquid had a soothing effect. Resting back in his chair, Margale announced wearily that he was ready to answer any and all questions.

From the start, it was plain that the law had a canny man with whom to deal.

Cardona asked Margale if he had murdered Nordham, to which the millionaire returned a serious negative headshake. Joe planked the bloody tarot upon the desk, asked if Margale had ever seen it before. The millionaire showed complete surprise.

"There's a fellow named Legrec passes these things around," announced Cardona, referring to the card. "Ever hear of him? Or his calling cards? He still has a lot of them left in his pack."

"There are no such cards here," assured Margale. "You may search the place, if you wish."

"How about seeing the inside of that safe? We've looked everywhere else."

"Certainly!" Margale gave the decision promptly; then looked about, a trifle nervous. By this time, police were plentiful. The millionaire smiled, as he decided: "I shall be well protected."

"Against what?" demanded Weston.

"Against robbery," returned Margale. "The contents of that safe are worth approximately five million dollars."

That statement, in Cardona's estimation, indicated that Margale was either a liar or a lunatic; possibly both. But when the millionaire began to open the safe, Joe gawked.

It wasn't one safe—it was four, each inside the other. All had tricky combinations, over which Margale mulled. The final safe was a comparatively small one; it was stuffed with packages of stocks and bonds.

Margale sorted them carefully, placing them in front of Weston.

"I shall hold you responsible, Commissioner," said the suspected murderer, dryly. Then, to Cardona: "There is the safe, Inspector. Empty!"

Weston was looking through the securities. Their total value was huge; probably equal to Margale's five-million-dollar estimate. Margale sat with a triumphant look, facing Cardona.

"So you never heard of Legrec's cards," snapped Cardona. "He puts them on his victims, Margale.

Your own servant, Nordham, was one. And there were some others, recently. Listen and tell me if you recognize any of their names."

Margale nodded seriously.

One by one, Cardona repeated the names of Elwood Balcray, Sylvester Lysand, Hastings Keever.

The effect was remarkable.

Cardona would have been happy with one hit. Instead, he scored three. With each name, Margale gave a gulp.

"So you knew them?" snapped Cardona.

"Of—of course!" panted Margale, his face harrowed. "But—but I thought—their deaths were accidents."

"That's what Legrec wanted people to think," informed Cardona. "He'd claim he fell for it, Legrec would, if we could find him. Maybe"—Joe added the words wisely—"maybe we *have* found him!"

Margale ignored the inference. He was thinking of another matter.

"Since all three are dead," he declared, soberly, "I can discuss my relations with them; although"— he looked toward Weston—"I do so only because it may help you clear matters, Commissioner."

Weston nodded, counting to himself. He was going over a stack of Margale's bonds.

"KEEVER was a promoter," explained Margale. "He obtained all these securities of mine. That's how I happened to know him. He was a smart man, picking up gilt-edged buys at special prices.

"So smart, in fact, that I depended upon Lysand to study all my purchases. Lysand was my banker. Occasionally, he loaned me money, with some of those bonds as security.

"I was not the only one who profited. Balcray bought some of these securities also. He sold real estate to obtain the money. I did the same, and Balcray helped me dispose of such property."

Margale's tone was convincing to all but one listener. His own niece was staring, in doubt. Eleanor was used to her uncle's varied moods. She was picturing him as she had often seen him: a raging tyrant. She thought of Nordham, her one friend during Margale's periods of fierceness.

She could see her uncle as a murderer, with Nordham as his final victim. She wondered what had happened to Harry Vincent. She recalled her visit to Roban's old house; mention of bonds brought the counterfeiter's boasts to mind.

It was all that Eleanor could manage, to hold back her story of that night. All that was needed was a spark to ignite the blaze of spoken memories. Before Eleanor realized it, the flame was touched.

Unwittingly, Commissioner Weston inspired it.

"An odd thing"—Weston spoke musingly from his side of the table—"something very odd, indeed.

This special bond issue—Supertransit Fives—did Keever buy them, Margale?"

"Of course," replied Margale. "I have already told you that Keever bought all those securities."

"You have a quarter million in those bonds alone."

"I suppose so. The list will tell."

Weston shook his head, puzzled.

"I know about that issue," remarked the commissioner. "It was originally intended as a million-dollar sale; but it was halted. Only two hundred thousand dollars of the issue was printed. You have fifty thousand more than are in existence."

Eleanor reached the table. That news was all she wanted. It meant that the truth would have to come out. Eleanor had been catching glimmers of it.

"Those bonds are counterfeit!" exclaimed Eleanor. "Those, and probably all others with them! I know the man responsible. His name is Rupert Roban!"

CARDONA had heard of Roban. The man was almost a myth; but his work was too famed to be ignored. Turning from Margale, Cardona started to quiz Eleanor. It wasn't necessary.

Eleanor was telling of the mystery call, with the spoken name of Legrec. She mentioned the address in the telephone table; her trip to Twentieth Street. By the time she had recounted her interview with Roban, Cardona was on his feet.

"That's plenty!" he shouted. "We raided that place on Twentieth Street! The story fits, Commissioner. Margale's story is phony. He's covering up how he got those bonds.

"Roban made them for him. Keever was the go-between who brought them here. Lysand and Balcray were the saps who were supposed to fall for them. But Margale got leery of the lot.

"He knocked off his own man—Keever—and handed it to the other two, besides. Tonight, he figured the trail was closing in on him. That's why he grabbed Vincent and Cranston.

"Out there in the hall"—Cardona made a dramatic gesture—"is the one man who might have told us facts we need to know. Nordham is that man, and he is dead. Murdered by you, Margale"—Cardona was pointing an accusing finger at the millionaire—"to cover up your biggest swindle game!"

Weston bounded up beside the table, shouted to Cardona:

"Arrest him, Inspector! Thomas Margale, alias Gautier Legrec, we charge you with the murder of—"

Further words were useless. Under the point of Cardona's finger, Margale was slumping as if the accusation withered him. His face was ashen; life seemed gone from it. Cardona shoved forward on the chance that Margale's sag was a fake.

It was Alan Rigby who suddenly intervened.

"Wait, Inspector." Rigby spoke coolly, solemnly. "We are mistaken. This man is innocent. He is not Legrec."

There was stunned silence. Rigby let it lengthen; then:

"The man we want," said Rigby, "is Rupert Roban. Find him and we shall at last have Gautier Legrec!"

CHAPTER XXI
THE CLUE FROM ABOVE

IT was an hour later, in Rigby's penthouse. The famed investigator was standing in the center of the room, with Weston and Cardona seated opposite him. Rigby was making a final review of a theory with which the others fully agreed.

"It wasn't Margale's collapse that broke the case," stated Rigby. "That was genuine enough—and no wonder! Poor devil—all his fortune is in those fraudulent securities.

"The real point was Keever. You gave me that, Inspector, though I don't think you realized it. Your theory was good, very good, but it made Keever out to be a crook. That made me see the clear.

"Keever a crook! Then why not Lysand? Why not Balcray? Victims of Legrec? Not a bit of it! Their game was to work together; to deprive poor Margale of his fortune. Keever brought the securities to Margale. Lysand certified them; Balcray bought, to encourage Margale.

"Promoter—banker—investor; what a combination! Behind it all the evil genius of Legrec, otherwise Roban. The long-forgotten counterfeiter, whose face is here!"

Rigby pulled down the chart that showed the composite face which he had formed to represent Legrec.

There was another point that Rigby added.

"An inside man was needed," he stated. "Nordham was that man. He sent the tip-offs to Legrec. That slip of paper that Eleanor found? Planted there by Nordham, in writing falsified to look like her uncle's. But Eleanor chanced upon it too soon."

"It led to Roban's own place," reminded Cardona.

"Of course," assured Rigby. "He wanted his old headquarters to be found later, to confuse the law. He is no longer Roban, to his own way of thinking. He is Legrec!"

"Quite clear," agreed Weston. "No wonder Nordham found Eleanor so easily. Once safe, it was wise to bring her back. She could not harm Roban, once his last great counterfeiting job was ended."

"Roban wanted to kill her," mused Rigby. "But that is Legrec's way. He has tricked me, badly.

Here he was, slaying his own duped confederates, making us think that they were innocent victims, with a death card placed on each!"

Rigby strolled to the French windows. The terrace was cool; he motioned the others to join him. Sight of Cranston's hat brought a tightness to Rigby's lips.

"Legrec was there, at Margale's," he recalled, "only a few minutes before we arrived. That was when he slew Nordham. But where did he go after that? If we could only find his hideaway!

"Vincent is a difficult case to follow. He must have been carried through that side door, to which Legrec had access. But Cranston—he never reached Margale's, so far as we know. Where was he intercepted?"

RIGBY picked up Cranston's hat, stared at it as though hoping that it held the clue. Something fluttered to the cement promenade. Weston picked it up.

"What's this?" he inquired. "It looks like an envelope, addressed to Vincent. Oddly disconnected. *L-e-g*—it must refer to Legrec. Here's Roban's name, too!"

Rigby wasn't listening. He was still speaking about Cranston.

"How—tell me how!" His tone was pleading. "How did Legrec know that Cranston was going to Margale's at all?"

"Look at this, Rigby!" Weston was excited. "Vincent's message puts it that Roban is Legrec! What does he mean by *bhang*?"

Rigby saw the word; his eyes stared.

"*Bhang*! The term for hashish! Vincent was drugged when he wrote this! Wait—that medicine at Margale's! That's how Nordham kept Margale half stupefied. The concoction was doped!"

Rigby's eyes reverted to Harry's message. He didn't seem to realize that Weston had just found it.

"Cranston talked to me," mused Rigby. "To no one else. He was here, on this terrace—no, in the penthouse living room. I wonder—"

Rigby looked upward. Above was the darkened wall of the penthouse second story; windows were black against it. Rigby squinted.

"Those look like Venetian blinds," he remarked. "That place is curiously cooped up, even though goods are stored there. Do you suppose, by any stretch of the most fantastic imagination, that Legrec—"

Cardona caught the suggestion. He snatched Harry's message from Rigby's hand, pointed to Cranston's hat, then to the chair.

"That's where it was!" exclaimed Joe. "The message was covered by Cranston's hat. Maybe he read it; maybe he didn't even see it, when he laid his hat down. But it's a cinch where it came from. Through one of those slats!"

Rigby nodded solemnly. He slid his hand to a pocket where he carried a gun. His eyes were straight upon the upper windows. His words were undertoned.

"It is fortunate that we are speaking out here," he asserted. "I see it all plainly, although it amazes me. Legrec has chosen his hideaway directly above my own headquarters!"

Weston gazed as though Rigby were insane. Cardona, however, approved with a grim nod.

"It's a cinch he's got your place wired," whispered Joe. "That's how he overheard Cranston talk to you."

"But Cranston called Margale's," reminded Weston. "He talked to Nordham."

"So he did!" exclaimed Rigby. "I had forgotten it. It is fortunate that I did. That mental lapse started me on the right route. That paper proves it."

RIGBY'S next action was a cool one. He lighted his pipe, strolled toward the door of the penthouse, with a slight shrug as though he found the terrace too cool.

Cardona caught the idea, did a pretense of his own. Weston followed.

Once inside, Rigby beckoned them. They went to the door that blocked the stairs to the upper story. Rigby tested the lock. He nodded. On a slip of paper, he wrote the words:

I can manage it. Keep up a conversation.

Weston and Cardona took the hint. They forced a discussion that became effective as they continued. All the while, Rigby was trying his hand as a locksmith; but without luck.

Finally, he pulled his revolver from his pocket, made a gesture toward the lock. It looked like the only way.

Cardona motioned for Rigby to wait. Joe went out and called in the headquarters man, to add strength to the raiding squad.

They were crouched, ready for a dash, when Rigby fired two quick shots. The first blew the lock askew; the second ruined it. As Rigby yanked back the door, Cardona took the lead.

There were dim lights above. From a corridor came the scuffle of arriving men. First at the head of the stairs, Cardona opened fire. Revolvers answered; but the opposition broke. Cardona headed for a turn in the hallway.

When he reached there, Weston was at his shoulder; Rigby and the detective were close behind. Cardona tried to give a warning; too late. Three gunners had rallied down the hall. Their fingers were on gun triggers.

It looked like curtains for Joe Cardona, even though his companions were on hand to avenge his death. An instant more, opposing guns would bark. Then, into that moment came a burst from an unseen gun.

It spoke from a transom that shattered with the thrust of steel. Down from the clattering glass tongued the flame from an automatic. A bullet clipped the foremost of the attacking gunners. Instinctively, the others aimed for the transom.

More shots volleyed. That down-tilted muzzle had the edge. Revolvers were belated in their answers. Weston saw the face of his friend Cranston at the transom; gave a welcoming shout. Cardona toned it with shots from his own revolver.

Three thugs were down. There were others, piling in from elsewhere. Bullets clipped them as fast as they came. Crooks had no chance with the spreading invaders—not with that supporting fire from the transom.

Shooting above the heads of Weston and Cardona, The Shadow took out the cream of the opposition.

AT the finish, there was a blast at the locked door. Copying Rigby's move below, Cranston had shattered the lock of his prison room. He sprang out into the hallway; before Weston could greet him, Cranston gave the quick question:

"Where's Rigby?"

A call answered. It was distant. Cardona was nearest to that direction. He led a dash to an open doorway. Beyond it, he saw two men grappling: one was Rigby, the other a white-haired old man who battled with fury: Roban.

The Shadow came behind Cardona. He was motionless, calm as Cranston always was. While Cardona stared helplessly, Cranston's automatic trained upon the fighters. He was awaiting a chance break in that struggle.

A muffled shot sounded while The Shadow aimed. It was Rigby's gun that gave it; the muzzle jabbed against Roban's ribs. A shrill shriek sounded from dried lips; the old counterfeiter rolled to the floor.

Panting, Rigby watched the others while they gathered. His eyes were fierce from the fury of the fight. Roban, too, was staring with embittered glare. His lips moved, to croak in challenging gasp:

"Legrec—Gautier Legrec—"

That proclamation of identity was all. As Roban's eyes glazed in death, it was Alan Rigby who pronounced:

"We have seen the end of Gautier Legrec."

Those were the only words. But there was an expression from another person present. It was visible, not spoken; hence no one observed it.

The gaze of Lamont Cranston sparkled.

His eyes were those of The Shadow.

CHAPTER XXII
THE SPOILS OF LEGREC

LAMONT CRANSTON received his congratulations later. They came when the victors reached Rigby's own living room. With them, they brought a rescued prisoner in the person of Harry Vincent.

Half stupefied from the dose of *bhang*, Harry could not talk coherently. That was new proof of Cranston's endurance. Although he had been similarly treated, he had resisted the ordeal.

The explanation was a simple one. Cranston, it seemed, had found Harry's note, but had not entirely grasped its importance until his capture. Realizing that he would be in for the hashish treatment, he had faked a rapid collapse for Roban's benefit.

His dose of the vapor had therefore been a mild one. His weariness, however, indicated that he felt some effect from it. He decided to leave now, taking his friend Vincent with him.

On the cool terrace, Rigby discussed the triumph with Weston and Cardona. Rigby had one regret: that he had been forced to give Roban that death bullet.

"It ended Legrec," he declared, "but it brought us nowhere in our next step: the reclamation of Margale's wealth."

"Roban didn't stow it up above here," put in Cardona. "We've scoured that place all over."

"Wherever it is," returned Rigby, "only Roban could tell us. Five million dollars—buried somewhere, as deep as that metal room in the old house where he counterfeited those bonds."

There was a stir from the penthouse living room, so slight that no one observed it. Shaded blackness glided across the floor, like the passage of a cloud before the sun.

"I wish you luck, Inspector," said Rigby to Cardona, "and I shall willingly give my cooperation. But the search for Legrec's spoils may prove a hopeless one.

"Margale converted his funds into those false securities, some weeks ago. That gave Legrec a long while to bury away the cash. What fools, those chaps who aided him! They let all those millions drift into his possession.

"But that proves the cleverness of Legrec. I told you, when I first arrived here, that he invariably disposed of helpers when he needed them no longer. This time, he annihilated them. Legrec intended to make this haul appear as his last."

Rigby stood by the parapet, gazing southward toward the bay and the ocean beyond.

"I shall be leaving soon," he remarked, "for my first real vacation in years. Keep me well posted, Inspector, regarding any clues to Thomas Margale's lost wealth—"

The telephone bell sounded from the penthouse. Rigby went to answer it. He called back:

"For you, Commissioner!"

CARDONA came in with Weston. Glumly, the inspector stared at a broken panel in the wall, where Rigby had uncovered the dictograph over which talk from Rigby's quarters had reached Roban's room upstairs.

Despite his puzzled thoughts regarding the location of Legrec's swag, Cardona became suddenly conscious of excitement in Weston's voice.

The commissioner clattered the telephone receiver.

"It was Vincent!" he exclaimed. "So hazy, I could scarcely make him out. But his import was plain."

Weston drew a troubled breath, then added: "Cranston has disappeared!"

Rigby eyed the commissioner closely, half smiling, as though the matter were a jest. Then:

"Impossible!" he exclaimed. "What could have happened to him, with Legrec dead? Who could have wanted to quiz Cranston—"

The name died on Rigby's frozen lips. He was staring across the living room. Weston and Cardona followed that gaze, but their ears brought news before their eyes could see it.

A strange laugh, chill and sinister, crept through that room. It crept from lips that were invisible, unlike the eyes above them. Those eyes gazed from beneath the brim of a slouch hat worn by a cloaked figure in black.

Despite the ominous tone of that laugh, Joe Cardona felt a sweep of exultation.

The Shadow!

All along, Cardona had been bothered by one mighty problem: The Shadow's odd absence from this case. Somewhere—probably in Eleanor's uncompleted testimony—Cardona had caught indications of The Shadow's work. That, in fact, was why Cardona had expected more.

It had come—The Shadow's entry into the quest for Legrec; but only after the case was solved. Cardona had one flickering hope—that The Shadow might help him in regaining Margale's millions; but that began to fade.

The search for Legrec had run ahead of The Shadow. The rest would probably be beyond his depth. With all his faith in The Shadow's prowess,

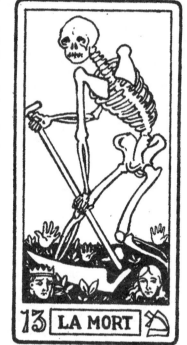

Cardona could not dispel his present doubts.

Weston showed actual anger.

The commissioner's thoughts were similar to Cardona's. His reaction went further. Weston looked upon The Shadow's arrival as a useless masquerade. He began to splutter that the cloaked visitor was not needed.

THE SHADOW'S eyes fixed upon Weston.

A gloved hand came from beneath the cloak. It bore an object that Weston recognized. It was the hat that Cranston had left on the promenade, but which he had worn later, when he departed with Harry Vincent.

"What has happened to Cranston?" demanded the commissioner. "If harm has come to him, you are responsible!"

From beneath the inner band, The Shadow plucked a card. He passed it to Weston, who stared at it, then showed it to Rigby.

The card was a tarot. It depicted a skeleton carrying a scythe; beneath, the grim legend: *"La Morte."*

"Death"—Rigby's tone was mechanical—"the one infallible card. But not from Legrec's pack—"

"From that pack!" spoke The Shadow. His tone was as sepulchral as the voice of death itself. "But not with Legrec's knowledge.

"The infallible card has failed. Yet there is another, Rigby"—lips phrased the name coldly—"that is even greater than the card of death.

"Receive it—not from Legrec"—The Shadow's laugh toned out—"but from The Shadow!"

Another card came to view, gripped by gloved fingers. The Shadow thrust it into Rigby's frozen hand. It showed a wanderer, moving toward the distance.

"Il Matto!" The name came from Rigby's nearly motionless lips. "The fool who gains what he deserves—"

"From The Shadow!"

At those words, Rigby took a frantic, backward spring. He had lost the last vestige of his former nerviness. His face, with its wild expression of fury, gave him away.

But his hand stopped short of its gun.

The Shadow held Rigby covered with an automatic. It had come from that black cloak with one amazing sweep.

"LEGREC disposed of all the men who aided him," declared The Shadow. "All, including Rupert Roban. Cleverly, Roban's part was changed. From a mere counterfeiter, approached by Keever, he was induced to pose falsely as Legrec.

"The real Legrec wanted the testimony of Eleanor Margale. Why did Roban try to murder her? Why did Roban once deny that he was Legrec, then make that claim?

"When did Roban go to Margale's to murder Nordham? Cranston can tell. From his transom, he was watching the passage from Roban's room above here. Cranston has answered that question. He states that Roban did *not* leave."

The muzzle was looming closer to Rigby's eyes, forcing the snarling man back toward his table.

"How did Legrec cover his presence in so many places where he engaged in crime?" quizzed The Shadow. Then, coldly, he answered: "By posing as a man who sought to find Legrec!

"When Legrec had chosen Roban as a scapegoat, how did he prepare for it? By framing that false picture, on this wall. And how"—The Shadow was pointing to the huge picture that resembled the dead Roban—"how did Legrec prevent Roban from finally betraying him?

"By murder! The last of many murders. One death that was not marked by a misleading card. There is the final answer—given to Gautier Legrec!"

Rigby's eyes bulged from a purplish visage. His game was ended; he, the real Legrec, saw his long-built schemes go fluttering like the fool's card that drifted from his fingers.

Moving away, The Shadow kept Rigby covered every instant, until, at last, the cloaked avenger stood by the shattered panel that wired this room with the floor above it.

His free hand thrust deep, The Shadow pressed a hidden switch, that proved how Rigby—not Roban—had been able to cut the circuit. The Shadow had not forgotten how Rigby's voice had begun in the middle of a conversation, over the loudspeaker above.

"As for the wealth gouged from Margale"—The Shadow's tone was mocking—"where better could it be, than here!"

Gloved fingers were probing the broken panel. There was a snap; the smashed woodwork slid aside. With it came the next panel to it, revealing another deep cache.

That recess in the wall was stuffed with bundles of currency: Margale's millions, that the dupe had converted into cash for Alan Rigby, the self-styled Gautier Legrec.

HANDS slumped behind him, Rigby made a move that only The Shadow saw. It was pressure of a button, the push signal that he had used to instigate Cranston's capture. Rigby waited, hoping that the motion had not been seen.

Words of admission gulped from Rigby's lips. He was admitting his crimes, to hold The Shadow's attention. But he could not keep his gaze from shifting toward the outer door. Rigby's own eye flash told The Shadow when the barrier wavered.

With a sardonic laugh of challenge, The Shadow wheeled to meet the last half dozen of Rigby's horde. They were men who had thought Roban to be Legrec, but who responded to the signal that had reached the elevator.

They would have rallied to Rigby, realizing him their master, had they encountered any foeman other than The Shadow. In their bewilderment, they thought that The Shadow had hoaxed them to the penthouse.

Two of the startled crew raised guns. The Shadow's quick shots crippled them. The rest flung away their weapons, thrust their hands high.

Rigby gave a cry of frenzy, breaking from the grasp of Weston. Shoving past Cardona, he sprang for The Shadow.

A gloved hand turned as Rigby's gun came out. In that instant, with Legrec's last followers ready to snatch up their weapons on a chance, The Shadow had a lone course. His gun spoke; its spurt arrowed for Rigby's heart.

A long, crashing plunge brought Rigby to the center of the room, a dead form when he struck the floor.

Turning from the body at his feet, The Shadow moved toward the door. Bowed crooks huddled while The Shadow passed.

Cardona clamped bracelets on a pair of them, covered the last pair with his revolver, while Weston pounced for the telephone to bring detectives from the lobby. As the commissioner called across the wire, he heard the dull *clang* of the elevator door.

That echo was toned with the throb of a final, solemn laugh. Mirthless, The Shadow had spoken his triumph over the multi-murderer, Gautier Legrec!

THE END

Coming soon in **THE SHADOW #41:**
CHAIN OF DEATH & DEATH'S PREMIUM

Spotlight on The Shadow
by Anthony Tollin

During the Summer of 1937, Street & Smith and the Ruthrauff & Ryan Advertising Agency began preparations to reintroduce The Shadow to a national audience in a radio revival showcasing the mysterious crimebuster from Walter Gibson's pulp novels. Edward Hale Bierstadt, a respected criminologist who had previously scripted Warden Lawes' *20,000 Years in Sing Sing,* was recruited to work with Gibson developing the scripts that would launch the revival. Decades later, Gibson retained fond memories of his first meeting with Bierstadt on Great Chebeague Island in Maine's Casco Bay:

> The place was stacked with *Shadow* magazines and Ed ... told me that he not only had read them, but had liked them. That marked the beginning of a warm and lasting friendship, particularly as I liked the script when he read it to me. He had featured a death-row scene, something that he was closely familiar with, and he had captured The Shadow's mystique as well. His experience as a criminologist had given him an insight into the ways and wiles of small-fry crooks that showed clearly throughout the script and caught the tempo of the earlier Shadow novels.

The first draft of Bierstadt's Shadow script concluded with a teaser announcing the next episode, "Serpents of Siva." When he learned that the scriptwriter hadn't developed a storyline beyond the title, Gibson offered to "write a Shadow novel called *Serpents of Siva* and then you can adapt it." Gibson's novel was submitted September 17, 1937 and published in the April 15, 1938 edition of *The Shadow Magazine,* while the second Shadow radio script actually featured a *servant* of Siva, Ram Lal, in a plot inspired by Gibson's 1933 novel, *The Crime Clinic.* The broadcast also featured a rare radio visit to the Cobalt Club and the second appearance of The Shadow's "constant friend and aide, Margot Lane," a distaff substitute for Harry Vincent created to provide a vocal contrast to Lamont Cranston's baritone.

The Shadow returned to the network airwaves on September 26, 1937 over the young Mutual Broadcasting System. The revamped series starred 22-year-old Orson Welles as Lamont Cranston, the "wealthy young man about town" of Gibson's pulp novels. The supporting cast included many of the *March of Time* actors who formed the nucleus of Welles' Mercury Theatre company that later followed Orson to Hollywood: Agnes Moorehead (as Margot Lane), Ray Collins (Commissioner Weston), Paul Stewart and Everett Sloane, while Broadway veteran Thomas Coffin Cooke voiced Blue Coal's fictitious heating authority, "John Barclay." Since the series was broadcast on Sunday when comedy ruled the airwaves and Broadway theaters were dark, *The Shadow* had its pick of the finest actors from both the New York stage and dramatic radio.

Since Welles was busy rehearsing his Broadway Mercury Theatre productions, *Shadow* producer Clark Andrews and director Martin Gabel allowed the mercurial star to skip rehearsals; during which his assistants Bill Alland and Richard Wilson read his lines and marked up his scripts. The show's star performed his dual role without having previously seen the script. "My God, I didn't even know what was going to happen to me when I was in 'em," Orson later recalled. "Not rehearsing— which was part of my deal with Blue Coal, the sponsor—made it much more interesting. When I got thrown down the well into some fiendish snake pit, I never knew how I'd get out."

Though he devoted less than an hour each week to *The Shadow,* the series helped launch his national reputation. *Time* titled its 1938 cover story on Welles "Shadow to Shakespeare" while *The New York Times* headlined its interview, "The Shadow Talks," and noted that when Welles "sent a road unit of 'Caesar' into the hinterlands he found that his claim to fame as producer-star of the Mercury Theatre was dwarfed among the playgoers by the overshadowing fact that he had played 'The Shadow' on the airwaves."

Throughout his life, Orson Welles remained loyal to the medium that gave him his first national fame, later regretting that he had devoted so much of his energies to filmmaking. "I wish I hadn't fallen quite so hard ... because movies take too long to make and cost too much money. I've spent most of my life, as it turns out, just *trying* to make movies. For me, radio's a personal loss. I miss it very much.... Radio was the biggest thing in my life...." •

"They keep talking and joking about Lamont Cranston and they don't know I was it. I keep wanting to say, 'That was me!'" —ORSON WELLES

THE SHADOW
"THE RED MACAW"
by Edward Hale Bierstadt
as broadcast October 3, 1937 over MBS

(MUSIC UP: "GLOOMS OF FATE" — FADE UNDER)

SHADOW: (FILTER) Who knows what evil lurks in the hearts of men? The SHADOW knows! (LAUGHS)

(MUSIC)

ANNCR: The Shadow, Lamont Cranston, a man of wealth, a student of science and a master of other people's minds, devotes his life to righting wrongs, protecting the innocent and punishing the guilty. Cranston is known to the underworld as The Shadow; never seen, only heard, his true identity is known only to his constant friend and aide, Margot Lane. Today's story—"The Red Macaw."

ANNCR: Ladies and gentlemen — be prepared for any kind of weather from now on. Stock up tomorrow with 'blue coal'— America's finest anthracite— the coal that is colored a harmless blue at the mines for your protection. Then, you'll be ready to keep your family comfortable and healthy this winter … with even, dependable heat … the kind of superior heat 'blue coal' always gives!

ANNCR: Blue Coal presents the SHADOW! The Mystery Man who strikes terror in the very hearts of sharpsters, lawbreakers and criminals. (FADE)

(MUSIC UP AND UNDER)

(MACAW SHRIEK)

RAM LAL: The master speaks. Attention, ladies! The spirit of Shiva is upon us … Quiet!

(MACAW SHRIEKS)

RAM: Put your hands up—all of you!

(WOMEN SCREAM)

(MUSIC UP AND OUT)

WESTON: Men, I have a very important announcement to make to all members of the police department this morning!

(MURMUR OF MEN'S VOICES)

I have become convinced that the man responsible for the crime wave sweeping our city is a character who is known as The Shadow! I have issued a warrant for his arrest, and I want him brought to justice!

SHADOW: (LAUGHS)

WESTON: Who's that!? Reilly— who was that laughing!?

REILLY: (AFTER A SLIGHT PAUSE) I don't know, sir— nobody seems to know!

SHADOW: The Shadow knows! (LAUGHS … BLENDING INTO …)

(MUSIC)

MARGOT: Lamont Cranston— the police have got a warrant out for The Shadow! .

CRANSTON: Really, Miss Lane? (LAUGHS)

MARGOT: Listen, Lamont, dear—you've played the role of The Shadow for five years! You've driven a large part of the underworld out of business—

CRANSTON: Yes— and there is still a large part yet to be driven out of business. You know, Margot, sometimes I suspect that there is one controlling mind back of the organized crime in this city— one master criminal; I'm certain of it, in fact. Someday— I'll find that man. Perhaps then we can talk of quitting.

MARGOT: But, Lamont, you can't fight the underworld and the police, too! You mean too much to me, and it must not happen. You must let The Shadow stop, for my sake, Lamont, please.

CRANSTON: Someday perhaps, Margot, but my dear, The Shadow still has too much work to do. But about this little piece of playfulness on the part of the police—this warrant for a man they've never seen and can't identify—it interests me. I think, if you won't mind my leaving you so abruptly, I think I'll take a run over to the Cobalt Club. It's just about the time my very good friend Police Commissioner Ralph Weston usually has a cocktail there.

(MUSIC)

WESTON: Hello there, Cranston. Have a cocktail?

CRANSTON: (COMING ON) Hello, Weston— don't mind if I do. A dry Martini. Well, how's the Police Department? Anything of special import preying on the master mind nowadays?

WESTON: Well— nothing we can't deal with.

CRANSTON: How delightful. There are so many things in life I feel myself incompetent to deal with.

WESTON: When you feel like that, you can always pay someone else to do the job. That's the advantage of being a millionaire.

CRANSTON: I have often consoled myself with the same thought. By the way, didn't I hear that there was a jewel robbery at the Chatham's last night?

WESTON: Cranston, if I permitted anything to bother me, it would be the series of jewel robberies this fall. Three in a row! Fortunately, we have our man. Or rather we know who he is!

CRANSTON: My dear man, you're infallible— positively infallible!

WESTON: It's The Shadow! We've got a warrant out for him now!

CRANSTON: You have a warrant out for a Shadow!

WESTON: Not *a* shadow, Cranston— *The* Shadow!

CRANSTON: So he's the one that staged those three jewel robberies, eh?

WESTON: Yes— I'm inclined to believe he is.

CRANSTON: Amazing! Who put you on his track?

WESTON: Well, we've had a pretty hard time of it. Although there were always plenty of witnesses at these robberies— they all took place at parties, you know, and most of the guests were women—

CRANSTON: Go on –

WESTON: Well, we never could seem to get a coherent story out of them. None of them could seem to tell us just what happened— acted almost as if they'd been hypnotized. Finally we found one man— highly intelligent— and he made the suggestion.

CRANSTON: And who is this brilliant intellect?

WESTON: His name is Ram Lal— poses as a mystic— occultism— wisdom of the East— all that sort of thing— been educated in the best Egyptian universities.

CRANSTON: Ah, yes— I believe I've heard of him.

WESTON: You must have. Terribly popular— goes to all the fashionable parties. The women are mad about him. Pretends to be a magician or something— goes everywhere with a big red bird who talks— it really says the most amazing things.

CRANSTON: I see. The police are now taking orders from a talking bird, eh?

WESTON:	Don't be silly— Ram Lal is a brilliant man. When we questioned him, he said it was obvious, from the way the robberies were accomplished, that no ordinary crook was at the bottom of it. In fact— there was only one criminal with the finesse— the occult ability to confuse witnesses—who could be responsible. And he is the great, almost supernatural magician and detective, *and* criminal—The Shadow!
CRANSTON:	Hmm—
WESTON:	And I think Ram Lal is right. It all hangs together. The lack of clues— the witnesses who can't remember a thing— the strange unkind methods used— it all points to a master criminal intelligence. So this time we're going to get The Shadow!
CRANSTON:	You sound very determined, Weston. I'm glad you're not trailing me.
WESTON:	(LAUGHS) Well, Cranston— what would you do if you were The Shadow?
CRANSTON:	If I were The Shadow, I think I'd have a heart to heart talk with this magician colleague— Ram Lal.
	(MUSIC)
RAM:	(HINDU CHANT— UNINTELLIGIBLE— MORE OR LESS TO HIMSELF)
SHADOW:	(LAUGHS) Ram Lal!
RAM:	Who calls?
SHADOW:	It is I, Ram Lal!
RAM:	And who are you? I am alone here!
SHADOW:	You are not alone— I am here with you!
RAM:	And who are you?
SHADOW:	The Shadow.
RAM:	(SLOWLY) Ah—The Shadow. (SARCASTIC) Welcome to my humble abode, dear master.
SHADOW:	You've heard of me, I see.
RAM:	But certainly! Who has not heard of The Shadow— the comic strip— that joke for children? (LAUGHS SOFTLY)
SHADOW:	Ram Lal—you have falsely accused me—and I do not easily forget—or forgive!
RAM:	No? and just what do you expect to do about it?
SHADOW:	You choose to defy me?
RAM:	Of course.
SHADOW:	Ram Lal, you are a fool!
RAM:	There are those who will not agree with you. And now, if you have finished— I just continue my devotions—
SHADOW:	I have not finished— I will never have finished, Ram Lal, until I have brought your downfall!
RAM:	And how do you propose to do that?
SHADOW:	There is no knowledge of the ancient world—no science of the modern that I will not bring against you!
RAM:	Really? (LAUGHS) What do you—what does any Occidental know of the Wisdom of the East, and as for your pompus modern science—bah! I have studied that too. You can prove nothing without witnesses—and the women who are my followers— they will not talk about me. They cannot. I have rendered them powerless!
SHADOW:	Perhaps I can give them back their power! Ram Lal—somewhere you have left something undone—some loose end—that, I will find! After that it will be easy!
RAM:	I shall await that discovery with delightful anticipation!
SHADOW:	I rather think, Ram Lal, you will not have to wait too long!

(LAUGHS, BLENDING INTO)
(MUSIC)

SHADOW: Margo Lane— stand by for ovelius—cultivate the acquaintance of Ram Lal Egyptian mystic—pay special attention to the talking bird— I will protect you.

(MUSIC)
HOOT OF FAR-OFF BOATS ON RIVER

RAM: The fog is heavy on the river tonight, Miss Lane. The ships are calling to each other like lost souls.

MARGOT: Your view over the Hudson is very beautiful, Ram Lal. It was kind of you to let me come and see it with you.

RAM: I am only happy that you enjoy it, Miss Lane.

MARGOT: Not everyone has the privilege of being the guest of the master of mystery.

RAM: You're very flattering.

MARGOT: Not at all! By the way— speaking of mysteries— I can't help wondering about the great silent bird of yours that sits on his perch between the windows. It looks at me with such blank, staring eyes.

RAM: Ah, yes—my red macaw. You like him?

MARGOT: A macaw? He's gorgeous— but so silent.

RAM: Silent? You think so?

MARGOT: Well, he hasn't made a sound so far.

RAM: That is because he is a good servant. He waits for orders.

MARGOT: Whose orders?

RAM: Mine— and only mine.

MARGOT: You mean he won't speak for anybody else?

RAM: Exactly.

MARGOT: May I try him?

RAM: With pleasure.

MARGOT: What is his name?

RAM: Hareen.

MARGOT: Hareen, what time is it? Do you know?

(PAUSE)

RAM: You see? He waits for me. Answer the lady, Hareen!

MACAW: Caw—caw—caw—caw—caw.

MARGO: Five. And it's just five o'clock. That is wonderful. But can he really talk, Ram Lal—pronounce words?

Agnes Moorehead and Orson Welles voiced Margot Lane and Lamont Cranston in "The Red Macaw."

RAM: Most certainly. Hareen, what is the end of life?

MACAW: De— ath!

RAM: And what is the end of death?

MACAW: Li-fe!

MARGOT: Incredible! Do you teach him the answers, Ram Lal?

RAM:	What need to teach? He knows.
MARGOT:	Will you ask him just one question for me?
RAM:	If you like.
MARGOT:	What is it that casts a shadow— and yet is only a shadow?
RAM:	Answer, Hareen!
MACAW:	Sa-tan!
MARGOT:	(SLOWLY) The Shadow of a shadow. I wonder.
RAM:	Tell me, Miss Lane— why did you ask that question?
MARGOT:	Why—I hardly know.
RAM:	You had no particular purpose?
MARGOT:	Why, of course not! Why should I?
RAM:	You lie, Margot Lane! You have come here as a spy!
MARGOT:	How dare you speak like that! Open the door— I'm going home!
RAM:	(SUDDENLY DROPPING SUAVITY, AND BECOMING VERY MENACING) You are going nowhere until you have answered my questions! Come here— Miss Lane!
MARGOT:	Don't— don't you touch me!
RAM:	I know how to deal with women!
MARGOT:	(FIGHTS OFF)
RAM:	Who turned off the lights? (PAUSE) Answer me!
SHADOW:	(SOUND OF DOOR UNLOCKING AND OPENING) The door is open, Miss lane. Go— you will be quite safe.
MARGOT:	Gladly.
	(SOUND OF RUNNING FOOTSTEPS, RECEDING)
RAM:	(SUAVE) The Shadow! So— it is you again! I might have known. Shadow, why do you not reveal yourself— so that we may meet, face to face?
SHADOW:	I am here, Ram Lal. Here in the corner.
RAM:	So? (THEN FAST) This time I am prepared for you! (TWO SHOTS)
SHADOW:	(LAUGHS) Ram Lal, your Hindu magic should have told you— you cannot shoot a shadow! (LAUGHS)
	(MUSIC)
SHADOW:	Margot Lane—a red Macaw can't talk— get me a list of all women under the influence of Ram Lal. Stand by for ovelius.
	(MUSIC)
RAM:	Miss Lane is a spy— a spy for the police, Sultra.
SULTRA:	Then she must die, master.
RAM:	Yes, she must die, and you, a servant of Shiva— a master of death by the noose— should know how!
SULTRA:	Tell me where she lives, master. Tomorrow she will be dead— gasping for air…
RAM:	It is well.
	(MUSIC)
MARGOT:	Why did you insist on coming home with me tonight, Lamont?
CRANSTON:	My dear, I have a curious feeling that you are in danger.
MARGOT:	But why? ˙
CRANSTON:	After all—Ram Lal suspects you and—
	(AN EERIE CRY OFF) (PAUSE)

CRANSTON:	Did you hear that?
MARGOT:	Of course. What was it— a night bird?
CRANSTON:	A night bird— here in New York? Well— perhaps.(EERIE CRY AGAIN OFF) There it is again. Where would you say it came from?
MARGOT:	From just outside my window. It couldn't be anything but a bird. This is the top floor. (REPEAT CRY)
CRANSTON:	(SLOWLY) I really think this extraordinary bird merits my attention.
MARGOT:	What are you going to do with that revolver?
CRANSTON:	It may put me on more equal terms with the bird who cries. (PAUSE) Listen carefully, Margot. I am going to open the window and lean out. When I do so— hold on to my belt. Brace yourself and hold with all your weight. Pull me back. You understand?
MARGOT:	Lamont— I'm frightened.
CRANSTON:	You needn't be. Now then— ready? (FADE) Here goes the window— up. (THEY HAVE BOTH MOVED A LITTLE OFF) (WINDOW UP ... EERIE CRY REPEATED MORE CLEARLY) Now, I'll lean out to see what makes that cry. (FURTHER OFF) Ah! (STRANGLING SOUND FROM CRANSTON) Ah-hhhhhh! (A SHOT) (LONG strange cry fading further and further off)
MARGOT:	Lamont! Lamont! Are you hurt?
CRANSTON:	(PAUSE) (GASPING) No— darling— throat rather sore— that's all.
MARGOT:	But what was it? What happened? I couldn't see.
CRANSTON:	An Indian strangler—on the roof. I knew the call. It's the call of Shiva, used by those who kill with noose. He used that cry to get me to the window—thought it was you, of course—and dropped his noose. I got him before he got me—fortunately!
MARGOT:	But what does it mean!?
CRANSTON:	Simply a delicate attention from Ram Lal to you.
MARGOT:	The man must be mad! You said he was clever.
CRANSTON:	He's mad with fear—that's all. Until this man is unmasked—you're not safe! So— we'll pretend that his little ruse tonight was successful. You'll go into hiding here in your own house. Tomorrow, the papers will have the story of your untimely ending. I'll arrange for that.
MARGOT:	But Lamont—
CRANSTON:	Please, darling— do as I ask. It'll only be for a little while.
MARGOT:	But when do I come to life again?
CRANSTON:	The Roger Berkleys are giving a party tomorrow night, aren't they?
MARGOT:	Yes— the invitation came last week. Ram Lal will be there.
CRANSTON:	You will go to that party.
MARGOT:	But what will everyone say? I mean, if my— my death has been announced?
CRANSTON:	The greater shock the better. Ram Lal is going to be there, of course.
MARGOT:	I know he will. Betty Berkley told me.
CRANSTON:	Good. Your appearance there ought to make Ram Lal believe in miracles. Margot, something tells me that tomorrow night we'll clear the name of The Shadow. But I'll have to act quickly from now on.
MARGOT:	What are you going to do?
CRANSTON:	I'm not sure what Lamont Cranston, well-known playboy and dilettante is going to do, but somebody else knows that you must fight fire with fire. The Shadow is going to give a séance.

(MUSIC)

SHADOW: (OFF A LITTLE) Ladies, please give me your attention! I know that all of you have been under the influence of Ram Lal.

MAUDE: Why— where is he? I don't see anybody!

RUTH: I'm scared!

ETHEL: Well, I'm not.

SHADOW: I have come to you this way, ladies, because I wish to demonstrate to you that matter cannot only be materialized, but that it can be dematerialized also. I am a voice— no more. Look around the room. It is not large. You will not see me— yet I am here.

RUTH: I don't like this at all!

ETHEL: Be quite calm, dear! It's only a fake of some kind. Any yogi could do it, if he wished.

SHADOW: If it is a fake, your highly intelligent minds should quickly uncover it. And, speaking of fakes, I know that you have all—every one of you—has been under the influence of that prince of all fakes—Ram Lal.

MAUDE: Didn't I tell you?

ETHEL: Don't worry, my dear.

RUTH: I wish I hadn't come.

SHADOW: You have nothing to fear. I bring you knowledge— knowledge that has been hard brought by years of training under the greatest mystics of the earth. Before I give you my message, I must know how greatly, if at all, your minds have been distorted from the truth by Ram Lal's teaching. You do not believe? Will you submit to a simple, harmless test?

MAUDE: No test will shake us. We have complete confidence in Ram Lal.

SHADOW: Very well. Attention! I turn out the lights!

(CLICK)

            Look at the end of the room. There is a wheel upon the wall and on the wheel are electric lights of various colors. You see them?

ETHEL: Certainly.

SHADOW: Good! Watch them closely as the wheel revolves. Ready?

MAUDE: Perfectly ready! Of course, it's cheap trickery!

SHADOW: I throw the switch—

(HUM OF ELECTRIC MOTOR)

            The wheel revolves. Keep you eyes fastened on it. Leave your minds free. Empty them of all error. Watch the wheel revolve— watch it! Watch it!— watch it! The lights have blended into one. You can see nothing else. Your minds are open to me. I can see your thoughts … (DREAMILY) I can see your thoughts (THEN SUDDENLY VERY STACCATO) … Mrs. Fowler! Listen!

ETHEL: (SPEAKING WITH MECHANICAL MONOTONY) Yes?

SHADOW: You were at all three parties at which jewel robberies took place this autumn, were you not?

ETHEL: Yes—I was.

SHADOW: And Ram Lal with his red macaw was at all of them, too, wasn't he?

ETHEL: Yes—he was.

SHADOW: Now, concentrate. Divest your soul of all error, and—now—let me see your mind. Tell me the last thing that happened before the masked thieves came into the room.

ETHEL: The—red macaw—was asked a question.

SHADOW: Ah! And what was that question?

ETHEL: Ram Lal asked it—he asked it—what was beneath the light?

SHADOW: And what was the answer of the red macaw?

ETHEL:	(PAUSE) The shadow—the shadow.
SHADOW:	The Shadow? (LAUGHS FADING)
	(PHONE RINGS) (RECEIVER LIFTS)
WESTON:	Hello-hello! Police Commissioner Weston speaking. Who is this?
SHADOW:	(OVER FILTER) The Shadow! (LAUGHS)
WESTON:	Hey, what is this— a joke? The Shadow wouldn't dare call me up. There's a warrant out for him now.
SHADOW:	I'm not taking that seriously, Commissioner.
WESTON:	You will when I serve it!
SHADOW:	You mean, I will *if* you serve it!
WESTON:	I'm not worrying about that!
SHADOW:	I will give you something else to worry about. You may know that the Roger Berkleys are giving a small party tonight.
WESTON:	Certainly I know it. So what?
SHADOW:	The fourth in the series of jewel robberies will be committed there. Are you interested?
WESTON:	Try to pull that. I'll surround the house, and have a raiding party ready to break in at any minute.
SHADOW:	Excellent! I could not ask for more. And, if you wish to choose the right minute for the raid, you will wait for the signal.
WESTON:	What signal?
SHADOW:	The signal given by the red macaw! When he mentions my name—that is the signal! (LAUGHS) Remember, "The Shadow." (LAUGHS)
	(MUSIC) (MURMUR OF VOICE, ETC.)
MRS. B:	So glad you could come tonight, Lamont. I was afraid this fearful news about Margot Lane might keep you away.
CRANSTON:	My dear Muriel— nothing could keep me away from one of your parties.
MRS. B:	So sweet of you. I think you know everybody here—Oh, have you met Ram Lal?
CRANSTON:	No—I haven't had the pleasure.
MRS. B:	Oh, Ram Lal— I want to present Lamont Cranston—
RAM:	Charmed, I'm sure, Mr. Cranston—
CRANSTON:	How do you do? I've heard quite a lot about you— sometime I'd like to see your famous bird.
MRS. B:	Ram Lal is showing off his red macaw for us tonight— Aren't you Ram Lal?
RAM:	I am to have that pleasure, I believe.
CRANSTON:	I would very much like to meet that bird. I hear amazing things about it.
RAM:	The mystic East is full of the unexpected.
MRS. B:	(SHE CLAPS HANDS TO STILL THE UNDERCURRENT OF AD LIBBED CONVERSATION IN THE BACKGROUND) Quiet, please! (SILENCE) We are to have a most unusual pleasure tonight! Ram Lal has brought his red macaw and has promised that it will answer questions!
	(APPLAUSE AND AD LIBS Isn't he wonderful!?, etc.)
RAM:	Ladies and gentlemen! I have the honor to present to you, Hareen, the sacred red macaw! (APPLAUSE)

Ray Collins voiced Commissioner Ralph Weston in 1937.

	(LINE OF GIBBERISH) Hareen— you will answer the questions I ask! Now—
MARGOT:	(COMING ON) Good evening, everybody!
	(AD LIBS OF AMAZEMENT)
RAM:	But I thought you were dead.
MRS. B:	Good heavens— Margot Lane!
MARGOT:	The reports of my death were somewhat exaggerated!
	(GENERAL CLATTER OF CONGRATULATIONS FROM CROWD)
	But I didn't mean to interrupt. You were about to listen to the red macaw as I came in. Please continue, Ram Lal.
RAM:	(GASPING) I— I cannot! I am ill.
CRANSTON:	Ah! Evening, Margot, old thing. If Ram Lal is— ah— indisposed —-do you mind…I wonder if I can do anything with the red macaw?
	(CROWD MURMUR) UP
RAM:	You are absurd … He—will not—cannot speak for you!
CRANSTON:	You'll be surprised, Ram Lal. Hareen! You hear me?
MACAW:	Ye-es.
CRANSTON:	(AMID MURMER OF ASTONISHMENT) Who is your master?
MACAW:	You— are!
RAM:	I protest at this—farce! It's—It's—
CRANSTON:	Just one more question, Ram Lal. Hareen— Hareen! *What is under the light?*
MACAW:	The—the shadow. The—shadow!
RAM:	A lie! A cheat!
CRANSTON:	Is it? Wait, dear master!
	(CRASH OF GLASS OFF)
WOMAN:	(SCREAM)
VOICE:	(OFF) Put up your hands— all of you! This is a stickup!
	(CROWD GASPS)
	(POLICE WHISTLE)
WESTON:	(COMING ON) Get 'em, boys!
REILLY:	Drop that gun, you!
???	What is this, Ram Lal—a trap?
RAM:	(HYSTERICAL) Yes—no! I do not know you!
???	Oh, you don't, eh? Well, take this—
REILLY:	No, you don't!
	(SOCK— BODY FALL)
REILLY:	I got him, Chief! And, we caught three others outside!
WESTON:	Good! Take them to headquarters.
REILLY:	Okay! Come on, you!
	(GENERAL CONFUSION)
WESTON:	Wait a minute, Reilly—take this one too!
RAM:	Keep away from me!
REILLY:	This Ram Lal guy?
WESTON:	Certainly— he's the leader! He tried to put me off the track!
REILLY:	Okay— Come on— get going!
RAM:	(PROTESTS, FADING)
	(GENERAL AD LIB)

WESTON: (FADING) He's someone else too, unless I'm very much mistaken.

            (MURMUR OF EXCITED VOICES)

MARGOT: (SOTTO) But Lamont—the macaw—it talked!

CRANSTON: (SOTTO) No, it didn't—Ram Lal talked for it—simple ventriloquism, that's all. And it just so happens I'm as good a ventriloquist as Ram Lal.

MARGOT: (SOTTO) Oh, Lamont—you're marvelous!

WESTON: (COMING BACK) Ladies and gentlemen, I have a surprise for you! It is one of the most satisfactory discoveries of my whole career in crime detection—You know the man taken here tonight as Ram Lal. His real name is—The Shadow!

            (EXCITED EXCLAMATION)

            Yes—and for once—the laugh is on The Shadow!

SHADOW: (OFF—LAUGH)

WESTON: What was that?

SHADOW: You're wrong, Commissioner. You've got Ram Lal, but The Shadow—has the last laugh! (LAUGHS)

            (MUSIC)

Thomas Coffin Cooke, a.k.a. "John Barclay"

ANNR: Before today's adventure with The Shadow comes to an end, John Barclay—'blue coal's own heating expert is here to say a few words … Mr. Barclay …

BARCLAY: Good evening friends. Before winter sets in, you folks want to be very sure of having a comfortable home this winter, don't you. Well, here's the way to insure proper home heating. Call your local 'blue coal' dealer and take advantage of the extra free service he can give you. Remember: He's more than a fuel dealer … he's an authority on modern home heating. For more than six years, I have trained service men for your 'blue coal' dealers. These John Barclay service men, as they are called, have shown thousands of families how to operate their furnaces in order to get better heat at lower coast. Here's what one satisfied customer says about 'blue coal' and the John Barclay Service. I quote his letter in part: "Having moved into my present home last fall, I tried many kinds of coal without satisfaction. Finally I got in touch with the 'blue coal' people, and they sent a John Barclay service man to my home. He thoroughly inspected my heating plant—making some minor repairs and also explaining in detail how to run my furnace for best results. I then decided to try 'blue coal', which gave me such satisfaction with so little attention that I would not think of using any other coal!" There you are, friends. That's how one home-owner successfully solved his heating problem. Your 'blue coal' dealer is not only interested in selling you 'blue coal', America's finest anthracite, but he is interested in helping you get all of the comfort to which you are entitled when using this splendid fuel. No matter what kind of fuel you are using now, or from whom you are buying, your heating problems can be greatly simplified by taking advantage of the services which every 'blue coal' dealer is equipped to render. The combination of 'blue coal' and John Barclay service, will, I am sure, warrant a trial by you. I thank you.

ANNR: The story you have just heard is copyrighted by *The Shadow Magazine.* The characters in this story are entirely fictitious; any similarity to persons living or dead is purely coincidental.

            (MUSIC "GLOOMS OF FATE"—UP AND UNDER)

SHADOW: The weed of crime bears bitter fruit. Crime does *not* pay. The Shadow knows! (LAUGH)